Elisabeth Fairchild won the 1995 *Romantic Times* Best Regency Novel Award for *Miss Dorton's Hero*. A newcomer to the Signet list, she has b_____ders and receives _____ titles are *The Rak_____olly and the Ivy*.

Carla Kelly is a highly regarded Regency author who recently received a Career Achievement Award from *Romantic Times* as well as RITA Awards in 1994 and 1996. Her latest book is *Miss Milton Speaks Her Mind*.

Allison Lane, a very talented newcomer, won the 1996 *Romantic Times* Reviewers' Choice Award for Best First Regency for *The Rake's Rainbow*. Her newest titles are *A Bird in Hand* and *Birds of a Feather*.

Edith Layton, critically acclaimed for her short stories, also writes historicals for Harper-Collins and has won numerous awards. Her last short story appeared in *A Regency Christmas*. She loves to hear from her fans and can be reached at www.edithlayton.com

Barbara Metzger, one of the stars of the genre, has written over two dozen Regencies and won numerous awards, including a Reviewers' Choice Award for Best Regency and a National Reader's Choice Award in 1995. Her latest Regency is *Miss Treadwell's Talent*.

SIGNET REGENCY ROMANCE

On Sale November 15, 1999

A Fine Gentleman by Laura Matthews

Lady Caroline Carruthers was enjoying her visit to the Hartville home. But one thing made life at the estate complicated—Lady Hartville was intent on convincing her son that Caroline would be the perfect wife for him. Who could think of marrying such an obstinate, infuriating man as Richard? But an unexpected surprise arriving on the doorstep turns a far-fetched plan of wedding meddling into startling possibility....

0-451-19872-7/$4.99

The Irish Rogue by Emma Jensen

Ailís O'Neill is not the average Dublin debutante. She spends time teaching English to Gaelic peasants—and painting the local wildlife. But with her brother running for British Parliament on behalf of Ireland, Ailís is expected to socialize with the political set. Her disdain for the English partisans is evident, but no more so than for Lord Clane. And she knows nothing of Lord Clane's notorious past—or that his future includes plans to steal her heart....

0-451-19873-5/$4.99

My Lady Nightingale by Evelyn Richardson

Mademoiselle Isobel de Montargis had a passionate soul, a strong will, and a proud determination to become more than music tutor to the dashing Lord Hatherleigh's niece and nephew. Her dream was to become an *actrice de l'opera*. But how could a lady, respectful of her reputation and social standing, be able to ever fulfill such a daring dream? Leave it to Lord Hatherleigh....

0-451-19858-1/$4.99

To order call: 1-800-788-6262

A Regency Christmas Present

Elisabeth Fairchild

Carla Kelly

Allison Lane

Edith Layton

Barbara Metzger

A SIGNET BOOK

SIGNET
Published by New American Library, a division of
Penguin Putnam Inc., 375 Hudson Street,
New York, New York 10014, U.S.A.
Penguin Books Ltd, 27 Wrights Lane,
London W8 5TZ, England
Penguin Books Australia Ltd, Ringwood,
Victoria, Australia
Penguin Books Canada Ltd, 10 Alcorn Avenue,
Toronto, Ontario, Canada M4V 3B2
Penguin Books (N.Z.) Ltd, 182–190 Wairau Road,
Auckland 10, New Zealand

Penguin Books Ltd, Registered Offices:
Harmondsworth, Middlesex, England

Published by Signet, an imprint of New American Library,
a division of Penguin Putnam Inc.

First Printing, October 1999
10 9 8 7 6 5 4 3 2 1

Copyright © "Heart's Desire" Susan Ann Pace, 1999
Copyright © "Christmas Wish List" Barbara Metzger, 1999
Copyright © "An Object of Charity" Carla Kelly, 1999
Copyright © "A Christmas Canvas" Donna Gimarc, 1999
Copyright © "The Last Gift" Edith Felber, 1999

All rights reserved

REGISTERED TRADEMARK—MARCA REGISTRADA

Printed in the United States of America

Without limiting the rights under copyright reserved above, no part of this
publication may be reproduced, stored in or introduced into a retrieval system, or transmitted, in any form, or by any means (electronic, mechanical,
photocopying, recording, or otherwise), without the prior written permission
of both the copyright owner and the above publisher of this book.

BOOKS ARE AVAILABLE AT QUANTITY DISCOUNTS WHEN USED TO PROMOTE
PRODUCTS OR SERVICES. FOR INFORMATION PLEASE WRITE TO PREMIUM MAR-
KETING DIVISION, PENGUIN PUTNAM INC., 375 HUDSON STREET, NEW YORK, NEW
YORK 10014.

If you purchased this book without a cover you should be aware that this
book is stolen property. It was reported as "unsold and destroyed" to the
publisher and neither the author nor the publisher has received any payment
for this "stripped book."

Contents

Heart's Desire
by *Allison Lane*

1

December 22, 1813

The guard's horn blared, warning the stable of the mail coach's approach and startling Emma Fairlawn out of her unproductive thoughts. Her eyes lit on the other passenger, a wizened vicar she had all but ignored since he'd boarded an hour earlier.

"A heavenly choir could hardly sound as sweet," he murmured, pressing her hand between his two. "I have arrived, my dear lady. Yet you remain adrift." His gaze sharpened. "You will face many choices in the coming days. But if you keep your wits about you and carry this, you will achieve your heart's desire. May your future be blessed. Happy Christmas."

"I—and Happy Christmas to you," Emma stammered, surprised into incoherence by his action. How had he possessed himself of her hand? He'd seemed harmless enough, but now she had to wonder.

She glanced down. An exquisitely plaited straw heart nestled in her palm. No larger than a guinea, its craftsmanship was finer than she'd ever seen. Her mouth curved in wonder even as a pang smote her conscience. She could hardly accept a gift from a stranger.

"Tha—" Her protest died. Mesmerized by the heart, she'd not felt the coach stop. The vicar was gone.

Her gaze returned to her hand. *Your heart's desire* . . .

She snorted. Even if the magic his words implied was real, it would do her no good. She had no dreams, having long since given up hope for a better future. Wishing was for children or the wealthy—people who knew little of life's trials. As for her, she was grateful to survive a day in reasonable comfort. Wanting more could only lead to pain. Especially now.

Her youthful dreams of being swept off her feet by a handsome gentleman had long since died. Though Robert had been a good husband, he'd never been the stuff of fantasy. And now he was gone. James's wife Agnes resented sharing the house with another woman, her antagonism finally driving Emma from Fairport. The reception that awaited her in Cumberland would be even colder, but she had nowhere else to go. She had failed to find a post. Prayer. Connections. Begging. Nothing had produced an alternative to this journey.

Unless . . .

She forced her eyes away from the heart. That flash of hope was irrational, demonstrating her desperation. Magic did not exist. No knight in shining armor would whisk her into a life of luxury. No Merlin would conjure up a governess post. No heavenly messenger would insert a heart into Agnes's avaricious breast. There was no escape from becoming a companion and drudge to a cold, sour woman and clutch-fisted man.

Cursing the vicar for reminding her of this dismal

future, she raised her hand to toss the heart onto the ground. But instead, she slipped it into her reticule. A new passenger was limping slowly toward the mail coach. To avoid questions, she would discard the token later.

Captain Craig Curtiss pulled his hat lower, then wrapped a muffler around his face until only his eyes were visible. The mail coach was approaching. He must be downstairs when it arrived, for swapping out the team would take no more than two minutes.

Dear Lord, he prayed as he had done so often in the past fifteen years. *Grant me the courage to face the next battle.*

This journey was worse than those he had endured in Spain, and the coming confrontation loomed larger than any military conflict. He would rather face Napoleon himself than the dowager who held his inheritance in her unyielding grasp.

Gingerly favoring his injured leg, he limped toward the stairs.

"Happy Christmas, my good sir," said the wizened little man who met him in the inn's doorway.

"And to you," he responded automatically, though he had seen nothing happy about the day in thirty-two years of living. He tried to step past, but the man's eyes stopped him. So mesmerizing were they that he barely felt the pressure on his hand.

"You will face many choices in the days ahead." The man's gaze bored deep into Craig's core. "But if you keep your wits about you and carry this, you will achieve your heart's desire."

"Wha—" His jaw snapped shut. The fellow had already escaped into the taproom. He glanced down to find a dainty grass heart nestled in his palm, nearly lost in the vast expanse of his glove.

Heart's desire? He nearly laughed. The man had seemed harmless enough until he'd raised this ludicrous idea. When had his wishes ever mattered? Duty had been his watchword for as long as he could remember, though even duty could make conflicting demands—the mountains of Spain hovered briefly before his eyes.

He shook them away. He had no more control over his destiny than a twig caught in a torrent. His life had never been his own. Even fighting the dowager was an unwanted obligation that would pile new duties onto his shoulders if he won.

The man was dangerous, spouting the sort of superstitious nonsense that tricked gullible girls into buying worthless potions from village witches. But he was not so naïve. Fifteen years of war and carnage had expunged romantic notions from his soul. How else had he survived?

He raised his hand to toss the heart aside, but the boarding call distracted him. Slipping it into his greatcoat pocket, he limped toward the waiting coach.

Three hours later, Emma's stomach lurched as the coach skidded off the road. Her head slammed into the wall. Wood cracked. The guard shouted. Screaming horses and cursing men added to the cacophony.

"Are you all right?"

Not until the question cut through the pounding of her heart did she realize that they had stopped moving. Though the coach was canted at a crazy angle, it had not overturned. She carefully flexed her arms, pressing anxious fingers over her head.

"Quite all right. And you?" It was the first time

she had addressed the other passenger. He had been belligerently aloof since boarding, though she had been too engrossed in her own thoughts to care. And too cold. She envied him his greatcoat and thick gloves, for the temperature had been falling steadily. Her threadbare cloak allowed the chill to seep into her bones despite the pelisse and wool gown she wore beneath it.

"Undamaged," he said, answering her inquiry as he reached for the door. But it refused to open. Scraping frost from its window, he swore. The coach was lodged against the side of the ditch. Escape was impossible.

"Anybody 'urt?" called the driver, rapping on the other window.

"No, but the door is blocked. Can the team shift us away from the bank?"

"Wheel's shattered," the driver reported. "One 'orse is down, another dead lame. The guard left with the mail. But there's a inn a mile on. If you can 'old out a bit, I'll fetch 'elp."

Emma shivered, but there seemed no alternative. She nodded.

"Very good."

The driver departed. Her companion made himself more comfortable, twisting to lean against the side wall and drawing his feet onto the seat. Only his eyes were visible, glittering between his hat and muffler. Emma met that gaze, suddenly feeling very isolated. He was so big! Tall. Broad-shouldered. With hands large enough to span a dinner plate.

She shivered, suppressing the urge to rip away his scarf so she could at least see his expression. "Will he be long?"

"Half an hour. Maybe more. The Bell and Tassle is

not a coaching inn, so it will take some time to harness a carriage."

"You know it?"

"I grew up near here. Allow me to introduce myself. Captain Curtiss, late of His Majesty's forces in Spain."

An officer. Thus, a gentleman. She relaxed. "Have you returned to recuperate?"

"No." The denial was more of a growl. "My brother died, leaving me the title—Earl of Blacktower," he added, seeing the question in her eyes.

An earl? "So what are you doing in a mail coach?" The question slipped out before she could censor her tongue, but his laughter cut off her apology. At least she hoped it was laughter. The sound grated as if he'd not laughed in so long he'd forgotten how.

"The letter announcing William's death demanded that I return posthaste. Since it had been considerably delayed in transit, I dared not wait for funds—my London solicitor is ill. Nor could I remain until the current campaign is concluded," he added bitterly.

"Forgive me," she begged. "The question was intolerably rude."

"Perhaps, but no matter. May I know your name?"

"Mrs. Fairlawn, widow of Fairport's vicar."

"I once knew a Fairlawn of Fairport." His voice was carefully neutral. "Was your husband related to the baron?"

She nodded. "His brother."

A gust of wind shook the carriage, widening a crack in the roof. Freezing rain dripped into the pool seeping under the door. Shivering, she followed his lead, twisting her feet beneath her.

"You are cold," he noted. After a moment's hesitation, he began unwinding his muffler.

"That isn't necessary," she protested, despite relief that she would now see his face.

"I will not forgive myself if you freeze, though I must warn you that I am not a pretty sight."

The muffler came free, exposing a scar slashing down one cheek from his right eye to his chin—an angry, red scar still in the early stages of healing. Had the saber that made it also injured the leg he favored? On horseback, the cut would angle toward his thigh.

"So you *are* recovering from injuries," she said calmly as he leaned closer to wrap the muffler around her neck and shoulders. "That is too recent to have happened at Vitoria. Was there a later battle that I know nothing about?"

"It does not bother you?" He sounded every bit as shocked as he'd apparently expected her to be. "Most people recoil in horror."

"I've seen worse. But perhaps you are misinterpreting surprise as repugnance."

"No." Shaking his head, he returned to her original question. "There has been no pitched battle since Vitoria, but we have been engaged in a running fight with the French since late summer. This resulted from a lapse in judgment two months ago when I failed to spot an ambush." He grimaced as if wishing to take back the words.

"A competent officer would arrange an ambush so it would remain hidden until it was too late. If the French were incompetent, this war would have ended long since."

"A competent officer would spot the potential for ambush and avoid the site," he snapped.

"Did you know the area well, then?"

He glared.

"Unless you were retreating—which I refuse to believe," she added as he stiffened, "a running battle must lead you into unknown territory. How can you blame yourself for not recognizing every hiding place?"

He snorted, but his face relaxed a trifle—or so it seemed in the dim light.

"My husband would have admonished you to leave the past behind. If you made a mistake, then learn from it and move on. Otherwise, accept the inevitable."

He stared at the frosty window above them, biting his lip. "Fairlawn," he finally murmured. "Your husband must have been Robert."

"Did you know him?"

"I knew of him. He was a good man."

"He was. He died in a carriage mishap last year. I stayed at Fairport to nurse his brother's injuries, but now that he is married, I am returning to my father's estate."

"And your father is—?"

"Lord Whittaker." She again shivered, though not from cold. Returning home was a last resort, but Agnes had made it clear that she was no longer welcome at Fairport. James would rue his marriage, she thought for at least the hundredth time. At twenty, Agnes was already a harridan. She resented James's friendship with his brother's widow, and she despised the staff's habit of consulting Emma whenever a problem arose.

But that was no longer her concern. James believed that Agnes cared for him, not understanding that she would have accepted far worse than a one-legged husband if doing so elevated her to the aristocracy. But Emma could no longer influence him. Thinking about it only invited blue-devils.

She would be better served to think about her own future. Even if this stormy weather continued, she would be home by Christmas—not that they would celebrate it. Tradition was expensive. Even distributing baskets to their tenants on Boxing Day irritated her father. He might well have ceased the practice by now.

She had no illusions about her reception. Her father had been so anxious to get her out of his purse that he had forced her to wed an impoverished curate she barely knew. Robert had wanted a wife to help with his new parish in Kent, but his gratitude for her assistance had never ripened into love.

She pushed the memory aside, wishing her own feelings had remained aloof. Grief still cast a pall over most of her days. And that could only grow worse. Her father's letter of condolence had strongly hinted that she should not return home. But for the moment, she had nowhere else to go.

Her mother would welcome her, of course. The woman had suffered megrims and spells for thirty years, often demanding a companion to fetch and carry. But Whittaker had refused, claiming that nothing ailed her but a wish to make herself interesting. Whatever the truth, her disposition had worsened with time.

Please let me find a governess post soon, Emma prayed, as she had done so often this past month.

Heart's desire . . . Her eyes fell to her reticule. Was a post really what she wanted most?

Captain Curtiss had also fallen into an abstraction, but his eyes suddenly focused. "Did something happen to George's first wife? I know that he married several years ago."

She frowned, then recognized his confusion. "You

must not have heard. George died in the same accident that killed Robert. James is now the baron."

"James died at Badajoz." His gaze drilled into her skull.

"Did you know him?"

"We were in the same regiment."

"Queen's Light Dragoons."

He nodded, his breath seeming to catch. "James was my closest friend from the moment I bought colors—in the early days, I didn't realize that forming attachments invariably led to pain." He paused, but his haunted eyes revealed how many friends he had lost. "I saw him go down at Badajoz. No one survives such extensive wounds."

"I am not surprised the death rate is so high. Robert and I went to Portugal the moment we heard of his injuries. Conditions at the hospital were appalling. Since it offered little care even to officers, we removed him to a house, hoping that a cleaner bed and attentive nursing might help. They'd removed one leg before we arrived, and he was in a raving fever for nearly a fortnight, but he eventually improved enough to bring him home. It took more than a year, but he is healthy again and has assumed control of the estate. Except for jumping, he rides as well as ever and can walk using a wooden leg and cane."

His eyes glistened, but he allowed no emotion into his voice. "I am glad to hear it. He was a good man and a good officer. I wonder why he never let us know he'd survived."

"He may have done so by now."

He raised his brows.

"His full recovery dates back only two months. Until then, he was suffering such deep melancholia that he would spend entire days staring at the walls.

At other times he was overcome by pain or recurring bouts of fever. He mentioned the war only when delirious, often screaming orders, warnings, and pleas to a host of invisible soldiers."

"Did he call to anyone in particular?"

She shrugged. "Not by name. When we first arrived in Portugal, his most frequent screams warned someone to take cover, and he would often mumble about craggy rocks. Someone mentioned that he had been cut down during a skirmish in a rocky area outside Badajoz. Later, he seemed to regress to Buenos Aires."

"My name is Craig," he said softly, meeting her startled gaze. "James went down when he swerved in front of me, shouting to take cover, for he'd spotted a force of Frenchmen hiding in the rocks. I took a hit in the shoulder, but I survived. He intercepted the shot that should have killed me. It was the second time he saved my life. The first was at Buenos Aires." He stared rather fiercely at the window as he struggled for control.

"Perhaps that explains his melancholia," she suggested. "He probably believes you fell with him."

"I will disabuse him of that notion immediately," he vowed, stiffening his back. "James was always protective of his friends. So why did he allow his wife to turn you out?"

"I never said—"

"But she did." His eyes bored into hers, easily reading her shock at the unexpected change of subject— and the truth of his charge.

"Not exactly. It was best that I move on. Agnes resents both my friendship with James and the months I spent running the household. George's wife moved to the dower house after the accident, refusing to have anything to do with James—she is the sort who does not deal well with illness—so I had to take charge. But the staff has been slow to transfer their allegiance to Agnes."

"I can read between the lines well enough to understand, but I won't press for details. So you are returning to your family?"

"For the holidays. I will then seek a governess position."

Another gust of wind shook the carriage. The temperature had fallen even further, turning the freezing rain to snow that clung to the window above them. But water still dripped through the crack.

The captain shivered. "You won't get far today, Mrs. Fairlawn. It would be better if you accompanied me to Blacktower. You can send notice to your family that you will be delayed."

"They are not expecting me," she admitted, then bit her tongue, wishing the words back. "Thank you for the invitation, but it would not do."

"Nonsense. There will probably be a hundred relatives gathered for the holidays."

"In a house of mourning? I doubt it. Even if the notice was grossly delayed, your brother cannot have died that long ago."

"It is true that his wife and our mother remain in mourning. But Grandmother does not, and she runs the household. One more guest will hardly matter. And someone may know of a post, if that is truly your desire."

Heart's desire . . .

She was tempted. How often had she prayed for an alternative to going home? Even passing the holidays in a house full of strangers was more enticing than the cold reception she faced in Cumberland. But it would not do. "You cannot have considered the consequences of introducing a stranger to a family gathering."

"I am just as much a stranger," he countered grimly. "I last set foot in Shropshire fifteen years ago."

"Then how do you know there will even be a house party?"

"Grandmother would never ignore tradition. She revels in family history and centuries-old glory. The earls have always hosted their relatives at Christmas."

She ignored the odd note that had crept into his voice, for she could hardly ask another personal question. This discussion had already moved well beyond propriety.

Captain Curtiss shifted his leg, shifting the thrust of his argument at the same time. "You will likely take an inflammation of the lungs if you remain on the road. James would call me out if I allowed you to proceed in this weather."

He was right enough on that score, but arriving in his company, unescorted, would create a scandal.

"Are you so anxious to see your family that you would risk your life to reach them?" he asked softly. His eyes gleamed at her instinctive recoil. "I thought so. Allow me to perform this service, Mrs. Fairlawn. I owe it to James."

"Very well."

She meant to suggest that they should at least arrive separately, but the coachman's return distracted her. A flurry of activity ended only when she'd been bundled into a carriage with the earl.

2·

Craig watched Mrs. Fairlawn as the job coach skidded through the gates of Blacktower Park. Her questions had focused his attention on the upcoming confrontation. William's death would have allowed the dowager to resume control of the estate, even if William had managed to oust her, as he'd claimed. . . .

He'd last seen his brother two years ago. Granted, William had chosen his own bride and escaped to London, but leaving the estate meant leaving their grandmother in charge. Had he really taken up the reins at the end of the Season? Craig didn't know. The family had rarely written to him. In fact, he had received only four letters in fifteen years—death notices for his grandfather and father, a note when William wed, and the missive that now brought him home. Since the first three had also berated him for failing to bring new honors to the Curtiss name, he had rarely mourned the neglect.

But he must learn the answer soon, he admitted. It would affect the tactics he must employ to wrest control into his own hands.

Mrs. Fairlawn smiled as the arched bridge appeared through the swirling snow. It was the loveliest sight on the estate.

Her news had stunned him. James's survival seemed impossible, but it lifted a weight he had borne for nineteen months.

James was the only one who knew his shame: Craig Curtiss, scion of a family boasting countless military heroes, was a coward. Even in sieges like Badajoz, where cavalry was less involved than infantry, fear clouded his thinking. As it had done that day.

An alert, competent officer would have spotted the French and ordered his men into a flanking maneuver. His blindness had cost him his last friend, for the only reason James had swerved in front of him was to protect him. The knowledge had gnawed at his conscience ever since. Sixteen of his men had needlessly died that day. Yet his own wounds had been relatively minor. Why had he survived when worthy officers like James had perished? The unfairness had added to his guilt and intensified his grief.

He and James had bought colors at the same time, along with three other youths. All had become friends. Though he had never shared their enthusiasm for military matters, they had accepted his abhorrence of violence, taking him under their collective wing.

He'd been grateful—until he'd lost two of them to disease and injury while putting down the Irish rebellion, and a third in the Buenos Aires campaign. The pain had taught him to remain aloof. His horror at the death and destruction wrought by war marked him as odd, so he had hidden it. Only James had understood, his support and friendship keeping Craig sane, his protection keeping him alive. James had even sacrificed himself to serve the friend who was closer than a brother.

He shifted, one hand brushing the small lump in his pocket.

Heart's desire . . .

Was James's life what that strange little man had meant—not that he could possibly have known that James's seeming resurrection would fulfill a wish he had never dared voice, even in the darkest recesses of his mind.

Easing his guilt unlocked memories he had suppressed after Badajoz. He sifted old conversations for any information on Mrs. Fairlawn.

Emma. That was her name.

James had remained close to his family, which accounted for his survival. Robert and Emma had actually traveled to Portugal to nurse his injuries.

He stifled a shudder. His own experiences with military hospitals made James's survival even more astounding. The places were cesspits of filth, disease, and death. Care was minimal as overworked surgeons labored to mend an endless influx of patients, a task large enough to stymie even Hercules.

James had often spoken of his brothers. George had been a dour man interested mostly in horses, though his wife had dragged him to London every Season. In contrast, Robert had dedicated his life to helping the estate dependents. Emma had thrown her heart into supporting Robert's efforts, her fame spreading beyond the parish. She'd found jobs for weavers put out of work by the mills, for fishermen barred from the most productive waters by war, and for maimed soldiers no longer fit for fighting. That last was a cause close to his own heart, and he had often wondered if she was as appealing as James had made her sound.

Forcing his mind back to the carriage, he studied her. He had ignored her until the accident, not wanting to inflict his scars on a stranger. Keeping his face hidden while conversing was rude.

She was pretty enough, her brown hair pulled into a neat knot, her green eyes brightened by gold flecks now that her terror had abated. Even before he had recalled her background, she'd proven to be an unusual woman. Everyone else in England instinctively recoiled when first seeing how disfigured he had become.

It was the other reason he had invited her to share Christmas with his family. He needed someone who looked at him without revulsion. And his habit of second-guessing himself often led to trouble. An outsider's voice could guide him through the coming battle. James had served that function for years. Now James's sister must fill in.

They could not have arrived at a more propitious time, he realized, checking his pocket watch as the carriage pulled to a stop. Everyone would be dressing for dinner.

"Welcome to Blacktower."

"Thank you, my lord."

He frowned as he escorted her haltingly up the steps. Either the staff had grown slack, or the footman assigned to watch for arrivals had been called away by an emergency.

Horner opened the door. The butler had aged badly in fifteen years. "We expected you a month ago, Master Craigmont."

Craig bristled. Just so had Horner spoken when he'd knocked over a suit of armor after escaping his tutor at age five. "I don't know why, since I sent no word to that effect." His tone declared that he was no longer a boy. Removing his hat, he stepped into the light, revealing the maze of scars that made the most recent slash appear worse. Little remained of the face many had once considered handsome.

Horner flinched.

"Mrs. Fairlawn is joining us for the holidays," he continued. "See that she is settled."

Horner's eyes hardened. "Lady Blacktower is in her sitting room."

So nothing had changed. His grandmother insisted on approving all guests.

"I will speak with the dowager at dinner," he said, emphasizing her position as a contrast to his own. Like it or not, this house now belonged to him. "See that Mrs. Fairlawn's luggage is carried to the best available guest chamber. And assign me a footman. I left my batman in Spain and have not had time to hire a valet."

"You will speak with me now." Ice dripped from each word as Lady Blacktower swept down the stairs. She was swathed in unrelieved black, her back unbowed. Fury blazed in her dark eyes. Fifteen years may have deepened the creases in her face and turned her graying hair pure white, but her determination was as indomitable as ever.

Fear flashed down his spine. *Damnation!* A single stab from those glittering eyes could still make him want to flee. But she was no longer the demon of his childhood, he reminded himself, or even the nemesis of his curtailed youth.

Keeping Emma's hand on his arm, he stepped forward. "This is Mrs. Fairlawn, who has been stranded by the weather. My grandmother, the dowager Countess of Blacktower."

The dowager bestowed one contemptuous glance on Emma, then pointedly ignored her. "You are late."

"Hardly. Dinner will not be served for another hour."

"And stupid. You should have returned more than a month ago. How dare you ignore your duty?"

He forced out a laugh, though confronting the dowager always made breathing difficult. "Have you no notion of how far letters must travel to reach the Spanish mountains? I did not receive notice of William's death until a month ago. It took me a week to convince the doctors that I was fit enough to travel and another to arrange transport."

She ignored his sarcasm, frowning at his face. "As reckless as ever, I see. What an absurd piece of negligence to fall prey to wounds when you were needed elsewhere. Or did you deliberately court them to spite me?"

Mrs. Fairlawn gasped.

"Is there a problem with the estate?" He brushed aside her remarks. She believed that everyone acted solely to please or annoy her, refusing to admit that most of the family had more pressing concerns than her desires.

"The estate has been in perfect order since I took charge of it thirty years ago, but I cannot assure the succession." She was clearly irritated at this lack of omnipotence. "William should have listened to me instead of wedding that atrocious woman. But he was always spiteful. And completely inept. To kill himself taking a simple jump . . ." She clenched her fists. "I am surrounded by incompetents. But no matter. You will wed Miss Fitzgerald on Boxing Day. I will expect an heir within the year."

"You are absurd, madam." But he could feel his feet slipping into the quagmire.

"Once that woman proved her worthlessness by birthing a puling girl, I had no choice. Stephen has become a great disappointment," she snapped, naming her second son. "So you must deal with the succession—as even you must admit. Everything is arranged. The family is here, Michael has agreed to stand up with you, and Lord Fitzgerald is anxious to see the matter concluded."

"You actually set this up without consulting me?" he demanded incredulously. Though he should have suspected such a scheme. It was not the first time she had meddled in his life. Or the tenth. Or even the twentieth. *You will never be free,* whispered a voice that sounded like William. *No one escapes her clutches.*

Her eyes drilled into his, just as they had always done, seeing every defect, binding him in the unbreakable chains of her unswerving will. "It is my duty. Someone must see that the family affairs are properly conducted," she intoned. "None of you are capable of making the least decision. You need help. An experienced hand to guide you. A leader to prevent foolish mistakes, to protect you from danger, to remind you of your duty whenever you forget."

Rage obscured his vision, though he could do nothing about it. His ears seemed stuffed with cotton wadding that dulled all but the sound of the mesmerizing voice. He was trapped. Again.

No one escapes her clutches. . . .

Emma stared, appalled, her gaze sliding from the dowager to the captain as his arm trembled beneath her fingers. In a flash of empathy, she realized that his injured leg was on the verge of collapse. Aside from the embarrassment of falling in public, any show of weakness could undermine his position in a house he had already warned her was run by the woman standing before them. Judging by the malicious satisfaction in the dowager's eyes, she would pounce on any excuse to shut him away. By the time his wounds healed, he would have lost any chance to assume control.

"Captain." She slid her free hand under his arm, taking some of his weight. "This is hardly an appropriate place for a family discussion."

He stiffened, his scar more prominent than ever. "Quite true. Propriety must be offended. We will talk later," he told the dowager. Turning away, he limped toward the stairs, leaning heavily on her arm.

"Lady Blacktower cannot force you into marriage,"

she murmured as they climbed. "Even if she was once your guardian, she can no longer legally sign your name—unless you made her your agent."

"Never." His fingers clenched. "And she was never my guardian, though Father always followed her orders."

"Then you are under no obligation to Miss Fitzgerald." She didn't pursue the bitterness that had crept into his voice, but she would stake anything that this was not the first time the dowager had made plans without consulting him.

"But how can I back out without harming the girl?"

"Talk to her father. You are of age, so only a contract signed by you or your agent is valid. Avoiding all scandal will be impossible, but it should dissipate by next Season."

"How? We will both be tarnished if I jilt her."

"Impossible. No one can claim jilt without a valid betrothal."

"True." He sighed. "I had best speak to him immediately."

"An excellent idea. Allowing it to stand even until morning could imply your consent." She cocked her head, wondering if she dared continue. But James would expect her to help. If James had willingly risked his life for this man, she could surely risk a rebuff. "If I might be a trifle forward, James had a small difficulty when he first returned to England that might affect you as well."

"What?" He narrowed his eyes.

"After so many years in the military, he was accustomed to issuing orders, as I am sure you will understand. But this situation requires tact rather than confrontation. Ranting will serve no purpose. And you do not yet know whether the Fitzgeralds schemed with the dowager or are also her unwitting victims."

"I see." He made an obvious effort to relax. "Thank you. I will make a suggestion in return. You are undoubtedly weary from your journey. I know I am. We would both benefit from having dinner trays sent to our rooms. I will introduce you to the family tomorrow."

He was right, she admitted once he turned her over to the housekeeper, though she suspected that he was ducking further argument with his grandmother. At least the housekeeper showed her to a well-kept bedroom. Either the woman had not learned of the dowager's opposition, or the servants' quarters were already overflowing. Not that she could blame the dowager for her impression. Arriving alone with a gentleman gave the appearance of impropriety. Only her widowhood held ruin at bay.

Craig summoned Lord Fitzgerald to the library the moment he had changed his clothes, then watched the man's face turn purple.

"What rig are you running, my lord?" the baron demanded, interrupting. "My daughter accepted your letter of proposal in good faith. How dare you renege now?"

"What letter? I made no proposal," he snapped before recalling Mrs. Fairlawn's advice. He moderated his tone. "I first heard of the girl an hour ago. The only recent communication I received from England was this." He handed over his grandmother's announcement of William's death. "It followed me from my regiment to a series of hospitals, finally reaching me in Lisbon a month ago."

Fitzgerald glanced at his face, grimacing as he had

done each time he'd dared look. But at least the full dress uniform drew a grudging respect.

Craig held himself erect with an effort. The cold had stiffened his gimpy leg and still throbbed painfully through the slash. Only Mrs. Fairlawn's support had gotten him out of the hall without humiliation. Thank heaven she had been there. He needed rest, but she was right. He had to make a stand now if he hoped to escape this trap.

"Then how do you explain this?" Fitzgerald handed over his own missive.

"Not my hand, though I would wager you can identify it." He laid the two letters side by side, then dashed off a sentence in his own hand for comparison. His fury made it difficult to keep either voice or pen steady. The dowager was more unscrupulous than he had ever imagined.

The baron cursed under his breath. "We were hoaxed."

Craig leaned against the mantel. "It would appear so. Lady Blacktower likes to think she is in charge, but despite the privileges extended by previous earls, she has legal authority over neither the estate nor the family. In particular, she does not possess signing rights to my name. I intend no insult to you or your daughter and will do what I can to see that blame for this fiasco is assessed where it belongs, but I have no interest in marriage at this time. My first priority is to discover the condition of my inheritance and address its problems."

"What can I say, other than to ask that you inform Constance of your decision."

If the baron hoped a scene would deter him, he was wrong. "Of course. If she possesses the slightest intelligence, she will be relieved. She would be miserable here. My grandmother rules the house with an iron fist, accepting no challenge to her authority. Since learning about my inheritance will require all of my attention, I will have no time to stand up for another."

He left out his appearance. Miss Fitzgerald could assess that for herself.

Which she did. Fitzgerald must have warned her, for she hesitated to look at him. The first glance sent her into a gasping recoil.

It was the reaction he had expected, for few members of society accepted deformity, and Miss Fitzgerald certainly considered herself part of society. Her evening gown was a frivolous confection of sarcenet and lace—French lace, he realized, his fury reviving. And she was far from demure. A riot of curls could not detract from the determination in her eyes. She might abhor him, but she still coveted the position.

"I am grieved to discover that you have been the target of so cruel a hoax," he began.

"How a hoax?" she interrupted. "We have both the signed contract and the letters in which you set out your settlement terms. We will have you up on a breach of promise charge if you renege."

"How many letters?" he idly asked.

"Seven, received over a two-month period."

"Each in response to one of yours?" He allowed incredulity into his voice.

"Of course."

"Fourteen letters exchanged in eight weeks?" he scoffed. "Seven trips by land from Shropshire to Portsmouth, by sea to Portugal, then by land again across the Peninsula to the mountains dividing Spain from France? And seven more in return?"

She blinked.

"The contract is worthless, Miss Fitzgerald. Not one

signature was applied by my authority. The letters are
forgeries that don't even attempt to copy my hand.
Even one would not have reached me in the time you
claim, for I have been absent from my regiment. Judging by the date affixed to the sample I saw, the first
was written well after William's death. Upon receiving
notice of that death, I left immediately and have only
now arrived home." She blanched, for he had adopted
the tone he used on inept recruits. He ignored her
discomfort. Not only was she a selfish schemer, but
the money spent adorning her frivolous gown might
well have paid for weapons that had killed his men.

"But Lady Blacktower signed, along with the family
solicitor. You cannot back out now," she shot back,
fury twisting her face.

"I am of age, Miss Fitzgerald. Only two people have
the authority to sign my name. One is my own solicitor, who is unknown to the dowager. The other is
myself. Before you say another word, I suggest that
you ask yourself what benefit you could derive from
forcing marriage on someone who wants nothing to
do with you, and who would have the authority to
lock you away from society if he chose. I will do what
I can to smooth this misunderstanding, but I will not
honor a commitment I had no hand in making. Bringing charges will mark you as a grasping fortune hunter,
for you have no complaint in the eyes of the law."

"I see that I have been misled about your character," she said, allowing her revulsion to show.

"Just as you misled Lady Blacktower," he replied.
"I can accept her misconceptions about me, for we
have not corresponded in fifteen years. But she does
know you. She would never have pursued this match
had she understood your ambitions, for she despises
anyone she cannot control. The fact that she believes

you to be acceptable proves that you deliberately lied."

She gasped, apparently shocked that he had seen through her facade. Did she think her stratagems invisible? But he thrust her games aside, turning to Lord Fitzgerald. "You are welcome to remain through the holidays. Doing so will mitigate any rumors and avert most of the scandal."

"Quite true," he agreed, shushing his daughter's protests with a furious glance that promised retribution for placing him in so mortifying a position. Perhaps he also suspected that she had known the letters were false.

Craig returned to his rooms for dinner. The situation was worse than he had feared. William's claims that he had wrested control of the estate were, at best, exaggerations. He may have escaped to London on occasion—which their father had never managed—but the dowager remained as deeply entrenched as ever.

That would have to change.

3

Emma slipped into the conservatory. A new storm raged outside, lashing the park with rain that had already melted yesterday's snow.

What was she doing here?

Accepting this invitation had been a mistake. She had no illusions about the scene with Lady Blacktower last night. The woman assumed that Captain Curtiss had brought his mistress into the house. Her cut had been a pointed reminder that courtesans did not belong at respectable family gatherings. And that very public announcement of the captain's betrothal had warned her against trying to snare him for herself. If she appeared in the drawing room, the dowager would strike harder.

Even the servants looked at her askance or averted their eyes as they passed her. The only exception was the maid who had delivered morning chocolate and toast. Not that Bess disbelieved the rumors. Her deliberate welcome and friendly chattiness had been a way to spit in the dowager's eye.

So remaining at Blacktower would cause trouble. Yet leaving was impossible, for howling wind and heavy rain would have closed the roads. Thus she had set about helping her host, questioning Bess closely about the house, the family, and the dowager's grip on both. Now she must decide what to do with the information.

"You must be Blacktower's friend," said a soft voice behind her.

Emma spun around as a black-clad lady rose from a bench nestled between two miniature orange trees. "Pardon me for intruding."

"The conservatory is open to all."

The woman's voice contained a familiar note of hope battling despair, just as James's had during the early days of his convalescence. James had needed months to accept his changed circumstances. Did this woman also face a terrifying future?

"Are you Blacktower's friend?" the woman asked again.

"Mrs. Fairlawn."

"I am Lady Blacktower." She sighed. "So confusing with three of us. Call me Lady Catherine." A tear leaked from each eye. "Forgive me," she begged. "I have been blue-deviled since Mary was born. The strangest things set me off."

"Not uncommon," said Emma. "Many new mothers

experience such problems. Losing your husband so soon afterward must make it worse."

"Actually, he died two weeks before Mary's birth." She blinked away more tears. "Have you known Craig long?"

Emma shook her head. "We met on the mail coach yesterday. But he was in the same regiment as my husband's brother, so when he learned that I was looking for a governess position, he insisted that I stop here, hoping someone might know of an opening."

"Oh." She seemed disappointed.

"Arriving together must have started rumors."

"I was hoping they were true." The moment she said the words, Lady Catherine blushed. "What I meant was that I was hoping you would know him well enough to approach him on my behalf."

"You wish a favor?"

She nodded. "The dowager won't allow me to move to the dower house. She likes everyone under her eye, and she would never let Mary leave the nursery."

"I doubt that her word will remain law much longer. Captain Curtiss seems an able officer. He would never relinquish his rightful command."

"He will have no choice." She sounded resigned. "The dowager has already arranged his marriage, just as she did for her sons and William. William rebelled, eloping with me instead of wedding the girl she had chosen, but that was the last time he asserted his independence. His realization that he had no hope of defeating her made him increasingly blue-deviled. His only escape was to ride neck-or-nothing over the countryside—with the inevitable consequences. I don't know how she mesmerizes people, but no one has ever successfully countered her. I do not want her influence extended to Mary, yet she will never allow me to leave."

"Nonsense. The woman is not all-powerful. Nor can she legally run anything, as the captain has already informed her."

Lady Catherine stared. "He actually stood up to her?"

"Upon arrival. She announced that he would wed on Boxing Day. He refused. According to the maid who brought my tray this morning, he has already informed the Fitzgeralds that no betrothal exists."

"How delicious!" She had brightened considerably. "I wish I had felt up to joining the company last night. The news must have shocked a great many people. But tell me about yourself. Why are you searching for a position?"

"I married ten years ago, shortly after Robert's brother George acceded to the title and offered him the living at Fairport—he had been curate to a parish near my father's estate until then. He and George died in a carriage accident fifteen months ago, leaving the barony to James, Captain Curtiss's friend. Now James has married, but his wife is young and inexperienced. She does not need me competing for the staff's loyalty. My father's estate is poor, so it seems best to look for a post." She shrugged.

"I am sure we can find something." The prospect of helping seemed to cheer her.

"Thank you."

Heart's desire . . .

Emma fingered the plaited heart she had slipped into her bodice. Could it possibly be working?

But her practical nature scoffed at such nonsense. Magical amulets made interesting stories for children—along with evil witches, good fairies, and assorted ghosts—but they did not exist in real life. Even if Lady Catherine miraculously produced a position, it would be mere coincidence.

They fell into a discussion of her training and background that lasted until breakfast. The dowager did not descend until ten, so food was never set out until that hour—which explained the toast that had accompanied her chocolate. Lady Catherine promised to ask her correspondents if they knew of any openings.

"There you are," said Craig, spotting Mrs. Fairlawn near the breakfast room. He owed her his thanks for rescuing him last night. If she had not been there, he would have already lost his bid to gain control of his inheritance.

Reflection had convinced him that it was no accident the dowager had met him in the hall. The absent footman would have fetched her. By accosting him when he was weary from travel, she'd expected to slide him into the same submissive role played by the three previous earls. Her indomitable will was difficult to ignore even when he was rested and alert. Thank God for Mrs. Fairlawn.

Now he stood a good chance of prevailing. He had arisen before dawn, still unused to the late sunrise of an English winter after his years in Spain. Irritated that no food would be available until ten, he had issued instructions that breakfast would henceforth be set out by eight. Horner must have recognized his determination, for he'd bitten off the protest trembling on his tongue.

"My lord," Mrs. Fairlawn murmured.

"You look rested this morning," he said, then chided himself for inanity before turning to her companion. "I'm afraid I don't remember you."

"William's wife, Lady Catherine," said Mrs. Fairlawn, making the introduction.

Catherine's eyes slid past his face, but that was her only reaction to his appearance. "My lord."

"Craig," he insisted, wishing he'd had time to meet her in London two years ago. But running into William had surprised them both. He'd been on his way back to Spain at the time, and even the half hour they had spent talking had nearly made him miss his ship. "My condolences on your loss, Catherine. William was a good man."

"Thank you."

He turned back to Mrs. Fairlawn, allowing Catherine to proceed to breakfast. "Is your room comfortable?"

"Quite."

"I must thank you for your help. Lord Fitzgerald agreed with your assessment. He and his daughter will remain through Twelfth Night to mitigate any scandal."

"I heard." She scanned his face. Apparently she was satisfied with what she saw, for she continued. "I also heard that the dowager rules the estate almost as a medieval fiefdom. Lady Catherine wishes to remove her daughter to the dower house, but she has been compelled to remain here."

"I will deal with it." Her smile washed him with warmth. She was wearing a green wool gown today, with long sleeves and a hint of a ruffle at the throat. The color made her eyes blaze like beacons. "I will check on its condition and have it opened," he continued to deflect his thoughts from the way the soft wool molded her generous bosom. Yesterday's cloak had hidden a delectable body.

"Thank you. She admitted to a prolonged melancholy that began with William's death. I believe that taking charge of her own establishment would help."

Fortunately, she had not noticed his straying thoughts—and eyes. "An excellent notion. And when I speak with her, I will ask for further details about the dowager's despotic rule—I assume Lady Catherine provided that information."

"Actually, I obtained much of my information from Bess, the maid who brought my chocolate. The dowager is turning her off after Twelfth Night."

"Why?"

"She tripped on a turned-up carpet, spilling ashes in the hall. Only the extra work required by the house party prevented the dowager from tossing the girl out immediately."

"A ridiculous reason for dismissing her, unless clumsiness is a continuing problem. I will check into it," he vowed, leading her into the safety of the breakfast room. The passion blazing in her eyes triggered an unexpected wave of lust that he quickly stifled. *This is your best friend's sister,* he reminded his unruly thoughts. *And she is only passionate about injustice.* She must have been a great asset to both Robert and James. Already, she had learned more about the problems he faced than he had. Inviting her for Christmas had been an excellent idea.

The news that the dowager was more autocratic than ever was no surprise, though he had hoped that William's boasting would prove at least partially true. To win, he needed all the help he could find.

Heart's desire . . .

Drat the man for planting odd ideas in his mind. He had meant to discard that silly grass heart, but somehow it had wound up in his waistcoat pocket. Could he truly gain control of his inheritance?

He had no idea how long his grandmother had run Blacktower. Her husband had slipped into senility ten years before his death, allowing her to publicly take charge, but her will had prevailed long before. And her sons had been under her thumb from childhood. Apparently Stephen had escaped her clutches—or so last night's tirade implied. But the eldest had married on her instructions, acquiring a wife who had quickly become her slave.

Craig shook his head. His mother was his grandmother's shadow, agreeing with every word the dowager uttered and leaving her side only to fetch something the dowager had left behind. He sometimes wondered how she'd found the time to conceive two sons.

Sleep had sharpened his mind. He had known from the moment he'd received the announcement that he would have to fight for his inheritance. The weeks of travel had given him time to plan, and his military service had taught him much about tactics. Now that he had survived the initial encounter, he would remain on guard. This time, he meant to win.

What a fool he had been over their last battle.

By the time he had finished at Eton, he'd realized that his interests lay in the church. But he'd kept the ambition secret, knowing his grandmother would never approve. Pressure could force his weak-willed father to sign the enrollment papers. All Craig had to do was catch him alone.

Naïve. His grandmother was obsessed by her concept of tradition. Second sons distinguished themselves in the military. Third sons became government leaders. Only fourth sons entered the church.

Somehow she had learned of his plans. Determined that a Curtiss would add new military honors to the family name, she had met his carriage in the drive, his commission in her hand. With both his father's and his grandfather's signatures affixed to the papers, he'd been helpless. Even after he reached his majority and could sell out without her permission, he lacked the means to pursue another career. She had seen to it that he remained impoverished, reliant on a paltry quarterly allowance that, when combined with his inadequate military pay, barely covered his expenses.

"Good morning," he cheerfully greeted the guests as he entered the breakfast room. Twenty people sat at the table. "This is Mrs. Fairlawn, widow of Fairport's vicar and sister of Captain James Fairlawn, the man who twice saved my life in battle. Bad weather has interrupted her journey, but I hope to compensate her by finding her a governess post. If anyone knows of one, please speak with her about it."

The dowager uttered a contemptuous epithet and deliberately started a conversation with his mother. At the same time, Catherine's face broke into a broad smile. She strode toward them, hands extended.

"My dear Emma. Welcome to Blacktower. I have heard so much about you. Your father is Lord Whittaker, is he not? I attended school with Pamela Hardcastle."

"One of Father's neighbors. Heavens! The last time I saw her, she was a grubby twelve-year-old who got into the most frightful scrapes. What has become of her?"

Catherine escorted her to the sideboard, chattering happily. Craig scanned the crowd. Most eyes swiveled between the outraged dowager and Catherine's pleasure. Others compared Mrs. Fairlawn's obvious gentility to his own monstrous appearance, apparently deciding that a delectable widow would hardly conduct an affair with a man so deformed. But to a person, each nodded coolly when Catherine introduced Emma. He could read their minds. Few were ready to snub the dowager. Those who supported him would want something in return.

Like Catherine. She might like his guest, but her own interests drove her to this public support. It was a masterful move that raised Mrs. Fairlawn's standing, but he had hoped to continue their discussion. He wanted to hear what other information she might have gleaned and to learn more about James's recovery. Stifling his irritation, he filled a plate.

"Is it true that you jilted Miss Fitzgerald?" asked Cousin Michael when Craig joined him at the table.

"A betrothal must exist before a jilt is possible," he answered shortly. "This is a clear case of putting the cart before the horse. I had never been approached on the subject, so allowing wishful thinking to progress into actual planning was rather presumptuous. Assuming control of the earldom will require all my attention. Miss Fitzgerald is relieved to be allowed some say in her future."

"The dowager will not be pleased," murmured Cousin Julia.

"She is reconciled," he lied. He suspected that Lord Fitzgerald had treated the woman to some scathing comments in the drawing room last night. She had summoned Craig to her private sitting room before retiring, where she'd delivered a tirade about duty, honor, and his own ineptitude—which he had largely ignored, having been too tired by that time to listen. She was powerless to reinstate the betrothal, but would undoubtedly dig in her heels on other issues.

How many confrontations would it take before she

retired from the field? And what revenge would she extract in the meantime?

Emma was unsurprised by the company's ambivalence. Arriving sans maid, in company with a gentleman, supported whatever insinuations the dowager had made. She had Lady Catherine to thank that most guests were withholding judgment.

Not that she could blame anyone for thinking the worst. Despite his many scars, Captain Curtiss cut a fine figure. He was wearing his dress uniform this morning, the scarlet facings on the silver-encrusted blue jacket a perfect foil for his dark hair and eyes. Illness and hard travel had done little to diminish powerful shoulders and legs. And there wasn't a man in the room who radiated such authority. He must have bought colors quite young, for several people seemed surprised at his imposing size.

Quit staring. She quickly averted her eyes, reluctant to add fuel to the fires of suspicion that already raged.

By the time Catherine finished introducing those in the breakfast room, two new gentlemen had come down.

"You seem more cheerful today, Lady Catherine," said Mr. Colin Langtree, maneuvering the four of them to the foot of the table, away from the rest of the company.

"Perhaps I was bored." A smile warmed her face. "Mrs. Fairlawn has given me a new purpose."

"Or Blacktower's arrival has given you hope for a better future," he said daringly.

Emma glanced up. The sparks flying between the pair were nearly visible. Allowing them to converse as privately as was possible, she turned to Mr. Reeves, the village vicar; who had claimed the seat on her other side.

"Your husband was Robert?" he asked.

The question jogged her memory. "Reeves . . . You must be Jonathan. Robert spoke of you often."

"It was a sad day when I heard of his death. We had remained close since school, though our postings were too distant for visiting. But how is it you are seeking a position? Surely the family made provision for you."

Robert had always assumed that she would live at Fairport if she survived him, but he'd made no formal arrangements. "From choice. James recently married and needs time alone with his wife. I could have moved into the dower house with George's wife, but she has never been comfortable with me. My failure to produce children reminds her too strongly of her many miscarriages."

Reeves was staring. "How can you describe that as *your* failure?"

She shrugged, ignoring the pain of not having a family despite nine years of marriage.

"Heaven above! Surely Robert explained." His face had paled.

"Explained what?"

"He was incapable of fathering a child."

She carefully laid her fork on the table lest it drop from her shaking hand. Incapable? How could that be?

He took in her strained face and shook his head. "I cannot believe he never told you. I know he felt guilty about wedding you, knowing that you longed for a family. But he knew how much work he would face in a parish as large as Fairport. And he feared your father would sell you to a degenerate if you did not wed soon—an improbable occurrence given the isolation of your estate and the impossibility of staging a come-out. When he ceased mentioning the subject in his letters, I assumed that he had confessed."

"He never did, but you must know how he was; he never overcame his aversion to facing trouble. He must have decided that confessing served no purpose, since neither of us could change anything."

How like Robert, she admitted as Reeves filled the silence with tales of school. Even in Portugal, he had left it to her to fetch James from the military hospital, to arrange for help with the nursing, to sit up night after night as James thrashed about in delirium, to deal with the seizure that had nearly killed him. . . .

If only she had known. How many tears had she shed as month after month passed with no sign of pregnancy? He could have spared her the grief, the guilt, the prayers that were never answered, and her conclusion that she was as unworthy as her father had always claimed. Did he know her so little that he'd expected her to blame him?

No.

Blame had never been her way, as he knew quite well. She would have been disappointed, but her most likely response would have been sympathy and compassion—emotions he had never learned to accept. His silence had protected him.

This explained so much that she had never understood: the barrier that prevented true closeness; his determination to excel at every endeavor, which must have balanced what he would have seen as his defect; the ambivalence he always displayed around children. . . . No wonder he had tried to shower her with luxuries they could not afford. She had thought it an attempt to mold her into his ideal wife. Instead, he had been trying to atone.

But a newer memory distracted her thoughts. George had given up thought of siring an heir after that last miscarriage. Since he had expected James to die in battle, he had often reminded Robert that it was up to him to secure the succession. No wonder Robert had been so blue-deviled the last year of his life. And no wonder he had insisted that they rush to Portugal to look after James. . . .

"Why did Robert's family know nothing of his problem?" she asked, interrupting an improbable story involving a flock of turkeys and a despised tutor.

Reeves showed no surprise at the question. "He was injured in a riding accident at age fifteen while visiting me during long break. The surgeon was unable to repair all the damage."

"I see." So he had never mustered the courage to tell the family.

Too many emotions jostled for attention. Sorting them out was best done away from suspicious eyes and hostile faces. Her appetite was gone anyway, so she excused herself from the breakfast room.

4

Craig fled the latest importuning relative, escaping to the safety of the library. The day had been an orgy of unpleasantness.

He had no idea why Emma had left breakfast without eating, but he feared she had met with too much antagonism. He had run into enough himself. Even his mother had left the dowager's side long enough to read him a blistering scold.

"What makes you think you know better than

someone who has dealt with the family problems for
years?" she had demanded after parroting the same
words his grandmother had hurled at him last night.
"You are impossible! It was bad enough that you
stayed away for fifteen years without a word, but over-
throwing all our plans is too much. We will never live
down the ignominy."

"The only ignominy will attach to Grandmother for
forging letters in my name," he'd snapped. "It is time
she admitted who is earl here."

"Craigmont!" Tears filled her eyes—a trick she used
to signify repentance after angering the dowager, but
one he abhorred. "If you try to foist that awful woman
on this family, you will lose the respect of every member of society. She does not belong in a proper
home—as she knows quite well. You saw how she fled
when the vicar explained her mistake."

"Enough, Mother. False tears never move me. Nor
do lies. You may vent your spleen in private, but this
is my home now. If you cannot welcome my guests
during this season of hope and good cheer, you must
remain in your room." He had cut off further dis-
course by leaving, but he had hardly reached the hallway before an uncle accosted him. Then a cousin.
Then another. Six hours later, he had yet to find a
moment alone to think.

Not until he locked the library door did he spot
Mrs. Fairlawn thumbing through a folio of wildflower
prints. He stifled the urge to bury his face in her
bosom. She was the only one in the house who wasn't
either berating him or begging favors.

"You needn't leave," he said as she rose to return
the folio to its shelf.

"You appear to be a man in need of solitude, my
lord."

"Not solitude as much as a respite from the greatest collection of fortune hunters, fribbles, and fools it has ever been my misfortune to encounter." He sank into a wing chair, relieving the strain on his leg.

"Fools, my lord? An odd description for your family."

"Please do not be forever *my lording* me. The courtesy grates upon my ears, for I have heard nothing but endless repetitions of it since breakfast—all of them attached to demands."

"That is inevitable, Captain. Few people would seek out the dowager. I heard that she rarely helps anyone, unless doing so leaves them financially dependent on her. Most of the family is now under her thumb. Many live here year around. She raised quite a ruckus when your Uncle Stephen escaped her clutches."

"What happened?"

"His wife unexpectedly inherited a fortune, allowing them to purchase an estate in Kent."

"A long way from Shropshire."

"Exactly. He has ignored the dowager's demands ever since. Now that you have dodged her marriage plans, some people hope you might succeed in routing her."

"And then what? Do they expect me to grant their every desire?" He shook his head. "I had not realized what a woeful family I am called to lead. Never have I seen a more ridiculous bunch of prancing puppies. Cousin Harold actually tortures himself with a cravat that prevents him from moving his head, and Cousin Edward cannot sit down due to the tightness of his doeskin breeches. How can he even wriggle into them?"

"With a great deal of help." She laughed. "You sound as disapproving as the crustiest graybeard.

Surely you cannot equate the fashion of the moment with a reduction in either intelligence or ability. When my mother was young, she had to wear enormous panniers and towering coiffures which were just as impractical as what today's dandies espouse."

"True," he conceded grudgingly, relaxing when she resumed her seat. "Yet how am I to judge their requests when everything about them seems alien?" The question was rhetorical, but she must have sensed his perplexity.

"Are they so different from the new officers you've dealt with on the Peninsula?"

"I suppose not. We had our share of witless puppies who think war is a game whose prize is fame and glory. They soil their breeches the first time they experience enemy fire and discover they face an army whose primary goal is to shoot them." He found nothing glorious in battle and held only contempt for those who enjoyed killing.

"Try to see past people's affectations," she advised, returning to his original problem. Perhaps she had recognized his bitter tone. "No one can expect an immediate answer, for you have had no chance to explore even the most basic questions. How extensive is your fortune? Are there estate problems that need attention? What prestige can you bring to bear on behalf of your dependents? Only after learning about your own position can you decide which requests are worthy of support. James faced a similar challenge, compounded by his injuries, which were still debilitating when he came into the title. Having expected to make a lifelong career of the military, he knew little of estate management, agricultural reform, the family investments, or his relatives' concerns. The steward was quick to take advantage of his ignorance. Once James

found out, he replaced the man and asked me to oversee the new one until he was mobile enough to do
so himself."

"Why you?" She hardly seemed a font of agricultural knowledge.

"His brothers were dead, he knew few of his relatives, and I had disclosed the original steward's failings." She shrugged. "Robert had long suspected the
man of pilfering, but George refused to listen—though
he kept a close enough eye on the books that the
steward could steal only an occasional shilling."

"Something else I must learn about," he said, moan-
ing. The magnitude of the job ahead nearly overwhelmed him. "I've never even seen an estate ledger."

"I doubt they are much different from regimental
records. James often complained about the many reports he had to write, so I'm sure you are familiar
with ledgers. And if your grandmother has been in
charge, as everyone claims, then I doubt there has
been any illegal activity. She seems the sort to severely
punish anyone who cheated her. I *would* question
whether the estate has adopted the latest agricultural
techniques, though. Doing so can increase both your
income and that of your tenants."

"In what way?" Here was another subject he knew
nothing about.

She explained the changes she had helped James
implement at Fairport, warning that some of them
might not work at Blacktower, which was both inland
and farther north. Her own study had begun as a way
to help Robert's parishioners survive ever-increasing
prices. "But I should hardly be instructing you in the
management of your estate," she concluded an hour
later.

"Why not? I asked." He smiled. "And I would

rather come to you for information. You are the only person in the house who is not seeking my favor."

"What demands have you endured so far?"

He shifted to relieve the knot forming in his bad leg. "Money. Support to convince a reluctant father to approve a betrothal. Investment in what sounds like a wildly improbable scheme for some sort of dray that runs on rails."

"A railway enterprise." She laughed. "Several men have been experimenting with mechanical horses. At least one colliery installed such a device, though the engine proved too heavy for the tracks. It now sits near the mine, pulling cars back and forth from the quay by means of a cable. You will wish to study the proposal carefully, though, for many are spurious, and even those that are legitimate may not succeed."

"When did this madness start?"

"I am not sure, though a small track was set up in London several years ago to demonstrate the Catch-Me-Who-Can. The squire's son thought it quite astounding, though George considered it poppycock."

Craig shook his head. "Perhaps I should have spent more time with the other officers. I wonder what else I missed."

"Nothing you cannot learn about now. What other demands have you received?"

"The females. The dowager is pressing two of my cousins to wed, so she invited several candidates. Now that they think me available, three of them have become shocking flirts, despite being unable to look me in the face without cringing." He grimaced at the bitterness in his voice. His complaints sounded like whining, and he suddenly wanted her to think better of him.

"Do not feel unworthy just because your shell

shows a little wear," she said, responding as to a child. "You're experienced enough to know that scars fade with time. Granted, you can never return to youthful perfection, but that matters only if you allow it to."

"You speak of things you cannot understand."

"Not at all." She slid up her sleeve to expose a forearm covered with jagged scars. His stomach turned over at the pain she must have suffered.

"What happened?"

She shrugged. "A dog attack ten years ago. They had to kill the animal to free me. That is how the slice happened." She pointed to a six-inch silver line. "Fortunately, it injured nothing vital. Nor did yours."

"I know, and I know they will fade—though it is difficult to hide a face."

"I assure you, my sleeves are fashionably short in summer. I have found that people cease noticing the scars after a few meetings."

"Not in society," he countered. "I have visited London often enough to know that the *beau monde* does not tolerate imperfection. They treat crippled soldiers abominably and will consider the latest addition to my collection monstrous—which makes determined flirtation even harder to bear."

"Very well, I will grant you your irritation. But you must expect such interest, Captain. Earls always attract attention from ladies like Miss Wheeler—I assume that she is one of those annoying you?"

He nodded.

"Her father recently lost a fortune at cards. With hopes of a London come-out dashed, she is frantic to attach a wealthy husband who will provide the life she has always expected. You are the most desirable *parti* available, though I would advise you not to take that personally. A blind ninety-year-old would attract her if he could offer a title and wealth."

"Cutting her should settle that problem." He shrugged.

"I doubt it. And it would create others."

"Why?" Was he to be beset by fortune hunters wherever he went?

"Whatever your reservations about society, you must assume your place in it, my lord." Her deliberate use of his title was a harsh reminder of his new responsibilities. "Cutting someone for trying to catch your eye will raise more scandal than your imperfect appearance. Everyone in your position faces the same problem."

"Then how can I discourage her? I can hardly remain in my rooms. Grandmother's insistence on tradition means that I must host a score of holiday activities, starting tomorrow. There will be no respite until after Twelfth Night." Forgoing his duties as host would weaken his position with the dowager.

"Mimic the other gentlemen. Remain polite but aloof. Treat every eligible female exactly alike. By spreading your favors evenly, you raise no expectations. Save your cuts for those who break serious rules. So far, Miss Wheeler merely makes a cake of herself, as everyone can see. They will judge her accordingly. Your only problem will be to remain alert, for desperate misses will sometimes resort to dishonor to obtain a particularly wealthy prize."

"One of my fellow officers bought colors to escape just such a schemer," he admitted. "He had to wed the girl, but he immediately installed her on his most remote property, turned over his affairs to his brother, then joined us in Spain. Yet his situation preyed on his mind and probably influenced his decision to volunteer for a particularly dangerous duty at Badajoz. He did not survive."

"The Forlorn Hope," she said, surprising him. Few outside the army knew of that company. Composed of volunteers, it led the charge into the teeth of an enemy position. The few survivors were well rewarded. It allowed common soldiers to win commissions, the impoverished to earn their next promotion, and those weary of life to honorably set it aside.

"James discussed it with you?" he asked quietly. He had often considered volunteering, and would have had they faced another pitched battle immediately after Badajoz. James had no longer been there to talk him out of it.

"Not really. He mentioned it in one of his fevers—was this officer named Harry?"

He nodded. "James was close to many men, though he grieved as deeply as I for fallen friends." He shook his head, then straightened his back and changed the subject. This one was too painful. "I can understand why Miss Wheeler has shifted her eyes to me. Grandmother had been throwing her at Cousin Michael, but he has only a comfortable income."

"Who else does she wish to see wed?"

"Her grandnephew Colin."

"Mr. Langtree?"

"Yes. He's a more distant cousin. I've not spoken with him, so I have no idea of his opinion."

"I believe he is enamored of Lady Catherine."

"But that's—"

"Nothing to fret about," she said firmly. "Lady Catherine has months of mourning to complete before she can consider her future. In the meantime, she is capable of rebuffing any unwanted advances, and her melancholy faded under his attention."

"Of course." He hardly knew what to say. Perhaps this attraction explained the dowager's determination to find Colin a wife. She would be furious if Catherine left Blacktower. Tradition again.

The dressing bell saved him from responding further, but he pondered their discussion as he limped toward his room.

He could see why everyone near Fairport loved Emma. She radiated peace, treating everyone as though their concerns were vitally important and using the information she gleaned to devise solutions to their problems. And unlike the dowager, she expected nothing in return. It was how he had once hoped to conduct his own affairs.

An hour later, Emma entered the main drawing room. Only the captain's orders had forced her downstairs. Her position as a would-be governess barred her from this august company, and she had not yet recovered from the shock Mr. Reeves had dealt her. What was she to say to the man?

But even that question faded as her thoughts returned to Blacktower. Their talk had triggered more old memories. One of James's letters had mentioned Captain Curtiss, describing him as a man forced into the military by a tyrannical grandmother despite his ambition to take holy orders. His abhorrence of violence had made enduring the rigors of war even harder. And a lifetime of oppression had left him unsure of his own judgment.

She could see that for herself. He was in considerable pain, and not all from his injuries. James's hints had not begun to reveal the captain's mental torment.

She pasted a false smile on her face, but her mind remained on her host. He was a sensitive man with a strong sense of justice and a burning desire to help others—both rare, even in the clergy. How had he survived fifteen years of death and destruction? Especially after James had left. He'd admitted avoiding other officers. Her visits to the Portuguese hospital, and the scenes James had described in his delirium, gave her a good idea of the horror the captain had faced.

She pulled her mind back to the drawing room lest her soft heart put tears in her eyes.

At least sixty others were already gathered. Many glowered when she entered, proof that deserting the breakfast room that morning had revived suspicion. But Lady Catherine rushed forward to greet her.

"You look lovely tonight, Emma."

She stifled any pleasure. Her gown was hardly up to society standards, being two Seasons out of date.

But Catherine's next words drove her appearance from her mind. "Mr. Reeves confirmed that Lady Melcor has not yet replaced her daughters' governess. If you are interested, he can broach your name to her. Their estate is about fifteen miles from here."

"What do you know of the children?" she asked, relaxing as the hostile crowd shrank to a handful of helpful people.

"The twins are energetic, but delightful. The previous governess was quite good, but she had to return home to tend an ailing mother."

They were deep in discussion when the dowager arrived. A wave of hesitancy swept the room, intensified when the woman stared coldly at Blacktower, then cut Emma dead. Several guests mimicked her actions.

Emma felt like running.

"Her power is slipping," said Lady Catherine, smiling widely.

"And she feels it," concurred an older lady, deliberately joining them. "I am Lady Langtree," she added, giving Catherine no chance to introduce her. "The dowager is my husband's aunt."

Emma murmured greetings. "I can hardly blame her for distrusting me. Arriving in Lord Blacktower's company with nary a maid in sight was quite suspicious."

"But innocent," Catherine reminded her. "Anyone speaking with you must see that you are an honorable lady."

"Of course she is," said Blacktower, joining them. He bent over her hand. "Please accept my apologies for failing to protect you. I was not thinking clearly that day."

"Hardly a surprise after suffering a coaching accident atop your other injuries." But she shivered—and not from any stain their arrival had placed on her reputation. His very public support in the face of the dowager's cut had brought their power struggle firmly into the open, establishing her as a pawn in their battle. From now on, anyone approaching her would be rebuffing the dowager. The situation would allow him to identify his true supporters, but she prayed that her role on the Blacktower chessboard would not prevent Lady Melcor from hiring her.

She could hardly believe a position existed at all.

Heart's desire . . .

She touched her bodice, which again sheltered the amulet. When had she begun to believe in its power?

5

"There you are," Mr. Reeves exclaimed, joining Emma, who was fashioning garlands in the great hall.

She had gathered greens with the rest of the party that morning. A largely sleepless night had convinced her that she must participate in every activity, no matter how many cuts she faced. Avoiding the other guests played into the dowager's hands by making her seem guilty of improper conduct, which in turn reflected poorly on the captain. As the rightful owner of Blacktower, he deserved her support.

But even the carefree search for Christmas greenery emphasized her odd position between two hostile parties. The dowager had remained in the house, but no one doubted that she would hear of every smile directed at Emma. The captain's duty as host had kept him too busy to speak with her, and Lady Catherine had passed most of the expedition with Mr. Langtree. Without their support, few people had been willing to talk to her, so Emma had turned her attention to the children.

Five-year-old Jenny was her favorite. They'd had a grand time racing up and down hillsides, poking about the forest, and admiring the jewel-like lake tucked into a valley. Squirrels had chattered at them from the treetops, annoyed by the invasion of shouting, squealing people. Several dogs gamboled through the crowd, raising laughter with their antics.

But exploration had filled only part of the morning. They had also dragged holly branches to the wagon, stripped ivy from its stranglehold around a tree, and watched the captain climb a huge oak to cut down balls of mistletoe.

It was the first time she had seen him happy. He would make a wonderful earl, for he honestly cared for people. And she could already see the effect of his return. Most of the guests had picked up on his mood, genuinely enjoying themselves for the first time since her arrival. The dowager had acted on the family like ivy on a tree, choking the life from everyone she dominated.

There was no trace of snow, but the children played hiding games among the trees. Servants built a fire, offering chocolate to anyone feeling chilled. Much of the company eventually gathered there to sing carols. All things considered, it had been an enjoyable morning.

Now the entire company was busily decorating the manor.

"Were you looking for me?" she asked Reeves. "Or are they ready for this garland?"

"Looking for you. The footman Lady Catherine dispatched to Melcor House has returned." He held out a letter.

Her hand shook as she broke the seal. The contents raised a lump in her throat. "She accepts your recommendation and offers me the position. What did you say? You don't even know me."

"Fustian. I feel as though I've known you for ten years. Robert sang your praises often enough. He felt blessed to have you at his side. I merely mentioned the school you started at Fairport and your prowess on the pianoforte. When does she want you to start?"

"Boxing Day."

"Then you will attend tomorrow's ball. Will you save me a set?"

"Of course."

Mr. Langtree rushed in to collect the garlands she had woven, then swept Reeves off to help hang them. She started a new rope, but fate's stunning reprieve filled her thoughts, drowning out the ladies' chatter, and even the children's laughter.

She need not throw herself on her father's questionable mercy after all. Relief nearly burst her heart. She wanted to dance and sing and shout for joy. Only now did she admit how heavily the prospect had weighed on her shoulders. What a tremendous Christmas gift.

Heart's desire . . .

How had the man known? She had said nothing of her hopes or fears, not even mentioning her destination in that brief exchange of polite greetings when he'd boarded the coach.

Keep your wits about you . . .

What had that meant? Little wit was needed to make this decision. No sensible person would choose a life of animosity and drudgery over a respectable position where she was both wanted and needed.

Yet a thread of uncertainty tarnished her euphoria. Perhaps it arose because she had yet to meet her new charges. Or it might be lingering uneasiness from the dreams that had interrupted her limited sleep last night.

Unsettling dreams. Troubling dreams.

If only she could remember the details. But she had brushed them aside as the inevitable product of the dowager's animosity. And they probably were. The whispers that had permeated the drawing room last evening mimicked her parents' criticisms. *Unworthy. Encroaching. Shockingly unsuitable. Vulgar. No manners and less sensibility . . .*

She had never been acceptable, first because of her gender—as the only survivor among a dozen stillbirths and miscarriages, she should at least have had the courtesy to be a boy so her father's title would not pass to a despised cousin—then for the cost of raising her when everyone knew she would never attract a wealthy husband who might improve the family fortune. So it was no surprise that the most nightmarish dream had featured the dowager and her parents mercilessly attacking her.

But why had Robert appeared? And why had he been battling Captain Curtiss over a cradle?

She shook her head. That couldn't be right. The cradle probably represented Robert's inability to father a child. But it was Reeves who had been upset by Robert's silence, so he must have been the figure in the dream. He shared the captain's dark coloring.

On the other hand, if the cradle depicted her search for a new life, Robert might well have argued with Captain Curtiss. The captain was helping her find a post, while Robert would not have wanted her working. But he had not known Agnes. . . .

Miss Wheeler's arrival pulled Emma out of her thoughts. She shivered at the girl's malevolent glare, though the animosity was hardly surprising. Miss Wheeler considered her a rival rather than a pawn, for everyone believed she was close to the captain. So far, the girl had joined neither side of the family struggle, though she was clearly courting both.

"What an artistic masterpiece!" she exclaimed, joining the dowager, who was putting the finishing touches on the largest kissing bough Emma had ever seen. It would grace tomorrow's ball.

Emma concentrated on her garland, but she could not shut out Miss Wheeler's voice. The girl must have quizzed the servants, concluding that the dowager's wishes always prevailed, for she was making herself as agreeable as possible.

"Your preparations have made this house party the most delightful I've ever attended, my lady," she said, simpering. "It is heartwarming to find someone who observes the old traditions. Too many people have let them slide into undeserved obscurity. Is it true that tomorrow's children's party will feature the Lord of Misrule?"

Emma cringed when the dowager accepted the praise as genuine. How many house parties could Miss Wheeler have attended? She didn't look a day over seventeen. This was probably her first adult gathering.

The girl's motives should be obvious to the meanest intelligence. She extolled the dowager's knowledge and experience, then rued the captain's willful blindness in ignoring that experience. Under her prodding, the dowager was soon listing Blacktower's virtues—or what she perceived to be his virtues.

Emma gritted her teeth through descriptions of his devotion to duty and respect for his family. The dowager gloated over the prestige that had attached to the Blacktower title since Henry VIII had bestowed it upon an ancestor three centuries earlier, listing in detail every honor received by an earl since that day.

"Blacktowers have distinguished themselves in Parliament for generations," the woman said, using the resounding tones of an orator. "And Curtisses have been honored for their military prowess since the first one set foot on English soil at the side of William the Conqueror. Craigmont will not be the first to be lauded for both endeavors. He has already served gloriously against the Corsican monster, and his plans for preventing such upheavals from ever occurring in this country will draw praise from every man in Parliament. We can ignore that recent bit of carelessness," she added lightly. "It will have taught him caution."

"Carelessness?" Emma could remain quiet no longer. "You make war sound like a stroll in the garden."

"What would you know of such things?" the dowager snapped, glaring at the intruder who dared question her claims. "War is a glorious crusade that proves one's superiority and earns undying fame."

Emma drew herself upright, ignoring the voice that warned against making an enemy of the Melcors' neighbor. "War may occasionally be necessary to protect the innocent from the greedy, but it is a vicious, filthy business fought in abominable conditions. The military hospitals are little more than antechambers for the hereafter. I would not condemn a rabid dog to their care. Given the severity of the captain's injuries, his survival is a miracle."

"What would a woman know of such things?" demanded a gentleman who had arrived to collect more decorations. Since she had overheard him making similar statements that very morning, his scoffing tone could only be an attempt to placate the dowager. Fool. Did he really expect the captain to lose this battle?

"My husband and I traveled to Portugal after his brother was injured at Badajoz. James would have died had we not removed him from the hospital. Many with lesser wounds were not so lucky."

"As I thought," drawled a young dandy. "Arduous travel affected your mind. Women should stay at home where they belong, lest their fanciful fears infect others."

"A true lady would refrain from vulgar exaggeration," said an older gentleman, also ranging himself against her. "It sets a deplorable example, needlessly frightening ladies of sensibility." He gestured toward Miss Wheeler, who was artistically swooning.

"And shows a deplorable lack of respect for her betters," snapped the dowager. But her eyes gleamed at this show of support.

Emma shrugged. She had seen this willful blindness before, particularly among society's fribbles. Gentlemen did not want the world's miseries intruding into their comfortable lives. Admitting that friends were suffering in service to their country raised guilt. And few bothered to enlighten them. Newly retired officers wanted to forget the horror, so most people's knowledge of war came from heroic paintings or from old men reliving the glories of youthful campaigns. They either ignored the worst memories or boasted of them, as old Colonel Potter so often did.

"Discomfort?" he would snort, waving a glass of wine at his companions. "You never saw such wretched conditions. Rained every day for weeks. Horrible muck underfoot. But we carried the day." He conveniently forgot that his regiment had ultimately surrendered to the American rebels.

6

Christmas.

Despite a lengthy evening of sharing punch with carolers, attending church services, lighting the Yule log, and finally eating and drinking until the wee hours, Craig had again awakened before eight. He had no plans, for tradition demanded that each family group spend the morning in private. They would eventually drift down for breakfast, then meet in the great hall for a children's party at noon. Those without children would likely remain in bed until well after that. It was yet another gulf between him and the others.

But he had no family—or none that he was close to. His mother had ceased to exist as a separate person. Catherine would be with her daughter. Where would Emma be?

The question conjured memories of last night's dinner. Busy with his duties as host, he had caught only glimpses of her during the day—helping a child gather greens, making garlands in the great hall, talking to Catherine in the drawing room—but her name had arisen over the port. The dowager had apparently described war as a glorious crusade, throwing Emma into one of her passions. If the men spoke truly, she had said little enough, but the furor continued as gentlemen scrambled to discredit her lest she overturn their comfortable perceptions.

Shallow fools.

He had said nothing, unwilling to share his own painful experiences with those who could never understand them. They formed yet another barrier between him and his family, for few of them would believe what he had endured for the past fifteen years. Nor could he understand the petty concerns that filled their days.

Damnation!

He paused in the breakfast room doorway.

Despite the early hour, Miss Wheeler occupied the table. Alone. The hair stood up on his neck. She must have quizzed the staff to discover his habits. He had no doubt that she planned to maneuver the servants away, then cry compromise. She had been frankly furious that he had ignored her last evening.

"I shan't bother Cook for a steak just now," he told Horner, preventing the butler from leaving. "I must deal with an emergency before I can eat a proper meal."

Grabbing a piece of toast—and cursing under his breath—he fled the house, grateful that the day was unseasonably warm. He would remain on the grounds until noon.

Miss Wheeler was becoming a nuisance. Perhaps he should avoid the guests from now on. Their antics were wearing thin anyway. Appearing amiable when he was surrounded by fools and fretting over the men he had left in Spain grew more difficult each day.

Striding past the last formal garden, he ducked into the maze. It had been a childhood refuge, offering escape from his grandmother's oppressive will.

"Good morning, Captain," said Emma, once he'd threaded the hedges.

"Mrs. Fairlawn!" Startled, his words came out in a croak.

The prize for reaching the center. William's voice again echoed in his head, recalling the game they had once played. And she was a prize, indeed, this morning. Tendrils escaped from her usually severe hairstyle, curling provocatively around her face and neck. He staggered under the urge to kiss those rosy lips, to throw her to the ground and ravish her, to spirit her away to a land of enchantment.

The otherworldly aura that permeated mazes must be affecting his mind. "What are you doing here?" he demanded, more harshly than he had intended, reminding himself again that she was James's sister and thus unavailable for dalliance.

"Taking the air." She cocked her head to one side. "Is the maze private?"

"Of course not. I was merely surprised to meet anyone at this early hour, particularly here. But you are welcome. Did someone give you the key?"

She smiled. "Actually, your maze is nearly identical to one near Fairport. I had not expected to reach the center, but managed it with only two wrong turns."

"Amazing. It is quite complex. William and I often escaped new tutors and unwanted visitors by dodging in here. There are topiary animals in blind corners that are more difficult to find than the center."

"Is that why you are here today?" She rose as if to leave.

"Don't go," he begged. "I was feeling harassed, but an intelligent ear is always welcome. If you are not cold," he added as she pulled her cloak tighter. It was the same threadbare affair she had been wearing on the mail coach, but knowing what lay beneath made it seem more flattering today.

"Not at all. But who would bother you on Christmas morning? Your grandmother?"

"Miss Wheeler was alone in the breakfast room."

"At this hour?"

He nodded. "She is clearly determined to snare my title, despite knowing we have nothing in common. None of them care a whit for anything important." His blue-devils returned with a vengeance as he limped restlessly about the clearing.

Emma returned to the bench. "What is really troubling you, Captain? Miss Wheeler's antics are easily avoided, and you must know that it will take time to feel comfortable in your new duties."

"My *duty* lies in Spain," he snapped, recalling his fruitless search for information. "Or perhaps France by this time. How am I to know? I've seen no reports of our push across the mountains. The papers don't even list the casualties from the skirmish that wounded me, though I know that several of my men died. I gleaned more news from new arrivals at the hospital than from the London papers. One article even questioned whether we should continue wasting money on a hopeless fight in so distant a place."

"Typical. The battle is so far removed from the readers' lives that few can understand its necessity. And news is always many weeks behind time. But you know that your duty lies here. You will have to adjust to hearing news in a less timely fashion."

"That will be difficult." He joined her on the bench. "Instead of blindly obeying Grandmother's order to return at once, I should have rejoined my men until success was assured. It cannot be much longer. The French were falling back when I was injured, and we had captured much of their equipment. But Soult is a canny general, so there is always the potential for disaster. Until Napoleon is locked away, no one is safe."

"If your troops are on the move, you would only hold them back," she reminded him, nodding toward his bad leg. "Surely you left good men in charge."

"Yes." He sighed at the reminder, but she was right.

"And you must admit that you have an important job here."

"Aiding frivolous idiots?"

"You are determined to be out of sorts today, aren't you."

"What?"

"You are an intelligent man, so why don't you cease moping and think. Yes, many gentlemen have no understanding of what you have been through, but that is because your endeavors were successful. Why is every Spaniard attuned to the horrors of war?"

He sighed. "Because they have lived in the middle of one for years."

"Exactly. Whether they joined the resistance, aided France, or merely avoided involvement, they could not ignore the fighting. Those who remained in England have never experienced war, because you kept Napoleon so busy elsewhere that he could not invade. Yet in keeping us safe, you also kept most of us innocent. Which would you prefer? Empathy with your suffering or the confidence that arises from peace?"

"Confidence, obviously. But how am I to live with such innocence? I have nothing in common with the rest of my family."

"I cannot imagine how you survived fifteen years in the military," she said, shaking her head. "Impatience should have killed you long ago."

"What is that supposed to mean?"

"How long have you been in England, Captain?"

"Ten days."

"Most of them traveling?"

He nodded.

"Do you recall your reactions when you first joined your regiment?"

He'd already suspected where her words were heading. She was right. "I was lost. It was an alien world full of alien beings speaking a language I barely understood. I was convinced I could never fit in."

"Because it was completely different from the world in which you had been living."

Her piercing eyes raised shame for the first time. "I railed at fate," he admitted. "I had planned to pursue a career in the church, so I cursed Grandmother from dawn until well after dark for condemning me to a life of violence. Though Father's signature purchased my commission, her orders were responsible."

She shook her head. "You are still cursing fate, Captain. Like the dowager, you do not relinquish control willingly. But what if you had followed your heart fifteen years ago? Would you have railed against God if He had installed you in a remote parish? After all, Robert had no interest in serving as a Cumberland curate when he took holy orders."

He laughed. "I never thought of that. My dreams always led to the archbishop's throne in Canterbury— in record time."

"Visions of grandeur." She joined his laughter. "I should not be surprised after hearing your grandmother's sermon on the power and glory your ancestors brought to the title. You must have been raised on that history. But life rarely plays out as we expect. We can only make the best of whatever fate hands us. In your case, that means occupying a seat in Parliament and taking responsibility for hundreds of dependents. Learning about those duties will keep you busy for some time." She rose. "I must return to the house. I promised to speak with Lady Catherine this morning."

"She will be in the nursery." He offered his arm, then laid his hand over hers, irritated to find her fingers stiff with cold inside her thin gloves. He should not have kept her talking for so long. Even unseasonable warmth could chill to the bone in December. But she was the only person he could speak his mind to.

"Thank—" Her response died as Miss Wheeler appeared, the maze key clutched tightly in one fist.

"My lord," she gasped in feigned surprise. But the look she bestowed on Emma could have slain armies.

"I know you have urgent business, Captain," said Emma, giving him no chance to reply. "Thank you for showing me the way in, but you needn't stay. Since Miss Wheeler has a key, she can lead me out. In return, I will repeat the fascinating history you told me."

Dropping his arm, she smiled guilelessly at Miss Wheeler. "Have you heard about the white lady who haunts this maze? Shortly after it was built, tragedy claimed the life of an innocent maid seeking the treasure rumored to be at its center—though some claim she was really a cold-hearted schemer."

She had somehow maneuvered Miss Wheeler away from the entrance while uttering what promised to be a very pointed parable. Smiling in gratitude, he made good his escape. Miss Wheeler might be overwhelmed for the moment, but she would recover in short order.

He considered riding out to the ruins, but that had been another childhood refuge. Miss Wheeler undoubtedly knew them all. The dowager's hand had produced that key.

Reaching the house, he locked himself in the estate office. Emma was right. His preoccupation with the unfinished business in Spain prevented him from performing his new duties. He could no longer affect the outcome of the war—if he ever could. The officers who led his men were better than he had ever been. Even after fifteen years, he had never shaken his terror at facing fire. How many nights had he lain awake, fearful that others recognized his cowardice or haunted by men who had died from his mistakes? He had done his best, but it had never been good enough. Now it was over.

It's over. The realization burst through him in a growing wave of euphoria. His hand brushed against the token in his waistcoat pocket.

Heart's desire . . .

It was over and time to move on.

7

Craig limped around the great hall. The ball that marked the beginning of the twelve days of Christmas was another tradition. At least no one expected him to dance. He spoke mostly to gentlemen who owned nearby estates, but his eyes constantly searched the crowd for Emma. Where the devil was she?

He had not seen her since leaving the maze. He'd remained in the office all morning, studying the estate ledgers. Once Horner confirmed that Miss Wheeler was assisting the dowager with the children's party, he had moved to the library, where he ate a belated breakfast, then summoned assorted relatives to demand details about earlier requests. He asked uncles about the agricultural reforms Emma had mentioned and sought information about the politics and ideas prevalent in England at the close of 1813.

His mind reeled under this onslaught of facts, but he persevered. One day of study would not make up for fifteen years of ignorance, but it was a start. And his willingness to seek advice had warmed more than one face. The few decisions he'd already made seemed sound—not that his grandmother would agree. She had previously turned down some of the schemes he now condoned.

They were headed for a final confrontation, though he hoped to postpone it until after Twelfth Night. But she would have to accept that he was now in charge.

"My lord, I need your help." Miss Wheeler laid a pleading hand on his arm. Her scandalously low-cut gown offered a generous view of the assets nestled in its gaping bodice. But as usual, her eyes never strayed above his cravat.

"Is there a problem?"

"My sister has escaped the nursery, probably to play in the garden. I must find her before my father discovers her prank and punishes her."

"You hardly need my permission to leave the house," he said shortly.

"The search would go much faster if you accompanied me."

"Hardly. The footmen know every inch of the grounds, while I do not." That brought her eyes up, revealing a flash of fury. He drew her apart from the crowd. "I will be frank with you, Miss Wheeler. I am tired of your childish scheming. You make a cake of yourself by hanging on my arm, for I have no interest in schoolroom chits. And your attempts to wrest an offer from me are so dishonorable that I would never consider accommodating you."

"You would betray your class to that extent?" she demanded.

"They betrayed me long ago."

Fury flushed her face.

"Let me be perfectly clear," he continued. "You care nothing for me, as anyone can see. Thus your flirtations only reveal your greed. If you knew anything about me, you would never consider this course. I abhor London society and prefer a Spartan life. I believe that wielding the power of a title to avenge petty insults is unworthy of both ladies and gentlemen. My fortune will help my tenants and better the lives of the unfortunate. My attention will be on implementing the latest agricultural techniques and convincing the government to support the men maimed in its service."

Her hand quivered.

"Slapping me will only draw unwanted attention," he said quietly. "I would do whatever was necessary to stop you. Is that the sort of scene you want? Face the truth. Even if society's leaders discovered us in bed together, I would refuse to offer for you. Their opinions do not matter, for I respect none of them."

"You have ruined my holiday," she said through clenched teeth. "I was meant to make a splendid match at this party. Now Father will be furious. May you rot in the hottest corner of hell. May children run screaming from you in horror. I should have known that a crippled monster would not understand honor. I hope you suffer at least half as much as I have." Lips artistically trembling, she flounced off.

He nearly laughed at the idea that she knew anything about suffering. Infant. She had no concept of life's trials.

"What insult have you paid Miss Wheeler?" demanded the dowager several minutes later. "Will you never learn to control your loutish manners? Avoiding the children's party was bad enough. But how could you make that sweet child cry?"

"That sweet child is an unscrupulous fortune hunter who has successfully pulled the wool over your eyes about her character. It seems your vaunted perspicacity has diminished with age, for that is the second girl who has tricked you lately. We both know that you would never champion a chit who shares your determination. Nor would you support one who covets only the family purse. My insult was to point out that compromising me would merely destroy her reputation, since nothing would prompt me to offer for her."

"Appalling manners." She glared at him. "I cannot imagine how you became so uncivilized."

"From living in the mud, filth, and disease you condemned me to fifteen years ago," he snapped before reining in his temper. This was no place for an argument.

The dowager sputtered in indignation.

"Have you seen Emma this evening?" asked Catherine, joining them.

"No, though she should have come down an hour ago."

"Absurd boy!" The dowager snorted. "No trollop would dream of attending a society ball."

"She is no trollop and had already accepted my invitation," said Catherine stonily.

"But you have no authority to augment the guest list, as she obviously knows."

"Catherine *does* hold that authority." His tone made the dowager step back a pace. Fury swept every pore of his body. He forgot their audience, forgot the day, forgot everything in the realization that this woman had barred Emma from the ball. The lowliest governess was welcome, but a baron's daughter was not. "As William's widow, Catherine is chatelaine of Blacktower until I marry—an aspect of proper manners that you have ignored since Grandfather's death fourteen years ago."

"You understand nothing, Craigmont," she snapped.

"I understand that you have overstepped your authority. Outside of the dower house, you have none. Since you have chosen to live here, you must defer to Catherine, for she is in charge. If that is too onerous a prospect, then leave. I will not countenance disharmony under my roof."

"How dare you order me about!"

"I dare because I own this estate and everything on it. I dare because ordering people about has been my job for fifteen years, thanks to your meddling. Did you forget that the military trains its officers to follow the proper chain of command? Or did you willfully ignore that, as you have ignored so much else?"

"You cannot walk into my home and depose me," she spat. "The family will not stand for it. Nor will the staff."

Her shouts were drawing notice. Silence swept the ballroom. Even the musicians fell quiet. Every eye stared at the tableau in the corner.

The dowager's eye swept the crowd, demanding a show of support.

No one moved. No one breathed.

Finally Lord Langtree stepped forward. "Welcome home, my lord." Pointedly cutting his aunt, he smiled at Craig and extended his hand. "You are a credit to your position, Blacktower."

"Senile imbecile," she gasped, gesturing Horner to her side. "Summon the magistrate at once, Horner. This man is perpetrating a monumental fraud. Craigmont died serving his country. A deserter hoped to get his hands on the family wealth by impersonating him, but disfigurement has proved an ineffectual disguise. Lock him up, then ask Stephen to join me in the library. He is now the earl."

Horner turned his back on her. "Should we move her bits and pieces to the dower house, my lord?"

"Tomorrow will be sufficient. I trust it has been properly aired?"

"As you ordered."

She gasped, her eyes again sweeping the room, but though they paused on each guest in turn, no one met her gaze. One by one, they acknowledged Craig before resuming their conversations. Two retired officers saluted him. His great-aunt winked. The musicians struck up a sprightly country dance. Stephen's lighthearted laugh floated above the crowd noise.

Her face crumpled, showing every one of her eighty-two years. Without a word, she fled.

Craig relaxed for the first time in years. He had won. There remained the battle to modernize the estate, but that would be easier than anything he had faced in a very long time. Sending Catherine and Colin for a breath of fresh air on the terrace—Emma had been right to suspect a future there—he turned to rectifying the dowager's latest outrage.

Emma jumped when Blacktower entered the library. "You should be in the ballroom, my lord."

"I just learned of my grandmother's pettiness. You are welcome to join us. She will move to the dower house in the morning."

"Congratulations."

He raised his brows.

"You have taken charge of your life."

"For the moment. Will you join me at the ball?"

She shook her head. "I have nothing suitable to wear, and I will be leaving at dawn in any event. Lady Melcor offered me a post teaching her twins. Thank you for your assistance."

"What?" His face twisted in shock.

"You do not consider me worthy to be a governess?"

"Of course you are worthy. But how could you find a position this quickly?"

"Mr. Reeves and Lady Catherine. You did ask them to help me. The Melcor estate is only a few miles from here. And you will benefit from my leaving. Making peace with those closest to the dowager will be easier once I am gone."

"Fustian! I know I offered to help, but you deserve better than a life of service." He ran his fingers through his hair. "Marry me."

"How absurd." She had trouble forcing the words past the heart pounding in her throat. He could not have considered his offer. Either he thought to deflect Miss Wheeler by announcing a betrothal or defeating his grandmother so quickly had unhinged his mind.

He glared at her. "What is absurd about it? I cannot think of anyone who is better suited for the position. I have already come to depend upon your good sense. And your knowledge is far broader than mine."

"So could any decent steward say. Now enough of this silliness. I must retire if I am to get an early start." She rose.

Craig blocked the door. His proposal had startled him as much as it had her, but the more he thought about it, the better he liked the idea. "It is hardly silly," he countered. "I truly wish to wed you."

"You cannot have thought it through, my lord. I am far beneath your touch. Such an alliance would be scandalous."

"Your father is a baron. Your mother was fourth child to the Earl of Whitewater and granddaughter to the Duke of Bellingham." He grinned at her surprise. "I looked you up so I could counter the dowager's spite, but I wouldn't care if your parents were tenants. War taught me to judge people by their accomplishments. In battle, a man's station means nothing. What matters is whether I can depend on him to do his job."

"But society does not operate on those principles." She sighed. "You need to adjust to your new life and learn society's rules before you consider taking a wife."

"Is it my scars?" he demanded suddenly. "I thought you did not care about them."

"I don't." But her heart froze. "So that explains it. Instead of using me to sidestep Miss Wheeler's pressure, you are convinced that you deserve no one better."

Craig stared at her white face. His thoughtless words had hurt her. His stupid, thoughtless words. A stab of pain drew his hand to his stomach, brushing his arm against his pocket.

Heart's desire . . .

Knowledge streaked through his mind. Striding close enough to grasp her shoulders, he stared into her eyes.

"Miss Wheeler has realized the folly of her schemes. She fled my side after delivering the most juvenile curses I have heard in years. Nor does your tolerance of my appearance mean anything. I love you, Emma. I need you. I want to marry you. Is that clear enough?"

He loved her? Emma's heart stalled. Was he hon-

estly offering her another chance for children of her
own? Her hands clasped against her bodice.

Heart's desire . . .

His eyes were open, their depths clear of cunning.
Warmth flowed from his touch, building joy in her
heart.

*You will face many choices . . . keep your wits
about you . . .*

Could a man experiencing so much turmoil truly
know his own mind? She could not allow her own
desires to lead her astray. His claims were suspect
enough without twisting them further.

"You cannot have considered the consequences."
Only determination kept her voice calm and its tone
neutral. "Society would never accept me, as everyone
in this house knows quite well. My presence has already driven a wedge into this family. Wedding me
would create a rift that could last for generations."

"You refine too much. Granted, Grandmother will
not welcome you, but after tonight, she will never accept me either—her latest charge is that I am an im-
postor scheming to steal the family fortune." He
shook his head in disgust. "Now that she is vanquished, the rest are tripping over their feet in their
rush to welcome me. Langtree cut her dead just now,
and her son laughed."

She glared at him. "I know nothing about being
a countess."

"I know nothing about being an earl."

"But you have no choice. Even Shropshire society
would shun me. You cannot risk alienating your
neighbors by elevating a governess so far. I have fallen
foul of ladies often enough to know how they will
react, and my position was higher then."

"If you are referring to Lady Dumford, she insults

everyone." He smiled at her shock. "I know all about the woman. James claims she would spread calumny about Christ himself if He dared contradict her."

Despite herself, she laughed. It was such a perfect description.

"According to James, everyone else admires you greatly, and many consider you a saint. I can see why. You are the most caring woman I've ever met."

She tried to pull away, for his nearness was making it difficult to think. "That was an entirely different situation, my lord."

"Craig."

"My lord. Behavior admired in a vicar's wife would be shocking in a countess."

"Craig. I love you, Emma. Accept it."

She closed her eyes.

He glared at her shuttered face. She might be caring, but she was also stubborn beyond belief. Yet he needed her. His hands burned where they gripped her shoulders.

"Look at me, Emma." He repeated the command until her eyes opened. "There is only one excuse I will accept. If you can look me in the eyes and swear you care nothing for me, I will leave you now." He could see her struggle, but counted on her honesty to carry the day.

"I do care," she said at last. "But this will never work."

"It will. I love you," he said again. "With you at my side, I can handle anything fate throws at me. You have given me the courage I have always lacked."

"You lack nothing, Craig. You would not have survived fifteen years of war without courage. Hating violence does not make you a coward, though it must have caused you much pain."

He stared, amazed at how differently she interpreted his shame—and at how well she knew him. "You have given me the greatest gift of all, Emma—you believed in me, even when I could not believe in myself. You have healed my spirit and revived a faith I misplaced years ago. Please share my future."

She hesitated another long moment, then finally smiled. "Very well, I will wed you. Because I love you. You care for people in a way I rarely see."

He kissed her, pulling her close, relishing the rightness of it—until he felt an odd lump pressing against his chest.

"What—"

Her blush cut off his words. But she turned away to retrieve something from her bodice. "And oddity I received a few days ago." Her hand opened to reveal a heart.

"From a strange little man who promised you your heart's desire," he finished, pulling out his own.

They were identical.

She stared, then walked to the window to look up at the Christmas star. "I wonder . . ."

"I had just finished praying for help with the confrontation I knew I faced," he admitted.

"I had prayed for an alternative to going home."

"We are truly blessed." He gazed deep into her eyes. "My heart's desire was peace and someone to share it with."

"Love and children of my own," she admitted.

"And an end to loneliness."

"Happy Christmas."

"Happy Christmas, my love."

His lips covered hers. As their hands clasped, the hearts tangled, merging into one.

Christmas Wish List
by Barbara Metzger

1

"Christmas is coming," proclaimed the vicar. "Rejoice." His voice rose in volume and in fervor as he expounded on the holiday season, the holy child, the princely gifts, the hope for mankind. "And we must not forget the less fortunate at this time of sharing," Reverend Buttons went on. And on, reminding his parishioners of the indigent, the ill, the orphans, and how much more blessed it was to give than to receive. As his voice rose, his eyes did too, directing the congregants' gazes to the water-stained ceiling of the old stone chapel. "Be generous, my friends."

Or be wet when the roof collapsed, Miss Geraldine Selden correctly interpreted the vicar's unspoken message. Well, she and her brother were having too hard a time keeping a roof over their own heads to contribute much to the church fund. While Reverend Buttons started to decry the selfish greed rampant in the world, his favorite theme, Gerry let her mind wander. She mentally counted the jars of jams already put up, the shirts she'd been sewing for months, the shillings she'd managed to set aside for the Christmas boxes. There were apples and tops and cornhusk dolls for the children, packets of sugar tied in pretty ribbons for their mothers, a twist of tobacco for Old Man Pingtree who lived behind the livery. The Seldens were doing what they could, despite their own meager finances. But Gerry would *not* think of their straitened circumstances, not now.

So what if she and her brother Eustace, or Stacey as everyone called him, were forced to live in their former gatekeeper's cottage? They had each other, didn't they? And the rents from Selden House went to pay the mortgage and their father's other debts, so Stacey's patrimony would not be lost entirely. They had their health, their friends, enough food to eat, and enough funds to celebrate the holiday season.

Without repining over what used to be, Gerry daydreamed about what was to come: the smells of fresh-baked gingerbread and fresh-cut evergreens, the red velvet ribbons she was going to wind around the bannister railing, and the red-berried holly she'd gather for the mantel. There would be caroling and wassail and the annual ball at Squire's, the children's Christmas pageant, the Christmas Eve lantern walk to church, and the Christmas pudding she and Mrs. Mamford would put up this afternoon, after everyone in the small household had made their wishes. Christmas was coming, what joy!

"And what are you going to wish for, Miss Gerry?" the cook-housekeeper asked. "You'd ought to be asking for another London Season, where some handsome nob will sweep you off your feet and carry you away to a life of luxury." Then Mrs. Mamford and her husband, who acted as butler, groom, and valet to Sir Eustace, could retire to a little cottage near her sister's, without regrets. That was Mrs. Mamford's wish, anyway, and her husband's.

Gerry looked up from the nuts she was chopping and laughed. "What, Mamie, you think some wealthy peer is going to fall madly in love with the dowerless daughter of an impoverished baronet who'd driven his wife to an early grave and his son's inheritance to the money-lenders? Not likely. No, I shan't waste my wishes that way. Besides, I like keeping busy. What would I do as a lady of leisure?"

"I know what I'd do," swore Annie, the maid, from next to the sink. "I'd never look at another pot or pan or potato peel again. I'm going to wish for a new dress, I am, to catch the eye of Rodney, over at the smithy's. He can afford to take a wife now, and I aim for it to be me, instead of that red-haired Kitty Trump."

Gerry made a note to purchase Annie a dress length of calico. She might have to forgo new gloves for her own Christmas outfit, but every young girl deserved to have her dreams come true. In years past, Gerry remembered wishing for a special doll, a new cape, and once wanting to be older, so she could attend the holiday parties with her parents, foolish chit that she was, trying to hurry her adulthood. She might as well ask for those years back, but at five and twenty, Miss Selden knew better than to wish for what could never be. Another Season? No, she never missed the silliness, the empty chatter, and the endless gossip. She did not miss the fancy clothes either, for who would see her in the country in her homemade dresses, to titter behind their fans? The money was better spent on new equipment for the Home Farm, to add to their paltry income.

"So what are you going to wish for, Miss Gerry?" Annie wanted to know.

Gerry tucked a long brown lock of hair back into its braid before attacking the bowl of raisins. "Oh, I suppose I shall wish for peace on earth, an end to war, an easy winter."

Mrs. Mamford clucked her tongue and tossed a sliver of fruit to the cat at her feet. "Go on with you, Ranee, and you, too, missy. Them's for bedtime prayers. Pudding wishes are for something special, something for yourself."

Gerry stopped chopping to think. She might secretly dream of a house and family of her own, but that was as goosish as wishing for the pot at the end of the rainbow, and the past years had made her much more practical than that. She was actually hoping that this season of hope would bring her something far more substantial than a castle in the sky, something like a new student for pianoforte or painting lessons, something that would add to her small cache of coins, so that she could buy her brother a horse.

Gerry regretted the family's decline much more for Stacey's sake than for her own. They'd come about, he always declared when she worried aloud about their future, and she believed him, but how was he ever to find a bride or support a family? He swore he did not mind working the fields alongside his farmhands, nor tutoring Squire Remington's doltish sons for extra income, but Gerry saw him look out the window every time a rider went past, and knew he was missing the Selden House stables. The most promising filly to be auctioned off for their father's debts had been Jigtime, Stacey's favorite. Gerry smiled as she added her raisins to the batter. For today, she would not wish for the moon, only for a mare.

*   *   *

Christmas was coming, alas.

Sir Eustace Selden put off answering his sister's call to the kitchen as long as possible. He could hear the women's laughter and smell the scents of cooking, but he had to force himself to put on a smile when he entered the narrow, cluttered room. He knew what he'd find: his sister up to her elbows in flour, smudges on her apron, with her cheeks flushed from the oven's heat and her hair undone, looking no better than the maid, Annie. But his sister was no scullery maid, dash it. Gerry was a lady of quality, and every time Stacey saw her working at tasks his mother never dreamed of, he felt another pang of guilt. Christmas time was the worst, for he'd recall the celebrations at Selden House and know what she must be missing. Her merry grin only added to his remorse, for his sister was a regular Trojan, never complaining of her lack of opportunities buried in this tiny cottage, never whining over the life they'd lost. Gerry's many sacrifices deserved so much more, more than he feared he'd ever be able to give her. By the time he reclaimed Selden House, Stacey worried, his sister would be too old for a dowry to matter, if she wasn't worn to the bone with all her lessons and charities, the scrimping and saving they had to do for the simplest of celebrations. Deuce take it, she was five and twenty already. And he was a year older, and no closer to providing for his only kin than he'd been at nineteen.

"Come, Sir Eustace," Annie called when she saw him lingering in the doorway. "It's time to stir the pudding batter and make your Christmas wish. I wished for a new dress, I did, so now I'm sure to get it."

Gerry's wink told him the frock was as good as in

Annie's trunk. "And did you wish for a new gown too, sis?" he asked. He could afford that for her, at least, so she wouldn't have to go to Squire's Christmas party in last year's dress.

"Oh no, I already have a length of green velvet that Mr. Cutler couldn't sell because of the water marks. Once I've embroidered flowers over the spots, no one will know the difference. And no, I will not tell you what I wished for. Go on, make your wish."

Stacey took the mixing spoon from Mrs. Mamford, stalling while he despaired over his sister making her own gown out of inferior goods. She should be dressed in moonbeams and dancing on clouds. Or at least dancing with some eligible *parti,* instead of the apothecary or the vicar's nephew at Squire's country ball. Wishing would not make it so, no matter how hard he stirred the confounded concoction. The rent money was not going to increase, nor the farm's income, not this year. But perhaps, just perhaps, someone new would attend the ball. In that case, the baronet wanted his sister to shine. So he wished for a necklace for her, but not just any bauble. Her own pearls with the diamond butterfly clasp were the one bit of finery their father hadn't managed to find to sell before his death. Gerry had put them on the auctioneer's block herself, to help pay off his debts. Their sometime neighbor, Lord Boughton, had purchased the pearls, likely for one of the licentious lord's London ladybirds. Nevertheless, Stacey wished the earl would come home for Christmas, bringing the necklace, and agreeing to permit Stacey to pay him back over time for their retrieval. Meanwhile, Sir Eustace decided to ask if he could add Latin lessons to Squire's sons' schooling, even though he thought he'd have better luck teaching Caesar to Squire's pigs.

*   *   *

Christmas was coming, thought Squire Remington. Botheration. No hunting, no fishing, and every man jack in the county coming to celebrate the season at the Manor, same as they had since his grandfather's time. Only his grandfather hadn't been a widower with three young sons to raise. This year, not only did Squire have no wife to handle all the details of the annual ball, but he had no housekeeper either. His hell-born brats had seen to that. Something about a fire in her apartment. No, that was the last one. This one was the snake. And Vicar thought he'd ought to rejoice? Hah! As for charity, Squire swore he'd give everything he owned just for a little peace and quiet.

What he really wanted this Christmas was a competent chatelaine, someone to take his boys in hand until they were old enough to send away to school, if any institution was desperate enough to take them. Squire wanted someone to make sure his mutton was hot, his ale was cold, and his bed was warm. Was it too much to ask that his dogs were permitted in his house, and his sons' vermin weren't? He wished he had a loyal housekeeper, but he supposed he'd settle for another wife. A wife couldn't up and quit.

"So what do you think, Miss Selden? Can we make a match?"

Gerry twisted the ribbons of her sash between restless fingers. "This is so . . . sudden, Squire."

"Sudden? M'wife's been gone these three years. None of the old tabbies can find fault with that."

"That, ah, was not what I meant. It's just that I never thought to . . . You and I . . . ? Not that I am not honored by your offer, of course," she hurried to add, offering the plate of tea biscuits. "Just that I need some time to consider your proposal."

"What's to consider?" Remington waved one beefy hand around the tiny parlor, taking in the threadbare carpet, the faded upholstery, the mended curtains. "I'm no Midas, but I'm no nipcheese either. You'd have the household allowance and your pin money. A house of your own, mayhaps children of your own, too, though I just know my boys'll take to you like their own ma." He also knew enough not to bring the brats along, not wanting to scare her off afore he'd said his piece. Squire was so determined to conclude what he saw as an advantageous arrangement for both of them that he didn't notice Gerry's shudder, whether at the thought of mothering his hellions or of begetting a babe with him. "I'll even throw in that mare you want for your brother, as a marriage settlement."

Now that was horse-trading. Gerry told him she needed a few days to decide, with which Squire had to be content. On his way home, though, he passed young Selden, who asked him for additional work.

"I'll tell you what, my boy. You convince your sister to accept my hand and I'll see you don't have to be giving lessons anymore. I'll make you my factor or something. With a horse of your own. You think on it."

Sir Eustace did think, about how his sister's future would be secure, how she'd never want for anything again.

"Anything but love," Gerry replied to his suggestion that she carefully consider Remington's offer, for she was not likely to receive a better one. "And you know we promised each other that neither of us would wed for mere expediency, no matter what other sacrifices we have to make. Our parents' unhappy marriage of convenience was lesson enough. Besides, Christmas is coming. Anything can happen.''

2

Christmas was coming, blast it. The government was nearly shut down, most of his friends had decamped for their country seats, and even his secretary had taken a long vacation to visit with family. Bah! Now Albrett Wouk, Lord Boughton, was left with an alpine mound of correspondence, an awesome list of dependents, an ambitious mistress, and absolutely no inclination for any of the argle-bargle. Everyone wanted something at this time of year, confound it, from the social-climbing hostesses to the suddenly solicitous servants. What did Lord Boughton want for Christmas? He wanted it to be over. If he desired something, he'd have purchased it for himself, no matter how extravagant. If he wished to visit somewhere, he would have gone, no matter how far. And if he wanted to put on leg-shackles again, well, he would have shot himself.

There was not one deuced thing that Brett could think of to make this season the least bit enjoyable, much less endurable. Merry and bright? Mawkish sentimentality and base avarice. Comfort and joy? Forced conviviality and just plain gluttony. Jolly? Fah. Without the la-la-la.

The earl shuffled through the stack of mail, sorting out the invitations. He supposed he'd accept one fashionable house party or another, the same as he did every year, for lack of anything better to do. He'd find the same overabundance of food and drink, the same overripe widows, the same overwhelming tedium.

Gads, last year the Sherills had trotted out three unmarried nieces to serenade the company at the Yule log ritual. The chits had been as entertaining as the log, though less talented. Hell and damnation, none of the invites sounded in the least appealing.

Even his current mistress was growing less appealing by the day—or night. If he stayed in Town for the holidays, Charleen would take the opportunity to cling even tighter to him and his purse. She'd expect him to do the pretty, naturally, and Lud only knew what she'd expect after that. Brett did not intend to find out.

Lord Boughton flipped through a few letters until one caught his interest. "Presumptuous puppy," he muttered to himself, tapping the page on the edge of the desk. That Bartholomew babe Selden from Upper Ossing wanted to purchase back, at cost and over time, a necklace he'd sold at auction. What did the cabbage-head think the earl was, a money-lender? Father Christmas? Brett ripped the note in half and tossed the pieces on the floor with the rejected invitations. Let the bumpkin buy his own baubles.

His lordship frowned, remembering the sale at Selden House. He'd arrived too late to bid on the cattle, but the pearls had caught his fancy. As soon as he had the necklace home, though, the earl had realized it was a pretty trifle, but not extravagant or showy enough for the birds of paradise he usually decked in diamonds. Well, the confounded necklace must still be in his vault somewhere. He'd send it to Charleen, Lord Boughton decided, along with a check. That way, he'd be saved the aggravation of Christmas shopping and, with any luck, an emotional scene when Charleen realized that was all she was getting from him, ever.

*   *   *

Christmas was coming, by Heaven, and the New Year after. That meant another birthday in her dish, and the devil take them all! Charleen, Lady Trant, was getting old. It must have happened when she wasn't looking, for just yesterday she'd been an Incomparable, a Toast. Today she was a slice of toast, dry and hard. Charleen swept her diamond-braceleted arm along the top of her dressing table, knocking scores of bottles, jars, and tins to the carpet. What good were all the lotions and potions? They couldn't make her two and twenty again. One bottle had escaped her wrath, so she tossed it against the wall. Why not? She could barely read the label, anyway.

Charleen was not looking forward to another year of trying to cover the gray hairs, the fine lines, and her living expenses. If she didn't snabble herself a new husband soon, the men wearing a path to her door wouldn't be eager suitors, they'd be bailiffs and bill collectors. Maybe she could marry one of them. Lud knew she wasn't getting any closer to bringing Lord Boughton up to scratch. Hell, her bosoms would reach her waist before he reached the conclusion that he needed a new wife. Charleen, on the other, ruby-ringed hand, had decided she needed to be Countess Boughton ages ago. The earl was well-mannered, well-favored, and most important of all, well-breeched. What was in his well-tailored breeches was not half bad either.

Well, Christmas was coming, and she'd make deuced sure the earl did his gift selection at Rundell and Bridge's. Charleen really wanted a gold band and all that it entailed, but being well-versed in reality, the lady allowed as how she'd settle for a diamond necklace. She could always sell the sparklers and invest in the Funds. The future had to hold something besides stiff joints and swollen ankles, something that would last a lot longer than her looks.

Christmas was coming, at last! Lady Samantha Wouk sat up in bed and practiced her cough. She was not going to let such a golden opportunity get past her, not another year. This holiday, the earl's seven-year-old daughter vowed to herself, was going to be different. She and her governess were already at The Boughs, fortuitously deposited there a month ago when Aunt Jane came down with the influenza. That was the excuse given for packing her off, bag and baggage, anyway. Not that Lady Samantha wished the lady ill, but being sent off like a sack of dirty laundry suited her down to the ground, so long as the ground was her father's country estate in Ossing. Now all she had to do was get that elusive gentleman to come visit his own home.

According to the servants, Lord Boughton seldom rusticated, but seldom was better odds than never, in Samantha's book. He never came to Aunt Jane's at all, not once since Samantha had been taken there as an infant on her mother's death. Not that the earl's daughter blamed him. Oh no, Samantha knew how much Aunt Jane disapproved of Lord Boughton's extravagant lifestyle, with his clubs, his horse races, and his parties, all of which sounded perfectly delightful to the gentleman's offspring. Aunt Jane always clucked her tongue when his name was mentioned in the newspapers. That was how Samantha knew to sneak a look.

Samantha did not mean to interfere with what Aunt Jane called the earl's hedonistic pursuit of pleasure. She did not expect the stranger who happened to be her father to play at dolls' tea parties or know how to braid hair ribbons. She only wanted to remind him of her existence. What she really wished for this Christmas—and had, for all the ones that came before—was a mother, someone to whom she wouldn't merely be a responsibility or a paid chore. Someone who wouldn't pass her off to distant relatives or, worse, a boarding school. According to Aunt Jane and the servants, though, when they did not think she was listening, the earl did not like women. He never danced at coming-out balls, and he never escorted the same lady for very long. From what Samantha had gathered, Albrett Wouk hadn't much liked her mother, either. Theirs had been an arranged marriage, more for the begetting of heirs than for being life companions. In fact, and according to her old nurse-maid who'd been left to help look after Aunt Jane, the earl had abandoned his countess in the country as soon as she was breeding. Most likely he'd have returned to try again for a son, but Lady Boughton had not long survived her daughter's birth. Nanny said they'd all heard the earl swear he'd never marry again, but would let one of his cousins succeed him. He hadn't changed his mind in seven years, and Samantha didn't think he'd change it for a girl-child he never bothered to visit, no matter how lonely she was.

Well, Christmas was coming, and if she couldn't have a mother, Samantha had decided, she'd settle for a cat.

In truth, Lady Samantha didn't mean to get truly sick. She coughed under the covers until her throat was sore, and she made sure her toes came out of the blankets, into the chill night air. She picked at her food, dragged her feet during walks, and rubbed her temples, the way she'd seen Aunt Jane do. Unfortunately, her charade thoroughly convinced Miss Musgrove, her governess, who immediately sent for the local physician. When Mr. Weeks found nothing wrong, Miss Musgrove ordered the cook to start brewing healing draughts from an old herbal tome in the library.

Either the recipe was in error, or the ingredients were mislabeled, or perhaps the proportions were simply not suitable for such a tiny mite of a miss, but Lady Samantha took a turn for the worse. Now she couldn't keep any food in her stomach, and could barely lift her head off the pillow. The physician shook his head and ordered her bled. One look at the leeches, and Lady Samantha started screaming for, of all persons, her father. Then she fainted. The doctor proceeded for five days after that, as the earl's daughter lay limp on her bed, growing paler and thinner and weaker.

Christmas was coming, dear Lord, and the child was dying. Miss Musgrove spooned another dose of the latest concoction down her charge's throat, then watched as the brownish liquid dribbled out of Lady Samantha's mouth. She scrubbed at the untidiness with a damp towel, wishing she could make the entire unpleasant situation disappear as easily.

Miss Musgrove smoothed out the skirts of her black bombazine gown, frowning. Now she'd never have that school of her own where her pupils did not outgrow her teaching or her discipline. Goodness, a person got tired of looking for new positions, of being relegated to the wasteland between the servants' hall and the family rooms. Was it too much to ask to wish for a bit of security, a touch of independence? Now she'd not even get a reference from the earl or his sister-in-law, not after letting their kin die in this god-forsaken place with its one incompetent doctor.

The governess's hands trembled to think that they might even blame her. The earl was an influential man. He could have her sent to Botany Bay. But no, she'd followed the directions carefully, to the best of her ability. And the servants could tell him that she'd called for the doctor immediately. It was the old charlatan's fault that the disease had progressed so rapidly. If Weeks had treated the girl when they'd first sent for him, perhaps Miss Musgrove would not find herself in such a coil. No, they couldn't blame her. Besides, everyone knew the earl didn't much care what happened to the chit anyway. It wasn't as if she were his heir or anything. Miss Musgrove cared. Horrors, Christmas was coming and she could find herself out of a position.

After much hand-wringing, Miss Musgrove did what she'd been hired specifically never to do: she wrote to the earl. His sister-in-law Jane was too weak, and the earl was the one who paid her wages. Let him come take responsibility, and let him see what a good job of nursing the governess had done, certainly worthy of a bonus.

Brett finally reached the bottom of the pile of correspondence, vowing to raise his secretary's salary, if the chap ever returned from his vacation. The last letter was addressed in distinctly feminine, perfect copperplate. Brett held it to his nose, but the scent was indecipherable. The seal on the back was also unrecognizable, being common red household wax. The sender was definitely not Lady Trant, for Charleen could barely read the opera program, much less write such an elegant hand.

Unfolding the page, the earl let his eyes drop to the signature. He did not recognize that either. He almost tossed the letter to the floor with the rest of useless drivel, but the name "Samantha" caught his eye. As in "your daughter, Samantha." Brett read the letter, then read it again, swearing at the bone-headed woman, his missing secretary, his negligent sister-in-law, and his dead wife. Then he called for his carriage. No, his horse would be faster. The coach could follow with his bags, with his own Harley Street sawbones, with the contents of the nearest apothecary shop. While he was waiting, Brett scrawled a note to his solicitor, directing him to see to Charleen, the check, and the necklace. And to hire a temporary secretary to handle the rest of the mess.

Somewhere in the furor of his departure, whilst changing his clothes, gathering together money and his pistol and a hastily packed hamper for the journey, Lord Boughton discovered that he knew what he wanted for Christmas after all. He wanted to be a father.

3

"What does Mactavish want now?" Gerry asked her brother when she saw the note he was holding. Only one person of their acquaintance wrote with such a bold, sprawling hand. Besides, she'd seen the writing all too often enough in the past years. Mr. Euan Mactavish was the India nabob who was leasing Selden House. It suited the wealthy merchant to live in a gentleman's house. It did not suit him to live with falling tiles, smoking chimneys, or leaking drains. Sir Eustace was frequently summoned to their old home to listen to the latest disaster, and to renegotiate the terms of Mactavish's lease in recompense. Lud knew the Seldens could not afford the repairs and renovations Mactavish insisted upon. Gerry couldn't help her suspicions that the self-made mogul liked having a titled gentleman at his beck and call, even if Stacey was a mere baronet. "What does he want you to fix this time?"

"I have no idea. The message is addressed to you, sis."

"Goodness, what could Mr. Mactavish want with me?"

"Perhaps he wants to make an offer for your hand, too," Stacey teased. "Just think, you could move back to our old house and live like a princess. A much better bargain than Squire and his three imps of Satan."

Mr. Mactavish was short and bald and took snuff. He was loud, demanding, and used to giving orders. He was also old enough to be Gerry's father. "Don't be absurd," Gerry told her brother, taking the letter from him and slitting the seal on the back. "I cannot imagine what's on the man's mind now."

What was on the canny Cit's mind was a title. Christmas was coming, and he hadn't gotten rich by letting the grass grow under his feet, no sir. Who knew what bucks and beaus Squire might assemble for that annual ball of his? Mactavish meant for his little girl to meet all of them and marry the most elevated of the lot. If Squire couldn't produce anything better than young Sir Eustace, at least his Ginger would get her feet wet in the social waters. Mactavish meant to bring her out in London in the spring. Not all doors would be open to a tradesman's daughter, of course, but enough would, an' he make her portion generous enough. The problem was, his little Ginger'd been at a fancy seminary for young females until now. With no wife and no permanent home, Mactavish hadn't been able to have the rearing of the chit. Now that he had her home, he realized he'd made one of his few miscalculations. Ginger was as pretty as she could stare, and well educated, for a female. The price of her wardrobe could have clothed entire Indian villages. But there was no getting around the fact that his little gal was no dasher. She was a shy, wispy thing who didn't know how to go on in company. So Mactavish wrote to Miss Geraldine Selden, who was one of the few ladies in the neighborhood, and the only one who gave lessons in the village. Pianoforte and such, Mactavish recalled. She'd even had a London Season before that ne'er-do-well father of hers popped off. Surely Miss Selden would know just what to do to put some life into the little puss.

"He wants me to be a kind of companion to his daughter, who is finally home from school," Gerry told her brother after reading her letter. "And listen to this: he is willing to pay me handsomely, just for showing her how to go on, introducing her around the neighborhood, that sort of thing so she won't feel such a stranger."

Gerry twirled around and kissed her brother's cheek. "Our luck is changing, Stacey, I just know it is! And right in time for Christmas!" Now she might even earn enough blunt to buy Stacey's horse back from Squire.

Stacey was not quite as excited. He was sincerely happy for Gerry's windfall, of course, and hoped she'd use her wages to purchase some luxury he couldn't afford for her. Still, he hated to see his sister going out to work as an upper servant. And a moody young miss who sat mumchance could be as difficult a pupil as Squire's threesome, who only sat when they were tied to their chairs. "The chit might be a hopeless antidote, you know, besides shy. She could be short and bald like her papa."

"Heiresses are never the wrong height or hair color, silly. And Mactavish can afford to purchase her a wig!" Gerry was not going to be discouraged. "I'll call on them this very afternoon. And I'll bring along a special gift, so Miss Mactavish understands that I wish to be her friend, not merely another instructor. The poor girl must be tired of lessons after all these years. Of course, I'll have to make sure she can do the country dances, and I know she'll be asked to entertain the company at some party or other. I'll have to see what she can perform on the pianoforte. And if she knows the proper way to pour tea, how low to curtsey, that type of thing. Goodness, there's not a moment to spare, with Christmas right around the corner."

Unfortunately, Christmas was not the only thing coming around the corner.

Sir Eustace went off about estate business, leaving Gerry to dither about which gown to wear for the visit, not that she had a great many to choose from. 'Twould never do to appear dowdy, not when Mr. Mactavish was counting on her—and paying her—to bring Miss Mactavish into style. In the end she selected her newest walking dress, a dainty sprigged muslin copied directly from the pages of *La Belle Assemblee*. The fact that the frock was more suited to a September stroll than to a winter's walk was irrelevant. What was warmth compared to making a good impression? Gerry pulled her heavy brown wool cape on over the gown, instead of her more fashionable but thin pelisse. The niffy-naffy butler who had taken

Mamford's place at Selden House was the only one who would see such a plebeian article. Besides, the voluminous cape had pockets both inside and out to hold pencil and paper for making lists, the latest novel from the lending library, and the gift she was bringing to welcome Miss Virginia Mactavish to Upper Ossing.

Rather than trudge the entire two miles along the winding carriage drive, Gerry decided to walk the short distance along the high road to the gap in Selden's stone wall. From there the house was a mere stone's throw away. The high road, though, was in poor condition after the recent rains and yesterday's market day traffic. Gerry stepped through the gate and picked her way carefully between puddles and ruts and piles of horse droppings. The pair coming from the other direction took no such precautions.

The horse was huge and black, and covered yards with every pounding step. He wasn't at an all-out gallop, but a steady gait that could last for miles. The rider sat tall and straight, with his caped greatcoat billowing behind him like some dark angel's wings. He was bare-headed, with his black hair pulled back in a queue. Together they were a magnificent sight, one she was sorry Stacey would miss. Gerry stopped walking to admire the superb pairing of horse and rider as they neared, until she realized that they were going to pass altogether too near. She'd be pelted with the gobs of mire and muck tossed up by the stallion's hooves. She was going to arrive at Mactavish's looking like a wet, filthy mudhen. With a yelp, Gerry leaped backward. Only there was nothing beneath her feet, behind her. She screamed as she skidded to an ignominious seat in the roadway, almost under the stallion's feet.

The rider tried to stop, truly he did, shouting and

pulling the horse back on its hind legs till it was a miracle he stayed aboard. But now a frightened, confused mass of black muscle was towering over her, with metal shoes about to descend. Scrabbling for purchase in the mud, Gerry heaved herself away and rolled to safety—in the ditch.

She was sopping wet, covered head to toe in filth, and stank like a midden heap. All because some London toff was in too much of a hurry to mind where he was going. Gerry had no doubt the rider was from the City, as full of himself and his importance to the world as her half boots were full of stagnant water. "Damn you to hell!" she shouted to his receding back, as she tried to pull herself out of the ditch.

Lord Boughton had ridden just far enough past the fallen female to let Riddles gain his footing, then he turned and sped back, leaping off the stallion, dreading what he might find. Thank God the woman was standing, not lying with her head against a rock, or her limbs twisted, or her neck broken. Brett did not even hear her curses over the pounding of his heart. He reached down to lift her from the knee-deep scum.

Gerry couldn't help but notice that the gentleman's boots, at her eye level, were still gleaming. And the hand he held out to her was gloved in immaculate York tan kid. She took great satisfaction in putting her own sodden mitt in his. And greater satisfaction in telling the arrogant bounder just what she thought of such reckless, irresponsible, cow-handed riding. "How dare you act as if you owned the very roadways! Are you so high-and-mighty that no one else is allowed to share the very air you breathe?"

The air surrounding the bedraggled female was none too aromatic, so Brett quickly released her hand, once she was back on the roadway.

She did not even pause in her diatribe. "Don't you even bother to look where you are going, or are we lesser mortals supposed to anticipate your presence and run for safety?"

He'd seen the brown dab of a girl step through the little cottage's gate, of course, but naturally assumed she'd get out of the way, not stand and gape at him and Riddles like a bacon-brained booby. She'd cost him enough time already, though, so rather than stand arguing in the ill-kept road, Brett reached into his pocket and tossed the chit a coin. "For your inconvenience," he said.

"Inconvenient? You call this inconvenient?" Gerry gestured to her befouled cape, the bonnet that was floating, upside down, in the ditch water, her ruined shoes. Now she could not go to Mactavish's this afternoon at all, and this great gawk of a so-called gentleman thought it was an inconvenience! "You puffed-up popinjay! I could have been killed!"

"And still might be," Brett muttered under his breath. What a little shrew! Some poor fool might have been saved a lifetime of misery if the archwife had drowned in the ditch after all. He tossed her another coin so he could be on his way. The infuriated female caught the gold piece and tossed it back in his face, along with a dollop of mud. At least Brett hoped it was mud. He closed the distance between them and took her shoulders, growing angry himself at the delay. "You should learn to hold your temper, girl, before your betters."

"When I come upon someone better, I shall know precisely how to behave, sirrah! Unhand me, you dastard."

This close, Brett couldn't help noticing that her thick brown hair was fallen like a velvet shawl over her shoulders, and flame sparked from the depths of dark brown eyes. The petite country hoyden would be quite an attractive armful, he decided with a connoisseur's eye, except for her waspish tongue. Well, he knew how to still a woman's mouth, all right. He kissed her.

Her lips were cold and wet, but Lud, they sent a fire through him. There must be something about rustic wenches and their very earthiness, Brett thought, that moved him as no hothouse London beauty had in ages.

Miss Selden was stunned. She'd never experienced more than a timid peck or a chaste salute, hardly kisses at all when compared to this . . . this ravishment. Good Heavens, no wonder so many girls came to grief in the City! Of course, this devilishly handsome rogue, with his blue eyes and cleft chin, had to be an expert at the art. Why, she'd felt that kiss down to her toes—her waterlogged and frozen toes, the cad! How dare he take such unfair advantage of what he undoubtedly thought was some poor milkmaid or a farmer's ignorant daughter. So she slapped him.

Rubbing his cheek, and incidentally spreading dirt from his no longer pristine gloves, Brett drawled, "My apologies, miss." He was not about to tell this rag-mannered wench how affected he'd been by her innocent, unaware sensuality. "It was only a kiss, so you can stop sputtering now. Not a very proficient kiss, as these things go. Perhaps you'd like lessons, my dear?"

Not very proficient? That was more insulting than the stolen kiss! "How dare you bring your licentious ways to a decent neighborhood, you rakehell. You libertine, you immoral bas—"

So he kissed her again, longer and deeper. Then he stepped back to wait for the slap, knowing he deserved it, knowing the kiss had been worth it. Instead the girl gasped, patted her pockets, and shouted, "Bandit!"

Brett glanced both ways along the road, searching for the danger, until he realized she meant him. "Dash it, I stole a kiss, nothing else. I admit I was riding too quickly, but I am no highwayman."

She wasn't paying him the least attention, rushing around in a frenzy. "Not you, you clunch. Bandit's a kitten. He was in my pocket." She bent over to peer into the ditch, leaving him with a draggle-tailed but delightful view.

Brett knew he should be on his way, but there was just something about this female that made him reluctant to leave. And he was, in truth, responsible for her difficulties, to say nothing of the liberties he'd taken with her person. So he stepped nearer, to help in the hunt, poking with his boot toe behind fallen branches, echoing the chit's "Here, kitty, kitty." And feeling like a prize fool on all counts.

"There you are!" she exclaimed, tearing her befouled mittens off to lift something out from behind a rock.

"That?" Brett asked, staring at the handful of lint she held. "That's no cat, that's what's left in the currying comb after I brush my horse." But she was cooing to the palm-sized dustball with blue eyes and a pushed-in face like a pug dog's. "Great Scot, did it get squashed in the fall?"

Without taking her eyes off the ridiculous creature, Gerry told him, "No, that's the way he's supposed to look. It's a rare type of long-haired cat from Malukistan, along the Silk Route. My uncle sent a pair back from his travels, and now I and a few other cat fanciers are trying to establish them as a special breed, without weakening the strain through too-close matings."

Brett believed he now knew more about long-haired cats than he ever needed to. He also believed that he might have made an error. A serious error. His little rustic beauty was not quite as young as he'd thought, and he noticed that her accent, now that she was not shrieking like a banshee, was educated and refined. And her fingers bore no rings. Bloody hell.

"Yes, well, I am glad to see that the animal has not come to any harm. Now I really must continue my journey, Miss . . . ah, Miss . . . ?"

She had already turned her back to him and gone through the gate toward the cottage. She was the first woman to cut him in his memory. Brett shrugged and remounted. He wasn't here for any country dalliance, he told himself. Nor duels with irate fathers.

4

The earl was in Ossing, in time, thank goodness.

The child looked as pathetic as any undernourished, disease-ridden scrap of humanity he'd seen in London's stews and kennels. Lud, how many times had he tossed such a creature a coin? And how much good had that done? he wondered now, for surely this ashen, enervated child was past praying for.

Brett prayed anyway, using words and phrases from his childhood, making bargains he didn't know if he could keep, with forces he didn't know if he believed. She couldn't die, this black-haired piece of himself, she simply could not. "Do you hear me, Samantha?" he whispered, fearing a shout might still the shallow breaths altogether. "You cannot die. I forbid it! I have come all the way to see you, miss, and see you I shall.

Don't you dare leave me before I have even discovered the color of your eyes. Dash it, Samantha, wake up and look at me."

Her eyes were blue, the same as his. But they were vacant, unfocused, as though she were staring at a light he couldn't see.

"No, you can do better than that, Samantha. Try, sweetheart. You've got to get better, you know, because . . . because it's almost Christmas. Come on, Sammy, you can do it. Wake up. Please."

Butterfly lashes fluttered, then opened wider. "No one ever calls me Sammy," she whispered back.

He leaned closer to hear. "No? Not your aunt or Miss Musgrove?"

"Oh, no. They say that would be common. I am a lady, you know."

He nodded. "Yes, I did know that, Lady Samantha Wouk. Is that what you wish me to call you?"

Her brows knit in confusion. "I think you must, sir, as we have not been introduced. That's one of the rules, you know." She sighed. "There are so many I cannot remember them all. But you won't tell Aunt Jane, will you, sir?"

"What, tattle on a new friend? Never. Besides, sometimes I forget some of those silly rules, too."

"You do?"

"Of course. Word of a gentleman. No, word of a Wouk. That's even better, you know, for we might forget a few plaguey manners, but we never forget a promise."

Her blue eyes widened. "Are you really my father, then? You really came?"

"I came."

"Then I suppose you can call me Sammy." She smiled, showing a missing tooth and a dimple.

Lud, Brett thought, she was going to break a hundred hearts in a few years. "And I would be proud if you would call me Papa."

"Not 'my lord'?"

That's how Brett had always addressed his sire, with proper respect for the cold, sanctimonious stranger. "Definitely not 'my lord.' Now you rest and get better, my girl, all right?"

"Word of a Wouk," she murmured contentedly before drifting back to sleep.

The earl was in Ossing, thank heaven, thought a much relieved Miss Musgrove. At least she was relieved until Lord Boughton dismissed the doctor, tossed out the tonics, and announced that he would sit by Lady Samantha's bedside from now on. How was she supposed to prove her dedication and devotion to the brat? How was she supposed to get a reference from him, or a Christmas bonus? Drat.

The earl really was in Ossing, for her! The next time Samantha awoke, he was asleep in the chair next to her bedside, with his bare feet on a stool and a dark shadow on his chin. He was her father, in truth, not a fever dream, because he looked just like his portrait in the library downstairs, only much handsomer. How absolutely, positively glorious! Her plan was working even better than she'd expected. Samantha almost clapped her hands in excitement.

Her slight movement was enough to startle Lord Boughton awake. "Sammy? Are you thirsty, sweetheart? Would you like some fresh lemonade? I've been keeping it cool near the window. Or perhaps some hot broth?"

She wrinkled her nose. "Not one of Miss Musgrove's potions?"

He'd thrown them out the window, after one smell of the noxious brews. The nearby hedges were already withered. "No, you don't need them anymore, now that you are doing so much better."

She wasn't well enough for him to leave yet! Samantha shook her head and whimpered, "I do not feel like anything right now, thank you. I'll just lie here awhile."

"Well, don't plan on staying abed for too long, for we've a lot to do if we're going to be ready for Christmas."

"We do?"

"Of course. We need to gather greenery to decorate, and ribbons to tie around everything. We'll have to search through the attics for my mother's ornaments and such, and we'll have to find us the biggest Yule log in Upper Ossing." What he used to disdain at friends' house parties now seemed eminently desirable, if he could tempt the child from her sickbed. The rituals and rigamarole of the season might even be pleasurable, if seen through those blue eyes, raised to him so trustingly. Why, once she was recovered—and he refused to consider that she might not—he could take the poppet skating and sledding, if the weather were not too cold, and if she were bundled tightly enough. And if they got snow. He found himself wishing for a blizzard like the veriest schoolboy, for his daughter's sake, of course. Perhaps sledding was too rough a sport for such a delicate little sprite, though. How should he know? At least he could teach her to make snow angels, something he was certain neither his starched-up sister-in-law nor the proper Miss Musgrove would have taught her. How much else had she missed because he was such a wretched parent? He thought of all the other activities his hosts and their families had delighted in through all those interminable holiday gatherings, to his aggravation. "Oh, and we'll have to make at least one kissing bough, if you promise not to get up any flirtations with the footmen."

"Papa! I am only seven years old!"

"Ah, then I suppose it's safe to have mistletoe in the house. And candles in every window. And caroling. We definitely must have caroling. You'll like that, won't you, poppet, all the trappings and trimmings?"

In her dreams, Samantha could not have imagined a more perfect holiday. She'd never even seen anything like what he described, not at her puritanical aunt's house. They'd prayed on Christmas and had a goose for dinner; that was all. She thought she'd like this celebration much better, if he was there with her. "You'll stay?"

He wouldn't lie to her, not after boasting that a Wouk's word was his bond. "I cannot stay forever, Sammy, for I have business in London and other properties to oversee." Deuce take it, he was a conscientious landlord; how could he have ignored his own child for so long? But she'd been an infant when his wife died. Sending the babe to her aunt had seemed the best solution. Now remorse made him say, "But I will be here as long as you need me."

Samantha sighed and the earl grabbed up her tiny hand, as if to keep her from drifting off again, whence she might not return. Desperate to focus her attention on the future, so that she'd fight to have one, he asked, "Surely there is something special you want to do for Christmas, some magical gift you are looking forward to? Perhaps a new doll? A pony?"

She had a closet full of dolls. His secretary sent her

one for each birthday and holiday. She had a pony, Jessie, because Aunt Jane considered equestrian skills to be part of a proper female's education. But she'd never had a pet of her own. "I've always wanted a kitten, but Aunt Jane says they are dirty, sneaky creatures."

"Your aunt's opinions do not matter here, Sammy. This is my house, and yours."

"But Miss Musgrove would never permit an animal in the nursery."

"If Miss Musgrove disapproves"—and the poker-backed governess seemed to disapprove of everything!—"she will have to leave."

"You can do that, Papa?"

"Of course I can. I'm an earl, remember. I cannot toss her out in the cold, for that would be ungentlemanly, but if you don't care for her, and she does not care for your pet, then we'll find her another position or something. What do you think about that?"

"Would I have to go away to a school?"

"Eventually, so you'll meet other girls your age. You'll like making new friends."

"I've never had a playmate. Aunt Jane says the village children are too vulgar for an earl's daughter."

Brett was growing heartily sick of Jane's dictates. And feeling guilty as hell for leaving the little mite with Miss Prunes and Prisms for so long. No pets, no friends, nothing but lessons and prayers? The earl might know tuppence about being a parent, but he'd wager he could do better than that. Medea could do better than that! He patted his daughter's hand. "You'll just have to make a speedier recuperation, then, so we can go pick out your kitten. I'm sure the tenants will have any number for you to choose from if there is no kitchen cat with a litter here. And I'll ask the grooms about the barn mousers. We'll find the prettiest one in the bunch. Maybe a white one, so you can call it Snowball. How would that be?" He vowed he'd find her a purple one, if that was what she wanted.

"Oh, no, Papa, I don't want just any old kind of cat."

Suddenly Brett was feeling a draft on the back of his neck. Or was that a prickling of doom? "No? You wanted a lion cub or a tiger, perhaps?"

"No, silly. I want a special, *special* cat."

Oh, Lud, he was about to be punished for all his sins. "And I suppose you know exactly where to find this doubly special feline?"

Samantha sat up in bed, showing more energy than she had since he'd come. "Of course I do! Miss Selden raises them, you see, at the old gatekeeper's cottage."

"Miss Selden from Selden House lives at the gatehouse?" He'd been too concerned with his daughter's health to ask about anything else. "The baronet's sister?" Let there be another Miss Selden, he prayed, almost as fervently as he'd prayed for his daughter's return to health.

"And Sir Eustace, also. Mr. Mactavish rents the big house. Miss Musgrove thinks he is common, but Miss Selden and Sir Eustace are Quality, she says, so we went to call on them once, when we first arrived. And I saw the most adorable kitties in the whole wide world. I want one of those kittens, Papa."

Once, when he was swimming, the earl had stepped on an eel. That almost described what he was feeling now.

The earl was in Upper Ossing? Confound his craven heart, fumed Charleen, Lady Trant, as she peered again at the letter from Brett's solicitor. Where the deuce was that anyway? And could the message really say that Boughton was going to be indefinitely detained in the country on account of a sick girl child? Her vision must be worse than she'd thought. By all that was holy, though, Charleen would *not* purchase spectacles. And she would not be cast aside like yesterday's mutton. A skimpy string of pearls, that's what he thought she deserved after she'd served his needs for all these months? Never mind his generosity at the dressmakers, the milliners, and the wine merchant, she was entitled to more. To his title, in fact.

Blast! Even with the diamond butterfly clasp, the necklace wouldn't bring enough blunt to keep her in candles for a month. Her eyesight was good enough to count the diamond chips, but not to notice the folded bank draft that was tucked beneath the pearls. Perhaps he'd meant the necklace as a token of his esteem, until he could purchase a more worthy gift, Charleen decided. Yes, that was it: he'd left in such a hurry he'd delegated his fusty old man of affairs to send her a trifle, to show his regrets at being away from her over Christmas.

Of course, there was no good reason for them to be apart. The earl was certain to grow bored in the country. Lonely. He'd need a companion, perhaps a lady to act as hostess to the local gentry. Why, Charleen would be doing him a favor by traveling to . . . Where the devil was that place? Osier? Orange? And she could help with the sick child, too. She could, ah, read to her. No, that wouldn't work. Charleen could play at dolls. Well, her maid could sew up some doll clothes, at any rate. Boughton would see what a good mother she'd make, what a good wife, what a good countess. What a good idea!

5

The earl was in Ossing, drat the man. Miss Selden had slapped one of the foremost members of the beau monde. She knew it even before the rumor mills started to grinding. After all, she'd heard the little girl was ailing, and what kind of unnatural father would leave a child alone on Christmas anyway?

Aside from the logic of Lord Boughton's appearing at this time, there simply could not be many other such nonpareils as her highway accoster. But if by some chance there should ever happen to be a more handsome, more virile, more commanding gentleman—not that she thought he was gentlemanly, not by half—well, he wouldn't be riding through Upper Ossing.

The libertine from the lane was the earl, all right, from his famous elegant tailoring to his fabled standing among the demimonde. And now he was standing in Gerry's shabby parlor with a bouquet of flowers in one hand. Roses, no less, and this December. If his clothes or his confidence did not proclaim the rogue's worth, the roses would have. And there she was, in a faded gown, likely with stains and spots from the ivy she'd been braiding for the mantel. At least she'd managed to wash away the stink of yesterday's dousing; now if she could only get rid of his lordship so easily. He was everything she disliked in a man: arrogant and immoral. Like others she'd met during her London Season, the earl thought his wealth and title could buy him respect and affection. Likely they did. Then he'd gamble it all away on the turn of a card or a turned-down sheet, while others did his work, his worrying. No, Gerry did not admire his lordship's ilk at all. Of course the earl's dark good looks were another matter altogether.

She made him her best curtsey without offering her hand, which was all scratched from the holly's prickers. Then she indicated the best chair. No, Ranee had been sleeping there this morning and the pillows were covered with tawny cat hair, just the color to show well on his midnight blue superfine coat. She sat in it herself before her knees gave way, nodding him toward the uncushioned wooden desk chair.

The earl didn't sit, but took to pacing back and forth in front of the fireplace. What, the rug wasn't threadbare enough? But Gerry felt reassured by this sign of his lordship's unease. So the care-for-no-one nobleman had a conscience after all. Feeling generous, she began: "Lord Boughton, there was no need for you to come here. I assure you our previous encounter is better forgotten by both of us."

"No," he said. "I had to come, Miss Selden, to ascertain your well-being and that of your, ah, small companion."

"We are both unharmed by the incident, my lord, thank you." She was not about to tell him how stiff and sore she was, nor how half the scratches on her arms were from Bandit's bath.

"Yes, well, I am pleased to hear that. I most sincerely apologize, both for my careless riding and . . . and the other."

"The other?" Generosity only went so far.

"For, ah, mistaking you for a country lass, Miss Selden."

"You 'mistook' me for one of your light-skirts, my lord."

"I can only beg you to excuse my behavior on the

grounds that I am not used to ladies wandering around by themselves or dressed with such practicality."

He must mean frumpish, Gerry thought, frowning, and ignorant of polite behavior. "Your so gracious apology is accepted, my lord," she snapped at him. "And my conduct was less than genteel in return. There, now we are quits, and you do not have to keep looking at the doorway to see if my brother is going to rush in and challenge you to a duel over my honor. I would not be so nonsensical as to mention the contretemps to anyone, and I trust you will do the same." She stood, declaring the visit at an end. "Will that be all?"

"Not precisely." Boughton started to shred one of the roses he still held in his hand, so Gerry took the bouquet away before he damaged the perfect blooms. "Oh, yes, quite. With my regards."

Taking pity on his discomposure at last—truly she'd thought a nonesuch would have better address—she asked after his daughter. "A charming child. I was sorry to hear she was ill. I trust she is improving, else you'd not be out making calls."

"Yes, Sammy. Thank you. Quite a remarkable recovery, actually. That's why I've come, you see."

Gerry frowned. "Not to tender an apology?"

Devil take the woman, Brett thought. Must she make everything so deuced difficult? "Of course that was first in my mind. But I did have another mission also. I should like to purchase one of your kittens for my daughter."

"No."

"No? Just like that? Come now, you cannot hold my behavior against an innocent child. Sammy has her heart set on a kitten." And he had his heart set on seeing the last of this plain-speaking pocket-venus who seemed to rob him of his manners, his morals, and his masterful way with women. "Surely you'll reconsider, for a price."

So now he thought she was mercenary! Gerry strode toward the door, leaving him to follow. "For one thing, my lord, my kittens are not for sale. I *give* them to those who will love them and care for them, and not let them breed with the kitchen Tom or a stray. You do not fulfill my requirements, my lord, with your hedonistic, pleasure-seeking way of life. Look how you cared for your own child."

He chose not to. "Then think of that child. You cannot be so heartless as to deny a dying girl her wish, can you?"

"You said yourself she is recovering nicely. And if she were not, the last thing she'd need is a helpless creature to take care of."

"I have a battalion of servants, Miss Selden. Surely you do not have to worry that the kitten will not be cared for."

"What, after Lady Samantha returns to her aunt's and you return to your travels, do you really think those servants are going to brush the cat daily, and make sure it never gets lost? My cats are used to a great deal of affection. Can you swear that your servants will provide that, too?"

Brett countered with the one argument he was sure of: "Sam will not be returning to her aunt's. She'll be lonely here in Ossing."

"Then she needs playmates, sisters and brothers, a parent's love. No, you shall not use one of my cats to make up for your own failings. Good day, my lord."

Lud, how had such a simple thing as purchasing a cat become so involved? Since when did a fellow have to pass a court-martial to be deemed worthy of a ratcatcher? And how the devil was he going to tell Sam there would be no pug-faced furball for her on Christmas? "I beg you to reconsider, Miss Selden, for Sammy's sake."

"And I beg you to leave, my lord. I don't like you and you don't like cats."

"Of course I do." He couldn't recall being in the same room with one of the creatures, but saw no reason to mention the fact. He couldn't recall being in the room with a woman who disliked him, either, but that was a problem for a different day. "The little bugger, ah, baby in the ditch surprised me, is all."

"If you liked cats, you'd have one."

Her smug tone was grating on Brett's temper. And her pursed lips were crying out for kisses, which would not help his cause in the least, he was sure. He took a deep breath and said, "I like giraffes, Miss Selden, and I do not have one of those either. Try me with a cat. That's the only fair test."

Gerry nodded, and went into the hall, making odd bird-call noises. In a moment, a large, extremely fluffy black cat with a plume of a tail and a nub of a nose strolled into the room, wrapping itself around Miss Selden's legs. "This is Mizra Khan, the sire of most of the kittens I breed. If you sit down, he will come to you."

He sat on the sofa, and sure enough, Mizra Khan leaped up alongside him, butting his head against the earl's sleeve. The earl tried to school his features into not showing distaste at the innumerable cat hairs left on the fine wool. "There, it likes me."

"He wants his ears scratched."

So Brett scratched the cat's silky ears, and was rewarded with a loud rumbling purr. Then he took out his quizzing glass on its ribbon and let the cat bat at it awhile. He grinned up at his hostess, his puss-prowess proven, when Mizra Khan stepped closer, onto his lap, in fact, and began to knead the earl's thigh with his front paws. The claws dug in, catching on the fawn-colored breeches, catching on the earl's skin beneath. Brett gingerly lifted the cat down to the floor in a controlled hurry, then glanced at Miss Selden to see if she disapproved. The cat, meanwhile, had discovered the tassels on Lord Boughton's Hessians and was swatting at them. "Playful chap, isn't he?" the earl asked, bending to pat the cat and subtly push him away from the mirror-surfaced boots. Mizra Khan had other ideas. He stood on his back legs and started to use those unblemished boots as a scratching post. "I say!" Brett said, giving the cat a firmer shove, at which Mizra Khan sank his teeth into Lord Boughton's thumb.

"Bloody hell!" he shouted, clutching his bloodied finger. "Now I suppose I'll have to worry about contracting some dread disease!"

Gerry was already cuddling the cat. "Silly kitty, now we'll have to worry about you contracting some dread disease. Good day, my lord."

The earl was in a taking when he rode back to The Boughs. He did not even visit the nursery until he'd had half a bottle of brandy, and soaked his thumb in the other half.

"Did you get it, Papa? Did you get my kitten?"

"Hush, poppet. You wouldn't want to ruin your Christmas surprise, would you?"

The earl was in Ossing, thought Eustace. How fortunate. Now he could go ask about Gerry's necklace in person.

Interrupted amid the new stack of correspondence that had been delivered from London, Brett did not believe young Selden wanted the necklace for his sister. The handsome young baronet likely had a ladybird somewhere and was too embarrassed to admit it, the mooncalf. For sure the woman Sir Eustace was describing bore no relation to the harridan Lord Boughton had twice encountered. Good-natured and giving? Hah! She hadn't given him one of the blasted cats, had she?

And the necklace was undoubtedly in Charleen's grasping hands by now. He could easily get it back, the earl knew, by promising a more expensive bauble, but the lad had no money and no claim to the pearls. He did, however, have something the earl wanted very badly.

"You'll trade me the pearls for one of m'sister's kittens?" Sir Eustace scratched his head. "I don't know, she's that particular about where they go. If she turned you down, she must have had good reason." He paused, but the earl was not about to discuss Miss Selden's mutton-headed motives. "Technically, the cats are half mine, as our uncle meant the first pair for both of us. But I would never go against m'sister's wishes in the matter." From what he'd seen of the earl's grand estate, though, Stacey could hardly imagine a better home for anyone, feline or otherwise. And he realized how foolish his attempt to purchase the pearls had been. Why, the earl had more blunt than Golden Ball. "I'll have to think on it, my lord."

"You do that," Boughton told him, going back to his paperwork. Damn, what he wouldn't give for a secretary! "I say, you wouldn't perchance be interested in a position, would you?"

*   *   *

The earl was in Ossing, what an opportunity! Euan Mactavish was not one to let an opportunity slip by, b'gad. He hadn't made his fortune by waiting for it to fall into his lap, by Jupiter, and he wasn't going to let this chance, or this earl, pass him by. The chap just might be looking for a sweet young thing to mother his little girl, an unspoiled beauty who wouldn't mind being left in the country while the earl pursued his own pleasures. Boughton might be above his Ginger's touch, but Mactavish had nothing to lose by trying, and a title to gain. So the merchant decided he'd throw a fancy dinner to welcome his nibs back to the neighborhood. Ginger would have a new gown, and sparklers enough to dazzle even a London buck, and she'd impress the nob with her ladylike ways and her ability to run a gentleman's household. The only problem was, his Ginger could barely order herself a cup of tea, much less a dinner for a top-of-the-trees toff. He sent for Miss Geraldine Selden.

Gerry did not mind in the least being hired on to plan a lavish entertainment at her old home, in addition to her sessions with Miss Virginia, and she was pleased with the extra income. She was that much closer to being able to make Squire a respectable offer for the mare. What Gerry could not approve, however, were the plans Mr. Mactavish confided in her for his daughter's future. Miss Virginia was a sweet child, and Boughton would eat her for breakfast. Whatever poise Gerry had managed to instill in the lovely innocent would be drained away by one of the earl's dark scowls. And if he kissed her, as the rake was wont to do with every female who crossed his path, Gerry supposed Miss Mactavish would dissolve in a puddle of tears. She was already red-eyed and swollen-faced, likely from crying over her father's ambitions to throw her at the neighborhood's most eligible and elevated gentleman. Fortunately, in Gerry's mind, Ginger now had the kitten Bandit to console her.

The earl was in Upper Ossing, and what a pawky little village it was, too, with barely a decent shop. But if Boughton was at The Boughs, that's where Charleen, Lady Trant, was bound.

The earl was not pleased to see her. He didn't used to be so stuffy, she told him, but he didn't used to think of himself as a parent, either. A gentleman simply did not stable his convenient alongside his family. Charleen was deuced inconvenient, in fact, even if she had brought her old auntie along as chaperone to satisfy the conventions. That wouldn't satisfy one brown-eyed beldam who already thought he was a womanizer. Besides, the aunt was stone deaf, and twice as short of sight as Charleen. Damn. And he couldn't throw them out until he had the blasted necklace. Young Selden had turned out to be an excellent secretary, for one thing, and Brett still had hopes of trading for the kitten, for another. But Charleen was not parting with the gewgaw, not even when he said that his solicitor must have made an error, that he'd meant the pearls as a gift for his daughter. Not even when he said a diamond and ruby necklace would be waiting for Charleen in London. No, now she wanted more before she'd leave him in peace. Now she wanted one of the blasted exotic cats Sammy was raving about. Double damn.

The earl was in Ossing, good heavens, and his mistress was there with him! Miss Musgrove found the situation unpalatable, unprincipled, and untenable. Even if she could not tell from her bedroom in the nursery wing if the earl was winging toward his paramour's suite every night, Miss Musgrove was mortally offended. In fact, if Miss Musgrove had somewhere else to go, she'd be out of this house of licentious depravity in an instant. The idea of a cat in the house was bad enough, but a courtesan?

6

The earl was in Ossing, by George! Squire Remington was delighted. At last, a decent hand of cards! Boughton accepted the invite—he never had been high in the instep, Squire reflected—and arrived one evening after his daughter was asleep. Squire politely inquired into the little miss's health and raised his glass to her continued recovery.

"And your fine family?" Brett asked, savoring the cognac and cigars, away from the disapproving Miss Musgrove or the clinging Lady Trant or her old deaf auntie. Conditions at The Boughs were not precisely congenial. "What is it, three boys?"

Squire sighed. "Aye, my good wife Rose blessed me with three healthy sons: Tibold, Corcoran, and Diogenes. She bore 'em and gave 'em jumped-up names, then had the good sense to shuffle off this mortal coil afore she had to raise the limbs of Satan. No matter, I call 'em all Sonny, on account of they never sit still long enough for me to figure which is which." He sighed again and refilled his glass.

"It sounds as if they need a firm disciplinarian," Brett suggested from a superior position. *His* daughter would never cause a groat of trouble.

"Aye, but the village schoolmaster won't have them back, even after the school is rebuilt, the vicar refuses to let them come near him except on Sundays, and young Selden is too tenderhearted. I tried to convince his sister to take them in hand, but it 'pears Miss Gerry knows them too well."

"You tried to hire the baronet's sister as governess?" He knew they were fallen on hard times, but never thought things had come to such a pass. He could not envision the proud little beauty in some menial post.

"Governess? Hell, no. Offered to marry her, don't you know. Governesses can up and quit; wives can't. Fine gel, Miss Gerry. Everyone hereabouts adores her. She helps run the orphanage and the Ladies' Aid Society, besides assisting vicar with the parish."

"A veritable paragon." Brett was having to revise his opinions of Miss Selden in light of his own daughter's near veneration of the female. The servants, the tradesmen, the local shopkeepers, all sang her praises. Unfortunately, the lady showed charity to everyone but him.

Squire sighed yet again. "Aye, she is that. Would have suited me to a cow's thumb, having her around. She turned me down, though, even when I offered to pay some of the brother's expenses."

"Why? Was she holding out for a better offer?"

Squire scowled at him. "Miss Gerry? The gel ain't greedy, if that's what you're hinting at. Said she wouldn't feel right marrying without her heart coming along."

Brett raised his glass, and his estimation of the lady. "To an honest woman."

After a few more hands of piquet, which mostly went in the earl's favor, Brett reintroduced the topic. "You say you are looking for a governess, then?"

"More like a warden, till the lads are ready for boarding school." Remington put his cards down and looked at Brett like an eager puppy. "D'you know of any?"

"I just might know a respectable woman in need of a position. Not in the first blush of youth, mind, but she has high standards, and will not tolerate any nonsense in her house."

"Just the thing! I'd be mightily obliged if you'd give me her direction. Obliged enough to lose another fifty pounds to you."

Brett waved aside the money. "Would you be obliged enough to beg a favor from Miss Selden? I want one of her kittens, but don't seem to pass muster."

"Sorry, Boughton, but she won't part with them for an abbey." He rubbed his chin. "Happens though that I do have something she wants, a horse her brother raised up from a foal. Jigtime ought to be racing, but I'm more interested in hunters, don't you know. I figured to let my oldest have her when he's ready. Seems Miss Gerry's been giving lessons and such just to pay the price. It's a shame really. She's a game little mare."

Jigtime or Miss Selden? Brett wondered. It seemed that the hard-working brother and sister really were that devoted that they would make such sacrifices toward the other's happiness. Damn, and he'd given her pearls to his particular! He made a mental note to send to London for an even costlier necklace for Charleen. "And you say Miss Selden wants to get the horse back for her brother?"

"Aye, a Christmas present. If you're serious about finding me a caretaker for the cubs, I'll trade you the horse for m'gaming vouchers, when your woman takes the job. If you offer the horse, mayhaps Miss Gerry will look on you more kindly." He shrugged. "Didn't work for me, but you might have better luck. After all, you only want a cat. I wanted a keeper for my boys."

Miss Selden was not seeing the earl in a better light. Oh, the light was better, thanks to the new chandeliers Mr. Mactavish had installed at Selden House, and the countless oil lamps on every surface. And the earl was looking bang up to the mark, as her brother would say, in his formal evening dress, with his black hair combed back, except for one dark lock that fell on his forehead. That forehead might as well have sprouted horns when she heard his latest offer.

"A kitten for the horse, that Squire owns, but might trade for your daughter's governess? That's . . . that's diabolical!"

The earl studied his manicured fingers. If Miss Selden thought this negotiation was demon-spawned, he prayed she never heard the rest of the bargain. Charleen had agreed to give up the pearls if he produced an expensive bracelet, a new protector, and a kitten. So he had to get the horse from Squire, so he could trade Miss Selden for a kitten, which he would give to Charleen, in order to get the pearls for Sir Eustace, who was then supposed to get another kitten for Samantha. And everything hinged on musty Miss Musgrove surviving a week of Squire's sons. Deuce take it, why couldn't Miss Selden just give him the blasted cat before his wits went begging altogether? And why did she have to look so deuced pretty with her hair done up in a crown-like coil atop her head, held by a ribbon that almost begged a man to tug loose, so he could see the brown locks flow down across her shoulders, across his pillow. Lud, where had that come from? He was supposed to be thinking of exchanging livestock with the woman, not heated kisses!

"It's a trifling matter," Brett lied. "I have something you want; you have something I want. A simple transaction among friends."

They weren't friends and nothing was simple. Except perhaps her brother, for acting the mooncalf over Miss Ginger. Mactavish was furious, dinner was a disaster, and Gerry had the headache.

The first catastrophe was the cook's tantrum in the drawing room where the company was taking sherry before dinner. No, that wasn't even the first crisis. The first calamity was Boughton bringing his mistress to Selden House for supper! Ginger was tongue-tied, Stacey's eyes never strayed above Lady Trant's inadequate neckline, and Gerry was outraged. How dare he! Then the old auntie tripped over the kitten, which by rights should not have been in the parlor and for which Mactavish loudly berated his daughter and Gerry both, in front of the company. The shout sent Lady Trant's aunt careening into the end table, spilling the sherry.

Ginger started to cry, naturally, clutching Bandit to her—compared to Lady Trant's expanse—girlish bosom. Her eyes, already red, started to overflow. Stacey went to her, out of kindness, and removed the kitten from her grip to make sure it had taken no harm, handing over his own handkerchief. Whether it was his gentle smile, despite her being quite out of looks, or the way he held the kitten without the least regard for his dark coat, Miss Mactavish was smitten. Anyone listening hard enough could have heard Ginger's heart fall at Stacey's feet, which were five feet off the ground by this time. He'd received a timid smile from an angel, and he was lost. He never even looked at Lady Trant's bosom again.

And Ginger never thought to send for a servant to

clean up the mess, so Gerry had to, and asked that dinner be set forward, which caused the irate chef to appear, which sent Ginger into strong hysterics, which led Stacey into putting his arms around her, which led Mactavish to turn even redder in the face than his daughter. And which caused the dastardly earl to wink at her!

A downy one such as Lord Boughton had to have known Mactavish's ambitions to snabble him for a son-in-law, just as he had to notice his mistress eyeing the lavish appointments—added to Selden House by Mactavish—with an appraiser's eye. He found it amusing! He even smiled at her throughout the longest dinner of Gerry's life, as if asking her to share the joke. Some joke, when she would lose her prize pupil at the best, and they might lose Mactavish as a tenant at worst. There was no way he would tolerate an alliance between his princess and a pockets-to-let baronet. Gerry would not have been surprised if he'd ordered them from the house, instead of ordering the next course, when Ginger neglected to do so.

Seated at the foot of the table as hostess, Ginger had eyes—and words—for Stacey only. Heaven knew what they found to talk about, as Gerry hadn't wrung more than a few sentences out of the girl all week, unless they spoke of cats. Perhaps that's what Stacey had found to amuse the heiress, tales of the family pets. Either way, the girl ignored her other, intended dinner partner, the earl. Gerry was too far away to kick her under the table, so could only pray Mactavish did not notice his daughter's rag manners.

She needn't have worried. At the other end of the mahogany table, Lady Trant was serving up a generous display of bare flesh for the merchant's delectation, and Mactavish was seasoning his conversation with talk of investments, when he wasn't pouring the butter boat over the dashing widow. Across from Gerry, the aunt dipped her hand in the soup instead of the finger bowl. Gerry prayed for dessert.

When the ladies finally withdrew, after the butler had to remind Miss Mactavish to lead the women from the room, Lady Trant made much of the kitten, who hadn't ought to be in the Green Salon, either, sharpening its claws on the Aubusson carpet, and asked Gerry for one of her own.

"For it's sure to make a splash in London, don't you know. I'd like to be the first to have one of the newest breeds."

Gerry wasn't sure about the kind of home the kitten would have, or what would happen when Lady Trant grew tired of the latest fancy.

"And don't think the little darling would be left alone. Auntie is home most of the time. She would love a kitty on her lap. Wouldn't you, Aunt Forbish?"

"Eh?"

"Cats, I said. You love cats, don't you?" Charleen shouted.

"Eh?"

Lady Trant then offered to do Gerry a favor in exchange: "I'll convince our host that his chit is never going to do better than a baronet, not even with all his blunt greasing her way, and that he'll never find a lad who'll treat the gal better. Just seeing the pair of them makes me want to weep."

Gerry, too. "You'll never convince Mr. Mactavish. He has his heart set on a viscountcy at least."

Charleen pulled up a dangling curl, and pulled down the lace at her bodice. "You just watch, my dear. At the least I can distract him for a bit. Otherwise he's liable to toss you and your delightful brother out before the tea tray is brought in."

When the men returned, Stacey went straight to the heiress, the nodcock, leading her and the kitten to the pianoforte. Giving Gerry a grin, Charleen draped herself over Mactavish's arm and begged him to show her the collection of carvings he'd brought back from India, in the other direction. The aunt was snoring. And Gerry was alone with the earl.

Rather than permit him to bring up the issue of the cats again, she waved toward Lady Trant's departing trills of laughter. "Your, ah, friend seems to have abandoned you." Then she felt her cheeks flush with her impertinence.

"Greener fields, don't you know." The earl brushed her embarrassment aside, as if he made a practice of speaking about his ladybirds to ladies of quality. Or as if Gerry were a mature, intelligent female who understood the ways of the world. She understood nothing, except that his broad shoulders were close to hers on the sofa, and his well-muscled thigh was almost touching her leg. Good grief, she could not be attracted to such a here-and-thereian! Although her opinion of him was changing with each report Stacey brought home from The Boughs about the number of worthy charities that his lordship supported, and how he was having Stacey make lists of needed improvements to his tenants' holdings. And how his daughter thought he'd hung the moon.

"I did not invite Lady Trant to The Boughs," he was saying. "I encouraged her to leave, in fact." He wasn't sure why he felt he had to explain away his onetime inamorata, present-time houseguest, but he'd given over wondering why he'd wish to look better in this woman's eyes. Big, beautiful brown eyes they were, eyes a man could get lost in. He caught himself leaning closer, bending lower, breathing in the scent of her. Roses and something else, perhaps evergreen, from all the garlands around the room. He put another inch of distance between them, for safety's sake. "I just gave my blessings for Mactavish to hunt on my coverts anyway."

"Hunt on your . . . ? Oh."

"I had thought she'd be more eager to return to London if she had one of your kittens to show off." Along with the diamond and ruby bracelet he'd ordered. "But now I doubt if she'd go, until she's got her claws firmly into the wealthy Cit."

"You don't mind?"

"What, that she's finding a new protector? That's why I asked to bring her tonight. It was either Mactavish or Remington. I am relieved."

So was Gerry.

"Oh, and I put in a good word with Mactavish about your brother. Told him I thought the lad would do well in politics, with the right backing. And that Prinny was handing out titles like tea cakes, to those who made significant contributions to the regent's coffers. No reason a baronet couldn't be elevated to baron or some such. I agreed to use my influence in Town."

He hadn't only hung the moon, but the stars along with it. "You did all that? For Stacey?"

"No, for a Christmas kitten for my daughter." And one for Charleen.

7

Miss Geraldine Selden wished she had more time, alas. With Christmas right around the corner, there were never enough hours for all the shopping, sewing, baking, and decorating, much less choir rehearsals, children's parties at the orphanage and the school, and informal gatherings at the neighbors'. Every year she vowed to start earlier, and every year she enjoyed every minute of the frantic rush. This year, however, she truly needed a few more weeks to try to earn enough money to reclaim Stacey's horse. He would be so disappointed when Mactavish banned him from Selden House as a suitor for the heiress, he'd need cheering more than ever. The mare couldn't take the place of Miss Mactavish's hand in marriage, of course; then again, Jigtime wouldn't soak his shirtfront with constant tears, as Miss Ginger seemed wont to do.

Gerry decided to make one more attempt to bargain with Squire Remington. Sadly, he no longer owned the horse, but he did want a kitten. Under no conditions would Gerry give one of her darlings to a house full of unruly, uncivilized little heathens, to say nothing of the hard-drinking squire and his flea-bitten hounds. He said he wanted the kitten for his sister in Bath, however, a poor invalid who could never travel. That was the excuse she gave for never visiting Remington Manor, at any rate. Gerry said she'd think about it.

Squire wished he had more time, blast it. With that confounded ball coming faster than a bull with a burr up his nose, Remington needed help. He put on his Sunday clothes, having washed his hands and face and behind his ears, and took himself off to Boughton's place. At The Boughs, he made Miss Musgrove a handsome offer, which she handily accepted. The governess moved into the manor; Jigtime moved to the earl's stables. Suddenly there was peace and quiet.

Suddenly the servants were not threatening to leave.
Suddenly Squire could take a nap in his own book
room without barricading the door and hiding the key
to his gun cabinet or his wine cellar. Glory! And the
woman had done it all in . . . jig time. Squire slapped
his knee. Damn, things were looking up. He was feeling so in charity with the world, in fact, that when
Miss Selden called, he asked for one of her infernal
cats. Silly creatures, they were, all hair and no nose,
with enough airs to shame a duchess, but if she was
too stubborn to trade with the earl, Squire decided,
he'd see they both got what they wanted. They might
even get a bit more than they bargained for. He
slapped his knee again, which a mangy brindle dog
named Squeaky took as invitation to join him on the
couch.

Miss Musgrove wished she had more time, by
heaven. The whole county was invited to Squire's ball
and she'd barely begun to get the little savages in
hand—a hand which incidentally held a birch rod—
much less the servants, the sty of a manor, and Squire
himself. The dogs had to go, as soon as she had a
firmer grip on the reins, but at least Miss Musgrove
was only sharing her quarters with unmannered mon-
grels, not mistresses.

Charleen, Lady Trant, wished, once again, that she
had more time. But there was another wrinkle in her
mirror every day, so she dare not wait much longer.
She was no closer to melting Boughton's heart, if he
had one to melt, and her bills were no closer to being
paid. Most likely she'd never had a chance of bringing
the top-sawyer up to scratch, no, not even if she'd
managed to get one of those curtain-climbing cats for

his sickly little brat. His gratitude would extend only so far. So far he had presented her with a necklace she wouldn't be ashamed to walk into a pawn shop with, and the promise of a check waiting for her in London—if she left, and left him the pearls. His patience was growing as thin as Charleen's hair, from all the bleaching. Aunt Forbisher's kissing the antique armored knights, hoping for one of the footmen under the mistletoe, wasn't helping. So Charleen powdered her nose and rouged her cheeks, and went to see Mr. Mactavish. The bald old man couldn't hold a candle to the earl, but he did hold a king's ransom in Consols.

Mactavish wished he had more time, by George, time to show his little girl off in London and time to make a noble match for her. But she was getting her heart set on young Selden more every day. And turning into a blotch-faced watering pot, besides. With her looks so off, it was a wonder even the baronet came to call. Mactavish wanted her married, he wanted her a lady, but more and more, he wanted his mewling daughter and her meowing cat off his hands. Especially now, when he could wrap his hands around the tidiest bit of willing woman he'd encountered in years—if his daughter were not underfoot. That was why he got so excited when Lord Boughton came to make an offer. Unfortunately, the offer was for Ginger's cat, not Ginger.

"What, part those two? Be easier to part the Red Sea, my lord. The widgeon ain't been the same since she got the puss, but I've got enough woe trying to get her mind off young Selden without sending her into a decline. But happens I might be able to persuade Miss Selden to give me another, to sweeten me toward the family, like. I could say I got so used to having the little blighter underfoot that I want one of my own, for when Ginger goes off on her wedding trip."

"You get the cat for me, Mactavish, and I'll get Selden a higher title, even if I have to give him one of mine."

The earl wished he had more time, by Jupiter. Christmas was just days away and he was no nearer to getting one of the wretched little beasts for his daughter than he was to flying. He'd even inspected every litter of kittens in the shire, it seemed, in hopes of finding one that looked peculiar enough to pass for one of Miss Selden's misfits. He had his London solicitor make inquiries at the Royal Feline Fanciers Society, with no luck. Drat the woman for being a pig-headed prude when it came to giving away the Malukistan mousers. And drat her for intruding on his dreams, too. She was not mistress material, and she sure as the devil would not make a comfortable wife, if he were in the Marriage Market, which he was assuredly not. Therefore, she had no business in his thoughts, his imaginings, his Christmas wishing. Brett vowed to put Miss Selden entirely out of his mind—as soon as he'd gone to the gatekeeper's cottage one more time.

Sir Eustace wished he had more time, hang it. At first he worried that Mactavish would scoop Ginger off to London for presentation to every fortune hunter in town, or arrange a marriage for her with some ancient aristocrat. He didn't think the merchant could outright ban him from the doorstep of Selden House, since Stacey still owned the pile, but he could make sure Ginger wasn't home to receive him. The old man seemed to be leaning toward favoring his suit, though, with the earl's influence, Stacey didn't doubt. At least he'd stopped slamming doors and throwing things, according to Ginger, who was adorably ablush as she offered him tea. Before the old crab could change his mind again, Stacey meant to make a formal offer for his darling Ginger. He was fairly certain she'd accept, too, if her father gave permission. She'd whispered to him after church that she missed him. What joy! Stacey had walked into a tree, waving goodbye. Lud, he wanted his sister to know such happiness. Furthermore, he wanted her to have a comfortable future, without having to share the cottage with him and Ginger. Even if Mactavish let them all move back to Selden House, the baronet knew Gerry would not be content as a poor relation in another woman's home.

Sir Eustace desperately wanted his sister to shine at Squire's ball, his last hope that a particular nobleman would take notice. He wanted her pearls.

Gerry was out delivering baskets to the needy when Boughton called, but Sir Eustace was glad to see his employer, even if he was a shade embarrassed to have to wipe cat hairs off the chair before he could invite the earl to sit. Once he'd poured a glass of brandy, he put forth his new offer. As he explained to the earl, if Stacey could gain Mactavish's blessing, then the bank would surely make him a loan against future expectations, with which he could pay Lord Boughton back for his sister's necklace. Not that he was interested in Miss Mactavish for her father's money, he made sure the earl knew.

"I never supposed such a thing, not with the two of you making sheep's eyes at each other across the church aisle all through vicar's sermon." He reached into his coat pocket and withdrew a velvet pouch.

"No, the pearls should never have been sold. I understand the need at the time, and I only blame your father for that, not you. But they belong to Miss Selden. So, here, take them, for her. You've worked hard enough to earn them. They're yours, no strings attached. The only thing is, if you could see your way clear . . ."

"You still need a kitten for your daughter."

So Stacey asked his sister for one of the cats as soon as she returned home. "You just have to trust me on this, Gerry. You know I'd never do anything to hurt one of them."

Since he was sitting on the sofa with Ranee on his shoulder and Mizra Khan playing with his watch fob, and kittens tumbling in his lap, she could not refute his love for the creatures. Nor how happy and carefree he seemed, for the first time in ages. "I'll think about it," was all she said.

"Don't think for too long. I mean it for a Christmas present."

Gerry wished she had more time. And more kittens.

Lady Samantha Wouk wished she had more time, but she was not giving up hope. Her father was here, Miss Musgrove was not, and Sammy needed only one more miracle.

"Papa, why don't you ask Miss Selden to call, so she can see what a nice home we'll give the kitten?"

"You know I cannot invite an unmarried woman to my house, poppet. That must have been one of Aunt Jane's rules you forgot."

"You could if we invited Sir Eustace and Miss Mactavish to tea, also, couldn't you?"

"I suppose that might suit, if you are sure you are well enough for it."

"Papa, I am feeling fine!"

She was looking less peaked every day, and had, to his mind, an inordinate amount of energy for a sickly child. One more game of Hide and Seek would have him taking to his bed. Company tea sounded lovely. The invitations went out, were accepted, and Lady Samantha threw herself into planning her first party.

First to arrive, Gerry and her brother were met at the door by two footmen who took their wraps, and a bewigged butler who escorted them to the nursery parlor, where another footman threw open the door, so the butler could announce their names with every ounce of pomposity he could muster. Lady Samantha giggled. So did Gerry.

A gentleman playing with his son was always an affecting sight, but a lord presiding at his daughter's dolls' tea party was sheer magic. The earl was seated at a child-sized table, his knees almost touching his chest, balancing a tiny teacup. How had Gerry ever thought him stiff and careless of others, arrogant and unloving? His affection for the little girl shone through the embarrassed flush at being caught in such an undignified pose. "We, ah, that is, Sammy thought you should see where the kitten would reside, before taking tea downstairs. Perhaps you would care to wait below, Sir Eustace, in case Miss Mactavish arrives soon and wonders where her host and hostess have disappeared to."

Stacey was down the stairs before the hoped-for cat could lick its ear. Gerry did not have time to feel the awkwardness in the situation—although she did note that there was no impropriety, with the young housemaid mending one of Lady Samantha's pinafores in the corner—before the child took her hand and led her to the nursery bedroom. Gerry was encouraged to inspect the wicker basket, lined with the softest flannel, that was to be the kitten's bed. Pretty porcelain bowls were already set out on an embroidered table runner, waiting food and water.

"And behind the screen in the schoolroom is where its earth box will go. Jed Groom is building it. What do you think?"

"I think you and your father have thought of everything," Gerry noted, except, of course, how devastated the child would be if no kitten appeared on Christmas morn. Now this was blackmail in the worst degree. Gerry glowered at the earl, who merely shrugged his shoulders, but he couldn't hide the dimpled grin, the same one Samantha wore. Gerry conceded, as they all knew she must.

"I can see you will make an admirable cat keeper, my dear. I am sure one of Ranee's kittens will be happy to come live with you."

The child threw her thin arms around Gerry's legs, almost toppling her, in her excitement. "Oh, but Papa said it's to be a surprise."

"I'll wager he did," Gerry said dryly, trying not to smile at the shamefaced earl. "Have you decided on a name for this Christmas surprise?"

"Why, I—Papa! Mistletoe!"

"That's a lovely name for a—" Gerry started, until she noticed the little girl was pointing upward. There, above her head in the doorway of the room, was a lopsided ball of crudely woven vines, with a ribbon-tied spray of mistletoe dangling from one twig.

"Gentleman's duty, don't you know," the earl teased, taking her by the shoulders. He meant for the kiss to be a quick touching. It wasn't. Gerry meant to offer her cheek for the ritual. She didn't. They both intended to remain unaffected by the forced contact.

They weren't. Warmth and wanting mingled with their breaths, tenderness and unspoken yearnings.

The kiss went on and on, touching eternity, touching paradise. Then Samantha was touching them. "Papa, won't Miss Mactavish and Sir Eustace think we are rude if we don't go down soon?"

8

Christmas wishes did come true. Just ask anyone at Squire's country ball. Why, there was hardly a dry eye in the place.

Squire wiped away tears of pride to see his three boys polished up like bright new apples, and his house gleaming. Even his hounds had had baths. Almost bursting his buttons, he welcomed his friends and neighbors, and bade them share a toast to his forthcoming nuptials to dear Ermintrude.

"Who the deuce is Ermintrude?" murmured more than one of the company. Then Remington brought forth Miss Musgrove, her black bombazine exchanged for a dove-gray merino that made her look more like a pouter pigeon than an old crow. Not that the ex-governess would be guilty of showing such emotion in public, but she nobly restrained tears of satisfaction, that she would never have to seek another position.

After a few more toasts, Mr. Mactavish cleared his throat and, despite tears of chagrin, announced the betrothal of his daughter Virginia, to Sir Eustace. Ginger was as damp-eyed and sniffly as usual, but no one doubted her happiness, the way she beamed at the young baronet through her tears. She never left her fiancé's side.

At Mactavish's side, Charleen, Lady Trant, sported a new ruby bracelet besides the new diamond necklace, with stones so big she didn't need spectacles to be dazzled. She kept bottled up inside the tears of relief that she wouldn't end her days in the poor house. Nothing ruined a woman's looks faster than weeping, she'd always believed, or made a man more uncomfortable. Charleen was going to make sure that Mr. Mactavish stayed very comfortable indeed.

Her aunt kept dabbing at tears of mirth. That old uncle of the squire's was more shortsighted than she was, and the two were having a high old time under the mistletoe boughs. At least she told the old coot it was mistletoe.

Sir Eustace was also enjoying the kissing balls, and the congratulations of all his friends and neighbors. He'd actually gone and won the hand of the sweetest, most adorable girl in all of England. By sheer luck, she'd turned out to be one of the wealthiest heiresses. Now he'd never have to worry about losing his heritage, his family home. And he'd be able to look after his dear sister, too. Why, just seeing Gerry in her green velvet gown, with the string of pearls at her throat, made him almost as watery-eyed as his beloved. To add to his joy, Gerry had made him shut his eyes that afternoon, as Jigtime had been brought round by the earl's groom, with red bows woven in the mare's mane, and bells on her bridle. Truly this was the finest Christmas in memory.

It was positively Lady Samantha's best yuletide ever. Her first real party, held in her father's arms as Squire lit the Yule log in the manor's huge fireplace and blessed all the company. She was so tired, though, that she nearly fell asleep there on her father's shoulder during the caroling, almost weeping that she'd be sent home with Maggie and the footmen, without seeing Papa dance with Miss Selden. Her only consolation was that when she awoke in the morning, she'd have a cat of her own.

Everyone would have a cat of their own. Gerry had seen to it. Mr. Mactavish was getting Tiffany, the gold-colored kitten. Squire was to have placid Coco, for his sister in Bath. Gerry thought her brother should have Speedwell, the kitten with the bluest eyes, for they almost matched his Ginger's eyes, when they weren't swollen shut. Lady Trant was a perfect match for Sheree, the prettiest kitten, the one that Gerry had thought to keep for herself. And the smallest, Mistletoe, of course, was asleep in her lidded basket, waiting for Lady Samantha. Gerry wished she could see the look on the child's face on Christmas morning. But this evening would be enough, if she didn't take to blubbering with gladness over her brother's bliss.

The Earl of Boughton was not crying, of course. If his eyes were moist, it was likely due to the game of snapdragon he'd played earlier, trying to win Samantha a raisin from the flaming bowl. Brett could not deny, though, that his heart was overflowing. Never had he known such contentment over such simple pleasures as he was finding among friends and family. He'd never felt such satisfaction, not without being castaway, winning a fortune at wagering, or being sexually satiated.

He could make this joy last, Brett knew, longer than this one night, longer even than the Twelve Days of Christmas. All he had to do was give up his freedom, place himself and his child at the mercy of a managing female he barely knew—and could barely keep his hands off, in her green velvet gown. *Now* he felt like crying.

But he'd do it, humble himself, for Sam's sake. That Miss Geraldine Selden fit perfectly beneath his chin,

or that she had the softest skin in the kingdom and
the most generous nature on earth, had little to do
with the fact that she doted on his little girl and Sam
adored her. Like hell it didn't.

"Would you care to look at Remington's portrait
gallery?" he asked sometime later, when she was resting between vigorous country reels.

"Oh, Squire doesn't have a formal gallery. He keeps
a few ancestors in the book room, where the card
tables are set out."

"A trip to the refreshments room, then?"

"No, thank you, my lord. Mr. Heron just brought
me a glass of lemonade."

"A walk outside?" Lud, he was getting desperate.
It was colder out than Charleen's heart. Gerry just
smiled, handed him her lemonade, and went off to
dance with the curate. Brett's patience came to an end
altogether when the party ended and he hadn't had
one minute alone with Gerry. He suggested, therefore,
that Sir Eustace escort his betrothed home. He would
see to Miss Selden's return to the cottage.

Too enamored to question the propriety of such a
happy notion, Stacey went off with Ginger. How much
could happen between Remington Manor and the cottage, anyway?

One kiss. One kiss lasted the entire journey, with
infrequent pauses for breathing, for shifting Gerry
onto Brett's lap. One kiss, and her hair and bodice
were both disarranged.

"Oh, dear, I cannot go home like this."

"Good." Brett rapped on the carriage roof and in-
structed the driver to stop by The Boughs first. "To
deliver the kitten," he added for the driver's benefit.
"I gave the servants the night off," he added for
Gerry's.

The earl waited in his library, counting his blessings, while Gerry tidied herself in one of the spare bedrooms. They went up to the nursery together, the kitten complaining at being in the basket so long.

Gerry spoke softly: "Hush, Mistletoe. It's not every cat that gets to be a Christmas wish come true."

By the light of the oil lamp left burning, they could see that Samantha was fast asleep. Gerry tucked one hand under the covers, and then she tucked the kitten under the child's chin.

Brett raised an eyebrow. "What about the cat bed, on the floor?"

"Don't be a gudgeon," was all she said. "Mistletoe will end up here anyway." She kissed the kitten on the nose, and the child on the forehead, and stepped back. "There, that's done."

"And what about your Christmas wishes, my dear?" Brett asked.

"Did you see how pleased my brother was? He intends to start a racing stud, so he won't be so dependent on Mactavish's money forever." She touched the necklace at her throat. "And I got my pearls, something I never expected at all. It's a perfect holiday already. And you? What did you wish for?"

Brett looked at his sleeping daughter, and the beautiful woman at her bedside. "I was too blind to know what to wish for. I couldn't have described it or given it a name in words. But it seems fate knew what I needed for my happiness, far more than I. Now there is only one thing missing from my perfect holiday."

"Goodness, what could that be? You can have anything you want."

"Can I?" He took a ring from his pocket, a huge diamond set with emeralds. "Will you accept?"

Gerry had never seen a diamond so big, not even

on Lady Trant. "Heavens, you aren't offering me *carte blanche,* are you?"

"With the Boughton engagement ring? I'll find something more to your taste if you don't like it."

"Oh, no, I love it." She was already admiring the ring on her finger.

"And me?"

Now she turned to admire the anticipation she saw burning in his eyes. "Oh, I must have loved you from the moment your horse pushed me into the mud. My wits have gone begging ever since, don't you know."

He knew very well, having suffered the same condition without the excuse of a knock on the head. "And I love you, my precious Miss Selden. Will you do me the honor of becoming my wife, my countess, my happily-ever-after?"

Despite the absence of nearby mistletoe—the berries, not the cat—they sealed their engagement with a kiss. Sometime later, Gerry heard the hall clock chime. "Gracious. I must be getting home. It's almost time for church. And I'll have to fix my hair again."

He was searching the carpet for her missing hairpins. "Before you go, I have a problem that requires your expertise."

"A problem?"

He nodded as he led her downstairs to the library. "A person can have too many, ah, blessings, it seems."

There in the corner of the room, barricaded behind hastily rearranged chairs, pillows from the couch, and piles of books, was a laundry basket, filled with kittens. Long-haired, short-nosed, blue-eyed kittens.

"But . . . ?"

He bent to put one of the kittens back in the basket. "But Squire had no sister in Bath, and Mactavish doesn't even like cats. Lady Trant has no need to make a splash in London, now that she's got her nabob. Your brother only wanted to exchange one for the pearls." He held up Bandit. "And Miss Mactavish has concluded that she'd rather not spend the rest of her days sneezing and wheezing."

"It was the cat all along?"

He nodded. "It seems all of our friends wanted Sam to have her kitten. More than that, I'd guess half were playing at matchmaker. And they were right. I can't do without you. I could manage to raise my daughter, and I could even survive the emptiness I knew before you." He gestured toward the wriggling kittens. "But this? Only you can help."

She knelt by his side. "Will you mind?"

"What, that your brother gets to raise prime horse-flesh and I get to raise push-faced hairballs? Not at all, sweetings."

Gerry knew he was teasing by the way he was rubbing a kitten's belly, with one gentle finger. "I wish . . ."

"Anything, my love."

"I wish you would kiss me again."

So he did, because Christmas wishes really do come true.

An Object of Charity

by Carla Kelly

Captain Michael Lynch never made a practice of leaning on the quarterdeck railing of the *Admirable,* but it hardly seemed to matter now. The crew—what was left of them—eyed him from a respectful distance, but he knew with a lift to his trounced-upon heart, that not one of them would give less than his utmost, even as he had.

His glance shifted to that spot on the deck that had glared so brightly only last month with the blood of David Partlow, his first mate. One of his crew, when not patching oakum here and there to keep the *Admirable* afloat, or manning the pumps, had scrubbed that spot white again until all trace was gone. Still he stared at the spot, because now it was whiter than the rest of the deck.

Damn the luck, he thought again. Damn the French who had sailed to meet the *Admirable* and other frigates of the blockade fleet, gun ports open and blazing a challenge rare in them, but brought about by an unexpected shift in the wind. Most of all, damn the luck that fired the *Celerity,* next ship of the line, and sent her lurching out of control into the *Admirable.*

And maybe even damn Partlow for rushing to the rail with a grappling hook just in time for the *Celerity*'s deck carronade, heated by the flames, to burst all over

140

him. Another *Celerity* gun belched fire then, and another, point blank at his own beautiful *Admirable,* one ball carrying off his sailing master, and the other shattering the mainmast at its juncture with the deck. "And they call that friendly fire," he murmured, leaning on the railing still as the *Admirable* inched past able ships in Portsmouth harbor.

There would be an inquiry, a matter of course when one ship had nearly destroyed another. He knew the Lords of the Admiralty would listen to all the testimony and exonerate him, but this time there would be no *Admirable* to return to. It would be in dry dock for three months at least, and he was sentenced to the shore on half pay. The lords might offer him another ship, but he didn't want any ship but the *Admirable*.

Lynch was mindful of the wind roaring from the north, wavering a point or two and then settling into a steady blow. He couldn't fathom three months without the wind in his face, even this raw December wind.

At some exclamation of dismay from one of the crew, he looked up to see the dry dock dead ahead. Oh, Lord, he thought, I can't stand it. He didn't mind the half pay. Even now as he leaned so melancholy on the rail, his prize money from years and years of capture and salvage was compounding itself on 'Change. If he chose, he could retire to a country estate and live in comfort on the interest alone; his wants were few.

The scow towing his ship backed its sails and slowed as it approached the dry dock. In another minute a launch nestled itself alongside. His bosun, arm in a sling but defying anyone but himself to do this duty, stood ready to pipe him off the *Admirable*. His trunk, hat case, and parcel of books were already being transferred to the launch. The bosun even forgot himself enough to lower the pipe and suggest that is was "better to leave now, sor."

"Damn your impertinence, Mays!" he growled in protest. "It's not really like leaving a grave before the dirt is piled on, now, is it?"

But it was. He could see the sympathy in his bosun's eyes, and all the understandings they had shared through the years without actually calling attention to them.

"You'll be back, Captain," the bosun said, as if to nudge him along. "The *Admirable* will be as good as new."

And maybe it will be a young man's ship then as it once was mine, he thought, stirring himself from the rail. I have conned the *Admirable* for fifteen years, from the India Wars to Boney's Orders in Council that blockade Europe. I am not above thirty-six, but I feel sixty, at least, and an infirm sixty at that. With a nod to his bosun, he allowed himself to be piped over the side.

Determined not to look back at the wounded *Admirable,* he followed his few belongings to Mrs. Brattle's rooming house, where he always stayed between voyages. He handed a coin to the one-armed tar who earned his daily mattress and sausages by trundling goods about town in his rented cart. It was almost Christmas, so he added another coin, enough to give the man a day off, but not enough to embarrass him; he knew these old sailors.

And there was Mrs. Brattle, welcoming him as always. He could see the sympathy in her eyes—amazing how fast bad news circulated around Portsmouth. He dared her to say anything, and to his relief, she did not, beyond the communication that his extra trunk was stowed in the storeroom and he could have his usual quarters.

"Do you know how long you will be staying this time, sir?" she asked, motioning to the 'tween-stairs maid behind them to lay a fire.

He could have told her three months, until the *Admirable* was refitted, but he didn't. "I'm not entirely sure, Mrs. Brattle," he heard himself saying, for some unaccountable reason.

She stood where she was, watching the maid with a critical but not unkindly eye. When the girl finished, she nodded her approval and looked at him. "It'll be stew then, Captain," she said as she handed him his key.

He didn't want stew; he didn't want anything but to lie down and turn his face to the wall. He hadn't cried since India, so it didn't enter his mind, but he was amazed at his own discomposure. "Fine, Mrs. Brattle," he told her. He supposed he would have to eat so she would not fret.

He knew the rooms well, the sitting room large enough for sofa, chairs, and table, the walls decorated here and there with improving samplers done by Mrs. Brattle's dutiful daughters, all of them now long-married. His eyes always went first to the popular "England expects every man to do his duty," that since Trafalgar had sprouted on more walls than he cared to think about. I have done my duty, he told himself.

He stared a long while at the stew, delivered steaming hot an hour later and accompanied by brown bread and tea sugared the way he liked it. Through the years and various changes in his rank, he had thought of seeking more exalted lodgings, but the fact was, he did not take much notice of his surroundings on land. Nor did he wish to abandon a place where the landlady knew how he liked his tea.

Even to placate Mrs. Brattle, he could not eat that evening. He was prepared for a fight when she returned for his tray, but he must have looked forbidding enough, or tired enough, so that she made no more comment than that she hoped he would sleep better than he ate. Personally, he did not hold out much confidence for her wish; he never slept well.

The level of his exhaustion must have been higher than he thought, because he slept finally as the day came. He had a vague recollection of Mrs. Brattle in his room, and then silence. He woke at noon with a fuzzy brain. Breakfast, and then a rambling walk in a direction that did not include the dry dock, cleared his head. He had the city to himself, possibly because Portsmouth did not lend itself much to touring visitors, but more likely because it was raining. He didn't care; it suited his mood.

When he came back to his lodgings, he felt better, and in a frame of mind to apologize to Mrs. Brattle for his mopes. He looked in the public sitting room and decided the matter would keep. She appeared to be engaged in earnest conversation with a boy and girl who looked even more travel weary than he had yesterday.

He thought they must be Scots. The girl—no, a second look suggested a young woman somewhere in her twenties rather than a girl—wore a plaid muffler draped around her head and neck over her traveling cloak. He listened to the soft murmur of her voice with its lilt and burr, not because he was prone to eavesdropping, but because he like the cadence of Scottish conversation, and its inevitable reminder of his first mate.

As he watched, the boy moved closer to the woman, and she grasped his shoulder in a protective gesture. The boy's arm went around her waist and she held it there with her other hand. The intimacy of the gesture rendered him oddly uncomfortable, as though he intruded. This is silly, he scolded himself; I am in a public parlor in a lodging house.

Never mind, he thought, and went upstairs. He added coal to the fire, and put on his slippers, prepared for a late afternoon of reading the *Navy Chronicle* and dozing. Some of his fellow officers were getting up a whist table at the Spithead, and he would join them there after dinner.

He had read through the promotions list and started on the treatise debating the merits of the newest canister casing when Mrs. Brattle knocked on his door. She had a way of knocking and clearing her throat at the same time that made her entrances obvious. "Come, Mrs. Brattle," he said, laying aside the *Chronicle* which was, he confessed, starting to bore him.

When she opened the door, he could see others behind her, but she closed the door upon them and hurried to his chair. "Sir, it is the saddest thing," she began, her voice low with emotion. "The niece and nephew of poor Mr. Partlow have come all the way from Fort William in the Highlands to find him! The harbormaster directed them here to you."

"Have you told them?" he asked quietly, as he rose.

She shook her head. "Oh, sir, I know you're far better at that than I ever would be. I mean, haven't you written letters to lots of sailors' families, sir?"

"Indeed, Mrs. Brattle. I am something of an expert on the matter," he said, regretting the irony in his voice, but knowing his landlady well enough to be sure that she would not notice it. What I do not relish are these face-to-face interviews, he thought, especially my Number One's relatives, curse the luck.

"May I show them in, or should I send them back to the harbormaster?" she asked, then leaned closer and allowed herself the liberty of adding that while they were genteel, they were Scots. "Foreigners," she explained, noticing the mystified look that he knew was on his face.

He knew that before she said it. David Partlow had come from generations of hard-working Highlanders, and he never minded admitting it. "Sturdy folk," he had said once. "The best I know."

"Show them in, Mrs. Brattle," he said. She opened the door and ushered in the two travelers, then shut the door quickly behind her. He turned to his guests and nodded. "I am Captain Lynch of the *Admirable,*" he said.

The young woman dropped a graceful curtsey, which had the odd effect of making him feel old. He did not want to feel old, he decided, as he looked at her.

She held out her hand to him and he was rewarded with a firm handshake. "I am Sally Partlow, and this is my brother Thomas," she said.

"May I take your cloak?" he asked, not so much remembering his manners with women, because he had none, but eager to see what shape she possessed. I have been too long at sea, he thought, mildly amused with himself.

Silently, her eyes troubled, she unwound the long plaid shawl and pulled it from her hair. He had thought her hair was ordinary brown like his, but it was the deepest, darkest red he had ever seen, beautiful hair, worn prettily in a bun at the nape of her neck.

He indicated the chair he had vacated, and she sat

down. "It is bad news, isn't it?" she asked without any preamble. "When we asked the harbormaster, he whispered to someone and gave me directions to this place, and the woman downstairs whispered with you. Tell me direct."

"Your uncle is dead," he told her, the bald words yanked right out of his mouth by her forthrightness. "We had a terrible accident on the blockade. He was killed, and my ship nearly destroyed."

She winced and briefly narrowed her eyes at his words, but she returned his gaze with no loss of composure, rather like a woman used to bad news.

"Your uncle didn't suffer," he added quickly, struck by the lameness of his words as soon as he spoke them. He was rewarded with more of the same measured regard.

"Do you write that to all the kin of your dead?" she asked, not accusing him, but more out of curiosity, or so it seemed to him. "All the kin of your dead," he thought, struck by the aptness of the phrase, and the grand way it rolled off her Scottish tongue.

"I suppose I do write it," he said, after a moment's thought. "In David's case, I believe it is true." He hesitated, then plunged ahead, encouraged by her level gaze. "He was attempting to push off the *Admirable* with a grappling hook and a carronade exploded directly in front of him. He . . . he couldn't have known what hit him."

To his surprise, Sally Partlow leaned forward and quickly touched his hand. She knows what he meant to me, he thought, grateful for her concern.

"I'm sorry for you," she said. "Uncle Partlow mentioned you often in his letters."

"He did?" It had never before occurred to him that

he could be a subject in anyone's letters, or even that anyone on the planet thought him memorable.

"Certainly, sir," she replied. "He often said what a fair-minded commander you were, and how your crew—and he included himself—would follow you anywhere."

These must be sentiments that men do not confide in each other, he decided, as he listened to her. Of course, he had wondered why the same crew remained in his service year after year, but he had always put it down to their own fondness for the *Admirable*. Could it be there was more? The matter had never crossed his mind before.

"You are all kindness, Miss Partlow," he managed to say, but not without embarrassment. "I'm sorry to give you this news—and here you must have thought to bring him Christmas greetings and perhaps take him home with you."

The brother and sister looked at each other. "It is rather more than that, Captain," Thomas Partlow said.

"Oh, Tom, let us not concern him," Sally said. "We should leave now."

"What, Thomas?" he asked the young boy. "David Partlow will always be my concern."

"Uncle Partlow was named our guardian several years ago," he said.

"I do remember that, Thomas," Lynch said. "He showed me the letter. Something about in the event of your father's death, I believe. Ah yes, we were blockading the quadrant around La Nazaire then, same as now."

"Sir, our father died two weeks ago," Thomas explained. "Almost with his last breath, he told us that Uncle Partlow would look after us."

The room seemed to fill up with the silence. He

could tell that Miss Partlow was embarrassed. He frowned. These were his lodgings; perhaps the Partlows expected him to speak first.

"I fear you are greatly disappointed," he said, at a loss. "I am sorry for your loss, and sorry that you must return to Scotland both empty-handed and bereft."

Sally Partlow stood up and extended her hand to him, while her brother retrieved her cloak and shawl from the end of the sofa. "We trust we did not take up too much of your time at this busy season," she said. "Come, Thomas." She curtseyed again and he bowed and opened the door for her. She hesitated a moment. "Sir, we are quite unfamiliar with Portsmouth. Do you know . . ."

". . . of a good hotel? I can recommend the Spithead on the High."

The Partlows looked at each other and smiled. "Oh, no!" she said, "nothing that fine. I had in mind an employment agency."

He shook his head. "I couldn't tell you. Never needed one." Did they want to hire a maid? he wondered. "Thanks to Boney, I've always had plenty of employment." He bade them good day and the best of the season, and retreated behind his paper again as Miss Partlow quietly shut the door.

Two hours later, when Mrs. Brattle and the maid were serving his supper, he understood the enormity of his error. Mrs. Brattle had laid the table and set a generous slice of sirloin before him when she paused. "Do you know, Captain, I am uneasy about the Partlows. She asked me if I needed any help around the place."

Mystified, he shook his napkin into his lap. "That is odd. She asked me if I knew of an employment agency."

He sat a moment more in silence, staring down at the beef in front of him, brown and oozing pink juices. Shame turned him hot, and he put his napkin back on the table. "Mrs. Brattle, I think it entirely possible that the Partlows haven't a sixpence to scratch with."

She nodded, her eyes troubled. "She'll never find work here, so close to Christmas. Captain Lynch, Portsmouth may be my home, but it's not a place that I would advise a young woman to look for work."

He could only agree. With a speed that surprised him, considering how slowly he had dragged himself to the rooming house only yesterday, he soon found himself on the street, looking for the Partlows and hoping deep in his heart that their dead uncle would forgive his captain's stupidity. He stopped at the Spithead long enough to tell his brother officers that they would have to find another fourth to make up the whist table tonight, then began his excursion through town. It brought him no pleasure and he berated himself for not being more aware—or even aware at all— of the Partlows' difficulties. Am I so dense? he asked himself, and he knew the answer.

Christmas shoppers passed him, bearing packages wrapped in brown paper and twine. Sailors drunk and singing stumbled past. He thought he saw a press gang on the prowl, as well, and his blood chilled at the thought of Lieutenant Partlow's little nephew nabbed and hauled aboard a frigate to serve at the king's good pleasure. Granted he was young, but not too young to be a powder monkey. Oh God, not that, he thought, as he turned up his collar and hurried on, stopping to peer into restaurant kitchens over the protestations of proprietors and cooks.

He didn't even want to think about the brothels down on the waterfront where the women worked day and night on their backs when the fleet was in. She would never, he thought. Of course, who knew when they had even eaten last? He thought of the beef roast all for him and cursed himself again, his heart bleak.

When it was full dark and his cup of discouragement had long since run over, he spotted them on the fisherman's wharf, seated close together on a crate. Their arms were around each other and even as he realized how awful was their situation, he felt a tug of envy. There is not another soul in the world who would care if I dropped dead tomorrow, he thought, except possibly my landlady, and she's been half expecting such an event all these years of war.

He heard a sound to his left and saw, to his dismay, a press gang approaching, the ensign ready with his whistle, and the bosun with a cudgel, should Tom Partlow choose to resist impressment in the Royal Navy. As an ensign, he had done his own press gang duty, hating every minute of it and only getting through it by pretending that every hapless dockyard loiterer that he impressed was his brother.

"Hold on there," he called to the ensign, who was putting his whistle to his lips. "The boy's not for the fleet."

At his words, the Partlows turned around. Sally leaped down from the packing crate and stood between her brother and the press gang. Even in the gloom, he could see how white her face was, how fierce her eyes. There was something about the set of her jaw that told him she would never surrender Tom without a fight.

"Not this one," Lynch said, biting off each word. He recognized the bosun from the *Formidable,* whose captain was even now playing whist at the Spithead.

To his irritation—he who was used to being

obeyed—the young officer seemed not to regard him. "Stand aside," the man shouted to Sally Partlow.

"No," Sally said, and backed up.

Lynch put a firm hand on the ensign's arm. "No."

The ensign stared at him, then looked at his bosun, who stood with cudgel lowered. "Topkins, as you were!" he shouted.

The bosun shook his head. "Sorry, Captain Lynch!" he said. He turned to his ensign. "We made a mistake, sir."

The ensign was almost apoplectic with rage. He tried to grab Lynch by the front of his cloak, but in a moment's work, he was lying on the wharf, staring up.

"Touch me again, you pup, and I'll break you right down to able seaman. This boy is not your prey. Help him up, Topkins, and wipe that smile off your ugly phiz."

The bosun helped up his ensign, who flung off his assisting arm when he was on his feet, took a good look at Lynch, blanched, and stammered his apologies. "There's those in the *Formidable*'s fo'castle who'd have paid to see that, Captain Lynch," the bosun whispered. "Happy Christmas!"

Lynch stood where he was between the Partlows and the press gang until the wharf was deserted again. "There now," he said, more to himself than them. He turned around to see Sally still standing in front of her brother, shielding him. "They won't return, Miss Partlow, but there may be others. You need to get yourselves off the streets."

She shook her head, and he could see for the first time how really young she was. Her composure had deserted her and he was embarrassed to have to witness a proud woman pawn her pride in front of practically a stranger. He was at her side in a moment.

"Will you forgive me for my misunderstanding of your situation?" he asked in a low voice, even though there was no one else around except Tom, who had tears on his face. Without a word, Lynch gave him his handkerchief. "You're safe now, lad," he said, then looked at the boy's sister again. "I do apologize, Miss Partlow."

"You didn't know because I didn't say anything," she told him, the words dragged out of her by pincers. "No need to apologize."

"Perhaps not," he agreed, "but I should have been beforehand enough not to have needed your situation spelled out for me."

Tom handed back the handkerchief, and he gave it to the boy's sister. "But why were you sitting here on the dock?"

She dabbed at her eyes then pointed to a faded sign reading FISH FOR SALE. "We thought perhaps in the morning we could find occupation," she told him.

"So you were prepared to wait here all night?" he asked, trying to keep the shock from his voice, but failing, which only increased the young woman's own embarrassment. "My God, have you no funds at all? When did you last eat?"

She looked away, biting her upper lip to keep the tears back, he was sure, and his insides writhed. "Never mind that," he said briskly. "Come back with me now and we can at least remedy one problem with a meal." When she still hesitated, he picked up her valise and motioned to Tom. "Smartly now," he ordered, not looking over his shoulder, but praying from somewhere inside him that never prayed, that the Partlows would follow.

The walk from the end of the dock to the street seemed the longest of his life, especially when he heard no footsteps behind him. He could have sunk to the earth in gratitude when he finally heard them, the boy's quicker steps first, and then his sister's steps, accompanied by the womanly rustle of skirt and cloak.

His lodgings were blessedly warm. Mrs. Brattle was watching for him from the front window, which filled him with some relief. He knew he needed an ally in such a respectable female as his landlady. Upstairs in his lodgings she had cleared away his uneaten dinner, but it was replaced in short order by the entire roast of sirloin this time, potatoes, popovers that she knew he liked, and pounds of gravy.

Without even a glance at his sister, Tom Partlow sat down and was soon deeply involved in dinner. Mrs. Brattle watched. "Now when did the little boy eat last?" she asked in round tones.

Sally blushed. "I . . . I think it was the day before yesterday," she admitted, not looking at either of them.

Mrs. Brattle let out a sigh of exasperation, and prodded Sally Partlow closer to the table. "Then it has probably been another day beyond that for you, missy, if you are like most women. Fed *him* the last meal, didn't you?"

Sally nodded. "Everything we owned was sold for debt. I thought we would have enough for coach fare and food, and we almost did." Her voice was so low that Lynch could hardly hear her.

Bless Mrs. Brattle again, he decided. His landlady gave Sally a quick squeeze around the waist. "You *almost* did, dearie!" she declared, turning the young woman's nearly palpable anguish into a victory of sorts. "Why don't you sit yourself down—Captain, remember your manners and pull out her chair!—and have a go before your brother eats it all."

She sat without protest, and spread a napkin in her lap, tears escaping down her cheeks. Mrs. Brattle distracted herself by admonishing the maid to go for more potatoes, and hurry up about it, giving Sally a chance to draw herself together. The landlady frowned at Lynch until he tore his gaze from the lovely woman struggling with pride and took his own seat next to Tom. He astounded himself by keeping up what seemed to him like a veritable avalanche of inconsequential chatter with the boy and removed all attention from his sister until out of the corner of his eye, he saw her eating.

Having eaten, Tom Partlow struggled valiantly to stay awake while his sister finished. He left the table for the sofa, and in a minute was breathing quietly and evenly. Sally set down her fork and Lynch wanted to put it back in her hand, but he did nothing, only watched her as she watched her brother. " 'Tis hard to sleep on a mail coach," she said in a low voice.

He didn't know why it should matter so much to him, but he felt only unspeakable relief when she picked up her fork again. She ate all that was before her like a dutiful child, but shook her head at a second helping of anything. Weariness had stamped itself upon all the lines of her body. She seemed to droop before his eyes, and he didn't know what to do for her.

Mrs. Brattle came to his aid again. After the maid had taken the dishes down the stairs in a tub, his landlady sat next to Sally Partlow and took her by the hand. "Dearie, I have an extra room downstairs and you're welcome to it tonight," she said. "Tom will be fine right here on the captain's sofa. Come along now."

Sally Partlow looked at him, distress on her face

now, along with exhaustion. "We didn't mean to be so much trouble," she said. "Truly we didn't."

She was pleading with him, and it pained him that he could offer her so little comfort. "I know you didn't, Miss Partlow," he assured her, even as Mrs. Brattle helped her to her feet. "Things happen, don't they?"

It sounded so lame, but she nodded, grateful, apparently, for his ha'penny wisdom. "Surely I will think of something in the morning," she told him, and managed a smile. "I'm not usually at my wit's end."

"I don't imagine you are," he commented, intrigued by the way she seemed to dig deep within herself, even through her own weariness. It was a trait he had often admired in her uncle. "This will pass, too. If you have no objections, I'll think on the matter, myself. And don't look so wary! Call it the Christmas present I cannot give your uncle."

After she left, he removed Thomas's shoes, and covered the sleeping boy with a blanket, wondering all the while how someone could sleep so soundly. He sat by the boy, asking himself what on earth David Partlow would have done with a niece and nephew thrust upon him. Tom could be bought a midshipman's berth if there was money enough, but Sally? A husband was the obvious solution, but it would be difficult to procure one without a dowry.

He spent a long time staring into his shaving mirror the next morning. His Mediterranean tan had faded to a sallow color, and nothing that he knew, short of the guillotine, would have any effect on his premature wrinkles, caused by years of squinting at sun and sails and facing into the wind. And why should I ever worry, he considered, as he scraped away at his face.

He had waked early as usual, always wondering if

he had slept at all, and moved quietly about his room. When he came into his sitting room, Tom Partlow was still asleep. Lynch eased into a chair, and gave himself over to the Partlows' dilemma. He knew she could not afford to purchase a berth for Tom, and oddly, that was a relief to him. Life at sea is no life, laddie, he thought, as he watched the boy. After all, you might end up like me, a man of a certain age with no more possessions than would fit in two smallish trunks, and not a soul who cares whether I live or die.

But I did have a mother once, he reminded himself, so I did. The idea hit him then, stuck, and grew. By the time Tom woke, and Sally Partlow knocked on the door and opened it for Mrs. Brattle and breakfast, he had a plan. Like some he had fallen back upon during years of toil at sea, it had holes a-plenty and would never stand up to much scrutiny, but it was a beginning.

"Miss Partlow," he announced over bacon and eggs, "I am taking you and Tom home to my mother's house for Christmas."

On his words, Mrs. Brattle performed an interesting juggling act with a teapot, recovering herself just before she dumped the contents all over the carpet. She stared at him, her eyes big in her face.

"We couldn't possibly intrude on your holiday like that," Sally Partlow said quietly, objecting as he had no doubt that she would.

Here I go, he thought. Why does this feel more dangerous than sailing close to a lee shore? "Miss Partlow, it is not in the nature of a suggestion. I have decided to visit my mother in Lincolnshire and would no more think of leaving you to the mercies of Portsmouth than, than . . . writing a letter of admiration to

Napoleon, thanking him for keeping me employed for
all these years!"

She opened her mouth to protest, but he trod on
inexorably and felt himself on the firmer deck of command. "If you feel a burning desire to argue, I would
not recommend it. I suspect that your uncle has funds
on 'Change. Once the probate is done—and I will see
that it is going forward—you should have funds to
repay me, even with interest. Until that moment, I
won't hear of anything else."

He returned to his eggs with what he hoped was
the semblance of serenity. Miss Partlow blinked, favored him with a steady gaze, and then directed her
attention to the egg before her. "Captain Lynch, I
suppose we will be happy to accompany you to . . .
where was it? Lincolnshire?" she murmured.

"Lincolnshire," he said firmly. "Yes, indeed. Pass
the bacon, would you please?"

They finished breakfast in silence. He knew that
Mrs. Brattle was almost leaping about in her eagerness
to have a word in private with him, so he directed
Tom and Sally to make themselves useful by taking
the dishes belowstairs to the scullery. To his amusement, the Partlows seemed subdued by his plain-
speaking, a natural product of years of nautical
command.

The door had scarcely closed behind them when
Mrs. Brattle began. "I never knew you had a mother,
Captain Lynch," she declared.

He looked at her in mock horror. "Mrs. B, everyone
has a mother. How, pray, do you think I got on the
planet?"

His landlady was not about to be vanquished by his
idle wit. "Captain, I am certain there are those of your
crew who think you were born fully grown and stalk-

ing a quarterdeck! I am not numbered among them. I am not to be bamboozled. Captain, is this a good idea?"

"I don't know," he was honest enough to admit. "They have nowhere to go, and I have not visited my mother in twenty-two years."

She gasped again and sat down. "You would take two perfect strangers to visit a lady you have not seen in twenty-two *years*? Captain . . ." She shook her head. "Only last week I was saying to my daughter that you are a most sensible, steady, and level-headed boarder, and wasn't I the lucky woman!"

"Yes?" he asked, intrigued again that he would come to anyone's notice. "Perhaps it is time for a change."

"It's been so long, sir," Mrs. Brattle reminded him. "Twenty-two years! Is your mother still alive?"

"She was five years ago," he told her. "I have kept in touch with the vicar, at least until he died five years past and my annual letter was returned."

She looked at him with real sympathy. "A family falling out, then?"

"Yes, Mrs. Brattle, a falling out."

And that is putting too kind a face upon it, he decided, as he sat down after noon in the post chaise with the Partlows, and they started off, with a call to the horses and a crack of the coachman's whip. Even after all these years—and there had been so many— he could not recall the occasion without a wince. It was more a declaration of war than a falling out.

"Captain?"

He looked up from the contemplation of his hands to see Sally Partlow watching him, a frown between her fine eyes. "What is it?" he asked, clipping off his words the way he always did aboard ship. As he regarded the dismay on her face, Michael regretted the sharpness of his inquiry.

"I . . . I didn't mean any disrespect," she stammered. "I just noticed that you looked . . . distressed," she concluded, her voice trailing off. She made herself small in her corner of the chaise and drew her cloak more tightly about her.

"I am quite in command, Miss Partlow," he replied, the brisk tone creeping in, even though he did not wish it this time.

She directed her attention to the scenery outside the window, which amounted to nothing more than dingy warehouses. "I didn't mean to intrude."

And she did not intrude again, through the whole long afternoon. He heard her sniff once or twice, and observed from the corner of his eye that she pressed her fingers against her nose several times; there were no tears that he could see. She put her arm about her brother with that same firm clasp he had noticed yesterday. When Thomas drifted to sleep, secure in his sister's embrace, she closed her eyes as well, with a sigh that went directly to his heart.

I have crushed her with my grudging generosity, he realized, and the revelation caused him such a pang that he longed to stride back and forth on his quarterdeck until he wore off his own irritation. But he was trapped in a post chaise, where he could only chafe and wonder how men on land ever survived such confinement. *I suppose they slam doors, kick small objects, and snap at well-meaning people, as I have done,* he decided, his cup of contrition full. He couldn't think of a remedy except apology or explanation, and neither suited him. *Thank God my father forced me to sea years ago,* was the thought that consoled him. He found himself counting the days when he could be done with this obligation to the Partlows, which had forced him into a visit home that he knew he did not want.

The time passed somehow, and Sally Partlow was obliging enough to keep her eyes closed. Whether she slept, he had no idea. Darkness came even earlier than usual, thanks to the snow that began to fall as they drove north toward Lincolnshire. Inwardly he cursed the snow, because he knew he could not force the coachman to drive on through the night and end this uncomfortable journey. When after an hour of the slowest movement he saw lights ahead, he knew the driver would stop and insist that they spend the night.

The village was Firch, the shire Cambridge, one south of his own, but there was no budging the coachman, who looked so cold and bleak that Michael felt a sprinkling of sympathy settle on the crust of his irritation. It was an unfamiliar emotion; he almost didn't recognize it.

"We have to stop here," the coachman said, as Michael opened the carriage door. "No remedy for it, Captain."

"Very well." He joined the man outside the carriage, grateful for his boat cloak and boots. He noticed the other carriages in the yard, and made the wry observation that Christmas continued to be a challenge for innkeepers. "Can you find a place for yourself?" he asked the coachman.

"Aye, sir. I'll bed in the stables with t'others." The man scratched his chin. "You're the one who might not be so lucky, beggin' yer pardon."

He feared the man was right. With no allowance for argument, Lynch told the Partlows to move along smartly and follow him inside. He started across the yard, leaning against the snow and wind, and wondering as he had before on the Portsmouth docks if they would follow him. He slowed his steps, hoping they would catch up with him, but they did not, hanging back, not wishing—he was sure—to trouble him beyond what they were already doing.

Hoping for the best, even as he suspected the worst, he asked the innkeep for two rooms and a parlor. "Sorry, Captain," the man said, properly cowed by what Lynch suspected was the height of his fore and aft hat and gold braid, if not the look on his face. The keep glanced beyond him, and he felt some relief that the Partlows must have followed him inside.

His relief was momentary. The keep asked him, all hesitation and apology, "Can ye share a room just this once with your son and daughter?"

"She's not my daughter," he said before he thought.

"Sorry, sir," the keep apologized. "Then you and your lady'll have to have"—he hesitated, as if trying to determine the relationship—"the boy on a pallet in your room, I'm thinking. There's no parlor to be had. Once you take that room, there won't be another for anyone else, it's that full we are."

"Very well," Lynch said, disconcerted right down to his stockings, but determined not to make it worse by saying more. "It seems we have no choice."

"None, sir," the keep replied.

Lynch was too embarrassed to look at Sally Partlow so he ignored her and followed the keep's wife up the narrow stairs to a room at the back of the inn. Again he listened for the Partlows behind him, because he knew that only the weather outside was keeping them tethered to his side.

The keep's wife apologized for the size of the room, but he could find no fault with the warmth from the fireplace and the general air of comfort in small places that he was used to, from life aboard a man o' war. When the woman left the three of them, Sally removed the plaid about her head, shook the flakes into the fireplace, and put the shawl on the narrow cot.

"I was thinking I should take that berth," he told her. "You and Tom can have the bed."

"Nonsense. I am fully a foot shorter than you, sir," she said, and nothing more; he had the wisdom not to argue.

He knew he would dread dinner in the common parlor, but he did not, even though the setting was not one he was accustomed to. No matter how rough his life at sea, his infrequent sojourns on land, in whatever port of the world, had always meant private parlors and deference. He sat at the long table next to Sally, and followed her lead, passing the common dishes around to the next diner, and engaging, eventually, in small talk with the farmer to his left, an act that would have astounded his late first mate. He decided to enjoy conversation about crop prices, and even yielded far enough to tell a sea story.

He never embellished tales, and he did not now, so he was amazed that anyone would care to listen to his paltry account of life at sea. Maybe he was trying to explain himself to Partlows; he didn't understand either, beyond a sudden need to offer some accounting of himself.

When dinner concluded, he could beat no retreat to a private parlor; before he could say something about sitting for a while in the public room, Sally told him that she was going to settle Tom upstairs in bed. "It was a long day, sir," she murmured, and he realized with a start that it was only the second thing she had said to him since his unkindness at noon.

I suppose it was a long day, he thought as he

watched her escort her brother upstairs, her hand
upon his back, her motion on the stairs so graceful
that he felt like a voyeur. He went into the public
room, content to prop his booted feet by the fender
and enjoy the warmth of the fire. He even leaned back
against the settee and called it a luxury.

He had thought that his hearing was going after
years of cannonading, but he knew her steps on the
stairs when she came down later. Before he could say
anything—had anything occurred to him—she was out
the door and into the snow. He debated a moment
whether to follow—surely she would never leave her
brother behind—then rose, pulled his cloak around
him, and head down, went into the snow after her.

He could barely see her in the dark, but he watched
her pause at the fence beyond the high road. The wind
swirled the snow, but she raised her face to it, as
though she hated super-heated rooms as much as he
did. He walked across the road to stand beside her.

"I was not running away, Captain," she said without
looking at him.

"I know that. You would never leave Tom."

"It is just that I do not like being an object of charity, sir," she said.

The candor of her words startled him, until he recalled her uncle, who never feared to tell him anything. "Who does, Miss Partlow?" he asked. "May I
remind you that you can repay me when your uncle's
funds on 'Change are probated."

"There won't be any funds, sir."

She spoke so firmly that he did not doubt her.
"How is this?" he asked. "He has always had his share
of the salvage."

"Uncle Partlow sent his money home for my father
to invest." She hesitated, then took a deep breath and

forged on. "My father had no more notion of wise investments than a shoat in a piggery." He could hear the tears in her voice then. "He wrote such glowing letters to Uncle Partlow, and truly I think Da believed that he could recoup his losses. Year after year he thought so." She sighed and faced him for the first time. "We are objects of charity, Captain. What will you do with us?"

"I could leave you here and continue by myself in the morning," he said. "Every town of any size has a workhouse."

The look on her face told him that was exactly what she expected him to say, and her assessment of him bit deep. She did not flinch or try him with tears, but merely nodded and turned back to the fence to lean upon it again, accepting this news as though he told her that snow was cold and winter endless.

"But I won't leave you here," he assured her. He surprised himself and touched her arm. "I have a confession of my own, Miss Partlow."

"You have not been home in years and years," she said. "Mrs. Brattle told me."

He leaned on the fence, same as she, and stared into the snowy field. "I have not," he agreed, perfectly in charity with her as though they were of one mind. What happened just then between them he never could have explained, not even at a court of inquiry convened by the Lords Admiral themselves.

"I suppose I should hear the gory details," she said at last, and he could not fail to note the amusement in her voice.

"Not out here in the snow. Your feet would freeze before I finished my tale of family discord, love unrequited, and blood in the orchard," he replied, turning toward the inn. He shuddered in mock terror and was rewarded with a small laugh.

Funny, he thought, as they ambled back together, but I have never made light of this before. Could I have made too much of it through the years? Surely not. He stopped her with one hand and held out the other one to her, which she took. "Let us be friends, Miss Partlow," he said, and shook her hand. "If you will help me keep my temper among my relatives, all of whom may wish me to the devil, I will figure out something for you and Thomas to do that won't involve the slave trade." It sounded so lame, but he had nothing else to offer that was remotely palatable. "Come, come, Miss Partlow, it is Christmas and we just shook on it. Have a little charity."

She laughed, and he knew he was backing off a lee shore. "This could be a Christmas of desperate proportions, sir," she joked in turn, and his relief increased. "Oh, very well, then!"

Once inside, he told her that he would remain in the parlor and give her time to prepare for bed. She thanked him with that dignity he was becoming accustomed to, and went upstairs. When he retired a half hour later, the room he shared with the Partlows was dark and quiet. By the light of glowing coals in the hearth, he undressed and lay down with a sigh, content to stare at the ceiling. His years at sea had conditioned him to brace himself against the ship's pitch and yaw, but the only movement was Tom sliding closer, seeking his warmth. He smiled and stretched out his arm and the boy curled up beside him. He slept.

Nightmare woke him an hour later or so, but that was not unusual. He lay in bed, his heart pounding, his mind's eye filled with explosions and water rising and the ship—his first ship, well before the *Admira-*

ble—slowly settling in the water: the usual dream, the usual time. After the moment of terror that never failed him, he closed his eyes again to let the dream fade, even though he knew he would not sleep again that night.

He opened his eyes in surprise. Miss Partlow had risen from her cot and was now perched on the side of his bed. Without a word, she wiped his face with her handkerchief, then pinched his nostrils gently with it until he blew his nose. His embarrassment was complete; not only had she seen his tears and wiped them away, she had made him blow his nose like a dutiful child.

"I would have been all right, Miss Partlow," he said in a whisper, unwilling to add Thomas to the audience. "Surely I did not cry out. I . . . I don't usually."

"You weren't loud, Captain," she whispered back. "I am a light sleeper, perhaps because I took care of Da for months before he died. Go back to sleep."

So he had cried out. The devil take her, he thought. He wanted to snap something rude at her, as he had done innumerable times to his steward, until the man never came into his quarters, no matter how intense the nightmare. But his steward was dead now, and he held his tongue in time.

"I thought your father was your ruin," he said without thinking.

She stared at him as if he had suddenly sprouted a dorsal fin. "And so why was I nice to him?" she whispered, after a moment in which she was obviously wondering what he was saying. "Captain, you mustn't throw out the bairn with the bathwater! He had his failings but he was my Da." She rested her hand for too short a moment on his chest. "Have you never heard of forgiveness, this far south?"

"See here, Miss Partlow," he began, but she put her hand over his eyes and he had no choice but to close them.

"Good night, Captain."

He must have dreamed the whole matter, because in the morning, Miss Partlow made no mention by blush or averted eyes that he had roused her from her bed. She was seated by the window, Bible in her lap, when he and Tom trooped downstairs to the common washroom, leaving her to complete her morning toilet in the privacy of the chamber. When they returned, she was still seated there, but her marvelous hair was now captured in a bun and she wore a fresh dress. And she looked at him—he couldn't describe the look, except that it warmed his heart.

He waited until they were some hours into their journey, and Tom was dozing, before he explained himself. "You wanted the gory details, Miss Partlow," he began. "Let me lay the bare facts before you."

She looked down at her brother, whose head rested in her lap. "Say on, Captain Lynch."

He told his story for the first time in twenty-two years of avoiding any mention of it, astounded how easy it was to talk to this sweet-faced woman. "I was young and stupid and hot-headed, Miss Partlow, and quite in love with my brother Oliver's fiancée," he told her.

"How old?"

He almost smiled, because in the actual telling, it seemed almost ridiculous. "Fourteen, and—"

"Heavens, Captain Lynch," Sally interrupted.

"Yes, fourteen!" he retorted. "Miss Partlow, have you never been in love?"

She stared back at him, and then smiled. "Not at fourteen, sir!"

"Is it warm in here?"

"No, sir."

"Miss Partlow, you are a trial. Amelia was eighteen, and I was a slave to her every glance. Did a boy ever fall so hard?"

"You were young," she said in agreement. "And did she . . . did she encourage you?"

"I thought she did, but I may have been wrong." He sighed, thinking of all the years he had hung on to that anguish, and wondering why now it felt so remote. "At any rate, Oliver found out and challenged me to a duel."

She looked up from her contemplation of her sleeping brother and frowned. "That does seem somewhat extreme, sir."

He nodded. "I can't say that Oliver and I ever loved each other overmuch before, and certainly not since. Twenty paces in the orchard with our father's dueling pistols. I shot him and ran away."

"Worse and worse," she murmured. When he said nothing more, she cleared her throat. "Possibly you could discard economy now, Captain, and fill in the narrative a little more?"

He could, but he didn't want to tell her about foggy days shivering on the Humberside docks at Hull, wondering if his brother was dead, wondering how soon his father would sic the Runners on him, and all the while eating potato peels and sour oats gleaned from ashcans in a city famous for its competitive beggars. He told her, and not even all his years, prizes, and honors could keep the distress from his voice.

As he spoke, Sally Partlow slipped out from beside her sleeping brother and came to sit next to him. She did not touch him, but her closeness eased the telling. "It's hard, not knowing what to do," she commented.

"And to be alone." She looked at Tom and smiled. "I've been spared that."

And why do you seem unafraid? he wanted to ask her. Your future is even bleaker than mine was. "The magistrate nabbed me after a week of dockside living," he said instead.

"And returned you home?"

He shook his head. "Father would not have me. He wrote that Oliver was near death, and what did I think of that?"

"Was he?"

"No." He looked down at his hands where they dangled between his knees. "I learned that much later from the vicar, who also told me that Oliver from his bed of pain had assured my father that the duel was all my idea, and that I was a hell-born babe, impossible of correction." He clapped his hands together. "That ended my career as son and brother, and I was invited—nay, urged, at age fourteen—to seek a wider stage beyond Lincolnshire."

He could feel Sally's sigh. "The world can be a frightening place, eh, Miss Partlow?" he said. He hesitated, and she looked at him in that inquiring way. "Actually, I sometimes wonder if I even shot him."

"I don't understand."

"Well, when the smoke cleared, Oliver was on the ground. I just ran, and do you know, I heard a shot when I was on the edge of the orchard." He shifted in the seat, uncomfortable as though the event had just happened. "I sometimes wonder if he shot himself after I left. You know, just the veriest flesh wound to paint me blacker than I already was."

She stared at him with troubled eyes, and then did lean against him for the smallest moment. Or perhaps the chaise lurched in the slushy snow; he couldn't tell.

"My father—bless his nipfarthing heart—did buy me a midshipman's berth with Nelson's fleet, even though I was a little beyond the usual age." He couldn't help a laugh, but it must not have sounded too cheerful, since it made Sally put her hand on his arm. "In the first and only letter I ever received from him, he said he was in high hopes that I could not long survive an adventure with the Royal Navy." Another laugh, and the pressure of her hand increased. "Deuce of it was, I did. I hope that knowledge blighted his life, Miss Partlow."

"Oh, dear, no," she whispered.

"He was a dreadful man!"

"He was your father."

On this we will never see eye to eye, he thought. He turned to face her then, sitting sideways. "I wrote to my mother every time we made landfall, but never a word in reply did she send, Miss Partlow! There is every likelihood that there will be no welcome for me, even at Christmas, even after all these years. And God knows I have wanted Oliver to suffer every single day of those twenty-two years." He wished he had not moved, because she had taken her hand from his arm. "If that is the case, then Miss Partlow, I've put you in an uncomfortable position."

"We can go to a workhouse and you can go back to sea, Captain," she said, as calmly as though they discussed whether to take tea in Barton or Fielding. She leaned toward him slightly. "But to harbor up such bitterness, Captain! Has your life been so horrible since that duel?"

What a strange question, he thought; of course it has. Under her steady gaze, he considered again, his thoughts directed down an avenue he had never explored before, but less even considered. "Well, no," he told her finally after he had thought through twenty-two years of war at sea, shipwreck, salvage prizes, foreign ports, exotic women, rum from tin cups, and the odd cat curled and warm at the end of his berth. He smiled. "I've actually rather enjoyed the Navy. Certainly I have done well." He lowered his voice when Tom stirred. "I doubt that Oliver's led such an exciting life."

"I daresay he has not," Sally agreed. "Uncle Partlow's letters were always interesting enough to share with the neighbors." She touched his arm again. "Think what a nice time of year this would be to let it all go, sir, and forgive Oliver."

"You must be all about in your head," he blurted without thinking. "Never, Miss Partlow. Never." He made no effort to disguise the finality in his voice, which he knew sounded much like dismissal. She sat up straight again and directed her attention to something fascinating outside in the snow.

"It was just a thought," she said quietly, after some miles had come and gone, then said nothing else.

"Rather a totty-headed one," he growled back, then gave himself a mental slap. See here, he thought, irritated with himself, can you forget for half a minute that she is not a member of your crew and doesn't deserve the edge of your tongue?

Furious with himself, he looked at her, and noticed that her shoulders were shaking. And now I have made her cry, he thought, his mortification complete. His remorse grew, until he noticed her reflection in the glass. She was grinning, and for some odd reason—perhaps he could blame the season—that made all the difference. I see before me a managing woman, he thought, observing her reflection. We scarcely know each other, and I know I have not exactly been making myself charming. Indeed, I do not know how. She is a powerless woman of no consequence, and yet she is still going to make things as good as she can. I doubt there is another woman like her.

"Miss Partlow, what on earth are we to make of each other? And what is so deuced funny?" he asked, when he nerved himself for speech. She laughed out loud as though her mirth couldn't be kept inside another moment, her hand over her mouth to keep from waking her brother. She looked at him, her eyes merry, and he knew he had never seen a prettier woman. "I tell you a sad story—something that has been an ulcer all of my adult life—and all you can do is ask me if I really minded the Navy all that much! Drat your hide, I'm almost thinking now that going to sea was probably the best thing that happened! It's your fault! And you want me to give up my grudges, too? Whatever happened to the . . . the shy commentary of scarce acquaintance? Have you no manners?"

"None whatsoever, I suppose," she told him, when she could speak without laughing. "Do I remind you of my uncle?"

That was it, of course. "You do indeed," he replied. "David would twit me all the day long." He paused to remember, and the remembering hurt less than it had a week ago. "I don't know . . . what to think at the moment, Miss Partlow."

She was silent a long time. "We are both of us in an impossible situation, and I say at least one of us should make the best of it. I am determined that you at least will have a happy Christmas."

My stars, but you have a way about you, he marveled to himself. "If I must, I must," he said. "Can you think of any subterfuge that will explain your presence and that of your brother?"

"Not any," she said cheerfully. "Paint us how you will, there's no denying that while Tom and I are genteel, we are definitely at ebbtide in our fortunes at present. Just tell them the truth, because they will believe what they want anyway. We are objects of charity, sir."

Who of us is not, he thought suddenly, then dismissed the notion as stupid in the extreme. I am not an object of charity! I have position and wealth, and every right to be offended by my brother. She is lovely, but she is wrong.

Thomas was awake then, and Sally moved over to sit by him again. Captain Lynch envied the way the boy so matter-of-factly tucked himself under her arm. He belongs there, Lynch thought, and could not stop the envy that rose in him.

"Do you know, Sally, I rather think I will give up the idea of the sea," Tom announced.

"That is probably best," she replied, "considering that I cannot buy you a midshipman's berth. What will you do then, sir?"

She spoke as though to someone her own age, and not to a little brother with wild ideas, and he knew she was serious. Lynch knew that this woman would never trample on a boy's heart and cause him pain. He watched them, and remembered a Benedictine convent, more of a hospital, in Tenerife where he had been brought during a terrible bout of fever. From his pallet he could see a carving in Latin over the door. He read it over and over, stupidly at first, while the fever still tore at him, and then gradually with understanding: "Care must be taken of the sick, as though they were Christ in person." That is how she treats people, he told himself, and was warmed in spite of himself.

"I think I will go into business in Fort William," Tom announced to Sally. "Wool. We can buy a large house and take in boarders and be merry as grigs."

"I think we should do that, too," Sally replied, and kissed the top of his head. "We'll serve them oatmeal twice a day at least and cut up stiff if anyone asks for hot water."

They both laughed, and Lynch wondered if that was their current lot. He wanted to ask them why they were not burdened down by their circumscribed life, or the bleakness of their future, but his manners weren't entirely gone. And besides, they didn't seem to be as unhappy as he was.

Sally Partlow was not a chatterbox, he knew, as they drew closer to Lynch Hall. She was content to be silent, and asked only one question as dusk arrived. "What is your mother like?"

He was irritated for a moment as she intruded on his own growing misgivings, then had the charity to consider her question. "I suppose you would call her a frippery lady," he said at last, "always flitting here and there, running up dressmaking bills, and spending more on shoes than you would ever dream of." He smiled. "I doubt my mother ever had two consecutive thoughts to rub against each other."

"But you loved her?"

"I did."

They arrived at Lynch Hall after dark. He wished the Partlows could have seen it in daylight. "I hope Oliver has not changed too much about the place," he murmured into the gloom. "Do you think anything will be as I remember?"

Sally leaned forward and touched his hand, and he had the good sense not to pull back, even though she startled him. "People change, Captain."

"I don't," he said quickly.

"Perhaps you should."

Cold comfort, he thought, and turned himself so he could pointedly ignore her.

"You never told me. Did your brother marry that young lady you loved?"

He sighed. How much does this woman need to know? "He did. I have this from the vicar. Apparently there have been no children who have survived even to birth."

"Seems a pity," Sally said, as the manor came into view. "What a large house, and no children."

He knew she was quick, and in another moment, she looked at him again. "Heavens, does this mean you will inherit someday?" she asked.

He nodded. "I suppose it does." He thought of the long nights standing watch and watch about on the *Admirable,* staring at the French coast and thinking about riding back to Lynch Hall in triumph. He never thought much beyond that, and the sour knowledge that Oliver would be dead then, and what was the point in triumph? "I suppose it does."

He was certain his voice had not changed, and he knew in the dark that Sally Partlow could not distinguish his features, but she leaned across the space separating them and touched his face, resting the palm of her hand against his cheek for a brief moment.

And then she was sitting up straight again, as though the gesture, the tenderest he could ever remember, had never happened. Her hand was grasping Thomas's shoulder as before, and she had returned her gaze to the window.

There were few lights burning inside Lynch Hall when the post chaise drew up at the door and stopped. He remembered nights with lights blazing in all the windows, and he wondered if there was some great shortage of beeswax this year, some wartime economy he had not heard of before.

"Does . . . does anyone live here?" Sally was asking.

"I believe so," he replied, no more sure than she.

The coachman said that he would wait there until he was "sartin, sor, that you'll not be needing me." Lynch helped Sally from the post chaise. He was prepared to let go of her hand, but she wouldn't turn loose of him. Or maybe he did not try hard enough. However it fell out, they walked hand in hand up the shallow front steps, Tom behind them. She did release his hand so he could knock.

After what seemed like an age, a butler he did not recognize opened the door, looked them over, informed them that the master and mistress were out for the evening, and prepared to shut the door. Lynch put his foot in the space. "I am his brother, and we will wait," he said. "Inside," he concluded, when the butler continued to apply the pressure of the door to his foot.

"I do not believe Sir Oliver has ever mentioned a brother," he said.

"I doubt he ever has," Lynch replied. "I am Captain Michael Lynch of the White Fleet, home for Christmas from the blockade."

The butler peered closer, as if to determine some family resemblance, then looked beyond him to Sally and Thomas, who were standing close together on a lower step. "Pray who, then, are these Young Persons?"

"They are my friends," Lynch said quietly, stung to his soul by the butler's condescension.

"Then may you rejoice in them, sir, at some other location." The butler pressed harder against the door.

"Where is my mother?" Lynch asked, his distress increasing as the Partlows left the steps and retreated to stand beside the coachman.

"If you are who you say you are, then she is in the dower house," the man replied. "And now, sir, if you would remove your foot, perhaps I can close this door before every particle of heat is gone."

Lynch did as the butler asked, but stood staring at the closed door, embarrassed to face the Partlows. He hurried down the steps and took Sally by the arm. "Miss Partlow, I do not believe there is a more top-lofty creature in all England than a butler! You must have formed such an opinion of this nation."

She leaned close to whisper, "I cannot think that Tom and I will further your cause with your mother, if the butler is so . . . so . . ."

She couldn't seem to think of anything to call the man, even though Lynch had half a hundred epithets springing to mind as he stood there in the snow. These two are babes, he thought. She is too kind even to think of a bad name, and Thomas, if I know that expression, is getting concerned. Look how closely he crowds his sister. He looked at the coachman. "Suffer us a little longer, sir, and drive around on the road I will show you."

No one spoke as the coachman followed his directions. They traveled through a smallish copse that he knew would be fragrant with lilacs in April. Somewhere there was a stream, the one where he sailed his first frigates years ago.

The dower house was even smaller than he remembered, and lit even less well than Lynch Hall. He took a deep breath, and another, until he felt light-headed. Be there, Mother, he thought; I need you.

The post chaise stopped again. He could see a pinpoint of light somewhere within, and he remembered the breakfast room at the back of the house. Silent, he helped down an equally subdued Sally Partlow. "I think I am home now," he told the coachman, walking around to stand by the box.

The man, his cloak flecked with snow, leaned down. "Sor," he whispered, "I know this trip has been on sufferance for you, wha' wi' your standin' an' all. No skin off me to take Sally and Tom wi' me. My missus'll find a situation for the girl wot won't be amiss, and Tom can 'elp me at stable."

Stables and Christmas, Lynch thought, and damn my eyes for acting so put upon because I have had to do a kindness. The man means well. "Thank you for the offer, but I will keep them with me," Lynch whispered back.

The coachman did not appear reassured, but after a moment of quieting his horses, he touched whip to hat and nodded. "Verra well, sor." With a goodbye to Tom and another touch of his hat to Sally, he was gone.

"Well, then, shall I knock on this door and hope for better?" he asked no one in particular.

"I think we are a great trouble," Sally said. "What will you do if no one answers, or if . . ." She stopped, and he could almost feel her embarrassment.

"Or if she will have nothing to do with me?" he continued. "Why then, Miss Partlow, I will marry you promptly, because I've compromised you past bearing already!"

He meant it to sound funny, to lighten what he knew was a painful situation for them both, but when the words left his mouth, he knew he meant them, as much, if not more, than he had ever meant anything. Say yes and then I will kiss you right here in front of

Tom and all these trees, he thought, filled with wonder at himself.

To his disappointment, she smiled. Come, come, Michael, you know that was what you wanted her to do, he told himself. "You're being absurd, Captain," she said.

"So are you, my . . . Miss Partlow," he answered. "I think we are both deserving of good fortune at this very moment."

"I know I am," she said in such a droll way that his heart lightened, and then sank again when she added, "But please remember that you are under no real obligation to us, no matter how you felt about my uncle."

It was just as well that the door opened then, because he could think of no satisfactory reply; she was right, of course. He turned his attention to the door and the old man who opened it.

Simpson stood there, older certainly, but Simpson. "You have aged a little, my friend," Lynch said simply. "Do you remember me?"

After a long moment of observation, the butler smiled and bowed. "I did not expect this day," he said just as simply. "Your mother will be overjoyed. Do, do come in." He looked at the Partlows, and Lynch could see none of the suspicion of the other butler in the darkened house. "Come, come, all of you! Coal's dear. Let's close the door."

They stood silent and close together in the small entranceway while Simpson—dignified, and yet with a little spring to his step—hurried down the hall. He listened intently, shamelessly almost, for some sound of his mother, amazed at his own discomposure. For the first time in his life, he understood why so many of his men died with the word "Mother" on their lips.

He felt a great longing that brought tears to his eyes. He could only be grateful that the hall was ill-lit. And then his mother was hurrying toward them from the back of the house, and then running with her arms outstretched. She threw herself at him and sobbed into his shoulder, murmuring something incomprehensible that eased his soul in an amazing way.

"Mother, I am so sorry for all those years," he managed, when her own tears had subsided, and she was standing back now to look at him.

Her eyes roamed him from hat to boot, assessing him, evaluating him. He smiled, familiar with that gaze from a time much earlier in his life. "I still have all my parts, Mum," he said finally, as he looked her over as well.

She was still pretty, in an older way now, a calmer way than he remembered, but her clothes were drab, shabby even, which caused his eyes to narrow in concern. She was no longer the first stare of fashion that he remembered, not the lady he never tired of watching when she would perch him on her bed while she prepared herself for a dinner party or evening out.

She must have known what he was thinking, because she touched her collar, which even to his inexpert eyes looked frayed. "La, son, things change. And so have you, my dear." She rose on her toes and he bent down obligingly so she could kiss his cheek. "Now introduce me to these charming people. Are you brother and sister?" she asked, turning to the Partlows.

"These are Tom and Miss Partlow," he said. "Next of kin to David Partlow."

"Your first mate?" she asked, as she smiled at the Partlows.

He stared at her. "How did you know that, Mama?"

he asked. "We . . . you and I . . . have not communicated."

She tucked her arm in his and indicated the Part-lows with a nod of her head. "Come along, my dears, to the breakfast room, where we will see if Simpson can find a little more coal, and possibly even another lamp. In fact, I will insist upon it."

This is odd, he thought, as they walked arm in arm. He remembered being a little taller than his mother when he left at age fourteen, but he fairly loomed over her now. The gray of her hair did not startle him, and then he remembered that the last time he saw her, she wore powder in her hair. It was another century, he thought in wonderment. How much had happened in that time!

As his mother sat them down in the breakfast room, he looked around in appreciation. Simpson was well ahead of the game. Even now he was bringing tea, and here was Cook, her sparse hair more sparse but her smile the same, following him with Christmas cakes. "One could almost think you have been expecting us, Mama," he said, taking a cup from the butler.

To his alarm, tears welled in her eyes. He held out his hand to her and she grasped it. "I have done this for twenty-two Christmases, son," she said, when she could manage. "Oliver and your father used to scoff, but I knew that someday . . ." She could not continue.

He sat back in amazement. "You astound me, my dear," he told her. "When I never heard anything, not one word from you, I knew that you must be of the same mind as Oliver and Father." He took a sip of the tea, then glanced at Sally, who was watching him with real interest. "After fifteen years, I quit writing to you."

His mother increased her grip on his arm until it became almost painful. "You . . . you wrote to me?" she asked, her voice so low he could hardly heard it.

"Every time I reached a port where the natives didn't have bones through their noses, or cook Englishmen in pots," he replied with a smile. "Must've been two times a year at least."

He knew that he wouldn't have started to cry, if his mother hadn't leaned forward then and kissed his hand and rested her cheek on it. "Oh, son," was all she said, but it wore him down quicker than any lengthy dissertation ever could. After a moment he was glad to accept the handkerchief that Sally handed him, and had no objection when she rested her own hand on his shoulder.

"You never got them, I take it," he said, after he blew his nose. "And you wrote?"

"Every week." She said nothing more, but stared ahead with a stony look. "God help me, Simpson, I left those letters in the bookroom, along with my husband's correspondence. Did you never see them?"

"Madam, I never did," the butler said.

Lynch felt more than heard Sally's sharp intake of breath. She dropped her hand from his shoulder and sat down heavily in her chair. "Simpson, none of my letters ever arrived here?" he asked.

"Never, Captain."

No one said anything. It was so quiet in the breakfast room that Lynch could hear the clock tick in the sitting room. Then his mother sighed, and kissed his hand again. "Son, if the scriptures are true and we are held to a grand accounting some day, your father may find himself with more debt than even Christ chooses to cover."

She spoke quietly, but Lynch felt a ripple go down

his back and then another, as in that long and awful moment before a battle began. He couldn't think of a thing to say, except to turn to Sally and say more sharply than he intended, "And weren't you just telling me about forgiveness, Miss Partlow?"

She stared right back. "Nothing has changed."

"All those years," his mother murmured. She touched his face. "You want to know how I am acquainted with your first mate?"

He nodded, relieved almost not to think of the hot tears he had shed—a man-child of fourteen—wanting her arms about him, when he lay swinging in his hammock over the guns. He thought of all the tears he had swallowed to protect himself from the laughter of the other midshipmen, some of them younger than he, and hardened already by war. "Mama, was it the vicar? I can think of no other."

"My dear son, Mr. Eccles was on his deathbed when he asked me to attend him. Oh, my, hadn't I known him above thirty years! He was too tired to talk, really, but he said he would not be easy if I did not know that for five years he had been hearing from you."

"It was never much, Mama, but I did want to know how you got on, even if you never wanted to speak to me . . . or at least, that was what I thought," he corrected himself.

She stood up, as if the telling required activity, and in her restless pacing, he did recognize the woman of years ago. I do much the same thing on a quarterdeck, Mama, he thought. To his gratification, she stopped behind his chair finally, and rested her arms upon his shoulders. He closed his eyes with the pleasure of it. "He woke and dozed all afternoon, but before he died that evening, he told me that you were well, and in command of a ship of the line." She kissed his head. "He told me a story or two that included David Partlow, and ports from Botany Bay to Serendip." She sat beside him, taking his hands again. "He never would tell me if you wanted to hear from me or not; indeed, he feared that he was betraying your confidence."

"I didn't know what to think, Mama, when I never heard from you. All I had ever asked of him in letters was to let me know how you were." He squeezed her hands. "And that he did." He hesitated a moment. "He told me that Father died ten years ago."

"He did," she said, and he could detect no more remorse in her voice than he felt. "Since then, Oliver has had the managing of me."

"And a damned poor job he has done, Mama," Lynch said, unable to keep his voice from rising.

To his surprise, Lady Lynch only smiled. "I thought that at first, too, son." She looked at the Partlows. "Thomas—does your sister call you Tom? I shall then, too. Tom, you're drooping! I hope you will not object to sharing a chamber with my son. Miss Partlow . . ."

"Do call me Sally," she said. "It's what everyone calls me, even if the captain thinks I should be Miss Partlow."

"And here I thought he would know nothing of the niceties, after all those years at sea!" Mama exclaimed, with a smile in his direction. "Sally it is, then. My dear, there is the tiniest alcove of a bedroom next to my room, with scarcely a space for a cat to turn around. How fortunate that you are economical in size." She looked around the table, and Lynch could see nothing but delight in her face. "We will be as close as whelks in a basket, but I dare anyone in Lincolnshire to have a merrier Christmas."

She had directed her attention to the Partlows, but

he followed them upstairs, leaning against the door-
frame of the little chamber he was to share with Tom
while Sally tucked him in. "I want my own bed," he
heard the boy say to his sister as she bent over him
for a goodnight kiss. "I want to be home." Don't we
all? Lynch thought, remembering years and years of
writing unanswered letters, letters where he pleaded
with his parents to forgive him for being a younger
son, for being stupid, for being a child who thought
he was a man, until the day came when he could think
of nothing that warranted an apology, and stopped
writing, replacing remorse with bitterness. I was intemperate and wild, he thought, as he watched the
Partlows, but these are forgivable offenses. Too bad
my father never thought to forgive me, and Mama was
never allowed the opportunity.

He thought his cup of bitterness, already full, should
run over, but he was filled with great sadness instead.
My parents have missed out on my life, he thought
with regret, but no anger this time. He remained
where he was in the doorway while Sally conferred
with his mother in low whispers. He heard "nightmare" and "mustn't trouble you," and looked away
while they discussed him. I am in the hands of managing women, he thought, and again, he was not irritated. It was as though someone had stretched out a
wide net for him at last, one he could drop into without a qualm.

He said goodnight to Sally there in the hall, standing
close because it was a small corridor, and then followed his mother downstairs, where she gave a few
low-voiced orders to Cook, and bade Simpson goodnight. She took his hand and just looked into his face
until he wanted to cry again. "Have I changed,
Mama?" he asked at last.

She nodded, her eyes merry. "You're so tall now, and—"

"That's not what I mean," he interrupted. "You've changed in ways I never thought you would. Have I?"

"You have," she said quietly. "How much, I cannot say, because you have only returned."

"For better or worse?"

"We shall see, Michael," she replied. "Oh, why that look? Does no one ever call you Michael?"

No one ever did, he realized with a jolt, as he heard his Christian name on her lips. "No, Mama. I am Captain to everyone I know."

She stood on tiptoe to kiss his cheek. "Then we will have to enlarge your circle of acquaintance." She pulled him down to sit beside her. "And you must not look at me as an object of charity, son! I am nothing of the kind."

He knew he must only be pointing out the obvious, but he did it anyway. "Mama, there is little coal in this house, few candles, and I have never seen you in a dress so shabby!"

But she only smiled at him in a patient, serene way he had never seen before in his parent, and tucked her arm in the crook of his. "I don't know that any of it matters to me, son, now that you are home for Christmas."

"That is enough?"

"Why, yes," she replied, even sounding startled at his question. After a moment, she released his arm and stood up. "My dear, morning comes early, and we can be sure that Oliver will be over soon."

He stood up with her, more bemused now than agitated. "I don't understand, Mama."

She kissed his cheek again and stood up. "I don't

know that things are ever quite as bad as we imagine they are, son. Goodnight."

Oliver was the last person he thought of when he finally slept, and the first person he saw when he woke hours later. He was dimly aware that at some point in the night someone came into his room and sat beside him, but he could not be sure who it was. He sank himself deep into the mattress and did not open his eyes again until much later, when he heard someone clearing his throat at the foot of the bed.

My, how you've changed, was his first thought as he stared—at first stupidly, and then with recognition—at the man gripping the footboards and glaring at him through narrowed eyes. "Oh, hullo, Oliver," he said with a yawn. "How are you?"

Comfortable in the way that only a warm bed and a venerable nightshirt allow, he gazed up at his older brother, and decided that if he had passed the man on the street, he would not have known him. He folded his hands across his stomach and observed his brother. So this was the object of my bitterness all these years, he thought, as he took in a man thin to the point of emaciation, but dressed in a style much too youthful for him. If I am thirty-six, then he is rising forty-four, Lynch thought, and there he is, dressed like a popinjay. Sir Oliver looked for all the world like a man denying age, with the result that he looked older than he was.

"Why did you think to come here now?"

To Lynch, it sounded more like a challenge than a question. "Well, Oliver, I have it on the best of authority that people who are related occasionally choose to spend certain calendar days together. I realize there's no accounting for it, but there you are," he replied. "And do you know, even though I am sure no one in the White Fleet believes me, I have a mother." He sat up then. "Is there some problem with the estate that she must dress like an old maid aunt no one cares about?"

Oliver smiled for the first time. "Economy, brother, economy! On his deathbed, our father made me swear to keep a tight rein on his widow, and so I did."

My word, two bastards in as many generations, Lynch thought. Vengeful even to death, was the old man? I imagine the next world was a jolt to his system.

"We have order and economy, and—"

"—tallow candles cut in half and coal doled out by the teaspoon!" He couldn't help himself; Lynch knew his voice was rising. "You won't object if I order more coal and beeswax candles for Mother, will you?"

"Not if you pay for them," his brother replied. "Through the years Amelia and I have been frugal with everything."

"You have indeed," Lynch agreed, remembering with some slight amusement that his brother had no progeny. "Last night we were even wondering if the manor was inhabited. Scarcely a light on in the place."

His brother shrugged, and sat down. "Why waste good candles when one is not home?" He leaned closer. "And when you speak of 'we,' brother, surely you are not married to that . . . that rather common person downstairs?"

Any manner of intemperate words bubbled to the surface but he stifled them all, determined for his mother's sake not to continue the fight where it had begun twenty-two years ago, over a woman. "No, I am not married to her. She and her brother were wards of my late first mate, with nowhere to go for Christmas."

To his further irritation, Oliver waggled a bony fin-

ger at him. "That's the sort of ill-natured charity that
makes dupes of us all! I'll wager you don't even
know them!"

Better than I ever knew you, he thought, or wish
to know you. He got out of bed and pulled down his
nightshirt at the same time that Sally Partlow entered
the room with a tray and two cups of tea. He wasn't
embarrassed because she seemed unconcerned. "Your
mother thought you two would like some tea," she
said, her glance flicking over him then coming to rest
on the wall beyond his shoulder. Her face was only
slightly pink, and dashed pretty, he considered. He
took a cup from her and sat down again, remembering
that this particular nightshirt—long a favorite—had
been from Bombay to the Baltic and was thin of material. "And you, sir?" she said, indicating his brother.
"Would you like some tea?"

Oliver shook his head. "Tea at midmorning smacks
of waste and profligacy," he said, so smug that Lynch
itched to smack him. "I ate my mush at daybreak, and
will make it last until luncheon."

Over the rim of the cup, Lynch glanced at Sally and
knew without question precisely what she was thinking. He turned his head so Oliver would not see his
smile. I do believe, my dear Sal, that it would not be
beyond you to tell my prig of a brother just where to
put his mush, he thought. You would probably even
provide a funnel.

He feared that Oliver must be wondering at the
expression on his face, but his brother was staring at
the tray Sally carried. The color rose up from his
scrawny neck in blotches. "I cannot imagine that Lady
Lynch would ever permit someone she cannot know
to be handling our silver!"

"Good Lord, Oliver, it's just that old teapot even I

remember," Lynch said, stung into retort. "I hardly think Sally will . . . will stick it up her skirt and trot to the pawnshop!"

"That is precisely what I mean!" Oliver replied. "We have had years and years of order and serenity and now you are back one morning with . . . with— heavens knows who this woman is—and things are going to ruin! I am going downstairs directly to tell Mama to count her—my—silverware carefully!"

Sally gasped. Without a word she picked up the teacup on the tray and dumped it over his brother's head. Oliver leaped to his feet, his hand raised, but Lynch was on his feet as well, and grabbed his brother's arm. "I wouldn't," he said.

"But she poured tea on me!"

"I don't blame her," Lynch replied. "You're dashed lucky this isn't the Middle Ages and it wasn't hot tar! How dare you accuse her of having designs on the family silver?"

Oliver looked at them both, his eyebrows pulled close together, his face in a scowl. "I'm going to talk to Mother about the wisdom of houseguests at Christmas," he said primly as he left the room.

Sally stared after him, then looked down at the empty cup in her hand. Lynch smiled at her and sat down. "You should have a little charity, Miss Partlow," he said. "Didn't you tell me only yesterday that it was high time I forgave my brother?"

He decided that she must not have realized what she was doing, because she sank down beside him on the bed. "Perhaps I was hasty," she amended. "I hadn't met him yet." Lynch shouted with laughter. After a long moment, she smiled, if only briefly. She stood up then, as if aware of him in his nightshirt. "He may be right, Captain," she said as she replaced both cups on the tray and went to the door. "I really don't have much countenance, do I?"

"Probably not," he agreed, in perfect charity with her, although he was not certain that she appreciated the fact. "It doesn't follow that the matter is disagreeable." To his utter delight, she made a face at him as she left the room.

He lay back down, hands behind his head, content to think of Sally, when she stuck her head in the room again. "Your mother said most particularly that you are *not* to do what you are doing now! She wants your escort to the vicarage this afternoon."

"Shrew," he said mildly. "When am I to have the nap I so richly deserve, after nine months of watch and watch about on the blockade?"

Sally Partlow sighed and put her hand on her hip, which only made him want to grab her, toss her down beside him, and abandon naps forevermore. "Captain, I believe that one must rise, before one can consider the next rest as a nap."

To his relief, Oliver was gone when Lynch made his appearance in the breakfast room. The table was covered with material and dolls, dolls large and small, with baby-fine hair of silk thread, and abundant yarn hair. Sally was diligently embroidering a smile onto a blank face, and even Tom was occupied, pulling nankeen breeches onto a boy mannikin. Lips pursed, eyes narrowed in concentration, his mother—who to his knowledge had never plied a needle in her life—pushed the last bit of cotton wadding into a disembodied leg.

He kissed her cheek, and cleared a little spot for himself at the table, which only brought a protest from Sally, and the quiet admonition of his mother to please eat his breakfast standing up at the sideboard. He didn't wish to spill eggs or tea on the dolls, did he?

Mystified at the doll factory on the table, he did as he was told. "Is this one of Oliver's cottage industries?" he asked finally, when he had finished and sat himself at the table.

"La, no," his mother said, as she attached a leg to a comely doll with yarn ringlets. "Ever year he complains when I ask for a few shillings to make dolls for the orphanage. He can be wearing, at times."

He leaned closer to her, wishing with all his heart that he had come home sooner. "I can change things for you now, Mother," he said.

If he expected to see relief in her eyes, he was doomed to disapointment. With a few expert stitches, she concluded the limb attachment and picked up another leg. "I suppose Oliver is onerous at times, son, but do you know, his nipfarthing ways at my expense have quite brought out a side of me I never knew." She looked around the table and Lynch could see nothing in her face but contentment. "When I think how little I used to do with much, and now how much I do with little, it fair amazes me!" She patted his arm, and then handed him an empty leg and pushed the stuffing closer. "And I owe Oliver this revelation of character."

"I . . . I suppose I never thought of it that way, Mother," he said, picking up the stuffing. He saw with a frown that his fingers were too large to make any headway on the leg. To his relief, Sally came to the rescue, moving her chair closer until her glorious hair touched his cheek as she expertly worked the stuffing in place with her own slim fingers. I'm in love, he thought simply, as he breathed deep of her fragrance—probably nothing more than soap and water—and tried to think when any woman had stirred him as completely as this one. The deuce of it was, he didn't think she had the slightest idea of her effect on him.

The thought niggled at the back of his brain all morning as he sat at the table and brought his mother up to date on twenty-two years of his life. He had no need to enlarge upon his experiences, because they were vivid enough with war, shipwreck, illness—which set Sally to sniffling, even though she heatedly denied it when he teased her—salvages, and exotic ports as his topics. Before he brought his recitation to a close, even Simpson and Cook had joined them around the table.

"The blockade is the least pleasant duty of all, I believe," he temporized.

"We will have it, too, son, since you have told us everything else," his mother said.

"No!" he exclaimed, rather louder than he had intended. Sally looked at him in surprise. "It's . . . it's not worth the telling."

He watched his mother gather the dolls together and motion to Tom put them in the pasteboard box Simpson provided. "And now the *Admirable* is in dry dock and I find myself in a strange position for a seafaring man."

"On land and hating it?" Sally asked, her voice soft. She hadn't stirred far from his side, but had continued to work on the doll in her lap.

Twenty-four hours ago, he would have agreed with her, but now he could not say. "Let us say, on land and not certain where to go from here," he told her, "or even what to do." He was deeply conscious of the fact that he was aware of every breath she took, so close there to him.

"Then that makes two of us," Sally murmured. She put down the doll. "Captain Lynch, do you ever wish, just once, that you could be sure of things?"

He shrugged. "Life's uncertain," he told her. "I suppose that is what I have learned."

"Not that it is good?" she asked. "Or at least satisfactory on occasion?"

"That has not been my experience, Miss Partlow," he said, his voice sharp. "If it has been yours—and I cannot see how, considering your own less-then-sanguine circumstances—then rejoice in it."

To his shame, Sally leaped up from the table as though seeking to put real distance between them as fast as she could. If he could have snatched his spiteful words from the air, crammed them back in his mouth again, and swallowed them, he would have, but as it was, Sally only stood by the window, her head down, as far away as the moon.

"That was poorly done, son," his mother murmured.

"I *told* you I had changed, Mother." Where were these words coming from? he asked himself in anguish.

"Not for the better, apparently."

The room was so hot, he wondered if he had been wise to order more coal. "Excuse me, please," he said as he left the table.

He kicked himself mentally until he passed through the copse and could no longer see the dower house. In his mind he could still see the calm on Sally's face, and the trouble in her eyes. It takes a thoroughly unpleasant customer to tread on a woman's dignity, Lynch, he told himself, and you've just trampled Sally's into the dust. Too bad the *Celerity*'s carronade didn't belch all over you, instead of her uncle. She'd certainly have a better Christmas.

He wanted to cry, but he wasn't sure that he could ever stop if he started, so he swallowed the lump in his throat and walked until he looked around in surprise, the hair rising on his neck.

He stood in the orchard, barren now of leaves, and any promise of fruit, the branches just twisted sticks. How does it turn so beautiful with pink blossoms in the spring, he wondered. I have been so long away from land and the passage of seasons. He closed his eyes, thinking of summer in the orchard and then fall, especially the fall twenty-two years ago when two brothers had squared off and shot at each other.

Why did I let him goad me like that? he thought. Why did I ever think that his fiancée preferred me, a second son, greener than grass, unstable as water in that way of fourteen-year-olds?

He stood a moment more in thought, and then was aware that he was not the orchard's only visitor. He knew it would be Oliver, and turned around only to confirm his suspicion. "Does it seem a long time ago, brother?" he asked, hoping that his voice was neutral.

Oliver shook his head. "Like yesterday." He came closer. "Did you mean to kill me?"

I was cruel only minutes ago, so what's the harm in honesty, Lynch wondered. "Yes. I'm a better aim now, though."

Oliver smiled. "My pistol didn't fire."

"I thought as much. And then you shot yourself later, didn't you?"

His brother nodded. "I wanted to make sure you never returned."

"It worked."

They both smiled this time. Lynch noticed that Oliver was shivering. "Your cloak's too thin for this weather," he said, fingering the heavy wool of his own uniform cloak. "Oliver, why in God's name do you live so cheap? Is the estate to let?"

He didn't think Oliver would answer. "No! It pleases me to keep a tight rein on things," he said finally. "The way Father did."

"Well, yes, but Father lit the house at night and even heated it," Lynch reminded him.

"I control this estate."

To Lynch, it seemed an odd statement. He waited for his brother to say more, but the man was silent.

They walked together out of the orchard and Lynch wondered what he was feeling, strolling beside the person he had hated the most in the world for twenty-two years. "You ruined my life, Oliver," he said as a preamble to the woes he intended to pour out on the skinny, shabby man who walked beside him.

Oliver startled him by stopping to stare. "Michael, you're worth more than I am! Don't deny it, I've checked the Funds. You've done prodigious well at sea. You aren't ruined."

"Yes, but—"

"And you don't have a wife who is so boring that you must take deep breaths before you walk into any room she is inhabiting. And someone damned unfeeling enough to . . . to drop her whelps before they're big enough to fend for themselves!"

"I doubt that Amelia ever intended to miscarry," Lynch said, startled, and wondering if now he had finally heard everything.

"And the deuce of it is, brother, I cannot unburden myself of her and take another wife who might get me an heir!"

Dumbfounded, Lynch could think of no response to such a harsh declaration, beyond the thought that if Amelia Lynch had been a horse with a broken leg and not a wife with an uncooperative womb, Oliver could have shot her. He had the good sense not to mention it. "No heir," was all he could say, and it sounded stupid.

Oliver turned on him. "Oh, I have an heir," he declared, "a by-blow got from the ostler's daughter at the public house, for all the good that does anyone. Naturally he cannot inherit. There you are, damn you, free to roam the world, tied to nothing and no one. As things stand now, you will inherit this estate."

As they walked on, Lynch felt a great realization dawning on him. It was so huge that he couldn't put it into words at first. He glanced at his brother, feeling no anger at him now, but only the most enormous pity and then the deepest regret at his own wasted time.

"Brother, can it be that we have been envying each other all these years?"

"I doubt it," Oliver snapped, but his face became more thoughtful.

"You were the oldest son and successor to the title, and you won Amelia's affection—my God, but I wanted her then—and Father's love," Lynch said. "Didn't you get what you wanted?"

Oliver sighed. "I discovered after six months that Amelia only loves lap dogs. Father never loved anyone. And Mama, who used to be such a scatterbrain, has turned into the most . . . the most . . ."

". . . respected and wise woman in the district," Lynch concluded, smiling at the irony of it all. "You and Father broke her of bad habits out of your own meanness, didn't you? And she became someone worth more than all of us. That must've been a low blow."

"It was," Oliver said with some feeling. "And look

at you! Damned it you aren't a handsome big fellow. I've been ill used."

The whole conversation was so unbelievable that Lynch could only walk in silence for some minutes. "So for all these years, you've either been wishing me dead, or wishing to change places. And I've been doing the same thing," Lynch said, not even attempting to keep the astonishment from his voice. "What a pair we are."

If it weren't so sad, he would have laughed. Father sentenced me to the sea, and I was the lucky one, Lynch thought. I've not been tied to a silly, barren woman, forced to endure years with that martinet who fathered us, or tethered to an estate when just maybe I might have wished to do something else. And Oliver thinks I am handsome. I wonder if Sally does?

He took his brother by the arm, which startled the man into raising both his hands, as though in self-defense. "Settle down, Oliver. I have an idea. Tell me how you like it." He hesitated only a moment before throwing his arm around the smaller man, enveloping him in the warmth of his cloak. "I've given some serious thought to emigrating to the United States. I mean, since I refuse to die and oblige you that much, at least if I became a citizen of that nation, I certainly couldn't inherit a title, could I? Who would the estate devolve upon?"

"Our cousin Edward Hoople."

"Hoople." Lynch thought a moment, then remembered a man somewhat near his own age.

"Yes! He has fifteen or twenty children at least— or it seems that way when he troubles us with a visit— and as many dogs," Oliver grumbled. "But I'd much rather he had this estate than you."

"Done then, brother. I'll emigrate," Lynch said. "At

least, I'll do it if I survive another year on the blockade, which probably isn't too likely. My luck has long run out there. That satisfy you?"

"I suppose it must," Oliver said. He looked toward Lynch Hall. "Do you want to put it in writing?"

Lynch shook his head. "Trust me, Oliver. I'll either die or emigrate. I promise."

His brother hesitated, then nodded, and hesitated again. "I suppose you can come to luncheon," he said, his reluctance almost palpable. "I usually only have a little bread and milk."

"I'll pass, Oliver. I think I've promised to take some dolls to the vicarage for Mama."

Oliver sighed. "That woman still manages to waste money!"

Lynch surprised himself by kissing Oliver on the forehead. "Yes, indeed. She must have spent upwards of twenty shillings on all those dolls for orphans. What can she have been thinking? Tell you what I will put in writing. I'll take care of Mother from now on, and relieve you of that onerous burden and expense." He looked at Oliver closely, trying to interpret his expression. "Unless you think you'll miss all that umbrage."

"No, no," Oliver said hastily, then paused. "Well, let me think about it."

They had circled back to the orchard again. Lynch released his brother, and put out his hand. "What a pair we are, Oliver."

Oliver shook his hand. "You promise to die or emigrate."

"I promise. Happy Christmas."

Oliver turned to walk away, then looked back. "You're not going to marry that chit with the red hair, are you? It would serve you right to marry an object of charity."

The only objects of charity are you and I, brother, Lynch thought. "That would please you if I married her, wouldn't it?" he asked. "You'd really think I got what I deserved."

Oliver laughed. "It would serve you right."

"I'll see what I can do," he offered, "but my credit with Sally is on the ground right now. I think she wants me dead, too."

Oliver was still laughing when Lynch turned away. He didn't hurry back to the dower house, because he knew they would have gone on without him. He sat at the table in the breakfast room for a long moment, wondering if it would be better if he just left now. He could make arrangements with his solicitor in Portsmouth for his mother, and add a rider to it for Sally and Tom, even though he knew that scrupulous young woman would never touch it. In only a day or two he could be back on the blockade conning another ship.

The thought of the blockade turned him cold, and then nauseous. He rested his forehead against the table until the moment passed. He knew that he needed Sally Partlow far more than she would ever need him.

The vicarage was much as he remembered it, but this new man—vicar since his old confidant had died five years ago—had taken it upon himself to organize a foundling home in a small house just down the road. "My good wife and I have no children of our own, Captain," the man explained, after Lynch arrived and introduced himself. "This gives us ample time to help others."

Lynch nodded, thinking of his own childless brother, who spent his time pinching pennies, denying his mother, and squeezing his tenants. "It seems so . . .

charitable of you," he said, realizing how lame that sounded.

"Who among us is not a beggar, sir?" the man asked.

Who, indeed? Lynch thought, turning to watch Sally Partlow bend over a crib and appropriate its inmate, a child scarcely past birth. He watched as the baby melted into her, the dark head blending into her own beautiful auburn hair. He thought of years of war and children without food and beds, left to shiver in odd corners on wharves and warehouses, and die. "I am tired of war," he said, his voice quiet. I need that woman.

"How good that you can leave war behind now," the vicar said.

"Perhaps," he told the man as he watched Sally. She has an instinct for the right thing. I wish I did. He sighed. If she turns me down flat, then my sentence is the blockade and I will die.

He shuddered at the thought; he couldn't help himself. The vicar looked at him in surprise, then touched his sleeve. "*Can* you leave it behind?" he asked.

That, apparently, is the question, he asked himself as he went to Sally. "Please forgive me," he murmured and without another word took the sleeping child from her. To his deep need and intense gratification, the baby made those small sounds of the very young, but did not even open her eyes as she folded into his chest, too. He felt himself relax all over. Her warmth was so small, but as he held her close, he felt the heat of her body against his hand and then his chest, as it penetrated even the heavy wool of his uniform. He paced up and down slowly, glad of the motion because it reminded him of his quarterdeck. The baby sighed, and he could have wept when her little puff of breath warmed his neck.

He wasn't aware of the passage of time as he walked up and down, thinking of nothing beyond the pleasure of what he was doing, the softness of small things, the impermanence of life, its little span. What would it have cost me to forgive my brother years ago? Nothing.

Stung by his own hypocrisy, he walked on, remembering the Gospel of Matthew, which he read from the quarterdeck to his assembled crew on many a Sunday, after the required reading of the Articles of War. With painful clarity, he recalled the parable of the unmerciful servant, who was forgiven of a great debt, then inflicted his own wrath on another who owed him a tiny portion of that which had been forgiven. " 'Shouldest not thou also have had compassion on thy fellowservant, even as I had pity on thee?' " he whispered to the baby.

He never prayed, but he prayed now, walking up and down in the peaceful room with a baby hugged to his chest. Forgive us our debts, he thought, as we forgive our debtors. How many times as captain have I led my crew in the Our Father and never *listened*? Forgive me now, Father, he thought. Forgive me, Sally. Forgive me, and please don't make me go back on the blockade. For too many years I have nourished my animosities like some people take food. Let us now marry and breed little ones like this sweet child, and walk the floor of our own home, and lie down at night with each other. Please, not the blockade again.

He stood still finally. The baby stirred and stretched in his embrace, arching her back and then shooting out her arms like a flower sprouting. He smiled, thinking that in a moment she would probably work up to an enormous wail. It must be dinnertime, he thought. She yawned so hugely that she startled herself, and retreated into a ball again. He kissed her hair and walked on until she was crying in earnest and feeling soggy against his arm. In another moment, the vicar's wife came to him, crooning to the baby in that wonderful way with children that women possessed: old women, young women, barren, fertile, of high station, and lower than the drabs on the docks. "The wet nurse is waiting for you, little one," she whispered. "And did you soak Captain Lynch's uniform?"

"It's nothing," he said, almost unwilling to turn loose of the baby.

She took the baby and smiled at him, raising her voice so he could hear over the crying, "You're a man who likes children."

I know nothing of children, he thought, except those powder monkeys and middies who bleed and die on my deck. "I think I do," he replied. "Yes, I do."

He stood another moment watching the woman with the baby, then took his cloak from the servant, put it on, replaced his hat, and soon stood on the steps of the vicarage. Sally Partlow waited by the bottom step, and he felt a wave of relief wash over him that he would not have to walk back to the dower house alone, he who went everywhere alone.

"I sincerely hope you have not been waiting out here for me all this time," he said.

She smiled that sunny smile of hers that had passed beyond merely pleasing to absolutely indispensable to him. "Don't flatter yourself! I walked home with your mama and Thomas, and then she told me to return and fetch you." She tugged the shawl tighter around her glorious hair. "I told her that you had navigated the world, and didn't need my feeble directions. Besides, this is your home ground."

"But you came anyway."

"Of course," she said promptly, holding out her arm for him. "You're not the only biped who likes to walk. The path is icy, so I shall hang on to you."

He tucked her arm in his gladly, in no hurry to be anyplace else than with Sally Partlow. "I am thirty-six years old," he said, and thought to himself, that ought to scare you away. Why am I even mentioning my years to this woman, was his next thought, followed by, I have not the slightest idea what to say beyond this point.

"Only thirty-six?" Sally said, and gathered herself closer. "I'd have thought you were older." She smiled at him.

"Wretched chit."

"I am twenty-five." She gripped his arm tighter. "There, that's in case my advanced years make you want to flee."

"They don't." To his gratification, she didn't let loose of him.

They walked on slowly, Lynch gradually shortening his stride to make it easier for the woman beside him to keep up. I'll have to remind myself to do that, he thought, at least until it becomes second nature.

In far too short a time, he could see the dower house at the bottom of the slight hill. Beyond was the copse, and then the manor house, all dark but for a few lights. It was too close, and he hadn't the courage to propose.

He sighed, and Sally took a tighter grip on his arm. "I hoped this would be a happy Christmas for you," she said.

He shook his head. "Perhaps we can remember this

as the necessary Christmas, rather than the happy one," he replied, then wondered at his effrontery in using the word "we."

She seemed not to even heed his use of the word, as though something were already decided between them. "Well, I will have food for thought, at least, when I return to the blockade," he continued, less sure of himself than at any time in the last decade, at least.

"Don't return to the blockade," she pleaded, and stopped.

He had no choice but to stop, too, and then made no objection when she took the fork in the path that led to the village and not the dower house. "You're going the wrong way," he pointed out.

"No, I'm not," she said in that unarguable tone that he had recognized in her uncle. "We're going to walk and walk until you have told me all about the blockade." She released his arm so she could face him. "You have told us stories of the sea, and personally I thank you, for now Tom has no urge to follow his uncle's career! You have said nothing of the blockade, beyond watch and watch about, and you look so tired."

"Say my name," he said suddenly.

"Michael," she replied without hesitation. "Michael. Michael."

"No one says my name."

"I noticed how you started the other day when your Mama did." She took his arm again, this time twining her fingers through his. "I can walk you into the ground, Michael. No more excuses."

You probably can, he told himself. He yearned suddenly to tap into her energy. "I'm tired. Watch and watch about is four hours on and four hours off, around the clock, day after week after month after year. We are a wooden English wall against a French battering ram."

She rested her cheek against his arm and he felt her low murmur, rather than heard it. "At first it is possible to sleep in snatches like that, but after a few months, I only lie in my berth waiting for the last man off to summon me for the next watch."

"You *never* sleep?" she asked, and he could have cringed at the horror in her voice.

"I must, I suppose, but I am not aware of it," he said, after a moment of thinking through the matter. "Mostly I stand on my quarterdeck and watch the French coastline, looking for any sign of ship movement." He stopped this time. "We have to anticipate them almost, to sense that moment when the wind is about to shift quarters, and be ready to stop them when they come out to play in our channel."

"How can you do that?" Her voice was small now. "It is not possible."

"Sally, I have stood on the deck of the *Admirable* with my hat off and my cloak open in the worst weather, just so I won't miss the tiniest shift in the wind."

"No wonder you tell us of fevers."

"I suppose." He took her arm again and moved on. "Not only do we watch the coast, but we watch each other, careful not to collide in fog, or swing about with a sudden wind, or relax our vigilance against those over our shoulders who would sneak in under cover of dark and make for shore."

"One man cannot do all that," she whispered, and she sounded fierce.

"We of the blockade do it." He patted her hand and they walked on into the village, strolling through

empty streets with shops boarded for the long winter
night. Through all the exhaustion and terror he felt a
surge of pride and a quiet wonder at his own abilities,
despite his many weaknesses. "We do it, my dear."

He knew she was in tears, but he had no handkerchief for her. I don't even know the right words to
court this beautiful woman, and flatter her, and tell
her that she is essential to my next breath, he told
himself. I've never learned the niceties because they're
not taught on a ship of the line. In the middle of all
my hurt and revenge, I hadn't planned on falling in
love. He knew he had to say something. They were
coming to the end of the village. Surely Sally did not
intend just to keep walking.

To his amazement, she did, not even pausing as they
left the last house behind. She kept walking on the
high road, as though it were summer. She walked, eyes
ahead, and he talked at last, pouring out his stories of
ship fevers, and death, and cannonading until his ears
bled from the concussion, and splinters from masts
sailing like javelins through the air, and the peculiar
odor of sawdust mingled with blood on the deck, and
the odd patter of the powder monkeys in their felt
slippers, bringing canister up from the magazine to the
men serving the guns, and the crunch of weevils in
ship's biscuit, and the way water six months in a keg
goes down the throat in a lump.

She shuddered at that one, and he laughed and took
both her hands in his. "Sally Partlow, you amaze me!"
He looked at the sky, and thought he saw the pink of
dawn. "I have told you horrible stories all night, and
you gag when I mention the water! If there is a man
alive who does not understand women, I am he."

Holding her hands like that, he allowed himself to
pull her close to him. If she had offered any objection,

he would have released her, but she seemed to like what he was doing, and clasped her hands across his back with a certain proprietary air.

"I'm keeping England safe so my brother can squeeze another shilling until it yelps, and . . ." He took a deep breath and his heart turned over. ". . . and you can lie safe at night, and mothers can walk with babies, and Thomas can go to school. Marry me, Sally."

She continued to hold him close. When she said nothing, he wondered if she had heard him. He knew he didn't have the courage to ask again. The words had popped out of his mouth even before he had told her he loved her. "Did you hear me?" he asked at last, feeling as stupid as a schoolboy.

She nodded, her head against his chest, and he kissed her hair. "I love you," he said.

She was silent a long moment. "Enough to leave the blockade?"

His heart turned over again and he looked up to see dawn. He had told her all night of the horrors of the blockade, and in the telling had come to understand his own love of the sea, and ships, and war, and the brave men he commanded. It terrified him to return, but he knew that he could now. With an even greater power than dawn coming, he knew that because he could, he did not need to.

"Yes, enough to leave the blockade," he said into her hair. "I will resign my commission with the new year." He waited for such a pronouncement to rip his heart wide open, but all he felt was the greatest relief he had ever known. This must be what peace feels like, he told himself in wonder. I have never known it until now.

She raised her head to look at him then, and he

wanted to drop to his knees in gratitude that for every morning of the rest of his life, hers would be the first face he saw. She put her hands on his face. "You are not doing this because I am an object of charity?" she asked.

"Oh, God, no!" He kissed her until she started to squirm for breath. "My dearest love, *you* are the one marrying the object of charity." He smiled when she did. "Of course, you haven't said yes yet, have you? You're just clarifying things in your Scottish way, aren't you?"

"Of course," she replied calmly. "I want to know precisely where I stand. Your brother will be horrified, your mother will be ecstatic, and Thomas will follow you about with adoration in his eyes. You've lived solitary for so long. Can you manage all that?"

"Actually, Oliver will be ecstatic. I'll explain later. I wish you would answer my question, Sally, before you start in with yours! My feet are cold, and do you know, I am actually tired right down to my toenails." That was not loverlike, he thought, but it didn't matter, because Sally was pressing against him in a way that sharpened his nerves a little more than he expected there on a cold road somewhere in the middle of Lincolnshire. "Where the deuce are we?" he asked.

"Somewhere in Lincolnshire, and yes, Michael, I will marry you," she said, then took her time kissing him. When they stopped, she looked at him in that intense way that warmed him from within. "I love you. I suppose I have for a long time, ever since Uncle Partlow started writing about you in his letters home."

"Preposterous," he said, even as he kissed her once more.

"I suppose," she agreed, after that long moment. "There's no use accounting for it, because I cannot. I just love you." She held up her hands, exasperated at her inability to explain. "It's like breathing, I think."

"Oh, Sally," he said, and then kissed her again, until even the air around them felt as soft as April.

They learned from a passing carter (who must have been watching them, because he could hardly contain himself), that they were only a mile from Epping. It was an easy matter to speak for breakfast at a public house, admire his blooming Sal over tea and short-bread, then take the mail coach back to Lynch. Pillowed against Sally's soft breast, he fell asleep as soon as the coachman gathered his reins. He probably even snored. Hand in hand they walked back to the dower house. He answered his mother's inquiries with a nod in Sally's direction, then went upstairs to bed, leaving his pretty lady to make things right.

She must have done that to everyone's satisfaction. When he woke hours later, the sun was going down and she was sitting in a chair pulled close to the window in his room, her attention on yet another doll in her lap. He lay there admiring her handsome profile and beautiful hair, and hoped that at least some of their children would inherit that same dark red hue. He chuckled at the thought; she turned in his direction to give him an inquiring look.

"I thought I would prophesy, my dearest," he said, raising up on one elbow.

"I almost shudder to ask."

"I was merely thinking that a year from now it will probably still be watch and watch about."

She put down her needlework and he recognized that Partlow glint in her eyes. "You promised me you were going to give up the blockade."

"I am! Cross my heart! I was thinking that babies

tend to require four on and four off, don't they? Especially little ones?"

To his pleasure, she pinked up nicely. She took up her sewing again, and turned back to the window, even as her shoulders started to shake. "I can see that you will be a great deal of trouble on land," she said, when she could speak again.

"I'll do my best."

She finished a seam on the little dress in her lap and turned it right side out. "I think it would be prudent if we don't settle anywhere close to Lynch, my love," she told him. "I'm sure Oliver thinks I am a great mistake."

"I'm open to suggestion," he said agreeably, then shifted slightly and patted the bed. "Let's discuss it."

She shook her head. "Not from there! My uncle Partlow always told me to beware of sailors."

"Excellent advice. See that you remember it."

They were still debating the merits of a return to the Highlands over a bolt across the Atlantic to Charlotte because he liked the Carolinas, when Mama called up the stairs that dinner was ready.

He took Sally by the arm as she tried to brush past the bed. She made not a single objection as he sat her down next to him. Sally leaned closer to kiss him. "I thought your uncle told you to beware of sailors," he reminded her, then pulled her closer when she tried to sit up. "Too late, Sal."

She seemed to feel no melancholy at his admonition, but curled up beside him with a sigh. "I am tired, love! I do not plan to walk all over Lincolnshire tonight."

"Let me make a proposal, dearest Sal."

"You already did, and I accepted," she reminded him, her voice drowsy.

"Another one, then. What do you say if after dinner we hurry to the vicarage, where I can ask about the intricacies of obtaining a special license? We can get married right after Christmas, and I will see that you get to bed early every night."

She blushed, even as she nodded. He folded her in his arms, and to his gratification, she melted into him like the baby he had held yesterday. He thought briefly of the *Admirable* in dry dock, then put it from his mind forever. He smiled to think of the Gospel of Luke, another favorite quarterdeck recitation—"and on earth peace, good will toward men."

"Happy Christmas, Sally," he whispered in her ear, as goodwill settled around him like a benediction, and peace became his second dearest companion.

A Christmas Canvas

by *Elisabeth Fairchild*

It was a grim place to spend his Christmas.

The dappled gray stopped uncertainly just inside the stone archway, belled pack horse jingling to a halt at its heels. Behind the horse and rider a fog-wrapped sun went down on All Souls' Day. Church bells tolled faintly from the vast, empty canvas of the misted moor.

Maitland trusted the animal's instincts. He eyed the courtyard and the graystone house beyond with suspicion. Savage Manor—a dour house in dour surroundings. The stone was as colorless as the day, the rooftop lichen covered. Crouching monkey-faced gargoyles scowled down at him from seven medieval gables. Mullioned windows, tall and narrow, with projecting lintels, like beetled brows above each set of three, frowned at him. The windows, hollow-eyed, held no light to welcome him.

He came by choice, by plan—here he sketched the future. Within these walls he thought to find, if not the perfect Christmas gift, at the very least, Christmas answers.

It did not, at first glance, look anything like a fortune hunter's haunt.

The pack horse shifted its weight, bells jingling too cheerfully, hooves clopping on cobblestone, the sound echoing. It was then he saw her, a flash of light and movement in the upstairs window, the pale, golden shape of a woman cut into a thousand diamonds against the darkness of the room beyond, one hand pressed to the pane, in the other a candle flickering.

Could this be she? The woman he had come to paint. He doffed his cap with a flourish, despite the misting rain. He could get no wetter.

The woman merely stood, watching, palm pale against the glass, the curve of her breast an enticing swell against the flat contrast of a fall of dark drapery. He could have painted her as she stood.

"I wish to commission a portrait, Mr. Gregory." Two weeks since Lord Savage had rubbed meaty hands together, eyes gleaming, gaze roving, up and down, up and down, as if it were Maitland's body he commissioned rather than the use of his hands. "A Christmas gift. You come highly recommended. A beauty she is, my Dorothea, though I do say so myself. I am not one to overstate the thing, sir, but when I say you will enjoy your subject, you may believe me."

His subject, he was sure it must be she, dropped her hand from the window, and stepped back, into the gloom of the house. Hair standing damply against the back of his neckcloth, he felt himself still watched as he chirruped the nervous gray into motion.

When the narrow oak door at the back of the house opened, hinge screeching, a thick, sweet smell met his nose. Cinnamon, cloves, citrus, and plums—a heady, yeasty brew. Soul cakes and plum pudding—Christmas come early.

A staid, plump woman peered out at him. " 'Ooo are you?" she demanded suspiciously.

"Mr. Gregory," he said. "I am expected."

She did not swing the door wide in welcome, merely eyed him narrowly a moment before she said, "You are late, sir, and wet. 'Tis a nasty day. You'll be leavin' yer boots and gear just inside the doorway to drip."

"My horses," he stayed her when she would have stepped back.

She frowned. "The lad will see to them."

He tipped his hat, water drooling from the brim. "If you please, marm, I prefer to see the poor beasts stabled myself. They have been good to carry me so far. If you will just tell me where to take them."

She pointed.

He nodded, surprised she called no one to help him. It took three wet trips to unload, everything dumped just inside the door.

He found the ancient stabling bleaker than the house—a chiaroscuro study in gray. The stable lad, thin scarecrow, stood in the doorway, wet and shivering, eyes squinting against the misting rain.

The place was blessedly dry inside, sweet smelling, the mangers full of hay. He got a good look at the none-too-impressive number and condition of cattle Gordon Savage kept as he relieved the dappled gray of her saddle and swabbed down her steaming sides. The lad saw silently to the pack horse.

Maitland snuck a peek at the Baron's antiquated vehicles, leather molding and worn, cushions splitting. Then he splashed across the courtyard to the house, where the smell from the kitchen set his stomach to growling.

The cook fed him mutton stew and All Souls' buns, the filling heat a blessing. The scullery maid, a child, wan faced, her hands raw as rare beef, took away his plate. The stout housekeeper who had answered the door told him her name was Tilly. He was to ask her should he need anything. She led him through the nighttime gloom of a darkly paneled hall, keys jingling, the faded tapestries of a former prosperity billowing in the breeze of her brisk passage.

Footsteps clacking on bare floors, she took him through three rooms emptied of furniture. They went through two shrouded in dust cloths before taking the servants' dark and pokey stairs to the first floor, where they made their way through a sudden wealth of furnishings, rows of Dutch school paintings, the soft warmth of jewel-tone rugs, a glow of pewter candlesticks.

"Your room, Mr. Gregory." She flung open the door. Echoing and chill, a long gallery stretched before them at far greater length than he had anticipated.

The first thing he saw was the faint smear of her handprint on the pane, the mark of her upon his future here.

"Thank you, Tilly," he dismissed her. "I will ring if I need anything."

She left him, the shadows of the house swallowing her, keys jingling. He crossed an ocean of canvas-covered floor, footsteps muffled, candles and fireplace flickering golden highlights on wood-paneled walls, drawn to the window he had seen in reverse. The view was a watercolor blur of fogged twilight. Not the view he was interested in. He raised his hand, measuring the stretch of his palm to her handprint. It fit neatly within, smaller than his. Big enough, he thought, greedy enough, to snatch up an old man's purse should it come within reach.

They had arranged a bed near the fireplace, and canvas to cover the floor, with a washstand and pitcher near the window. He moved the bed away from the warmth, the canvas on the floor helping him to slide the weighty mass of carved cherry and enswathing dra-

peries. Too lulling, such heat. His senses, his awareness, must remain keen.

The faintest of sounds, the feeling he was watched.

"Who might you be?" he asked before he turned
to find beauty framed in the dark doorway, watching
him, a young woman in a cheerful, persimmon gown,
golden hair bright as flame. The vibrant color of her,
the sweetness of her youth and unblemished beauty,
burned like candle flame in the dim gloom—a Christmas angel come early.

He wondered how long she had stood there, observing him, gaze steady, guardedly curious, assessing the
changes he had made in the furniture arrangement
without comment.

"I am Dorothea Savage," she said.

The firelight played in her hair.

"I understand this Christmas gift I paint is a wedding gift as well."

She nodded without the glowing enthusiasm of a
bride-to-be.

"Lord Lovell is a lucky man," he said perfunctorily,
not at all convinced luck figured in the match.

"You know him?" Curiosity colored her features.
Through light and shadow she came the length of the
gallery, no diminishment to her beauty on closer
inspection.

"We are well acquainted," he admitted. "An excellent gentleman."

She smiled, a small lifting of sweetly curved lips,
a look of vulnerability, of innocence. Maitland was
unprepared for such a sugar-spun facade. "I hear
nothing but good of him. He was kind on the occasion
we met."

He had expected a hint of the cunning so prevalent
in her father's features. There was none to be found.

She would be easy to paint. No lies to tell about face or features. No embellishment on her youth or physical appeal. It was only the impression of her innocence he doubted.

"Ah! Here at last, sir!" A handsome, floral-scented gentleman intruded upon the room, all forget-me-not paisley and well-stitched straw-colored kerseymere. A small, silk-haired dog pranced at his heels, nails clicking on hardwood. The gentleman's features echoed those of Miss Savage, but there was a trace of the old man's foxishness to the twist of his lips, a jaded quality to his eyes, and bored hand gestures. "Come to paint Dodo, have you?"

The dog sat, nose pointed skyward, adoring his master's every move. What did this fellow call the animal, Maitland wondered, if he would address this beautiful golden girl so callously? He disliked the man's casual, urbane sarcasm.

The girl stood, less animated than the dog, gaze fixed on the floor, no protest, no objection. Maitland's heart went out to her.

"I am commissioned to paint Miss Dorothea Savage," he said calmly, with a hint of reproof.

He defended her! She looked up, surprised. No one had ever dared challenge Dryden's right to call her what he would. Not even she. She knew better. To show he hurt her would only encourage her half-brother to more cruelty.

This London artist her betrothed had recommended, broad-shouldered, heavily browed, dark hair rain-plastered to his head, an unruly growth of stubble on his chin, would seem a gentleman in manner if not in looks.

Her brother strutted about him, a pale crested peacock, his equally pompous papillon trotting at his heels, tongue lolling. "I am Dryden Savage, Dodo's brother."

He used his horrible nickname for her again, just to prove he could. She knew well his ways.

"Have you all that you require?" He asked with mock solicitousness, hands spread wide. "I know you will understand when I say we cannot afford to heat two rooms for your convenience, nor have we the servants to keep them tidy. You do not mind too much sleeping in the same space you work. Do you?" He passed in front of the fireplace, playing lord of the manor in their father's absence, the dog a persistent shadow.

The painter's eyes glittered darkly. She could not yet determine their color as they locked on her, rather than follow her brother's parade.

"The room is splendid," he said, with a nod, as if he knew she had chosen it. "The windows promise good light." His brows rose, as if they shared a secret. "I wonder if I might request a bit of furniture brought in, as setting for your painting?"

He asked politely, without the faintest trace of obsequiousness, as if he spoke to an equal rather than his employer.

"What's left of it is yours to choose from," Dryden chuckled, as if it were no matter that the vast majority of the rooms echoed with an emptiness debt required of them, as family heirlooms were sold off, one by one, to honor the gambling losses he and her father suffered. "Whatever you desire. Dodo will see to it."

She was far too used to his ready delegation of her time and energies to do anything but nod. Soon, she thought, she would be free of his demands, free of this place, free of unending money concerns.

"My dear . . ." Her brother frowned at her.

She hated it when he used endearments. They always prefaced some form of complaint. She set her chin, waiting.

"You do not intend to wear that dress, do you?"

She smiled and shook her head, thinking of the gift of her mother's words. It had been Christmas, and she but a girl, and Dryden had set her to weeping with the dagger of his tongue.

Mother had knelt, arms encircling the two of them, her bosom a warm comfort. "We each of us choose, my loves," she had said, voice low, the words resounding in Dorothea's ears. "Whether we enjoy this life, or make of it a misery, whether we bring that same joy or misery to others."

Even when she knew she lay dying, Lady Savage had spent the too-brief hours joyfully.

Dryden had chosen a different way.

"Father suggested the burgundy velvet," she said. It did not matter, really, what she wore. She would be married soon to a kind man who would shower her with pretty things.

Dryden nodded, his gaze critical, condemning her current attire. "The burgundy better suits the occasion. You might fashion a kissing ball with matching ribbon. What could be better for Christmas, after all, than your charms displayed to best advantage with the temptation of a kiss?"

She cared little for the burgundy with its plunging neckline, drawing unwanted attention.

"A pity." The painter fixed his gaze on her, a trace of mischief in the tilt of his lips. He framed her with his hands. "I can picture you on canvas in what you wear. Posed in a window, the color of your dress bright as a candle, lighting the way for lost souls."

He glanced in the direction of the window from which she had first seen him. It was a sly compliment, more creative than most.

It left her unmoved. She had grown wary of compliments. Actions pleased her more than words.

Dryden flicked lint from his lapel, his expression soured. Unasked-for opinions were generally unwelcome from those he employed. His features sharpened. "I have in mind a second painting."

The painter's gaze abandoned her.

"Something enticing. If you are interested."

They could not afford the first painting. How could he think of commissioning a second?

Mr. Gregory cocked his glistening head. Rain dripped from the dark curls above his ear. "Lord Savage mentioned only the one."

She wondered if he was cold.

"Surely you would not balk at twice the commission?" Dryden generously promised nonexistent coin. He knew better than to look in her direction. Her displeasure in his spending habits he knew all too well.

Mr. Gregory shook his dripping head. What wet, cold painter could afford to refuse? But then he slid a quizzical look in her direction—as if he sensed her doubt—as if he knew better than to take Dryden, or his promises, seriously.

That surprised her. Dryden made a fine art of impressing strangers.

Her brother's lips curled importantly. "Proceed with haste then. Both paintings must be finished in time for Christmas."

The stableboy, forelock dripping, expression surly, a study in discontented servitude, interrupted them, bumping the door as he entered, dumping the first of

Maitland's packs on the floor with a bang. Dryden's dog scuttled for cover. Maitland feared for his vials of linseed oil.

"Ungainly oaf!" Dryden cuffed the boy on the ear as he plucked up the pup to soothe its fears.

The stableboy's lips tightened, but he kept his thoughts to himself, gaze lowered, and tugged his mousepelt of a forelock as Savage brushed past, taking his leave.

Dorothea Savage patted the lad's arm, saying, "Thank you, Duff. How thoughtful of you to bring Mr. Gregory's things."

Duff looked at her with the same slavish adoration the papillon had exhibited.

Maitland directed him where to put his things. Duff eyed him warily, his loyalties to Miss Savage and no other. She asked if there was any more. He set off obediently for another load.

Maitland unpacked.

Miss Savage stood, back to the window, candlelight in her hair, her gaze following his every move. He arranged oils, packets of pigment, brushes, a palette knife, and a tin of turpentine.

He enjoyed serving as her focal point, enjoyed the silent tension that built between them. She was, after all, his reason for coming. Every tool he unpacked was for her benefit, and hers alone. She knew it. His careful preparations bespoke his appreciation of who she was, what she represented, the time they would spend together. Without his saying a word, she recognized his respect for her, for the relationship just begun.

"Do you take joy in painting?" Her voice broke the turgid stillness.

"I do," he said. He had, from the moment he had first taken a pencil in hand, recognized the powerful spell art cast over its subjects. A tenuous, seductive power struggle from the start, that of painter and subject. He tried to explain. "I enjoy freezing time. I relish capturing truths—telling the secrets and lies people wish to see perpetuated."

"Lies?" she whispered, startled and intrigued. He had intended she should be. She came closer.

"And you?" he asked.

She blinked. "What *of* me?"

"What truths and lies do you take joy in? I shall have a much easier time painting a portrait you will appreciate if I know from the start."

She opened her mouth to reply, stifling her response as Duff made his second appearance—an annoying interruption. The lad sensed his intrusion, his gaze scooting from one to the other as he deposited stretchers on the canvas-swaddled floor. Maitland's easel clattered like a pile of old bones. A roll of clean, raw canvas carefully wrapped against the damp bounced away.

Maitland caught it up.

The lad edged his way out the door.

"I have no secrets, sir," she said. "I would tell you no lies."

He smiled and shook his head. "Ah, but you tell me one even now in saying such a thing."

Her mouth opened to object.

"Ah-ah-ah." He circled her, saying, "Is it the slope of your shoulder? Or the length of your neck? Perhaps the set of your chin?"

"What?" Her head swiveled that she might keep her beautiful puzzled eyes on him.

He leaned close to whisper. "I make adjustments. I take care in the posing of my subject, in the emphasis, or lack of same, that I place on certain features."

"I see." She smiled engimatically. "You like to play God."

His initial impulse was to defend himself. "Artists are creators, within the worlds of their invention."

"As are liars and madmen," she said, brow arching.

A clever girl. A clever response. He could not help but admire her.

"The difference being," he said, his manner unprovoked, "my lies are commissioned, paid for, and hung upon the wall for all to see."

"Touché." She acknowledged his win in their verbal skirmish. "You required furniture?"

"You would show me?" he asked.

"If you will follow me?"

Eyeing the sweet sway of her skirts as she walked to the door, he thought, any man would be happy to follow her.

"Anywhere," he said.

"Father wants a Yuletide theme." She sped along the ill-lit hallway with the haste of familiarity, a glowing will-o'-the wisp ahead of him, her voice drifting over her shoulder. "Perhaps a table with a wassail bowl. And holly, ivy, mistletoe."

"Ah! I see," he said. "An oasis of Christmas fertility."

She stopped so suddenly he almost walked right through her—too much flesh for the feat, her shoulders too solidly human beneath his hands when he reached out to catch himself from stumbling. Her face looked a pale moon in the shadows, her voice sounded thin as the wind.

"What did you say?"

He could not think with his hands upon her, could not speak, could not focus on anything but the anger and fear in her jasper green eyes.

He stepped back. His hands hung useless with longing for her missing warmth and softness. "Symbols," he said. "Fertility symbols."

She tilted her head inquisitively, chin rising. Her posture bespoke resistance.

He plunged in anyway. "Heaven-sent, mistletoe was believed to be."

"By whom?" Her eyes narrowed like a cat's.

"Druids."

"Druids?"

"To be gathered six days after a new moon. The mistletoe, I mean, not the Druids."

Her brows rose. Her eyes gleamed. A mocking tilt took possession of her wholly kissable lips. "And holly?"

He wished he had kept silent. "Uhm." This was going to sound foolish. "Considered the winter refuge for wood sprites. It protects against bad fortune, witchcraft, and uhm, lightning."

"Indeed?" Her tone mocked him. "You are fortunate. We've an abundance of all three."

He smiled.

"You fail to mention that ivy placed under a pillow brings dreams," she prodded.

"Of true love," he agreed flirtatiously. "Is it true? Do you dream of Lord Lovell?"

Her chin rose. Her eyes flashed fiery. "You take your interest in ancient custom too far, sir. Are we to make moonlight sacrifices while you are with us?"

"Only a virgin, it would seem." The words popped out without forethought. He regretted them the instant they were uttered.

She had the good grace to flush, a reddening painful to observe as she responded, without hesitation, "Only one, sir? I should think you more accomplished, so devastating is the thrust of your . . . wit."

She surprised him. He had been regretting how his tongue ran away with him, stood ready to apologize. She offered no opportunity. The swift barb of her sarcasm sank home a second time.

"How would you have me pose, I wonder? As the Madonna?"

"Touché." He tapped his chest, acknowledging the hit. She turned and set off, head high. Not so sweet as she had at first seemed, Miss Dorothea Savage. More like her name than he had imagined. And clever. She held her own in a battle of words.

Candlelight fingered the silk of her hair. The ripe, golden promise of her hips swayed, beckoning. Holy virgin, indeed. He followed, bewitched.

No wonder the old man was besotted.

She chose a carved table, heavy and dark, a settee to match. Ram's heads, clustered grape motifs and cloven hoof legs. To taunt him, he thought.

"I leave you now," she said with an impish smile. "Much to do."

Caldrons to stir? he considered asking.

She paused in the doorway, smile fading as she apologized. "You must tend your own fire. We've few servants."

"Of course," he said. "Will you come to me . . ." *On a broom?* "Tomorrow?" he went on. "We ought to begin the sketches immediately. We've less than two months to finish the painting. I would not deliver it, paint wet, to your betrothed."

"I am yours to do with as you will," she said.

All too suggestive, her promise, and yet her face read like a blank page.

He bowed, watched her go, called out as she reached the door. "Miss Savage."

She turned, "Yes?"

"What do you want?" he asked.

Her head jerked, tilted, as if he caught her off guard. Confusion shadowed her brow. "Pardon?"

"You tell me what your father, what your brother wants in this portrait, by way of dress and furniture and posing . . . you give me leave to do with you what I will, but you do not say what you want. How you see yourself."

She opened her mouth, shut it, thought a moment, and then smiled. "Does it matter?"

Her answer took him aback. That she should question the value of her opinion in the posing of her own portrait surprised him. "Only you can say," he said.

She studied him a moment, as though he suggested something unsettling. "How very kind of you to ask, Mr. Gregory. It is a question no one ever posed to me before. I must give it thought. Do you mind waiting for an answer?"

He did not mind at all.

He went to bed thinking of the sweet contradiction of her, awoke from dreams of her in his arms, in his bed, all of him stiff, cold, the bed, his arms empty, stomach growling, the fire gone out in all but his desire.

He rose to stir the ashes, shuddered with the room's chill as he shoveled the fireplace clean, relit the remains of wood, and threw on his clothes to search out breakfast.

The cook gave him sticky porridge, a tankard of twice-stewed tea, and a basin of hot water in which to wash. He stropped his traveling razor to a sharp edge and made himself presentable, his efforts received by empty hallways, an empty room, the feeling that his things had been touched, ever so slightly rearranged in his absence.

He stretched canvas, two large pieces, wondering if Dryden Savage had been in earnest in his suggestion that two paintings would be required of him. He prepared each canvas with burnt umber gesso, that he might draw Dorothea Savage forward from the darkness.

The morning passed, without sign of his subject, or her brother, until, the canvases set to dry, he went to the window about noontime, to study an indigo-stained sky for signs of the promised sun.

What he saw there, against backlit stormclouds, in a sterling light, stopped him cold. Another image for his canvas. A lad climbing a tree, a waif-thin girl beneath him holding wide the pale bell of her apron. He dashed to the table for a sketchpad.

Not a lad in the tree at all, he saw, but Miss Savage, in a wool sailor's middie and men's breeches, hair swept back beneath a plain wool cap. She scaled a goodly sized oak denuded of leaves, the only green on its branches in the balls of mistletoe above her head.

With a few strokes he captured the shapely line of her as she stretched upward, not boyish at all. The tension of her arm, he caught in crisp black charcoal, the bend of the tree, the ball of mistletoe trembling as she cut its stem. The first clump fell, berries exploding in the girl's apron, the lass from the kitchen, wan face upturned, expression solemn. She adjusted her stance, the better to catch the next bunch as it fell.

Above her, Miss Savage teetered, more mistletoe to be had, leaning farther. Too far.

The peril of her situation stilled the dance of charcoal, and stopped his breath.

The limb swayed.

The sketchpad slid from his hands, charcoal and conte bouncing into canvas sheeting determined to trip him in his dash from the room. Better traction along the dark hallway, his hip collided with a table's edge, bootheels skidding on a loose rug. He took the stairs at a gallop, two steps at a time.

Too many steps.

She lay sprawled beneath the tree, half-in, half-out of a puddle, alone, and motionless. The scullery maid had vanished.

A breathless darkness engulfed her in the moment after her fall. Then a splintered glimpse of blurred light. Pain radiated through her limbs. A chill wetness soaked hip and thigh. She gasped for air.

Sodden leaves had cushioned her fall. The ground, uncomfortably acorn strewn, stank of leaf mold.

A shadow flitted above her, a whiff of bay leaf and turpentine. Mr. Gregory, breathing hard, knelt beside her, his face beautiful with concern. His eyes were green, the brilliant color of polished jade.

She had not thought him handsome the day prior, his hair wet from the rain, face fatigue ridden and wary. Today, he was transformed, her rescuer, his concern for her painting him attractive.

"Lie still, lie still!"

He pressed her back to earth when she tried to sit, dark hair falling across his forehead, his freshly shaven jaw of an arresting firmness from such an angle.

"You've had a nasty fall."

As if she could forget, with her entire body complaining.

"Let me check first to see nothing's broken." His hands roved, too familiarly, arousing within her a strange blend of anticipation and annoyance, and yet his expression remained as dispassionate as a physician's. Concern there, but otherwise he appeared unmoved.

She did not argue, simply obliged him in stretching forth arms, bending each leg as he requested, and telling him where it hurt. A groan ended in a laugh, as she sought fresh position, rolling out of the puddle with his assistance, sitting up, avoiding putting weight on her soaked and aching hip.

"I've no more than skinned my hand." Gingerly she examined the stinging red spot. "Bruised elbow, hip, and knee. Nothing serious," she assured him. "But the seat of these breeches is soaked. Will you help me to stand?"

Dryden's dog vaulted into her lap, happy to find her at his level, tongue ready to bathe her cheeks.

Dryden spoke from behind them, voice mocking. "I vow you will be bruised as an old banana by Christmas, Dodo. A pity if Lord Lovell should turn you down. Damaged goods, don't you know. He is used to the best, I warrant. With his money he can afford to be. Would you ruin your chances with him, over a bit of mistletoe?" He kicked at the greenery.

"Your sister has taken a nasty fall."

For the second time Mr. Gregory championed her.

"Indeed! So good of you to rescue her, sir," Dryden drawled. "Do you mind carrying her inside, I wonder? I would take her myself, but I've a bad back."

Dryden—a bad back?

"Quite unnecessary, I assure you, sir," she protested when Mr. Gregory bent to oblige. "Really, do not trouble yourself. I am fine."

Eyes abrim with mischief, he slid an arm under her knees, another bracing her back.

"No trouble," he insisted. "No trouble at all." He looked her in the eye as he said it, could not help but do so, so close was the stance he had taken, kneeling, one leg bent, boot planted in the leaves beside her injured hip. His breath misted the air between them. And in that instant she knew he relished the moment, relished the idea of lifting her in his arms.

"Only help me to my feet," she insisted firmly. "Nothing is broken or sprained. I can walk."

One of his eyebrows canted skyward. Was it disappointment she saw behind the smile in his eyes? "You do not trust me?"

"It is not so much a matter of trust as of necessity."

"As you will. Arm about my neck, then."

She complied, with the feeling she ought not touch him so familiarly, his neck too warm, the thickness of his hair softer than she had expected. The smell of him weakened her knees almost as much as the pain when, rising, his body a fulcrum to help her, she put weight on the injured leg.

Wobbly, she leaned into him with a pained exhalation, the prop of his chest, his arm, an exhilarating comfort. He waited, his breath in her hair, warming the curve of her ear, allowing her time to collect herself.

"I shall just go and open the door, shall I?" Dryden suggested with a wry laugh.

"The mistletoe," she called. "Would you mind taking it in?"

"Too sticky," her brother complained. "It would surely ruin my gloves."

"I shall send the boy for it. Never fear." Mr. Gregory turned his head as he said it, his lips only inches from hers, the warmth of his breath a caress to her cheek. "Ready?"

She was ready. Ready for change, ready for her approaching marriage, ready for a man's breath on her lips. Mr. Gregory's breath smelled of cloves and tea. For an instant—young, supple, plump as plums—his lips were close enough for the tasting. Was she ready for an old man's withered mouth? Even a kind nobleman's, who had promised to take her away from this dreadful place?

Sour as an old man's breath, her thoughts—shameful, disloyal. She shook them away, fixing her attention, instead, on the fascinating sensations accompanying the pained slide of her body against the muscular length of Mr. Gregory's as they took their first united step.

She had lied. She was not ready, not at all prepared for the upheaval of her stomach, for the dizzying closeness of this young man, for the low burn that fired deep within her at his every move.

What feelings would Lord Lovell's aged fingers stir? This flutter of moths in her belly? This pounding thunder of pulse? This sense of anticipation, of imminent wonder?

Her legs seemed made of aspic, her arms of lead. She leaned into the brace of his arm at her back, his hand at her ribs. The rhythm of his body's movement became hers. With every step his hip thrust solidly against hers, thigh touching thigh, rib cage raking ribs, simultaneously painful, breathtaking, and blissful.

"Do you often wear men's breeches?" he asked, his gaze drawn to her legs, the rumble of his voice stirring body as well as ears, as much of a dilemma as their physical contact.

"One cannot climb trees with much success in a skirt," she pointed out. "Country ways, Mr. Gregory.

Do I shock you? I do assure you I do not do it when I think there is danger of anyone seeing me."

"Ah. That puts me in my place," he said.

"I could not know you would chance to look out of a window." He had her on the defensive, and she did not want to be on the defensive.

"Is there no one more suitable you could have asked to climb the tree, Miss Savage?"

She laughed. "Who? Duff?"

He nodded, his hand shifting its support, that slight adjustment raising gooseflesh. Too close to her breast, the pressure of his palm. She imagined him touching her, ached for the brush of his hand. Wicked thought! Unworthy of a young woman soon to be married to another man—a man whose touch she could not contemplate with matching anticipation.

"Duff is afraid of heights." She tried to put words between him and her wanton imagination. "And Dryden too fastidious to climb trees."

She stumbled on uneven ground. He was swift to brace her, hands and arms, the jut of his hip supporting hers. Wicked thoughts again, and wherever he touched her, an insatiable tingling heat.

"You did not think to ask me?" He turned his head, his pupils very dark.

They crossed the threshold, thus, into the plum-scented gloom.

"I did consider you," she contradicted.

"Did you?" His teeth flashed white in the darkness. "In what way was I deemed unsuitable?"

His face loomed too close, she thought. All of him too close, within the dark confining walls.

"You were busy with your canvases." Her words came too fast, too breathy. "I did not like to interrupt your business."

He chuckled, adjusting the weight of her, his hand drifting, a perilous pressure. "I had hoped to begin sketches of you this afternoon, Miss Savage."

"And so, I interrupt your work after all," she said, quietly contrite, longing for a chair, that she might relieve him of the burden she became, that she might relieve herself of the tensions he stirred.

"Sketches?" Dryden loomed in the darkness at the foot of the stairs. "Might not such drawings be done just as well with my sister seated, Mr. Gregory, her foot on a hassock?"

His leg tensed against hers.

"Do you feel up to such a thing?" he asked, his solicitousness endearing. Amused curiosity lurked in his eyes. He seemed always to be peeling back the surface of her, looking deeper than anyone else she had ever met.

"I am fine," she said. "More than happy to smile for Lord Lovell's painting."

But she could not smile when they reached the daunting obstacle of the stairs. Indeed, a gasp escaped her lips as she took the first riser. Her swollen knee threatened to buckle.

"On what floor is your room?" he demanded, stopping.

"Second." She stood hip-shot, like a brood mare put to pasture, favoring her bruised side.

"Is there none on the first or ground floor that you might use temporarily?" he asked.

"How logical your thinking," Dryden surprised her in saying. "The red room is right next to the gallery where you will be painting, Mr. Gregory. There is, in fact, a connecting door. All under dust covers at the moment, of course, but I shall send Tilly in to set it to rights."

"Fine," Dorothea groaned, amazed at his sudden housewifery.

"Until then, do you mind letting her rest in the gallery, Mr. Gregory?"

"Not at all," he said, and without a word of warning, he swept her off her feet and set off up the stairs, as if accustomed to carrying young women to his room.

"Put me down!" she blurted, unprepared for the alarming sensation of his arms crooked beneath her knees, her back, his hand upon her thigh. She was unprepared for the helplessness of a position in which the only appropriate prop for her hands would appear to be his neck. "Really, sir, this is most innappro—"

"Come, Miss Savage." He cut her short, breath fanning her face, lips too close for comfort. "Admit it." He paused, as if waiting for some declaration of her fluttery feelings. "You would never have made the stairs," he murmured. "Those bruises must hurt like the devil."

"I could have climbed them."

Her hip and knee throbbed in contradiction.

Her words provoked a skeptical gleam in his eyes. "Shall I put you down, after all?" He shifted her weight, as if prepared to do just that.

"No," she said quickly.

"No?" He shifted her again, this time a little higher in his arms. Their noses almost bumped. "So, you don't mind me carrying you, after all?"

His grin annoyed her. He seemed far too pleased with himself.

"How kind of you to play palfrey," she said primly.

He threw back his head with a hearty laugh, the rise of his chest tantalizing against the curve of her breast, the movement of his abdomen provocative against her hip. "So I am beast of burden, am I?"

He transported her through the doors to the gallery, to his curtained bed. It stood rumpled and unmade, evidence of their lack of sufficient servants, evidence of his former presence. He would have plonked her down amongst the tousled bedclothes had she not stopped him with a shriek.

"Not in these wet clothes!"

"We must have you out of them," he said, shockingly sensible.

She searched in vain for a lascivious twinkle in his eye.

"Put me down by the chair, and ring for Tilly."

"You would sit, dripping and aching, until she comes? Nonsense. You must strip down and climb under the covers."

"In your room, sir? In your bed? I think not."

"Come, now. You may pull the bedcurtains."

"Please ring for Tilly," she insisted obstinately.

"Better yet, I will go myself to fetch her," he said.

He left, the atmosphere of the gallery changing with his absence. Her body's responses changed too. She felt colder. Her bruises throbbed. Every move brought fresh pain.

Maitland had no intention of fetching Tilly as he had promised. He chose to head upstairs instead of down. He would fetch her clothes rather than the woman, and in the process he would explore Miss Savage's private chamber, where he hoped to gain some greater sense of who and what his uncle's affianced intentions really were with regard to the dear old man.

There were six chamber doors to choose from—the

first Dryden's room. When he peeped within, Dryden's silky little dog charged, barking furiously. He slammed the door in the animal's face and tried the next—a room under dustcovers.

Across the hall—her room—a chamber strangely spartan, the floor covered in a threadbare rug, once fine, as had been the bedhangings, now faded. The outside wall wore an ancient tapestry, its once bright threads faded to a whisper of suggested color; a unicorn downed by hounds, proud head still held high.

No smell of dust lingered here, no hint of mold, only her scent, elusive and tantalizing. She kept the place tidy. A branch of red-berried holly with a softening cascade of ivy graced a chipped stoneware pitcher at her gabled windowcasing, a cheerful reminder of Christmas's approach, carefully centered on an embroidered runner, white on snowy white.

He felt the intruder in crossing the room—a marauder come to ransack drawers and plunder trunks. He was a liar, here on false pretense. He did not relish the role.

Affixed to the wall, unframed, a half-dozen watercolor paintings—views of the moors at sunset, golden glow extinguished in a bleak landscape, a sunlit waterfall surrounded by thick, black forest, a dark pond, fallen leaves floating—in every one some brightness on a dark landscape.

Like she, herself, he thought, looking out of the window at the grayest and most unpromising of horizons.

Her wardrobe housed few gowns, three of them fine, the burgundy, the saffron, one of midnight blue. Window dressing, he thought, like the smattering of fine furniture in the front rooms downstairs. The rest of her dresses were as faded as the carpet, threadbare at cuffs and hem, a few carefully patched. He pitied her. Well he knew how women like frills and furbelows.

Dorothea Savage had few enough of these. He went through everything. A wardrobe, two trunks, one at the foot of her bed, the other by the door. A small cassock revealed a handful of inexpensive jewelry, three carefully rolled lace sets, collars and cuffs. She had an abundance of aprons and caps, no hatboxes to be seen, only two pair of shoes.

He gathered what she might need as he went, draped everything over one arm, a weight of faded femininity: chemise and petticoat, stockings and shoes, stays and tucker, the burgundy dress. Ironic, he thought. He took clothes to dress her, when he had it in mind it would be much more fun to undress her.

The unwrapping of her was another gentleman's Christmas gift. Lord Lovell's. The old man would kill him if he could see him in this instant, pawing through his betrothed's underthings. He laughed under his breath. This Christmas gift he gave the old fellow proved greater sacrifice than ever he had imagined.

She was in his bed when he returned, as he had suggested. The curtains were loosely drawn, a drift of blue that could not cut off entirely the vision of her.

He froze, given a glimpse, breath caught in his throat, pulse racing. She lay sleeping like a goddess given mortal form, nothing to clothe her but the bed-clothes loosely gathered at her waist.

His first reaction was to tiptoe out of the room, to leave her to rest in peace. She was too temptingly arranged. He feared someone else might walk in on her thus, stepped forward to better close the draperies, and found himself completely awestruck in the process, his best intentions dissolving.

She lay like a fallen angel, ready for seduction,

breathing deep and even, complexion pink with slumber, her hair fanned loose upon bared shoulders, golden waves upon the pillow, draping the creamy, rose-tipped swell of her breasts. She was a Botticelli Venus, a pearl to be plucked.

He ached to shed his clothing, envisioned sliding into the bed's warmth. His fingers itched to run through the silk of her hair. There was no question— he must capture the wanton promise of her.

The idea of such beauty, such supple youth, bedded by an old man, tore at something vital within him. His self-set task was to reveal her as a bride unworthy for his uncle, Lord Lovell, and yet, to see her thus revealed, he wondered if he got it wrong, and it was his uncle who was completely unworthy of her.

He went through three sticks of vine charcoal, a fistful of vellum, capturing first her face, her hair, from four different angles, the gentle sweep of her neck and shoulders, the dangerous rise of her breasts, and the sculptural fall of bedclothes over the tempting arc of her hip. Not a finger did he lay on her, but he caressed her every curve, nonetheless, by way of his art.

Through the soft touch of charcoal to paper he knew her intimately, every plane, every valley.

One foot peeped coyly from the covers. A hand curled like a shell upon the duvet. He drew all that was revealed to him, from every angle to be had.

He was not shy about rearranging the bedcurtains, about settling himself upon a stool that he might the more comfortably sketch her. It seemed odd she didn't stir. His shadow fell on her as he moved about. The paper rattled as charcoal rasped across page after page.

She slept too deep, too long.

It roused his suspicion, returned him to his senses,

made him question. He stopped drawing. He fell back a step to examine her objectively.

Too perfect her pose, too carefully the bedcurtains positioned, the careful fan of her hair, the suggestively arranged drape of the coverlet. He had been meant to find her thus. The idea chilled him.

His gaze darted to the door, swept the room. So many nooks and crannies, so much panalwork some- one might hide behind, might watch him from even now. There was no sense in him of the presence of another. No creak of wood to betray the betrayer. Long fled, he assumed. They had done their dark deed and left the rest to chance and the baseness of man's nature.

Who?

A glass stood at the bedside. It had not been there when he had carried her in. He lifted it to the light, tasted the milky fluid and made a face.

Laudenum.

Someone had given her the sedative. She had cer- tainly not gotten up to fetch it herself, nor had she carried it on her person.

Alarmed, he dared touch the creamy satin of her shoulder. Better to risk her anger than the possibility she had drifted into a faint from which she could not be roused.

"Miss Savage," he whispered.

She remained clasped in slumber's arms, an unusual pallor and heat to her skin and yet she breathed deep and even.

Troubled, he set down the glass, sat on the edge of the bed to check her pulse, mind whirling. More afoot here than he had ever imagined.

Disturbed now by her ill-clad form, he lifted the bedclothes to gently cover her, his every feeling one of protectiveness, and outrage. Pulling the bedcurtains shut, he carried his scattered sketches to the window.

She had been drugged and he had been duped. By whom? Who in this dark and mysterious place would do such a thing? Who would leave this beautiful, golden girl so vulnerable to a stranger?

She was beautiful. He had trapped the light and dark of her on the pages.

He ought to destroy them, he thought, his fingers curled to crumple the illicitly gained sketches.

And yet, he could not. He was a man to create and cherish beauty rather than destroy it. His nature rebelled at the thought.

Carefully, wondering if this was the closest he would ever get to the young woman in his bed, Maitland Gregory placed tissue between his drawings, and tucked them carefully away in the back of his portfolio before he rang for the housekeeper.

Dorothea Savage filled his waking thoughts that night as much as she had filled his bed that afternoon. The smell of her clung to the bedlinens. The scent of the soap she used in her hair drifted from the pillow. He buried his face in it, body aching. She was only steps away, in a room he might have reached, unde-tected, by way of a connecting door. So close and yet so far.

He had never intended to become infatuated with his uncle's bride-to-be. Someone here had intended he should be seduced. They had hoped he would succumb to his desires.

Who? Why? Was Dorothea Savage a part of it? He must uncover the truth.

The light of morning cleared head and heart, found him busy constructing a Christmas scene in which he meant to stage a Christmas bride's sitting. Holly and ivy in lush abundance, the settee draped with cloth of gold. An empty wassail bowl perched on the nearby table, rosy-cheeked apples clustered at its base.

Two could play at this game.

He had set the scene. He would find his answers. He would not be duped again.

She went to him.

It took a great deal of effort to rise, to dress herself, bruises aching, joints stiff, a strange lethargy dulling her mind—as if she had not slept well when she knew she had. It took effort to make her way from the red room to the gallery. She pushed herself. She wanted to see him again, wanted to begin the Christmas painting, wanted to continue their interesting verbal exchanges.

He was at his easel, dark head bent, brush in hand. He started when her shoe scuffed the floor. His hands rose immediately to drape the canvas, a strange look on his face, as if she interrupted him in a secret.

"Miss Savage," he said politely. "You look lovely. How fare your injuries this morning?"

"I am purpling nicely," she said.

His smile was lukewarm.

The room was greatly changed. She stepped into Christmas. Their remaining riches were gathered as backdrop for her portrait: rugs, wall hangings, a painting from downstairs, holly and ivy bristling atop its frame. A suit of armor proudly guarded the corner. The best of the silver huddled on an ivy-trimmed sideboard.

He would surround her in a life, she saw, a cheerful pocket of abundance, a picture of the kind of Christmas she had not known since her mother's death.

He fixed her with his gaze, a half-smile touching his lips.

"How would you have me?"

His smile widened, a mischievous twinkle lighting his eyes, as if she suggested something surprising—amusing. He waved his brush in the direction of the settee. "How would you have me see you?"

She settled at the end farthest from the punch bowl, her arm draped over the rolled arm of the furniture, face three-quarter turned, gaze fixed on the window's distant view of a horizon she hoped to soon put behind her.

"I would have you see me as I am," she said quietly.

He arranged fresh paper, fresh canvas upon his easel, looking up to remark coolly, "Trust me, I will."

He fell momentarily silent as he sketched. She could not sustain the stillness, could not allow the opportunity to speak to such an intriguing and provoking fellow slide by, unchallenged. They were to spend weeks doing this, after all.

"Tilly tells me you carried me to my room?" She held the pose, unable to look at him, sensing his sudden stillness.

"But of course. Who else?"

Defensive, the tone of his response. She wondered at it, turned her head to look. He almost sounded forbidding.

"I've no memory of it," she said, "but I would thank you."

He looked at her, eyes narrowed. "Can you hold that pose? No. Looking this way . . . not quite." He came swiftly from behind his easel to correct her. "Like so." One hand lifting her chin, the other cupping, tilting. The firm heat of his fingertips startled her heart to faster rhythm.

His gaze fixed briefly on the low neckline of the dress, further stirring her pulse. "Have you memory of who drugged you?"

She blinked, confused, then laughed breathlessly. What strange contradiction she met in the gentleness of his touch and the all-too-ungentle glint in his eyes.

"Do you mean the laudanum?" she asked.

He got an unexpectedly close-up look in her eyes as she said it. No guile there. No subterfuge, unless she was masterfully deceitful. Just alarm, and a growing awareness of how close they were. Her gaze broke contact and drifted to his lips.

He dared remain in almost uncomfortable proximity to her, his hands falling slowly away from her face, to her bare shoulders, which he turned slightly, not because they needed repositioning, but because he liked the tingling sense of connection that passed from her flesh to his fingertips.

The firelight cast her complexion in gold. The burgundy color of the cloth warmed her cheeks, her lips. Cloth-of-gold softened the edges of the settee, the contrast of color lush.

She had dressed her hair in an old-fashioned braided coronet, a twisted crown of gold. He longed to undo the pins, longed to see it spill in waves upon her shoulders, as he had seen it spilled before.

She shivered, pupils expanding. Her lips parted slightly.

He thought of kisses, dared think she thought of them, too, as they gazed at one another a long tension-fraught moment.

He wondered if she had ever kissed his uncle. He could not picture the exchange.

She lowered her gaze, lashes fluttering.

He stepped back. "Do you take the drug often?"

She glanced up, all innocence, if not true innocence at least she played her part well. "Dryden insisted it was just what I needed."

Dryden. He did not trust her brother in anything except his desire for her marriage to take place. Dryden would do nothing to jeopardize a solution to his debts, would he?

"And was it what you needed?"

Her tongue darted to the corner of her lips, to wet them. "I need . . ." She fixed her eyes on him. "I need . . ." The dampening of her lips proved stimulating.

He could think of a great many things she might need, none of them proper thoughts, given his intent.

"A rich husband?" he suggested wryly.

Flushing, she flew to her feet, wincing with her own sudden movement. "How dare you?"

"Ah! So it's love, is it?" The suggestion stopped her stumbling flight from the setee.

She turned to glare at him.

His head canted to one side, his eyes searching, a contrite smile hovering.

"It must be love if you would give yourself as a gift to Lord Lovell," he said.

"I give him likeness."

"More than that, surely," he murmured. "Do you not also grant him body, heart, and soul?"

She stood a little straighter, head high. "Ours is a bond of intellect, emotion, and spirit, Mr. Gregory. It promises a union of affection, of mutual respect." She spoke with finality, sure her answer must satisfy.

"Ah!" He nodded, as if he did, indeed, understand. He held silent long enough that she was lulled into thinking him silenced. "I wonder, Miss Savage," he broke the stillness. "Will Lord Lovell be content with so little?"

So little? The suggestion hung between them like the smell of turpentine and linseed oil—insulting her image of the future—a threat to her peace of mind.

"Come." He waved her back to the chair. "Forgive my unseemly suggestion. I'm sure you will be very happy."

"We shall be!" Her hands pleated the velvet of her skirt as she said it; like the hills and valleys she would put between this place and herself once she was married. "He is my future! My Christmas: a sense of security, of home, an honorable name, freedom from want. I offer myself in exchange. Would you call this such an uneven bargain?"

"And what of love? Passion?"

Outrage bloomed.

"Can you live a life devoid of both? I must admit I should be loath to do so." His pencil never faltered. He eyed her intently, awaiting her answer, his gaze roving as freely as had his hands when she had fallen, heat blossoming in her wherever his attention fixed itself, a blush firing in her cheeks. She must get used to him looking at her. What was his job but to look and draw what he saw? She must not allow him to discompose her with the piercing steadiness of his gaze, with his delving questions.

"You are impertinent," she said.

"I am," he agreed, lips twisting—unrepentant. "I beg your patience."

"But not my forgiveness."

One brow arched. "Have I wronged you?"

The unanswered question hung between them, his eyes on hers, searching, curious, an artist's curiosity.

Did he wrong her? Was her impending union not just what he assumed? A dispassionate convenience?

"I am fond of Lord Lovell—what I know of him," she said, voice low. "I have every respect for him. I . . ." She studied her hands, as if the lines in her palm gave her answers. "I do not know passion. Surely love comes in many guises?"

That stopped his sketching. His gaze passed over her, as intimate as a caress. "But of course."

She flushed, looked down, eyes drawn to the plunging darkness between her breasts. Odd, how much her own body startled her, revealed thus, an excessive abundance of palely exposed flesh.

He stared on occasion at her bosom, keen admiration in his bold gaze as he drew. But then, he examined all of her with equal appreciation, eyes never still, except when he spoke to her. Then he looked her straight in the eyes. Would his hands be the same, she wondered, touching every part of her, given the chance, focusing . . . where?

Was this uncomfortable welling of heat within, passion?

She could not imagine Lord Lovell touching the swell of her breast, could not picture intimacies of any kind with him. He had proposed to her in the library, after an evening of stimulating intellectual exchanges. It was thus she always saw him in her imaginings, his expression one of kindness, of joy in her company. Would he expect passion of her?

She rose, wincing with the effort, her bruises forgotten until now. She felt suddenly tired to the bone, uncertain on her feet, uncertain of her future.

"Have you enough for today?" she asked. Lord knew she had.

He set aside his charcoal, came out from behind the easel, arm extended, an offering of support.

She waved him away. "No, no, sir. Do not trouble yourself," she said. "I can manage quite well on my own."

"I regret to say I cannot," he said.

She paused, as much to catch her breath as to ascertain his meaning.

"I know other painters require less of their sitters," he said, "but I cannot progress with the required haste without your frequent and welcome presence."

"How frequent?" she asked warily.

"At the beginning, middle, and end most particularly." He touched her hand as she slid it into the crook of his arm, sending a splendid thrill all the way to her shoulder.

She laughed. "Does that not encompass the whole of the Christmas Season, sir?"

"At least an hour or two every day if we are to be finished in time for a Christmas wedding," he said with a smile. "I rely upon you."

They worked when the light was best, in the afternoon of the following day, and for that afternoon he refrained from asking provocative questions, loath to disturb the building sense of union between them.

He knew she entrusted the very essence of herself to his pencil, his brush—to the divination of his eyes— and he let the magic of that trust build quietly. Eternal youth and beauty was the gift he offered in return, this virgin eve of her marriage frozen forever in layered oil on canvas.

The weather shrank the world around them, a day of fog and drizzled rain, the windows misted, dripping moisture, their world contained, limited to the warm, golden bubble of contrived Christmas before the crackling fireplace in the painting gallery.

She had spent the morning making mistletoe balls for the hall, the prettiest one to be painted in her hand. It was beautifully done, two wire hoops bound in a sphere, trimmed in bits of lace and dangling velveteen ribbon, shades of creamy white and burgundy.

He admired her artistry, helped her to arrange it in the soft velvet folds of her lap, his hand briefly on hers, her eyes briefly on his. He might have kissed her in that moment, might have kissed her and gotten away with it. He was tempted. Indeed, he swayed toward her with that intention. But in the moment before he might have closed the distance and claimed her lips, he remembered his place and his purpose. Closing his eyes to the lure, he turned his head, and left the promise of kisses lie untested in her lap.

The afternoon unfolded nicely, nonetheless.

The lines on the paper unwound, thin threads of darkness, capturing the tender sweep of her throat, the retrousse tilt of her nose, the elegant turn of her wrist. His paintbrush and eyes became one, roving over her, recreating curves and planes, shape, light, and shadow.

She held silent, an uncomfortable, restless quiet largely due, he was fairly certain, to his former remarks. Not that she tapped toes or drummed fingers. No, it was only her eyes she could not hold still, and the tilt of her head. He could see it made her uneasy that he stared at her so relentlessly. She did, in fact, return his glances, stare for stare, which only served to draw his eyes to her the more.

An amusing way to pass time with a beautiful woman.

He formed questions in his mind as he formed her

cheekbones with a dash of flesh-toned pigment. A light touch. He would sketch his next round of questions as lightly as the pale slope of her shoulder. Only conversation would reveal the true essence of this creature, beauty or beast, pawn or player. He would go slowly, carefully, ever watchful, for he meant to capture the truth of her before he left this place, in his mind, for his uncle's sake, and on canvas, for his own.

Her chin, he decided as he roughed in its curve, must have been from the mother she had lost at birth. It spoke of a firmness, a sense of resolve to be found in neither brother nor father. Her gaze, too, he could not connect to them. It was of an unsurpassed calmness, as if she alone among her turbulent whirlwind of a family remained unmoved, calm as the weathered stone of the old pile in which she lived.

She brought out the best of his talent. The brushes felt good in his hand, his wrist limber as he framed in the outline of her cheek, the soft fall of curls.

He smiled. They had hours in which he might question her. He would unearth the truth.

Dryden, his little dog at his heels, wandered through the gallery halfway through the day to see how the painting progressed. He seemed pleased by what he viewed.

"Will you share a brandy with me this evening, Mr. Gregory?" he asked. "There is something we must discuss."

Maitland agreed. That evening he joined the heir to Savage Manor lounging before the fire in the drawing room he favored, his little dog at his feet, punch bowl near his elbow, a bowl of walnuts in his lap.

"I see the painting progresses," he called from this comfortable position.

"Yes. It goes well. Your sister is a fine subject."

The papillon growled softly. No response from his master other than the sharp crack of a walnut forced to give up its meat.

Dryden chided him, "You have not asked me about that second painting I enquired after, Mr. Gregory."

"No." Maitland's approach elicited a deeper growl from the dog. "I knew if you were in earnest you would not let me forget."

"And why should I not be in earnest, pray?" Another walnut surrendered to the jaws of the nutcracker.

The dog's disapproval rose to a warning bark.

"I thought you might want to see what I do before committing to the expense," Maitland stood his ground.

"Ah," Dryden sipped his punch. "Hush, Persephone." He waved a negligent hand.

Maitland squatted before the bitch. "Hello, girl. Shall we be friends?"

"Can you charm her, I wonder, as cleverly as you charm my sister?"

Maitland glanced up, confused by what sounded like approval. Why should this fellow be glad of his growing camaraderie? It made more sense that he would warn him away, as much as the dog did.

"Do you care for some punch?" Dryden rose to fill his cup.

Persephone eyed him warily, eyed her master's movements just as warily, before hesitantly sniffing Maitland's fingers.

"I would," Maitland said. As he rose, the papillon darted a swift lick at his hand.

Dryden noticed the exchange. "You've a magic touch where women are concerned. I thought it must be so from the moment I first laid eyes on you."

Maitland took the warm punch cup from him and accepted the chair indicated. "Something in particular you had in mind for this second portrait?" He took a sip of the punch.

"I should like you to paint my sister in the Classical style, Mr. Gregory. A nude."

Maitland choked on his punch. The image of Dorothea Savage lying near naked on his bed could not fail to come to mind.

"Do I shock you, Mr. Gregory, with such a request?"

"A little. It is not so unusual for a husband to ask for such a painting of his wife, or mistress, but . . ."

"But a brother." Dryden threw back his head and laughed. "I do assure you my request is not made for unseemly or prurient reasons. The painting is meant as a gift for Lord Lovell as much, if not more than the first. You will understand, perhaps, when I remind you he is rather advanced in years."

Maitland nodded. "I understand there is some discrepancy between their ages, yes."

"Indeed. Therein lies the problem." Dryden waved the nutcracker at him. "A fortune of magnitude tends to dwarf such differences, of course, but . . ." He plucked up a good-sized walnut.

"I confess, you confuse me."

Dryden planted the nut carefully in the mouth of the nutcracker, a wooden one, painted to resemble a little soldier. "Surely you will understand." His face contorted as he squeezed the soldier's wooden legs together until the nutshell cracked. "Dodo must bear Lovell a son."

Here it was, then, the ugly business he had come hunting, confirmed. The truth sickened him. They were fortune hunters after all. It stung. He had begun to like Dorothea Savage. Christ, he was half in love with the girl! He did not want to discover her a part of such plots.

Sick at heart he walked to the window, his view of a distant Guy Fawkes bonfire, the conflagration completely appropriate given their diabolical discussion. "Lovell's inheritance?" he suggested.

"Yes," Dryden seemed not at all surprised he should understand so swiftly. "Dorothea must bear a son before the old man dies, else her good fortune . . ." He repositioned the nut with a suggestive shrug, and cracked the shell from fresh angle.

"There is another contender, then, for Lord Lovell's inheritance?" Maitland asked, knowing full well there was.

Dryden picked the nut's flesh from the broken shell, popping bits into his mouth, offering tidbits to the dog. "A nephew."

"You think him heartless enough to cast off his uncle's widow?"

Dryden tossed the shell into the fire. "Money corrupts."

As does its absence, Maitland thought.

"You will do the painting, then?" Dryden asked. "I shall pay you well."

Inwardly Maitland sighed; outwardly he made every effort to appear eager. "If Miss Savage is amenable."

"Excellent!" Dryden offered him the nut bowl. Maitland refused it with a forced smile. "And if she is amenable to something else? Would you, I wonder, help us further?"

"How might I be of service?"

Dryden smiled, set aside the bowl, and patting his thigh, beckoned his Persephone. The dog jumped obediently, curling contentedly on her master's lap.

"Could you bed her?" he asked as he stroked the dog's ears.

Maitland could not believe he had been asked.

Dryden looked up. "Would you woo her?"

"Your question is most unusual, sir."

"Yes. Well, this is a most unusual opportunity. She is a virgin, still. You need not fear her poxed."

Maitland collected his wits. "The purpose of such a coupling?"

"Is it not obvious? To assure she has issue. One cannot assume the old man is still capable of producing an heir."

Maitland felt ill. Never had he met such a scoundrel. Such a plot was not wholly original, of course, but that a gentleman of some standing should suggest such an arrangement for his own sister, appalled!

He carefully contained his rage. "What of your father? Miss Savage? Are they of like mind?"

"Like mind?" he scoffed. "Father thinks it enough to entice the old fellow with a mistletoe portrait, and Dodo . . ." He sighed. "You will have to seduce her. She has never been in love. Lord knows the local lads have tried. It should not be so very difficult. She is ripe for it, and I think she fancies you."

Unable to respond in a civil tone, Maitland considered clouting the fellow, no, tossing him out of a window, better yet, he should beat him to a bloody pulp. He contained himself with some difficulty, pitying Miss Savage such a brother, such a father.

"You will give the matter due thought?"

Maitland thought he would be able to consider little else. He nodded stiffly, his eyes locked on the distant fire.

Remember, remember, the fifth of November! Gun-

powder, Treason, and plot! The words of the ditty passed unbidden through his thoughts.

The fifth of November became the fifteenth, every day Christmas day in the painting gallery—if only a mock Christmas, and yet Dorothea enjoyed the gift of Mr. Gregory's attention—of his time for her, and her alone.

More than anything else about him, she was fascinated by the way he watched her, a ceaseless watchfulness, as the drizzling days of November wound toward December.

Unending his gaze, it passed over her as palpable as a caress, day after day, week after week, his hand and the paint flying. Brief and assessing, the looks he snatched at the canvas, as if he were jealous of his own divided attention.

And as he watched, they talked—of the weather, the approaching holidays, the surrounding countryside—of the countryside where he lived in Surrey—the same countryside her affianced had mentioned.

They carefully skirted the subject of her impending marriage, speaking instead of childhood Christmases, of the Christmases he had spent in France and Italy where his art had taken him. He would not touch upon more serious subjects. As a result, she thought often of the questions he had once dared ask—questions for which she had no real answers. What of passion? What of love? Would her affection, her respect be enough for Lord Lovell? Would he expect more of her than she was prepared to give?

Throughout her mental musings Mr. Gregory held silent, his eyes alone conversant as he studied the line and shape of her, the turn of head, ankle, and wrist. She had never been examined by any man thus, hour upon hour, day upon day, as if he might never get enough of looking, as if he would know her every inch, as if he would plumb the depth and meaning of her: eyes, heart, and soul.

She became addicted to his searching gaze, enjoyed the building tension as his eyes passed over her time and again, measuring, judging, assessing, and yet nothing negative in the way he looked at her, nothing to make her feel small or inadequate, as her brother's gaze was wont to do, and on occasion her father's. They meant to change her, to shape and mold her, to question how she did things, what she made of herself—how they might use her to their advantage.

Even Lord Lovell had looked upon her as if he had plans for her—a use for her. Mr. Gregory simply drank in what he saw with a hungry, level, keen-eyed gaze, studying what she was, not what he could make of her. He seemed intrigued, as if he meant to go on looking until he had solved her every mystery.

Balm to her soul, his gaze.

She enjoyed their time together as the painting progressed, as Christmas and her impending wedding breathed down upon them.

"I should like to help," he offered, overhearing her plans for decorating the hall.

She knew not how to respond, other than to thank him, and set him to work.

His strength was needed in dragging in the Yule log, his height a boon in hanging holly, ivy, and mistletoe, his artistic touch remarkable in cutting paper chains and hearts and cornucopias. He even suggested the fashioning of Chinese lanterns.

"They are popular in London," he claimed as they added that happy glow to the hall, the stairwell—to the sparkle in his eyes. "The house begins to look like Christmas," he said.

She had to agree—they fashioned not the wealth of Christmas he had put together in the gallery for her painting, simpler than that—a shepherd's Christmas more than that of kings or wise men, yet festive nonetheless. She was pleased to see him enter into the spirit of the Season, his suggestions sensitive to her lack of proper funds. And yet, in every way Mr. Gregory helped her she realized that her husband-to-be, Lord Lovell, had neither strength nor height left in him for most of the simple tasks, the simple pleasures she shared with a painter, her housekeeper, and a stableboy.

On St. Catherine's Day, twenty-fifth of November, he helped her and Duff prepare baskets of apples from the orchard for the local poor.

The work went quickly, so quickly she felt loath to end their time together.

"The servants have a small party tonight in the kitchen," she said when all was done.

His head rose, his gaze pinning hers.

"You are welcome to come."

He said nothing, made no nod, and yet she read the answer in his eyes, in the curve of his lips. He would be there.

Russet- and golden-cheeked, the objects in the tub. A study in scarlet, vermillion, and canary yellow. He stared past the apples at his reflection in the water.

"Are these for bobbing?" he asked Duff, as the boy came up behind him, no smile as he nodded.

"Care to wet your head?" the lad's lip curled, as though the idea pleased him immensely to imagine Maitland facedown in the water.

"They are a pretty lot of apples," Dorothea Savage said, suddenly at his side.

The room came alive. The Season glowed in her eyes.

"Cook makes a wonderful pie."

He thought, not of pie, but the sweet promise of her lips. Her golden curls roused his jealousy, for they did kiss her cheek.

"Pippins, Quarrendens, and Pitmaston Pine Apples." She pointed to the fruit.

How provocative the puckering of her lips.

"Say that five times very fast," Maitland suggested. "Sounds like a Christmas game of forfeits."

"Will you forfeit your hands for tying?" Duff asked, brandishing string, gaze straying to Dorothea Savage's lovely face. *He is in love with her,* Maitland thought. We cannot help it, all of us, falling in love with her, young men and old.

He clasped his hands behind him. "Do you not believe in the honor system?"

"Not with the likes o' London painters, Mr. Gregory," Duff said.

Dorothea laughed. "We are a suspicious lot, sir. Trust is a thing you must earn among us."

"Will you join me?" He waggled his tied hands with a wink. "Test my trustworthiness? Have you no taste for a bite of something sweet? Or is it sour apples you tempt me with?" he asked Duff.

He knelt to tackle the tub, ready for a moment of merriment, a moment in keeping with the Season, an innocent moment in which he might forget her brother's proposal, and his own inclination to accept it.

The apples, predictably elusive, slid out from under him, slippery and wet. He lifted dripping head, shaking water from his hair, eliciting a mild shriek from Mrs.

Tilly, and the admonishment, "Come now. You'll make a mess of things, Mr. Gregory."

Did he?

He wondered, thinking of his uncle. Did he made a mess of his uncle's happiness, of Dorothea Savage's? Through water-beaded lashes he observed her kneel on the opposite side of the tub, pushing the golden curls away from her cheek, a bit of string to bind it back, her eyes straying in his direction with a mischievous twinkle.

"I am of a mind we may have more luck attempting the thing together," she said.

How beautiful she was, he thought. As ripe and golden as the apples he sought to sink teeth in.

"Mayhap you are right."

They leaned into the tub simultaneously, heads almost touching, his hair touching wet against her bright curls. He turned to look at her, breath rebounding from the water, that faint sound of their every inhalation and exhalation arousing, triggering thoughts of other circumstances in which they might listen closely to one another's breathing.

She focused on the apples, lips parted, ready for the chase. With a growing smile, a blooming sense of anticipation, he waited until she bent her head to the water, until her quarry slipped away. Then, with nose and cheek and chin he plunged in to nudge the fruit in her direction, through the apple-scented water, toward the clove and vanilla lure of her cheek.

She gasped, laughed, turned her head to take the thing, laughing more while he, breathing through his mouth, prevented the apple's escape. Wet cheek to wet cheek, her hair slid against her ear, his brow. He butted chins with her, tried to bite into the apple, savoring the sensation, the splashing, sliding forward-ness of their game.

The apple was wily, cunning, slippery. It rolled be-tween them, their heads bobbing in pursuit, laughter erupting in sloshy snorts that provoked more laughter. They soaked themselves, hair dripping, the game ridic-ulous and provocative. Too close to kissing—this.

He longed to abandon apples to pursue the fruit of her lips. The brush of her hair, her cheek to his, was almost too much to bear.

He bit at last into the apple, the sweet, watery tang of the juice sublime, the crisp snap of broken skin halting her attempt to claim the fruit. Her head rose, in fact, even as he made the effort to raise the apple from the water's clutch; she demanded to be untied.

"At once!" Her movements swift, she snatched up a linen cloth and set to work drying her hair, her face, her neck, as she walked away without a backward look. He, bleary-eyed, afraid to shake away the water in his eyes lest his movement loose his grip on the apple, watched her hasty leavetaking with surprise.

Why did she run away?

He caught up to her outside, beneath the oak from which she had cut the mistletoe. She leaned against the trunk, her back to him, face to the barren expanse of the moor.

He walked behind her, stripping the bond of string from his wrists, conscious of the mistletoe dangling above. "Have I offended you?" he asked.

She shook her head, sighed. "Would that you did. It would be easier."

"What would be easier?" he asked quietly, leaning into the tree, in the process leaning closer to her, his hand braced against the trunk, knowing the answer before she said a word.

"Being near you," she said, and stepped away.

He caught her hand as she moved, caught her off guard, pulled her back to him, into his waiting arms, against the immovable solidity of the oak. He bent to kiss her.

She turned her head away from his lips.

He whispered in the delicate shell of her ear. "Would you deny me the rites of the Season?"

"What do you mean?" Still she denied his desire, denied her own, though it hung between them thick as the mist on the moor.

"Mistletoe hangs above," he said. "Surely it permits me the pleasure of a kiss?"

Her gaze rose. She sighed again, turned, eyes closed, lips raised as if in unwilling sacrifice.

He leaned toward her, almost took a peck, resisted the impulse with a laugh, his breath on her face fluttering her lashes. "Open your eyes," he said.

She opened one, brow furrowing, as if his request disconcerted her.

"Both of them," he coaxed. "That's better."

She frowned. "Does one not close one's eyes in kissing? I had heard it was so."

He blinked, inhaled deeply. Was this—could it be— her first kiss? She was, after all, not wise to the ways of the world.

"One can shut one's eyes to the truth," he agreed, leaning closer. "But there is much of the best kisses to be found in looking deeply into the eyes of another—if one possesses a depth of feeling."

"And do you possess a depth of feeling?" she asked skeptically, gaze darting uneasily away.

"Can you not read the answer in my eyes, Miss Savage?"

She dared look up to meet his gaze squarely. He

saw himself reflected in green eyes, deep as a troubled ocean, dark as polished jasper, the facets of her emotions many. He recognized fear in her gaze, and questions, unanswered, and in the depths, as his own gaze strayed to her mouth and back again, unexpected heat flared, hidden passion smoldering, the passion all for him, and she afraid of what he might do with it.

Nothing more than a look, and she drew him in. He planted his lips on hers, gently, with every consciousness that this was a first, a beginning. It should be wonderful.

She saw what was coming in the depths of his eyes, the warmth, the glow, that part of his soul that opened up, reaching out to hers.

In his arms, in his eyes, in his lips, she caught a tantalizing glimpse of a home, a family, a passion and desire she had never known. At first it was just the link of their eyes and the warmth of his breath on her lips, then his lashes lowering, the light between them dimming as he drew closer. Anticipation hovered between them like a bird, wings beating in tandem with her heart. The soft, searching heat of his mouth met hers, seeking to mimic the union of their eyes, the link searching and deep, as he sought the perfect placement, the perfect pressure.

Longing caught her breath—parted her lips. She succumbed to the sweetest of exchanges, a melting, misted magic by way of his mouth.

She understood at last the meaning of desire. It flooded her, set her pulse racing, lit a flame deep within. She longed for more of him, clutched him closer, pressed herself more completely into his arms. Their closeness, far more intimate than any she had thus far shared, was not enough. The greedy abandon of her desire startled her.

She understood at last that she sacrificed much in agreeing to marry an old man with whom she would never share these feelings.

And in her awakened understanding, she pushed away from Mr. Gregory, away from what she had found, too late.

"No," he said. "Don't go." Regret painted his features, the staying motion of his hand.

Regret ruled her heart. It leant speed to her flight as she stumbled away.

"What have I done?" she whispered, the thought so vital she must voice it aloud to echo across the empty moor, to echo again in the stone archway, as she sought shelter from the vast, empty wildness of feeling that threatened to overwhelm her.

Above her, silhouetted in the window, Dryden stood watching, dog in arms.

"Oh, God," she moaned. "What a fool I have been!"

He did not sleep that night, though weariness dragged at his soul and sat heavy on his chest. His heart ached with longing. Given a taste, he was now ready to devour her, his purpose near forgotten, his lips bewitched and hungry for more.

He thought of her as she had once been, in this, his bed. He sought some trace of her scent in his pillow, his hands clutching at feathered softness as his mind conjured the memory of her waist, her ribs, the pillow a poor substitute.

He rose, unable to sleep, unwilling to forget, invigorated by the desires she roused. He lit lamps, lit candles, bringing to light the Christmas setting he had built for her.

She had been for him a month of Christmases, every day her presence a gift, his eyes filled with the sight of her—the Season personified—as between them burned a growing understanding and affection. He had captured that heated glow in her eyes. They sparkled brilliantly in the painting, warmer and more festive than the fire.

He uncovered the second canvas, begun in secret, the image kept hidden under oiled canvas cover, a painting he considered a Christmas gift, not to his uncle, but to himself. A nude, not as Dryden had suggested, of a Classical nature. No goddess, this, but his sleeping angel, carefully posed, from the drawings he had made while Dorothea Savage lay drugged. As much as he managed to capture her as a creature most fair, so too did he capture her vulnerable, and exposed.

Through the night he painted, his passion diverted to pigment, desires unfolding in light and shadow, shape and contour. Dawn found him paint spattered and exhausted, head drooping, Dorothea Savage come alive beneath his hands, skin glowing, hair unbound, the truth of her trapped forever on canvas.

His best work—she was his best work. She stirred the best of his talents. With a feeling of loss he abandoned his brushes, and became aware of the Christmas setting he had built and all it represented, all too aware of the approach of the real Christmas, time squeezing in on him—on them.

His uncle's painting stood half finished, on the easel beside his private work of art, pale shadow to the beauty he had just completed, harsh reminder of his original intentions in coming to this godforsaken house.

Too weary to so much as clean his hands of paint, he dropped his breeches and tumbled into bed, exhaustion claiming him as the sun pinked the horizon.

"You have what?" he heard her ask, stricken, her voice part of a dream. He was lost upon the moor following Dorothea Savage—lost in a mist, her name upon his lips.

Bleary eyed, head thick with sleep, he reached for her, found only paint-smeared bedclothes, roused further to her brother's voice, in the room now, both of them entering the gallery. He could hear their footsteps, Dryden's dog's toenails tapping.

"I have commissioned a nude, little sister. A companion piece to the portrait Father would give your husband-to-be."

Maitland sat up abruptly. Had he covered the painting? He could not remember. He stole a quick peek through the bedcurtains, eyes widening to find the canvas still exposed, glaringly vibrant, undeniably beautiful—not meant to be seen by either of his intruders.

He dove for the far edge of the bed, snaked his legs into his breeches as he slunk to the floor, and quietly skirted the easel, bent over, feet bare on the cold floor.

Her voice rose. "And do you mean to pose for it as well as pay for it, Dryden? I shall never do so. Nor can you convince me Father would wish it."

The papillon spotted him, with a little yip careened across the room to greet him.

"Father wishes to see you content in marriage, my dear, in motherhood." Dryden yawned, gaze following the dog. He caught sight of Maitland as he carefully dropped the spattered cover over the still wet canvas. "He wishes to dandle a grandson on his knee." His voice trailed away. His smiled broadened. He winked slyly at Maitland.

Miss Savage remained oblivious to his presence, her voice quiet but firm. "I will not pose for such a painting."

Smiling like a cat that has eaten a canary, Dryden waved a hand in his direction. "Would you cheat this man out of his living, Dodo?"

Dorothea whirled, surprise painting her features. "You!"

"Good morning." Maitland bent to pick up the papillon, who persisted in throwing herself against his legs. He held the animal to his shoulder like a baby, stroked its silky ears, looked into its trusting brown eyes.

"I had no idea you were here," she said, not brown eyed, but blue—just as trusting, and he completely undeserving.

"I am usually to be found here, Miss Savage."

She frowned and moved to study the unfinished Christmas portrait. "What think you of my brother's plan, Mr. Gregory?"

"The nude?"

She blushed. "Is it not unreasonable? Embarrassing?"

Would she deem his finished painting unreasonable? Embarrassing? "It is art," he said.

She sighed, exasperated, finding no ally in him, and turned to address her brother. "Do you expect me to flaunt myself before strangers?"

Before him, she meant.

"Don't be a ninny, Dodo. I am sure no one is more accustomed to viewing dispassionately the female form than an artist of Mr. Gregory's reputation. I trust him implicitly to get the job done to both our satisfactions." A certain lasciviousness hindered his brotherly tone. A sly glance at Maitland suggested he referred to something other than the painting. "Can you not convince her she is secure in your hands, Mr. Gregory?''

She turned, chin high, belligerent and embarrassed.

"Fear not, Miss Savage. I hold you in too high a regard to ask you to do anything that brings you discomfort.''

Dryden scowled at him. Dorothea's chin fell a notch.

"However," Maitland continued, "we might pose a study in such a way as to minimize both undue exposure, and any discomfort you feel in revealing yourself to inspection.''

"There, you see!" her brother coaxed.

"And what exactly is minimal exposure when it is a nude we discuss, sir?''

She was not to be easily pacified.

"We could set up a curtained area," he suggested as he grabbed up a pencil and sketchpad, the idea catching hold, stirring his own interest afresh. "You need not fear anyone walking in unannounced. A woman might be hired to sit nearby, ready with a robe.''

He made swift work of the sketch. "A seated or reclining three-quarter pose, thus." He held it out to her. "Your back to me, head turned, looking over your shoulder. A drape here." He shaded in the area over the sketched hip and buttocks.

"You think this would be attractive?" Resistance dominated her tone.

He could not believe she asked. "Beautiful," he said wholeheartedly, picturing the finished painting in his mind. "Breathtaking!''

"Lovell would not find it offensive?''

His answer came readily, his secret painting spawning a defensive reaction rather than allowing any true consideration of his uncle's feelings. "Miss Savage, no man who offered to take you to wife could be offended by a painting designed to capture forever the graces of the young woman who stole his heart."

It was not until the words were out that he wondered what in God's name he was doing, trying to convince her. He hoped she would say no, and he hoped she would say yes. His purpose wavered. He no longer knew what it was he wanted to discover for his uncle's sake. For his own. Her brother was a scoundrel. Her father little better. And he?

He had come, convinced he would discover his uncle's betrothed corrupt. To his dismay he uncovered only the corruption in himself. His fingers itched to do the painting. His heart leapt at the thought of her posing for a nude. He had to admit, his imagination took the scene further, to the unheard-of lengths her brother suggested.

To what end? That he might cuckold his uncle? That she might bear a son to disinherit himself? Ridiculous! And yet there was nothing ridiculous in his desire, his growing passion. He wanted to bed her, to make her his. He was completely infatuated.

"Let me think about it," she said, and in her eyes shone hint of sensibilities that made him think of Dryden's dog, Persephone, and he who sought to extinguish the innocent light of her in the dark underworld of his desire.

Dorothea Savage held a Bible reading and the singing of hymns in the keep's chapel every Sunday. The following morning, as December stole over the horizon along with the sun, proved no exception.

Maitland went every Sunday, that he might be near her, that he might gaze yet another day upon the object of his growing affections. Here, she was not the tempting beauty from his painting, potential model for another nude.

She wore blue, the color of the Madonna. He imagined her, thus, a lamb in her lap, as he slid into a pew behind Duff. Her gaze rose to meet his. He knew at once she had not forgotten their kiss beneath the mistletoe, nor the question of the second painting. Too high the color in her cheeks, the glow in her eyes. Too swiftly did that brightened gaze slide away from his, only to flutter in his direction again and again.

Duff turned to glare at him distrustfully, lips sullen, gaze unforgiving, as if he knew the whole.

They rose to sing "The First Nowell," and the Wexford Carol of "good people all, of noble virgin and her guide, of three wise men from afar with gifts of gold, of a Princely babe, and what our good God has done."

His gaze linked with hers as she sang. Her voice was clear and true. She took joy in her faith, in the Season, in sharing it with him.

When she opened her Bible, the others settled in their pews. She read to them from Luke—an echo to the songs they had sung, verses all too familiar, in keeping with the approach of Christmas.

"And the angel came in unto her, and said, Hail thou that art highly favoured . . ."

He thought of her as he had found her, asleep in his bed, like an angel. And he thought of the painting he had made.

"Blessed art thou among women . . ."

The beauty of her voice, of her mouth, as she read, entranced him. He heard naught, understood naught but the connection between them.

"Fear not, Mary: for thou hast found favour . . ."

She had certainly found favor in his eyes.

"And, behold, thou shalt conceive in thy womb, and bring forth a son, and shalt call his name Jesus. He shall be great, and shall be called the Son of the Highest . . ."

The full impact of what Dryden asked of him, what he intended for his own sister, for her offspring, penetrated the haze of temptation that had for the last few days clouded Maitland's thoughts. The walls of the chapel closed in on him.

He rose abruptly, turning heads, turning her head as she read. Her words, and the puzzled, disappointed expression that took possession of her features, followed him out into the fogged courtyard.

"And the power of the Highest shall overshadow thee . . ."

He stumbled onto the misted moor, gasping for breath, in need of solitude.

Rain pelted the windows of the gallery on the following day. Not sound, but scent gave her away. Maitland looked up from the background work he did on the Christmas painting when the faint trace of her perfume wafted into the room.

First sight of her took his breath away—it always did when she wore the burgundy velvet. Her father was right. If anything might make an old man's heart throb, it would be sight of her in that dress.

Her bosom was exquisite, her shoulders carved alabaster. The soft plush of the fabric begged touching. She was Christmas in that dress—his Christmas.

"Less than twenty days," she said, her tone vaguely pensive.

He turned from the canvas. "I am almost finished here."

She came to stand beside him, staring at the essence of the Season, and herself in the midst of it.

"And then?" she asked.

"And then, I go home for the holidays."

She stared at him intently, as if the thought had never occurred to her that he would go. With a frown she reached out to touch his mouth.

He caught her hand by the wrist. "You mustn't," he chided sadly.

Like a scolded child she bit down upon her lip, withdrew her hand, and said quietly, "You've a smear of paint."

He palmed his upper lip.

She shook her head, pointed, careful not to touch. "There."

He tried again, rubbing unsuccessfully with a rag.

She shook her head. "You have only made it worse. May I?"

He nodded curtly, closing his eyes as she clasped his chin in one hand and carefully daubed his lip with the rag in the other. When he opened his eyes, she looked right into them and said, "About the nude."

A moment's silence hung between them, her hand on his chin, rain tapping at the window. She parted her lips to go on.

He lost hold on the brush he had clenched between his fingers, its clatter loud enough to stop her.

He rose from his stool, the sudden movement distancing him from her touch and placing him in a position to tower over her.

"I don't think you should do it," he blurted, voice gruff.

"No?" Her chin tipped to one side. Her lashes starred wide in surprise. "Why? Are you in a such a hurry to leave?"

"No." He bent to pick up the brush.

"Tired, then, of looking at me?"

He looked her in the eyes a long, frozen moment. "Never."

She blushed and looked away. "I am confused," she persisted. "You seemed ready enough to convince me to pose, yesterday."

Thunder rumbled in the distance, a muted growl, before he admitted, gaze falling away, "Yes. Wrong of me."

She drifted quietly to the window, to stand gazing at the rain-grayed view, her finger tracing the dribble of a raindrop along the pane. "You were . . . convincing. What has changed your mind?"

"Miss Savage . . ."

"Dorothea."

He came out from behind the easel, motioning her to the gold-lapped chair. She sat obligingly in the midst of their sham festivities.

For a moment he stood arranging the positioning of her shoulders, the fall of her hair. Did he really want to explain?

She regarded him, steadfastly, unblinking, the green depths of her eyes disconcerting.

"Why not do the nude?" she asked.

He knelt to arrange the fall of her skirts. When he had redraped the fabric at her knee, she stopped his hands with her own.

He knew he should remove his hand from the velvet warmth of her knee, but could not.

"Mr. Gregory?" Her hand moved against the back of his.

"Dorothea," he sighed as he looked at her, at the Christmas that was not meant to be his. "I would not see you pushed in any way into something you are not really inclined to do," he said. "I would not see you persuaded, either by your brother, or by me, against your better instincts."

"Not even if it keeps you here?" she whispered.

It gladdened and pained him that she should say so. He gave her knee a light squeeze before he relinquished hold on it.

"No," he said faintly.

"Can you not think of good reason to stay?" she asked wistfully, her hands falling slowly away from his as he rose.

"To watch you marry another man?" he asked, voice flat.

She frowned and bit her lip, smoothing and smoothing the fabric at her knee. "Can you not think of any reason I should not marry him?"

"None," he said with a wince.

"Oh." Her voice sounded small. Her face looked too sad for the Christmas still life she played part of. She clutched her knees together like a child.

"None other than completely selfish ones," he amended. "As selfish as my reasons were in trying to sway you in favor of posing nude."

Her eyes held a world of curiosity. "Money? You need the money?"

He laughed, turned to look at the glowing embers of the fire with a sigh, pressed his lips together, and considered the wisdom of not telling her. But he could not let her go on in the misapprehension she did him out of a living. "Not money. Thought of you tempted me. Tempts me still."

That raised her head—pursed her lips. She rose swiftly from her Christmas throne in going to the window, as she pressed her forehead to the cool pane, eyes closing out the sight of him. Rain ran rivulets down the window, their shadow like tears on her cheek.

He followed her, heavyhearted.

In for a penny, in for a pound. "I am drawn to your wit, your beauty . . ." She turned to look at him. His eyes begged understanding. "I am drawn to your grace, to the very innocence I imagined undoing."

He leaned against the windowsill beside her, gently taking her hands in his, lifting one to press it to his cheek. "A fleeting treasure, this supple skin, dewy and smooth. And you stand poised to give it to another, to sacrifice youth, to abandon your greatest opportunity for passion—to what end? I would beg you do not do this lightly."

She withdrew from him, gaze uncertain, troubled and hurt, the world outside a melting watercolor.

He could not recall the words, could not deny his outpouring, there was no place to go but onward, deeper into the truth of it, hoping she might understand some part of his thinking, hoping she might forgive him.

"I am jealous of your betrothed! It is in some way criminal that no one else should ever see, never celebrate, all that you are."

She laughed, her mouth pulling to one side. "You . . . flatter me, sir."

"I speak the truth," he said.

"Your truth. I am not the paragon you would paint me."

He laughed. "Do not mistake me. I came here prepared to reveal your flaws, prepared to uncover a fortune hunter who had gulled a rich old man into marrying her."

"And now?" She fell back a step, away from the liquid magic of the window, out of his reach.

He followed her, in tandem, as if they began the fluid movement of a dance. "I dare to see you in my arms, my lips on yours."

He closed the space separating them without actually daring to touch her—the breath of space growing humid, close, and charged—the gray light from the window a distant thing.

"I dare to think I might steal you away from him."

Her breast rose and fell quickly, her breath urgent and rasping, as if they had run a race. She refused to meet his eyes.

"You should not say these things, Mr. Gregory." Her tone was remote. "I will not be untrue to the man I promised to marry."

He closed his eyes, passed his tongue over his lips, and kissed her lightly where firelight painted pale her forehead. "Not even for love, my dear? I would paint you permanently into the picture of my future."

A silence fell between them, weighty with potential.

He kissed her again, lips soft against the brushstroke of her brow. "You cannot marry him. You are meant to marry me."

His mouth hovered, another kiss in the waiting.

She swayed toward him, her eyes, troubled seas, locked on his. He thought she meant to kiss him, their lips approached within a hair's breadth of touching, but then, lashes fluttering, she closed her eyes and shook her head, undoing his picture of happiness.

"I cannot."

He fell back, stepped away, crushed. "You do not care for me?"

She stood unmoving as a statue.

"Not enough, it would seem." His voice rasped in saying it.

Her head moved, her gaze daring to meet his—her

eyes wounded—emotions raw. "I have never before felt this"—she raised a hand to her breast—"this quickening." Her eyes welled tears. "Every time you walk into the room, it is as if I have been given a gift."

He remained remote, too wounded by her ready refusal to say other than, "And yet, you are determined to be Christmas gift to another."

She smiled, the smile breaking joy to sadness in a way he had never before witnessed, could never hope to reproduce on canvas. "He is such a dear old man." Her hands fell to her sides, clutching at the deep red velvet, smoothing it restlessly. "When he offered it seemed a Godsend, the best, most joyful of arrangements."

She seemed in no way joyful now. Her voice caught on the word—her face crumpled tragically. Rain battered the windows with fresh enthusiasm.

"We talked, he and I—lovely, delving intellectual discussions. It was . . . divine. We spoke of family, of the nephew he has raised. We talked of politics, religion, current events—we spoke, of everything, from loneliness to limes. I had never shared such depths of thought, feeling, and philosophy with any man—until . . ."

The rain stilled at the window, as if the moor held its breath, waiting to hear more.

"Until you." Her gaze smote him afresh, brighter than the sun, warmer than the fire.

"Do you love me?" he asked. "You have only to tell me you do not and I shall desist in my pursuit."

In the fireplace a sharp pop and a shower of sparks. The window brightened as the sun peeped from the clouds.

She nodded, tears falling, the rain come inside.

He opened his arms to her, but she shook her head, expression forlorn. "I promised," she said wistfully.

Somewhere a lark sang greeting to the sun.

She sighed. "I . . . I have promised a dear, kind gentleman who would change my life in every way for the better that I will share his."

He thought of his uncle, thought of what he would take from his mentor and guide, as he said, "I will tell him that you have found another dear, kind gentleman who would make your life better in every way."

She burst into tears, shaking her head.

"Would you not marry me, then, my dear? Would you not ride away with me before Christmas comes?"

"She would not!" Dryden's voice interrupted them. "How dare you suggest such a preposterous future for my dear sister?" Stiff as a pikestaff he strode into the room, arms akimbo, Lord of the Manor. "Would she rather marry a painter than a well-heeled Lord? Live in a garret rather than a fine estate? I should think the answer to your ludicrous proposal would be self-evident, Mr. Gregory." He planted his heels as firmly as he had planted each word between them.

He caught them both off-guard. They stood slack-jawed, and speechless.

Maitland recovered first. Facing her, he asked bluntly, "Does he speak for you?"

Her brother gave her no room to respond. "Of course I do."

"If he does, I will go at once," he said earnestly. "Never to trouble you again."

"Off with you, then." Dryden swept the air with a shooing motion. "Pitiful little man, to think you might wheedle your way into my sister's affections. To think you might seduce her into marrying you."

"He did not wheedle. Nor seduce." She spoke at last, defending him!

"Oh but you are wrong, Dodo." Dryden shook both head and finger at her. "Entirely mistaken. For you see, I encouraged him to it."

"You what?" She cocked her head to one side, as if unable to believe her own ears. Her gaze flew to Maitland's face, seeking confirmation or denial.

He nodded, spread his hands. "He asked me to do what I could not."

Dryden snorted. "Oh, but you have succeeded, Mr. Gregory, beyond my wildest expectations. She is completely taken in."

Maitland ignored the outburst, his attention fixed on Dorothea's expression, on the light and shadow of emotions that passed over her troubled features. "He did not ask me to fall in love with you, which I have against my best intentions. I could not help myself."

"You could not help yourself from painting the nude, either, could you?" Dryden suggested snidely.

"There is no nude," she snapped, bristling, ready to defend him. Her gaze flew briskly from her brother's face to his.

"There is," Dryden taunted. "I have seen it."

"You go too far, Dryden," she insisted, waiting for Maitland to echo her disgust. When his ready confirmation never came, her face fell, disillusioned, even before he contradicted gently.

"There is."

He lifted the canvas from beneath the easel, throwing back the spattered covering.

"See!" Dryden crowed. "What did I tell you?"

She stood frozen, eyes wide, regarding herself unveiled with an inscrutable expression.

"You have given her wings," Dryden observed dryly. "But little else to clothe her."

"This is how you see me?" Her voice was hushed.

"One of many ways," he said with a nod.

"And all of them equally shocking, I'll warrant," Dryden needled.

Maitland was concerned only with Dorothea's reaction.

"You conjured this up out of your head?" she suggested. "This sleeping angel."

"No."

She blinked at him, nonplussed.

"I found you thus, in my bed."

"Good God, sir, how dare you take advantage of my beloved sister. I shall see you hanged for it!"

Maitland shot a disinterested look in Dryden's direction. "It was intended I should see you thus."

"What? Divine intervention?" Dryden scoffed.

"No." He locked eyes with hers. "Laudenum."

She turned to her brother in disbelief. "Dryden! Is this true?"

"How can you believe such a scoundrel? Do not tell me you will swallow whole his tripe!"

She said nothing, simply stood staring at him with a crestfallen expression.

Dryden went red in the face. "He did not have to look, to paint you, now did he?"

Maitland spread his hands. He could feel the fine sand of her regard for him slipping away. "He is right. I should have walked away, should have called at once for Tilly, should have shut the half-open curtains. I did none of these." He bent to pick up his portfolio. "I could neither walk, nor speak, only draw." He wrenched at the lace ties, undressing the leather case.

"What man could look away when faced with such artfully posed beauty?"

He thrust the drawings at her.

She backed away, stunned into silence, mouth slightly ajar, her breath shallow. When she refused to take them, he let them go, a fluttering white cascade. They floated to the floor at her feet, tissue rattling. With a muted cry she knelt to gather the drifted pages.

Dryden hovered, saying, "I told you so. He is the complete scoundrel. Only look at how many of these shocking drawings he has done."

She did look, silence drifting between them like the pages—looked away at last, without expression, as though numbed by what she had seen.

His eyes met hers, trying to communicate his regret.

"Posed?" She shuffled together the sketches, the tissue, carefully stacking, carefully replacing them in the portfolio. Her gaze rose. She cleared her throat, closed the portfolio, carefully tied it shut. "You said, 'artfully posed beauty'?"

He took a deep breath, looked to Dryden. "Yes."

"Utter nonsense," Dryden defended himself.

"Why?" She still looked to Maitland for answers.

He regarded her steadily. "You ask the wrong man."

"One of you must tell me. Why posed?" She slammed the flat of her hand against the portfolio.

"Why listen to him?" Dryden ranted. "He fabricates wild scenarios, unworthy of your consideration."

She ignored her brother's outburst, kept staring at Maitland, waiting an answer.

"Why do you think?" He turned the question back on her.

She studied the matter a moment, and shook her head.

"Tell me, Dryden," she said harshly. "Why did you give me the laudanum, then abandon me?"

"I wouldn't, Dodo. Didn't. You do not mean to take the least little thing he claims seriously, do you?"

She sighed, exasperated, looking from one to the other of them as if they were cut from the same cloth.

Maitland could see he was losing her, with every passing moment, that he might have already lost her over the painting—the sketches.

"He wanted me to get you with child," he said flatly. "He wanted to ensure the Lovell inheritance."

"Preposterous!" Dryden shouted. "Blasphemy! I shall sue you, sir, for defamation of character."

She pressed a shaking hand to her forehead.

"Lies," Dryden screeched. "All lies!"

"Money!" she said, voice low. "Would you sell my life away for thirty pieces of silver?"

Dryden, scowling, went to the painting. "You believe this painter? When he insults you with this abomination of nakedness?"

"You give me the headache, Dryden." She rubbed at her forehead.

"Shall I see it destroyed?" Maitland asked. "It is the best work I have ever done, and never meant in any way to offend you—but I give it to you—my Christmas gift—to be thrown upon the fire if you would, if it might make amends between us."

"It had best be burned." Dryden plucked up the painting and swung away from them.

"Put it down!" Dorothea ran after him, shouting.

Dryden turned, amazed at her tone. "What? You do not mean to burn it at once?"

"Leave it to me, Dryden," she insisted, grabbing the edge of the canvas.

"Ah! I see. You would set it aflame yourself."

"I would as soon throw you upon the fire," she contradicted him, returning the canvas to the easel.

"What?" Dryden grabbed her shoulders to shake her, saying, "Do not be a fool, Dodo."

"Unhand her." Maitland made a move to enforce the suggestion.

She turned and gently removed her brother's hand, gaze steady, saying softly, "We must each of us choose, Dryden, whether we enjoy this life, or make of it a misery, whether we bring that same joy or misery to others."

"Mother said that," he murmured, remembering.

She gazed at the painting, bright-eyed. "Do you not see? It is"—her mouth twisted—"beautiful. He has made me beautiful."

What's this? Maitland thought.

"Good God!" Dryden shouted at her. "How can you say so? It is obscene."

"No, brother," she said quietly, turning on him, her face that of the painting's—the angel awakened. "It is your histrionics that are obscene, your anger, your lies. That you plot against me . . ." Her voice failed, only to return with renewed vigor. "*That* is an obscenity. I see you with fresh eyes, Dryden, and what I see makes me long to weep."

Dryden fumed a moment before he turned on his heel and left the room, flinging back over his shoulder: "Turn on your family, then, you ungrateful slut. Let this poor man drag you away into obscurity, into poverty. I wash my hands of you."

They stood uncertainly in the charged silence Dryden left in his wake.

Maitland fell to his knees before her. "I have neither Lord Lovell's wealth nor his position, it is true, but I can well afford a wife. You will not suffer either obscurity or poverty if you come away with me. I offer you all that I have, all that I am, all that I shall be."

With a slowly dawning smile, she took his hand and said, "Gifts indeed."

In a lifting fog they mounted their horses, the air crisp and cold, the bells on the pack horses' harness cheerfully chiming, the cobbles slick beneath the horses' hooves. They had a few hours of daylight left to them, a few hours to take them away from Savage Manor. She turned the mare's head as they rode through the stone arch leading into the courtyard.

He drew in the gray, as well.

"Second thoughts, my love?" he asked.

"No," she said. "One last look."

She thought of the day she had watched him first ride into her life, gaze lifting to the gallery window. It stood empty, dimly golden with firelight. In the distance, faintly, bells rang, an echo of the noise the pack horse made.

"Any regrets?" he asked.

She drew in a deep, mist-laden breath. The air smelled of rain, wet stone, and drenched earth. It smelled of home, the only home she had ever known. What would her new home smell like, she wondered.

"Yes," she said, with a sigh.

"How so?"

"I regret that I break a promise I should never have made. I regret that an old man's feelings may be injured. I regret not standing up to my brother and making my feelings known all these years." She smiled up at him. "And you? Any regrets, Mr. Gregory?"

His answer was postponed by the increasing crescendo of ringing bells, by the noise of carriages entering the drive, hooves scattering gravel. Two coaches burst from the fog, dark horses straining against jingling harnesses as they climbed the incline.

"Oh dear!" she cried, pulling her horse closer to his.

"Lord Lovell," he said.

Snorting and blowing, their passage creating a wind that tossed hair and scarves, Lord Lovell's gold-crested, mud-spattered coaches pulled through the arch and ground to a stop, horses' hooves clattering on cobblestone, the cries of the coachman echoing from the stone face of the manor.

Four footmen leapt down to snap open the doors. A beaming, bright-eyed gentleman leaned his graying head out of one of the windows. "Miss Savage," he cried, with an impish smile. "Maitland! Where are you off to?"

"I steal away with your bride," Maitland said calmly.

The old man chuckled as his footman let down the iron step and helped him to alight. He bounced to the ground as if traveling agreed with him, eyes twinkling. "I had hoped you might like her," he said.

"Like her? I love her, my lord. I mean to marry her."

Behind Lovell the coaches erupted with a rash of activity. Out stepped his lordship's valet, two maids, a cook, and his assistants. Down from the carriages came an abundance of wrapped parcels, baskets filled with food, the unmistakable clink of wine bottles, a haunch of venison, a leg of lamb.

Lord Lovell smoothed the fur collar of his coat with a mittened hand, his chuckle contagious. "But she has promised to marry me, nephew. Has the lady a fickle heart?"

"Nephew!" she gasped.

"Did you not tell her, then?"

Dorothea turned to Maitland, bewildered.

Lord Lovell chuckled again. "I sent you the best painter I know, my dear. Did I fail to mention he is also my nephew?"

She gazed at Maitland as if regarding a stranger. Tilting her head, her breath misted between them as she said with a catch in her voice, "You should have told me."

Lord Lovell stepped close to her horse, still bubbling with good cheer and enthusiasm. "You must not let yourself be carried away by him, my dear Dorothea. I am prepared for a Christmas wedding, and a Christmas wedding there will be."

Miss Savage was neither cheerful nor enthusiastic in responding, "What trickery is this? Did you plot together to deceive me?" Evading Lord Lovell's outstretched hand, she slid from her mount.

"Dorothea!" Maitland swung from the back of his horse.

"My dear Miss Savage." Lord Lovell tried to stay her as she swept past him.

She turned a pained expression on both of them. "Why did you lie to me?"

"My dear girl." Lord Lovell's exuberance failed him. "You will remember our wonderful talks?" he asked gently, advancing on her slowly, reaching for her hand as if afraid she might bolt.

She allowed him to take it begrudgingly. "I remember," she said. "They meant a great deal to me."

"Well," he beamed at her. "It became absolutely clear to me as we spoke that you were a lonely young woman, of good character, and sweet temperament, a young woman whose sensibilities perfectly suited a young man I knew who was just as lonely—my nephew."

"What?" Maitland blurted, startled.

"But you asked me to marry you."

The old man tapped the side of his nose with an impish look of mischief. "If you will recall, I asked you if you would like to be married for Christmas."

"You never meant to marry me? You thought to play matchmaker?" Dorothea accused him.

"I thought . . ." He chuckled, well pleased with himself. ". . . you were made for each other. Sent Maitland to you, don't you see, knowing the two of you would fall in love. It was inevitable."

"But the portrait?" Dorothea and Maitland asked with one voice.

Lord Lovell caught up his nephew's hand, and pressed Dorothea's into it, his smile so wide it seemed his cheeks must crack, tears of joy adding fresh sparkle to his eyes. "The wedding, the portrait, these are my gifts to you. My Christmas gifts to the both of you."

They were married, of course, in a beautifully festive ceremony, on Christmas Day, a union that pleased Lord Savage and his son, Dryden, no end, for their debts were to be cleared, and the future of their gambling potential looked, in their own deluded estimation, rosy indeed. Dorothea had, after all, married into money.

The Christmas wedding pleased old Lord Lovell as well, for he had long thought his nephew a lonely young man, in need of a wife.

Of course, such a union pleased the wedded couple in ways far too many to tell, but most of all, it pleased Dorothea's mother, who looked down from heaven to see her daughter choose a life of joy.

* * *

And the paintings of Dorothea Savage, you ask?

They hang in famous art museums to this very day, along with more than a dozen additional canvases Maitland Gregory painted throughout the course of their lifetimes. Each brings untold joy to the hundreds of thousands who drift past the walls and niches where they are hung. They are, indeed, a visual gift to the passionate in everyone, for, you see, some part of the truth of the young Lord Lovell's incredible burgeoning love for the Honorable Dorothea Savage was forever captured in the portraits he painted of her, each one more beautiful than the last.

The Last Gift

by Edith Layton

It was twilight in the woods, morning everywhere else. But the winding path was so bracketed by brambles and buttressed by ancient trees that it was easy to forget the real hour of day. Brown and gray autumn leaves made a ragged carpet underfoot. Overhead, the bare branches they'd fallen from touched and linked, blocking all but a glimpse of the leaden sky. Brush and vines to either side of the narrow lane interlaced, forming dense thickets solid as walls. A few last ragged leaves rattled whenever the chill breeze blew, which was continually. It wasn't the best place to be on a bleak November morning. But so far as Skylar could see—which was admittedly not very far at the moment—there wasn't any better place to be right now. At least not in this dreary district he'd been stupid enough to decide to visit.

It was nothing like the place he'd just left. That had been the point. He'd thought it a clever one then. He didn't now.

London had been on the verge of Christmas the day he'd gone riding out of it. Even though the day was weeks off, London was a city of commerce and knew to a nicety how it should prepare for the holy day, and the unholy glee of all the money to be made from it. The streets, as always, had been filled with bustling people, beggars, shoppers, and strollers. But even now, the shop windows were beginning to sparkle with trinkets. The pavements in front of them were crowded with roving venders selling their usual goods, their ranks swelled by those crying Seasonal treats from chestnuts to pasties, pastries, and pies. Organ grinders, trumpeters, and carolers were already out in force, filling the frosty air with song. Children, monkeys, and bears danced for pennies. Pine, balsam, and fir, ropes of greens festooned windows, carriages, and buildings . . .

Skylar looked around, scowling. Even the greens were gray here. The only sounds were the dry leaves crunching under his horse's hooves. And the occasional cry of a rook. And the wind.

But he'd asked for this.

It was unfortunate he'd made the comment just as his friend took a sip of wine. "What?" Robert had sputtered, or tried to, gagging and hacking as the wine slid down the wrong way.

Heads turned. The hostess of the fashionable ball they were attending spun around. Their host hesitated, wondering if his guest's back wanted a good pounding, and worried about taking such a familiarity. There was no need. Skylar obliged as those in his vicinity were stepping back from the spray. The coughing soon dwindled to wheezing, and the partygoers went back to pretending not to have noticed.

It was, after all, what they'd been doing all evening. Skylar and his friend had been standing near the refreshment table at the side of the ballroom in the crowded London townhouse. But they were carefully and covertly watched—or rather, what they were watching was being watched. Not just because they were both attractive young gentlemen. But because they were both eminently eligible, as Skylar had just commented before he made the statement that caused his friend to choke.

This fashionable ball had been the bait; both of them were momentarily caught. Now there was much speculation on what would come of it. Netted by invitation, it only remained to be seen if they'd snap at any particular lure. But though they'd danced and chatted with the most popular young women present, the only sensational thing to happen so far was when one said something to the other to make him sputter and cough.

Not that they were hard to watch. When he wasn't red-faced from gagging, Sir Robert Pruitt was a handsome fellow. Fair, medium height, with a fresh face and an amiable grin. Of an old wealthy family, he was as charming and convivial as a man with half the income he was rumored to have. His companion that night, Skylar Cameron, now Lord Cameron, still "Skye" to his oldest friends, was another story altogether, a more dramatic one. He was new to Town, having lately come home from the wars to take on his titles and inheritance. Tall, lean, and dark, with strong clean-cut features, he still bore himself straight as the soldier he'd recently been.

"Lud!" Robert finally gasped, his eyes watering. He looked down at his previously pristine neckcloth, dragged out a handkerchief and began dabbing at it. "It's a good thing I was drinking Rhine and not a claret. I'm damp but not done for. Sorry if I showered you, Skye, but what a thing to say!"

"How much of it *have* you been drinking?" his friend asked curiously.

"Just this glass. But I couldn't believe my ears."

"I can't see why you'd even be surprised, much less start imitating a geyser."

"Can't see why?" Robert asked, amazed. "*You* saying such a thing? *No* one here interests you? Not one of these charmers? Instead, '*What I want is an old-fashioned girl*,' says you. *You?*"

"And why not?"

Robert stopped mopping his shirtfront and eyed his friend suspiciously, looking for a quiver of a lip or a glint of a smile, anything to show it was a jest. Lord Cameron's high planed face didn't show much emotion at any time. Now he only lifted an eyebrow over one of his long gray eyes to make an eloquent point of his interest.

Robert narrowed his own eyes, seeking a sardonic answer, aware his friend was better at such. "Well, confound it," he finally said irritably, "you said it so sincerely you had me half-believing you."

"Believe me wholly, my friend," Skye said with a wry smile. "I spoke truth."

"What?" his friend whispered, his round eyes rounder with astonishment, "With the Incomparable herself saving you dances? And our hostess, that adorable little Merriman chit, saving a place at her side at dinner for you? And that dashing Lady P. watching your every move? An *old-fashioned* girl? When you've got 'em all just waiting for you to say the word!"

"Yes," Skye agreed, "and that word is 'marriage.' But, Rob, my friend, they're not looking for love, or friendship, or even me, if it comes to that. They're looking for a husband, which is quite another thing. And I've a fancy for a female who wants my own poor self."

"Who says you won't find her here?"

"I can."

"Too cynical by half," Robert said, frowning. "I'll let it go for now. *That* didn't make me nearly cut my whistle. You said 'old-fashioned'! Huh! As for that, why, our grandmothers wed where their families said, and that was that, remember?"

"I do," Skye said on a small reminiscent smile, "because *my* grandmothers didn't. They flew in the face of convention to choose my grandfathers. One stayed determinedly single for so long that her parents finally had to agree to her choice. She was willing to outwait them even if it meant she'd have to use two canes to make her way down the aisle by the time she married. Or so she said, and they knew she meant it. The other compromised herself so thoroughly before the fact with her choice of husband that her parents didn't have any say in the matter. Both told me that with pride. That's the kind of old-fashioned I mean—a woman who doesn't care about Fashion or Custom. I'd like to meet such a one.

"But what are my choices tonight?" He shrugged one broad shoulder. "The eligible females here would rather fly in the face of a meat grinder than Fashion. It's all about appearances to them—in style and picking a husband to stay in that style. Their hair, their gowns, and especially their husbands must be in the latest, most enviable mode. Good for them, but not for the poor fellows they choose, I think.

"Take the Incomparable—for I won't. Yes, she's pretty and doubtless witty, but there's more calculation than admiration in those beautiful blue eyes when she smiles at me. This is her Season and she's out to make the most of it. I think I'd tally right no matter what I sounded or looked like. I don't blame her, but it don't move me to love her. Miss Merriman's more thoughtful, true. She covers all her bets, because she's equally charming to every eligible man here. She'll take the hand that offers most, no matter which body it's attached to. And Lady P.? She's looking for her next husband X, Y, or Z—or whichever name has the most social credit. This is a marriage market. But it occurs to me that no matter what we're led to think, we are the merchandise here.''

"That's the way of the world.''

"Not mine.''

"So where you going to find your old-fashioned girl?''

"I haven't the slightest idea,'' Skye admitted. "Thing is, I'd like to marry. I've thought of it for a while now—why else do you think I came here tonight? Uncle left me a fortune, but no family. That was what I missed most of all in Spain. But the problem seems to be that I'm weary of females I can negotiate for—in any way.''

"Huh!'' Robert said. "You've more than seven and twenty years in your dish. Time enough to have found a wife before this if you'd meant to, I think.''

"I've been at war too long. I suppose I counted too much on Clara,'' Skye added bleakly. "But what must the flighty chit do while I'm gone but take herself off to India with her family and meet that damned lieutenant and tie the knot what seemed like a week later.''

"Clara? Aye, she was sweet and demure,'' Robert mused. His expression changed to dismay, "You really meant to marry her?''

Skye's face relaxed in a smile so unexpectedly gentled it erased every vestige of distance from his face— and made several women covertly watching him over the tops of their fans wish to close the distance between them as fast as they could. "Don't pity me,'' he told his friend. "She was right to wed where she would. I meant to *think* about it, is all.''

"Well, you'll come to the Hall with me for Christmas. I'll stock the place with likely females for you to consider," Robert said stoutly. "Have my parents put their minds to it too. Aye, we'll have a regular Cinderella Ball! We'll invite society creatures and farmers' daughters, seamstresses and—and blacksmiths' sisters too! We'll find you that old-fashioned girl. And you know what? We'll scour London for her before we go as well!"

"That," Skye said, still smiling, "we will not do. I've had enough of Town for a while."

"So you want to come to the Hall with me now? Good. It's over a month to Christmas, but you'll be welcome."

Skye's smile faded. "No. I'll be glad to be there for Christmas, and I thank you for it. But now? No, I'm in a strange temper. I don't want to lose any old friends and know I'm in no mood to make new ones. Last month I was at war, tonight I find I can't make peace. The thing is, Rob, I'm tired of battlegrounds and I'm weary of Society, my own included. I don't want to hunt or be hunted. I just need some time alone.

"But not at Westerly," he added with a grimace, mentioning the great house he'd just inherited along with his honors. "Aside from the fact that it will be empty except for me and that's not the most festive way to spend the holidays, I'm not ready to shoulder that burden yet. And not here in London, either. With everyone gearing up for Christmas, the jollity is setting my teeth on edge rather than cheering me. Nor do I want to go abroad again so soon. All I think of when I think of the Continent is gunpowder and cannon fire. I need a place with no memories or expectations of me. I suppose I'm looking for someplace miracu-

lous, about as real as the smile on the pictures of
Father Christmas they've begun putting up in the shop
windows. You know—that smile that says 'Happy
Christmas if you've the price.' "

"You won't say that when you see what merriment
we get up to at the Hall! But you seriously want to
be quit of London now and don't know where to go?
Hmmm. Well, there's . . ." Robert's smooth brow furrowed. Then his eyes lit. "Wait! I know just the spot!"
he cried, smacking his head. "Seven Gates! You'll find
peace there, too much, maybe. You might even find
your old-fashioned girl there. Lord knows there ain't
no new-fashioned ones there.

"See," he said eagerly, "we have this cottage deep
in Wales, in the heart of Snowdonia. Not exactly a
hunting box, bigger than a cottage and smaller than
an estate. Belonged to great-grandparents on m'father's side. We used to visit when I was a lad, but no
one goes there much anymore. See, the place is too
wild for proper hunting, and there's too many twists
and turns in the forest for riding to hounds. The
wolves and elk and suchlike they used to track are
long gone. But there's waterfalls and glens and thickets, trees tall as mountains, and mountains that block
out the sky. It looks like Britain before the Romans
came, m'father always said.

"Sort of an eldritch place, really," Robert reflected.
"Hard to get to sleep there, I remember, what with
the noises in the forest and the way the wind carried
on. Still, when I was a lad, I loved the adventure of
it by day as much as I was troubled by it at night."
His eyes grew a faraway expression. "A boy could go
into the wood and get lost for hours, and then turn
and find himself on the front lawn!

"Aye!" he said with more excitement. "You need

a miraculous place? This is it. Mystical, really, with sudden fogs and shadows, winding paths that go nowhere, trails that end in mist, and hedges that seem to grow up the minute you turn your back. Ruins and follies deep in the forest—even a great manor house you could sometimes see from afar—but never from up close. I recollect one day I came upon this great iron gate—taller than my head when I was on my pony—with a lock on it. But no key. When I turned to search for it, I turned back to find no man-made barrier at all, but only briars growing thick as thieves, and shadows pretending to be anything you most feared.

"It's in England, but might as well be a thousand miles away. Well—it's yours if you're interested. Be glad to send word to the staff there. We maintain a few oldsters to keep the place up, no sense letting it fall to rack and ruin. Shall I say you'll be there?"

"I'll leave tomorrow morning," Skye said. "My man can come after, with my clothing."

"What?" his friend asked, amazed. "Don't say you've forgot the masquerade at Jameson's bachelor digs tomorrow night! Or the one the next night? And there's the one for the high flyers and then the one at the Seftons'—not to mention a public do at the Opera House I thought we'd drop in on. Can't leave tomorrow. It's Jameson's birthday!"

"And will remain so without me."

"Lud! You *are* gloomy. Well, so be it. I'll give you a letter to take with you to introduce you to the staff. Stay long as you like . . . No. Strike that. I'll come the week before Christmas to collect you. I'll haul you bodily to the Hall if I must. Because you might forget how to speak English if you stay longer. But if you want rustication, Seven Gates is just the place for you."

"Why, so I think it is," his friend said, smiling widely, "the very place for me."

But he hadn't been so sure of that when he left London the next morning, Skye remembered now as he sat his horse alone in the wood. Even then, as he'd passed under the arch of London's last wall, he'd been oddly uneasy. It seemed more like going into exile than out for a change of scene. Christmas was coming to the world's great metropolis, they were already getting ready for it, and he'd suddenly felt like a boy leaving the party before the birthday cake was brought out.

But he needed the quiet, he wanted the respite, he welcomed some silence. Or so he thought until he saw London fading like a dream into the brief afternoon he left behind him as he headed north and west into solitude. He'd had his first doubts then. And now, scant days later, he knew how wrong he'd been.

"Well," Skye commented aloud, "we could go home now, I suppose. Although Robert's home isn't that to anyone but those poor old citizens who keep it up for him. And no wonder. They're the only ones who can bear the solitude. Because they don't seem to know how to converse—or want to. Which may be why you're so content. They make *your* bed soft enough, my lad," he told his horse, who did him the courtesy of cocking back an ear at the sound of his voice. "The freshest hay for you, and good grain in your trough. But it lacks a certain something for me. Like pleasant company, good food, and diversion. Blast. I can light a fire in the library and I suppose there are books here I haven't read. But what's to do with the rest of the day then? It's only . . ." He took out his pocket watch and scowled. "Time doesn't *pass* here so much as it remains," he grumbled.

"Surely it said the same thing fifteen minutes ago? No. Still ticking." He tucked the watch away and stood in his stirrups to get a look around. All he saw were bushes and trees. "Well, there's nothing for it but to try," he sighed, "just as I always told the lads on the Peninsula, remember? Come on, Albion, let's see if there's another living being on this planet Wales with us, eh? There'd better be. Fine idiot I'll look coming home to London after only a few days in exile!"

Exile was exactly what it felt like, Skye realized. The staff at Robert's modest country home were willing. They were just not able to provide him with more than clean sheets and warm food. Unused to company, they seemed almost afraid of him. They did warn him to take care when he announced he was riding out yesterday, and then again this morning.

"Mind your way," the man of all work said dolefully. "Folks get lost here."

"Aye. Some never to return," the housekeeper warned him with a worried look.

"Probably because once they left the house, they returned to Civilization as fast as they could, without a word or backward look," Skye told Albion now. The great white horse nodded his head sagely at the observation. "Now then," Skye muttered, "yesterday we went east by northeast until we somehow wound up facing south. So, today, let's head west and see if we can see anything but brambles. . . . Well, here's a treat—a fork in the road. Hmm, which way shall we go? Most would turn right, wouldn't they? Since that's considered a lucky direction. Just as good a reason to turn left. But—look! There's actually light at the end of that lane. So whichever direction, it's right for us. Whoa!" he cried, ducking his head to avoid a low branch as his great white horse started down the narrowing path. "Take it slow—those thorny bushes to the side could pierce even your tough hide, my friend."

But then he fell still, and drew rein. Because Albion had taken him to a crossroads of sorts. And there was an old woman standing there, staring at him as though he'd dropped down from the sky instead of emerging from the dim tunnel of the tree-laced lane. *An ancient woman,* he corrected himself, taking her measure. She was bent almost double and had a face out of a children's nursery tale—the sort nannies used to threaten bad children with. Her face was so lined it looked like a winter apple the first day of spring. It was further creased now in a smile—a terrifying one. It might be a greeting, but it looked more sly than sunny, Skye thought, if only because all the seams in her wrinkled face went every which way when her thin lips turned up. The hooded eyes, however, were sparkling. And not with a delight that warmed him.

"Give you good morning, sirrah," she crooned pleasantly enough. "Be thou lost?"

He nodded. "Good morning, madam. Yes, I think I've taken a wrong turn."

"There are no right ones in this wood," she said, and sniggered.

Albion snorted and pawed the ground. He was the pride of Skye's life, taken home from Spain with as much care as antique glassware might have been, even though he stood hands higher than most horses and was wide as a barrel. But he was wiser than many men Skye had known, and the best conversationalist he'd found so far in this district.

"Then perhaps you might point me in the right direction?" Skye asked the old woman.

"Aye. Might do. If I knew where thou wished to be," the old creature said.

"I thought to explore the area, see some interesting sights. See something other than briars and brambles, at least."

"*See* more than that?" she laughed. "Hee hee. There's a thought. "But *interesting?* Oh, aye!" she answered eagerly. "Art on the right road for that! Go that way." She pointed a bent finger to the narrow path on the right. Skye squinted, trying to see more than gloomy shadows there. "But if thou dost not wish to go that way—why then, go t'other," the old woman cackled. "But don't be surprised to see thyself in the same place! Aye, *see,* indeed!"

Skye looked back to see what had caused such mirth. But the old creature was gone as though she'd never been there at all, as though she'd been only some figment of his imagination.

"Well, she could have been," Skye muttered uneasily. "No wonder Robert missed his sleep of a night! This place is more than eerie, it's uncanny. But I'm a grown man." Or so he told Albion, though he began to have his doubts. He turned toward the left path.

He hadn't gone more than a few paces when he saw another woman at the side of the road, gazing up at him. This one was as different from the other as day from night. She wasn't young, but in that vigorous middle age some fortunate women attained. Honey-haired, with a lovely unlined face, she wore a handsome gold cloak and a charming russet bonnet, and carried a wicker basket filled with apples and pinecones. In all, she looked elegant as any lady he'd ever seen tripping down the paths in Green Park. But this was the countryside, so he wasn't too surprised to see no accompanying servants or beaux. She'd have legions of both in London, Skye mused as he felt the charm of her surprised smile.

"Good heavens!" she said, considering him, her head cocked to the side, her smile becoming warmer and more welcoming, until she was positively beaming at him. "You're a long way from home, are you not, my dear sir? Lost too, I'd wager."

"Then you'd win, for I am, madam," he said, sketching a bow. "But I met another . . . woman . . . a few moments ago who told me that either path would get me to the same place."

"Did she?" She seemed amused. "And where is that?"

"Any way that would let me see the district. All I've seen all morning is shrubbery. Fascinating—if I were a botanist. But I'm only a gent on a repairing lease, at loose ends and looking for something of interest."

"There's not much of that here except for us locals, I fear. But she wasn't wrong, though she was likely only having her little joke. *You've* nothing to fear, though. Both lanes *will* eventually get you to the same place. And a very good place that will be." She gave him a youthful grin. "Don't doubt it. Things look bleaker than they are hereabouts. Especially today. Good day, sir. Have a pleasant visit."

She turned, stepped briskly off the road, and disappeared behind the tall hedge. Skye regretted it. She seemed like a pleasant woman who might have good conversation.

"And so, what such as *she* was doing here, I didn't

know," he grumbled to Albion as they paced down the winding road.

The breeze picked up. It gusted, feeling like a cold hand on Skye's back, propelling him down the lane. He put up his collar and ducked his head as it whistled past his ears and blew Albion's tail and mane ahead of him in streamers. But it also swept all the moldering leaves on the forest floor away before them. The wind was like an invisible busy broom clearing their way, exposing a surprisingly sound brick road, widening the lane until it no longer looked crooked or narrow.

As they rode on, it seemed to Skye that the hedges to the sides were growing shorter. He realized it was the effect of the road rising rather than the briars shrinking. But as the road grew wider, the trees seemed to step back as well. At least they stopped crowding together overhead. That let him see that the wind had chased the storm clouds, because it was growing brighter. The sun was definitely coming out. A mild sweet tang of spring flavored the air as the gusts slowed to breezes, and then became zephyrs. It felt more like April than November as he rode up the path and out of the dark wood.

And then he saw the iron gate.

It was exactly as Robert had described it. Skye felt like a boy on a pony too, though Albion and he must stand many hands higher than the boy Robert had been when he'd encountered it. The gate was formidable, even now. Tall and wide, dark with age and corrosion, secured with a huge hanging lock. The bars were thick and straight, except at the top. Skye bent back his head to see it was topped with intricate spirals and curlicues. Very decorative. And deadly. Because they ended in sharp points, enough to discourage any man mad enough to even think of climbing over. But it made a man consider just that. Because surely there must be significant treasure in a house requiring such defenses.

Robert said he'd turned away to find the key, then turned back to find it had all been a illusion wrought by the overgrown hedgerows. Skye nudged Albion forward. The great horse hesitated, but took a few nervous paces to the gate. Then balked. Skye had to lean over in order to grasp the lock. *Not* an illusion. Not hedges. Robert had likely been only too happy to declare it a delusion and ride away. It would have been daunting to a boy. Skye found it challenging.

There was wealth here. Which meant that whoever lived here, pirate or peer, had an interesting story to tell. And Skye was starved for diversion. He considered the matter. He dropped his hand and the lock swung down—and struck the gate—which jolted, then slowly swung ajar.

Even Albion's ears went up.

Skye rode slowly through the gate and down a meandering drive. The form of it was too gracious for chance, once it had been surrounded by a gracious lawn. Now the grass looked untended by anything but sheep. Skye expected to come upon a ruin, so he blinked when the house finally came into sight. It sat atop a gentle rise, a tall and gracious manor house of golden stone, in the style of the first George. It was fronted by a circular drive the wind had swept clean of everything but its cobbles. There wasn't a mark of fire or rot on the place, and as he rode close, Skye's spirits lifted.

"Well, well," he told Albion, "what have we here? A neighbor with taste and money? This visit might not be as blighted as I'd thought. We may be able to stick it out until Robert comes to rescue us, eh lad?

At least, the story of how Robert panicked and turned tail those years ago should amuse them. It's a good excuse for an impromptu call, isn't it?"

He rode up the drive. But no helpful lads came pelting from the nearby stables to greet him. No groom came to take the reins when he dismounted. No dog barked, no servant peered out of any of the many windows glinting in the sunshine. The only sound or motion was that of the wind, gently riffling through the lawn of tall dried grass, making it bow in waves.

Skye tied Albion to a post at the side of the drive, and went quickly up the short marble stair to the great golden oak door. He raised the knocker. It fell. And for the second time that morning a door opened by itself. Just a crack, but enough for Skye to realize it was unlatched. He felt the small hairs on the back of his neck rise. He cleared his throat. He coughed. He waited. Then, defenseless against his own curiosity, he raised one gloved finger to ease the door all the way open, expecting to see a deserted shell of a house inside.

But it was a handsome interior. The wind pushed past him and threw the door wide so he could see a hall with a grand rotunda and sweeping stair. Patterns of light from high windows at the sides of the stair illuminated the marble floor, showing off a checked gold, black, and white pattern. Vases in the niches of the wall held dried floral arrangements. And everywhere, there were strewn flowers, confetti, and ribbons. The breeze blowing in through the opened door sent them swirling in a gay dance of welcome.

Skye stood, pondering the empty house that seemed so full of life and beauty. No one was there, but it didn't feel deserted. He looked around the hall, his eyes adjusting to the leaping shifting light. . . . His shoulders leapt. He froze.

There was a man sprawled on the stair. He was dressed like a footman from another century, with a powdered wig tied back in a queue, a tight maroon jacket trimmed with lace, breeches, and silver-buckled high-heeled shoes. . . . His mouth hung open.

Skye had served on blood-soaked battlefields, but for a second, he hesitated to draw nearer. Domestic death was very different from what happened on a battlefield. But he didn't lack courage. He took a deep breath and stepped closer to see if the fellow was still breathing . . .

. . . and heard a light snore.

Skye grinned. Of course. It was early morning. The litter on the floor was the residue of gaiety. There'd been a party. A monstrous fine party, a masquerade from the looks of things. Of course! Masquerades were all the rage this season in London. Skye chuckled to himself as it all came clear. Everyone was likely still abed, sleeping it off. Except for the servants, who slept where they were supposed to serve. So even they must have joined in the fun. It would be unheard of in a well-managed home in London, but manners were freer deep in the countryside. Too bad he'd missed it, Skye thought, it must have been a grand fete. Because here he was, practically romping through a stranger's home, and no one yet the wiser.

An imp of curiosity, prodded by the knowledge of the certain boredom that awaited him if he decided to just turn and leave, made him decide to have a more thorough look around. If he woke anyone, he reasoned, all the better.

But a quick look in through a few doors showed him the revelers were still dead to the world. They were all in costume, and all asleep. Guests slept on, slumped, glasses still in hand, on chairs and settees, even on the sides of the ballroom floor. A pair of lovers curled in each other's arms on a sofa in the library. Revelers drowsed here and there in the coat-room. A peek into the kitchen made him yawn himself. The cook, also outfitted in gay regalia, sat snoring in a big chair by a dead fire, a trio of tumbled maids dreaming in their pallets on the hearth. Even the pot-boy dozed on his pallet, his arm round a yellow turn-spit dog, who didn't so much as open an eye when Skye peered in at them.

He was disappointed, but curiously reluctant to go just yet. The place began to remind him of a childhood nursery tale, of an enchanted kingdom, and a princess, pricked by a spindle, who slept for a hundred years. Skye chided himself. While comfortable, this place was no palace . . . and he was a grown man, for God's sake! He gazed up the long stair. He was an intruder. A prowler, truth to tell. He was, he supposed, looking for trouble. But trouble would be better than the lone-liness and gloom that were his only other options today. He took to the stairs.

The upstairs was still, every door to every room in the long hall closed. There was a limit to his audacity, so he turned to go . . . and saw sunlight streaming through an upper window shining on one oaken door, setting it blazing like glowing gold. It was like a sign. Or so he told himself. One look, Skye promised him-self, one last peek and then he'd be gone. That way, he could return tomorrow with an even better reason to visit, to regale them all with the story of this visit. Of how exhausted they'd been, and the foolish fancies that had entertained him because of it. But for now—one last look.

He lay a hand on the door and, not surprised to find it unlatched, pushed it slowly open.

And saw her.

She was the princess from the long lost tale. Dressed in the costume of a princess, at least. She wore a rose and gold gown, with a great bell of a skirt. The gown was nipped at the waist, and low at the breast. . . . Skye stepped closer. She was young, but not so young that the cut of the gown didn't show two shapely breasts that rose and fell with each slow breath. That exposed skin was pure ivory. The dreaming young lady's neck was slender, her face—enchanting. Long lashes covered tilted eyes. A straight little nose. Her brows were cinnamon, but he couldn't tell the color of her hair because she wore an ornate white wig, dressed with rosebuds the precise shape of that captivating, half-parted, pink mouth.

On impulse, because if he was thinking, he'd never have dared, Skye went to her. The fellow in that story had been a prince, and he was only a gentleman, but the impulse was as irresistible as her lips were. He bent, and kissed her.

Her lips were warm. He tasted cherry wine, and kept kissing those delicious lips until he felt her mouth quicken under his. Her steady breaths slowed and halted—and became a long soft sigh. Her mouth changed, trembling under his. Her lips parted further. . . .

He stepped back, rueful now.

It had not, after all, been a gentlemanly thing to do. But he couldn't regret it whatever the outcome. He gazed at her, bemused, and waited. Her eyelids fluttered open. Light-drenched amber eyes looked at him in confusion, and then with dawning comprehension. He awaited a screech, or a shout, and winced, readying himself for a commotion.

She stared at him. Those rosebud lips parted again. "Oh!" she breathed. "It's *you*!"

She'd been dreaming of a kiss. A long delicious kiss, unlike any she'd ever had, exactly like the one she'd always dreamed about. She sighed, opened her eyes—and saw him. Almost exactly the man she'd always hoped for. At least, a fascinating stranger. More than handsome. But alone with her. In her bedchamber . . . For a moment she thought of screeching, bringing the house down around his ears. . . . But they were such *interesting* ears. In that second of reflection she remembered. The party. The games. The costumes. Of course. Her parents had laughingly told her that if she didn't meet the man of her dreams at *this* party, she never would. So she'd gone to her room at last, disgruntled, because it looked as though she never would. But now, to open her eyes to *him*?

She stared, seeing him clearly in the morning light. Nothing she'd imagined. Everything she could have hoped for. Tall and well made. His dark hair was cropped, as though he'd recently recovered from a fever. Which might account for how lean his face was. A good face. Clean-shaven, with planes and edges, and astonishingly long-lashed gray eyes. A narrow high-bridged nose. Firm lips, now tilting in a ruefully amused smile as she felt her face warm, remembering just what those lips had felt like against her own. Not a boy. A man.

Dressed strangely, of course. The masquerade—a late guest then—surprising her in her bed! How embarrassing. She sat up, and felt her head whirl and the world spin round her. Strong arms went round her too.

"Whoa!" he breathed against her cheek. "Wait until your head and stomach settle before you move quickly. I know that feeling too well. Take a deep breath."

She did, and scented sandalwood and shaving soap. Not a whit of sweat and only a tint of horse. She was enchanted. She relaxed, happy to lie back in his arms, inhaling. And tingling.

"You arrived late," she finally said. "I'm sure we never met."

"Be sure of that," he said on a shaken laugh. "I'm sure I'm your latest guest too. I only arrived this morning."

"No!" she said, trying to sit up a little, and daring to look into his eyes. "Have you come far?"

"From the ends of the world," he said, his eyes tender as his voice. "London Town."

"No!" she said again, impressed. "And not afraid of the roads by night?"

"I didn't drive by night. I'm staying at the Pruitts' cottage, not far from here. Or perhaps far—I can hardly tell, the countryside's so thickly forested hereabouts."

"Only to you City folk," she rallied. "But . . . the Pruitts? Isn't Sir Pruitt in London Town now?"

"Yes. Do you know Robert? Trust him to know the most beautiful girl in any neighborhood—and not tell me. I've a score to settle with him now."

Her brow furrowed. "Robert? Nay, I do not know him. 'Tis only Old Master William and his wife who bide there now."

"Robert's my friend, I don't know the rest of his family very well," Skye explained. "I've only been at their house here for a matter of days. On a repairing lease. Town life got too much for me." Since she was still watching him with an adorable air of puzzlement, he added, "I've only recently returned from the war and haven't adjusted to civilian life as yet."

"Oh!" she said, her brow clearing. "Then I can't blame you. Poor fellow. You were in Spain?"

He nodded.

"Those curst Frenchies!" she exclaimed.

"But not so curst if they made it possible for me to meet you," he said, smiling at her again.

She ducked her head, blushing. His accent was strange, probably because he spent so much time in foreign parts. London! She didn't know anyone who actually lived there.

"You came costumed as a Roundhead, then?" she asked, noting his attire, peeping at him from under her lashes so as not to appear a bold minx.

"I'm not such a dull fellow as that, surely," he laughed, glancing down at his maroon and gold waistcoat. "In fact, this is almost gaudy enough to get me banned from Almack's—in London—it's *the* place to be," he told her, noting her puzzlement. "But I was in the Holiday spirit when I ordered it.

"Truth is . . ." he said uneasily, "I didn't choose a costume because I didn't know about the party until I got here. I'm afraid I'm entirely an interloper. I came to your house this morning on a different errand—I'll tell you about it someday. But the thing is, it's broad morning and no one was stirring. I was curious as to why everyone was still sleeping. Alarmed, as well. I suppose just because I'm so newly returned to peace and tranquillity I immediately leapt to the wrong, and worst conclusions. So I investigated the house to . . . to be sure nothing was wrong," he concluded triumphantly.

She gazed into his eyes. He looked down into hers.

"And found everything more right than I could have imagined," he added softly.

She colored and lowered her eyes. And raised them again.

He leaned closer.

"Mirabelle! Daughter!" a loud voice intruded, in horror. "And just who is this fine fellow I find in your bed, prithee?"

"Well, well, well," Squire Roundeville said merrily, slapping his hands on his knee, "a fine round tale, is it not, Wife?"

His wife shook her head, "Nay, not a round one so much as a rousing one, Husband. I vow I haven't been so entertained in weeks!"

"Years!" the squire countered, as they exchanged glances and burst into laughter.

But they were a jolly pair, Skye thought again with relief. They were the perfect hosts as they sat with him and their daughter in the front parlor before a blazing fire, sipping aged wine and chatting.

"The wine is good, but I'd have preferred tea—if things were halfway normal hereabouts," Squire said gruffly, looking down into the garnet contents of his glass. He sighed. "But the blasted kitchen staff is still rubbing sleep from their eyes. Would think they'd slept for a hundred years instead of a long winter's night," he added with another glance at his wife. She looked shocked, then embarrassed, and turned to see Skye's reaction.

He stared, his glass arrested halfway to his lips.

"Confess!" Squire chuckled. "That's just what you were thinking, eh? Had to be, right? What with your friend's story of an enchanted gate and whatnot, not to mention the look of the place when you got here?"

"And the enchanted princess I found, yes, of course," Skye said, looking at Mirabelle.

She grinned at him. "A princess, is it? Ho. Wait 'til you get to know me, sirrah, before you confer such titles on me."

"I can hardly wait," Skye said honestly.

She made a saucy face, but he noticed her color was still high. And it wasn't just the dusting of rouge on her cheeks. Well, he thought, no doubt his own face had been something to see when her father and mother had appeared in her bedroom doorway. He'd shot to his feet, stammering like a schoolboy, and then collected himself enough to make his apologies and give his explanations. But all the while he'd expected either to have to defend himself from the thrashing her father would have every right to try to give him— or prepare for the wedding her mother would have every right to expect to immediately arrange.

To be found sitting in a young woman's bedchamber, on her very bed, in fact, with his lips almost upon hers? He had compromised himself, and her. And was ready to pay the consequences.

But they'd waited. And listened. They'd looked long and hard at him, taking his measure. They must have liked what they saw. Because they'd exchanged a glance, and nodded in unspoken agreement. And then welcomed him to their home.

When he'd been sure he'd been forgiven, Skye said he'd be on his way. But in the same spirit of rural hospitality, Squire insisted he wait and have a visit with them this very day. Then they'd had to go see to their sleepy staff, and send their yawning guests on their way—or back to the bedchambers they occupied in the manor. As so often was the case when a party was given deep in the countryside, most were staying over, because travel was taxing, the roads difficult, the weather unpredictable, and the houses few and far between.

Now his hosts were back, and fully awake. But they were still in their costumes. They must have raided every trunk in the attic, Skye thought. They wore powdered wigs and lovely antique finery. Squire, a portly fellow with an engaging smile, looked as though he'd modeled his costume after some bucolic Justice of the Peace in Mr. Fieldings' naughty book *Tom Jones*. His wife, a comely woman, was his perfect partner in a panniered gown enlivened by gems and spangles. The little family looked like they'd stepped out of history. Skye half wished they'd remain so, if only because Mirabelle looked so rare and uncommonly lovely.

She was almost too theatrical for daylight. She wore jewels at her ears and on her fingers; even her high-heeled shoes were crusted with brilliants. She sparkled in the sunlight, glittering with every movement. Now, in the bright light, he could see her lips as well as her cheeks were dusted with rouge, and her eyelashes darkened with soot. In fact, she was as painted as an actress on the stage—or any tart on London's streets. But it fit her costume perfectly. And since the skin beneath the paint was perfect, and her eyes so clear, she looked dazzling, not tawdry.

Skye never thought he'd find a be-wigged, be-ringed, and painted lady so utter beguiling. But he found himself regretting the fact that next time they met she'd be a proper young lady of fashion—walking softly in silken slippers, pallid and correct in a demure pastel gown, the only dazzling colors permitted in her fan or shawl. He consoled himself with the thought that at least he'd get to see the color and texture of her hair.

"It's a simple tale, really . . ." Squire said now, and

paused. He stared down into his wine. "Thing is, we wanted to give a grand ball for our Mirabelle's eighteenth birthday. Something to talk about. So we *tried* to make the place look like an enchanted castle. Was the *theme* of the thing, don't y'know? Right down to the dust and spiderwebs and such. Overdid it, I suppose. Well, we didn't set a scythe to the grass for weeks, y'see. Tarted ourselves up too. Expect we look *antique* to you, don't we?"

"You succeeded very well, sir," Skye said. "You look like you might have stepped down from a family portrait."

Mirabelle frowned. "But what are they wearing in London these days?"

Her father laughed uproariously. Her mother looked down at her fan.

Squire frowned. "We *are* provincial, old-fashioned as the family of recluses we are. Don't have much contact with the outer world. There's a reason for that too." He shot a glance at his wife. She nodded. "Well, cat's out of the bag, ain't it?" Squire sighed. "The *other* thing is that I had an enemy. A powerful, unreasonable one. Oh, it's a sad tale and not for such a bright day. But there you are—one day I found I had me an implacable foe. Didn't know what would happen next. But I did know the best way to protect my family was to lay low. So we did. For years and years.

"Aye, missy," he told his daughter, who sat up straight and watched him, startled, "never told you neither. Didn't wish to frighten you. Just let you think me daft, or mean—didn't I, my poor honey? Don't deny it. Never let you go out with t'other lasses, or travel far, or even learn much about the wide world lest you desire it too keenly. The only folk we let you see were old friends and relatives, and most of them bided with us for safety's sake as well. Sad stuff, you said, and so it was for you. And for us. Me and your mama kept the peril to ourselves."

Squire grinned. "But the gladsome thing is I *had* an enemy. For I've learnt the danger's past! Aye! I thought it might be done with soon, which is why I made such a Ball for you, and made so merry at it. And we got word this very morning. 'Tis over! At last. Praise be!

"So we can come out of the shadows and live like normal folk again. You can stop your nagging," he told Mirabelle. "Aye, get to know our neighbors now, socialize like a young gel ought, do it all. Go to town—to Chester even, eh? Mayhap even London, someday. Get new gowns and suchlike . . . As to that, I've got to smarten myself up too. What *are* they wearing in London Town these days?" he asked curiously, looking Skye up and down. "Do I have to give up m'britches and put on a pair of them things? How *do* you get 'em on? Fit like a second skin, methinks, eh?"

Skye's eyebrow twitched as he fought the impulse to let it fly up. They were more outspoken in the country, and the fellow *had* just admitted how out of touch with Society he was. But no gentleman he knew would mention the fit of breeches in front of his ladies.

"Just so, sir," Skye answered calmly enough. "They're called 'inexpressibles.' Not only because they don't like to talk about them in polite company, but also because I think it's hard to express so much as a sigh when you're wearing them." He chuckled, to take off any hint of criticism. "Jackets fit close too. But you can keep your knee breeches. Shoes too, complete with buckles. They're too formal for everyday wear, but are still worn for the most elegant soirees and all affairs of state."

"And the ladies?" Mirabelle asked anxiously.

"Your beautiful gown would be fine for an elegant ball too," Skye answered gently, "or presentation at court. Not at informal parties. It's too grand. And not with the powder and paint, of course," he added with a chuckle.

"Of course," Mirabelle's mother echoed weakly. "Well, now we're free, we must get some fashion plates, mustn't we?"

"I took a stack of periodicals with me because I didn't know what my friend's library held," Skye volunteered quickly. "More than the *Gentleman's Magazine* too. I scooped up everything I saw at Hatchards. Would you like me to bring some over tomorrow?"

"Oh!" Mirabelle said, clapping her hands together. "*Would* you?"

"I can't think of anything that would stop me," Skye said, gazing into her amber eyes. "Except not being invited back, of course," he added with a great deal of false anxiety.

They all laughed. "Foxy fellow!" Squire said, rising to his feet to signal the end of the visit. "As though I'd dare not! My women would slay me! But now I needs must get the house back in order. The Ball's over. My worries too. Time to set the place to rights in every way, and the sooner the better, methinks!"

Squire walked his uninvited guest to the front door. Skye took Albion from an abashed-looking stable boy, obviously recently awoken to his duties. He swung up into the saddle, waved to his hosts, and took off down the drive. The wind had swept his path clean, the sun was shining brightly now, and he had no trouble finding his way. He grinned to himself, knowing he'd have no trouble finding his way back now either. Although it was only a matter of hours until he could do that, he could hardly wait. He let Albion have his head, and as they raced along the country road, Skye threw back his own head, laughing with pure pleasure.

"Sooth! But I look naked!" Mirabelle gasped when she saw her reflection in the mirror. But she gasped in shocked delight. "But it feels so good! I feel free as air, loose as a cloud, floating and unfettered and. . . ." Then she grew worried, and swung around to face her mother. "You're sure? Quite sure? I shouldn't want to look absurd."

"Well . . ." her mama said hesitantly, ". . . you do look lovely. Don't she, Samuel?"

"She looks a shame and a right trollop and a scandal to our name," Squire said, shaking his head. "But so they all look these days. Haven't I seen it with my own two eyes? Rode all the way to the village last evening and parted with a pretty price for the gown . . . Ho! *'Gown'!* There's a jest. Less fabric in it than it takes to make a handkerchief. So little it ought to have cost naught 'stead of the earth, as it did," he grumbled. "But it was all ready made— though how long it took to stitch such a meager thing up . . . never mind. I never did skint on my girl, did I? It ain't much, and it looks like even less on her. But I saw all the other lasses, and the fashion plates they showed me in the shop as well."

He sighed. "So if she looks a treat ready to spread on a Sultan's bed—why then, so does every last female in England these days. There we are, and there it is. And put down that rabbit's foot, missy," he told his daughter. "Nary a speck of paint, mind. It's just as the fellow said. For as he didn't say, only tarts wear it these days. And don't pull such a face, it will stick that way."

"Not even a dusting?" Mirabelle pleaded, touching her cheek. "But I look half dead, wan as a glass of new milk, I vow."

"That you do not," her father said. "We live out here in the neck end of nowhere, and I suppose we raised you too free, with every day a costume party and a frolic. But you're grown now and we're back in the world. Do you want to look freakish? Fashion changes like the wind, but this is a fair wind, for you look fine exactly as you are. . . . Stop frowning, Mother, you'll give her the wrong idea. I thought you agreed."

"I do, about her face," his wife said uneasily, "but the gown is so . . . drafty looking."

"It's all the crack," Squire insisted. "That's what the dressmaker said. Means it's what she should wear. Can't have her looking odd for the lad, can we? Now I think on, you'd best get yourself into that flimsy thing I bought back for you too. I don't want either of my gels looking old-fashioned. You'll look a treat in it too, I'll wager. Why, with two such sirens, I'll be beating the fellows off my doorstep!"

Her mother blushed like a girl. Mirabelle could only stare into the looking glass. The girl in the mirror was only veiled, not decently dressed at all. Her face was bare, but so was she. All that clothed her was a thin film of white muslin sprigged with yellow rosebuds. The gown had a round neck and puffed sleeves. That was all it had. The rest was all Mirabelle. Her bosom was covered, but it might as well not be. The thin undershift she had on hid some of the more obvious points, but pointed up most of the others. It didn't support her high breasts, so they moved when she did. No corset hugged her narrow waist, no belled skirt hid the swell of her hips. And when she moved, everything under her gown did too. She giggled. "I'm expected to actually stand in company in this?"

"But you wear this too," her mother said, handing her a beautifully patterned paisley shawl.

Mirabelle threw it over her shoulders and snuggled into it. It was scented like the garden of the Sultan her father mentioned, and for all she'd celebrated her freedom, it made her feel more secure. She sighed as she drew it close, still gaping at herself. "I knew we were backward and retiring before, and I suppose I understand why, and am glad to be free at last. But now!" She spun around to face her parents. "How will I get on?" she asked in sudden fear. "I don't know a thing about Fashion or Society!"

"You have manners and breeding, a brain and a heart, my girl," her father said. "You'll learn fast, and know more. Can't have you looking like a . . . *quiz*. . . . Aye, such it was the dressmaker said a dowd was called these days in London Town."

Mirabelle's face remained sober. "Papa . . . this enemy you spoke of. You're sure the danger's past? Now I think on, it must have been fierce. You kept me so close all these years. Was it something to do with your brother who died so long ago? Or maybe Mama's family? You said they were at odds with the Queen?"

"Neither. I don't wish to speak of it now," her father said sternly. "No point to it. Rest easy knowing it wasn't our fault—not really. And it's over. Now. Best get yourself ready. The lad should be arriving soon. . . . You do like him, don't you, lass?"

"I do, though I hardly ought. At least not so soon. For I don't know him, do I? It's just that he seems so *right* . . ." Mirabelle's eyes grew wide. " 'Od's Fish! Is he the one you said I'd meet at the ball?"

"Never in so many words," Squire said merrily, shaking a finger at her. "Just said it wouldn't surprise me if you met the man of your dreams. Your dreams did the rest, lass."

But they didn't do justice to her caller, Mirabelle thought when she saw him again.

He was so much of that outer other world she'd been protected from that though she thought he looked wonderful, he looked equally strange to her. Not for him the powdered wig country gentlemen affected when they went calling on a lass. Nor even a plain unpowdered queue. Short shorn hair instead. Glossy dark hair brushed forward, shining so clean in the sunlight it made her fingers itch to touch it. Nor did he wear a voluminous jacket that swung away from his body with every step. Nor baggy breeches, high stockings, and stout shoes. All his clothing—from jacket to waistcoat to britches—were fitted so close it made him look slender as a whippet, while showing he was strong as an ox. He'd wide shoulders and a deep chest and . . . sooth! The legs on the man! And in skintight knit breeches! They were cased in high shining boots with gold tassels to further tease the eye toward them. . . . Unless a girl used her good sense and looked away before she showed her appreciation too clear. Mirabelle did—and hoped she hadn't let him see how much she'd been impressed before she did.

But he didn't notice. He was too busily drinking in the sight of her dressed in the latest fashion. However lovely she'd looked before, he couldn't regret the loss of her antique finery. Because now there were no stays or hoops or panniers to disguise her shape. Her gown showed every delightful line of it, from her high breasts to her rounded hips. The pale peach blush of

color was echoed in her unpainted cheeks. At last he
lifted his gaze and saw her soft nutmeg brown hair,
pulled back and drawn up in a mass of curls at the
top of her head, to crown that lovely face.

He realized she must have seen the stunned admiration in his eyes, because she averted her gaze, in mod-
esty, no doubt. He was enchanted anew. She might be
in modern dress but she was obviously an old-fashioned
girl. He'd have to go slow. But time was all he had
here in the countryside . . . time, and her. He hoped.

"Mirabelle," he said, and took her hand. "Mirabelle," he breathed as he brought his lips to it. "Mirabelle," he sighed as he gazed down into her
wondering eyes.

"Come, fellow!" she laughed. "Is't the fashion in
London Town to only tell a lass what you think she
wants to hear? I like sugar, but I need a little spice.
I know my name—it makes no matter how nicely you
say it. Tell me something I haven't heard before!"

He chuckled appreciatively. Old-fashioned, perhaps.
But not backward. He put a hand on his heart. "I
spoke from my heart. But it's not the best conversationalist. What would you like to talk about then?"

"Tell me what's new, what's happening in the world.
If I'm to enter it now, I have to know. Tell me about
London. About Spain. About everything!"

He did. Or tried to. They sat in the front parlor and
he told her about the war, the hopes for peace, the
fashions and trends. She sat, entranced, asking questions now and then.

"Tsk! 'Tis a terrible thing," she exclaimed at one
point, shaking her head. "Why cannot our Good King
George set down this upstart, Napoleon?"

"Because the gossip is that he can't set down so
much as his own cup now, Mirabelle," Skye said.

"They say he's run quite mad. Perhaps soon his son will get a chance to do it."

"Huh!" Mirabelle said. "That one! He likes his pleasures as much as he hates his father. *There's* a scandal we heard about even here in the wilds of nowhere!"

"But he's our only hope. He, Wellington, and our good men. We'll see. The latest news isn't bad. At least we've got the French on the run at last."

"And the Spanish?" she asked.

He smiled. "Poor people. But we're doing our best for them, I saw that with my own eyes."

"It's clear you're a compassionate fellow," she said, looking at him with admiration. "But enough sad stories. Tell me what plays you've seen, what music you've heard . . . Oh! I'm starved for news! I feel as though I've lived in—the Antipodes, or on some far-off star, I'm so far from what is happening."

"You look as though you've dropped down from a star," he said, and laughed as she crinkled her nose. "No, don't give me a set-down, I can't help complimenting you. I think I'll dole out my news so you'll want me back again soon."

"But I want you back even though you haven't left yet," she said earnestly.

Now, no London lady would ever have admitted *that*! Skye thought later, as he took Albion down the road toward his cottage after the luncheon they insisted he stay for. That absolute honesty of hers. It was only one of the things he liked about her. That, and her quick wit. Her quaintly curious air. Her honest reactions. Her face, her voice . . .

Skye visited every morning, took luncheon with the little family every other day, and dined with them every night. He and Mirabelle went for bracing walks,

they engaged in bracing talks, they played at cards
and the old harpsichord in the music room. He taught
her new songs, she reminded him of old ones. They
played like children, and were treated by her family
as such. Skye was amazed at how much her father
trusted him, and resolved to be worthy of it.

Her education was remarkably extensive for a girl
of her age and situation, but as her father had desired,
it stopped short of current events and fashions. She
knew all the doings of the Greek goddesses, but nothing of the Prince's mistresses; could converse prettily
in French but knew nothing of their latest styles;
played the harp like an angel, but couldn't even hum
Haydn. She could quote Shakespeare profusely, but
knew not one word of the most popular wicked farces
on the London stage. She danced like a sprite when
her mother played the pianoforte for them. But her
eyes grew round and she was literally breathless when
Skye taught her to waltz, long before he whirled her
around the room, humming the tune so she could keep
to the steps. He liked to think it was he, and not the
dance, that took her breath away. Holding her in his
arms certainly robbed him of his.

Her one-sided education gave her a curiously knowing but innocent perspective on life. Her father had
kept her ignorant of much so she wouldn't miss it or
desire it there in their country fastness. Skye didn't
mind, even if she obviously did. It lent her an otherworldly air that enchanted him. And gave him an excellent excuse for his constant visits.

Her family let him run tame at their home. He
wanted to be nowhere else—except in her arms, and
she in his bed. But she was young, he was the experienced one, and there was a way to go about these
things. Or so he kept reminding himself when he was

in danger of drowning in the depths of her eyes, or drifting along the currents of her sweet scent until he had to forcibly pull himself back from pulling her into his embrace. He wanted her conversation, her good opinion, her lips, her breasts, her . . .

November slowly drifted into December, and he realized he never wanted to leave.

Neither did Mirabelle want him to.

"Yes. I know it's only been a matter of weeks," Mirabelle told her parents seriously, after they'd asked, "but I feel I've known him forever. Still, you're right. What I don't know is how serious he is about me."

"All we were trying to say, my love," her mama said gently, "is that though he's charming as may be, he's not from hereabouts, in manner or . . . perhaps morals."

"Aye," Squire put in. "He's as different from the lads you've known as a man from the moon might be, because London Town—and the times he's known there—are as different from what you're used to as that would be."

"Sooth," her mama put in, "I confess we're wondering if he's merely amusing himself until spring."

"*You* are wondering, my dear," Squire said. "I don't think he's a trifler."

"Mayhap he's not," his wife admitted. "But Mirabelle, I'm just wishful of reminding you that your cousins Philip and Harry and our good neighbor Edward all came for your birthday party and have stayed on because of you."

"Fiddle!" Mirabelle laughed. "That they did not! They came with their families, and stayed because of them, for they know they haven't a prayer of getting more than a 'Happy Christmas' from me. Haven't I told them so for years?"

"But you haven't known Lord Cameron very long," her mama said, watching her closely.

Mirabelle nodded. "Aye, but time doesn't matter. The strangest thing, but it's as though I knew him from the moment I opened my eyes and saw him—and so whether I knew him for a thousand years or a thousand seconds makes no matter."

Squire frankly grinned. But his wife still worried. "You've not had much experience with the wide world," she persisted, "or the men in it."

"You think I should cast him aside and look to see if I find others I prefer more?" Mirabelle asked, incredulous. "When the plain truth is I never had eyes for any man until I met Skylar . . . or is it that I'd only met lads and no men at all until him? So it seems to me now. But don't fret! My head's squarely on my shoulders," she said, hiding her own doubts, hoping what she said was true. "If he's merely amusing himself—then so be it. I'm enjoying myself in his company, and am content to wait to see what happens."

Her parents exchanged a look, and small smiles.

"So be it," her mama said.

"So it will be," Squire agreed.

But for all her brave talk, Mirabelle was worried. Because though she lived for his every visit, she too wondered which might be his last one. He never spoke of the future. But then, they were always so busily living in the present. They laughed, they chatted, he flirted, she teased. Sometimes she thought he was on the verge of something warmer. . . . But he was always the perfect gentleman. She'd see the warmth kindle in his eyes and feel the pull of attraction between them tighten—and he'd change the subject or move away.

The only kiss they'd even shared had been their first one, and that had been given only on a whim of his, she realized now. Sometimes, she wondered if she *had* dreamed it. He never gave *her* cause to worry that he was trifling. And that began to make her anxious.

But not so anxious that she didn't look forward to every moment with him. It was as though she'd been asleep in every way until he'd come into her life—and went right back to dozing whenever he left her.

"So late?" she cried in frustration one evening as they sat alone in the parlor before the fire and she heard the clock striking his usual time for departure. "And you must leave, I suppose? Zounds! I wish you didn't have to go! Not ever."

Startled, Skye looked up from contemplating her lips. Candor was one thing. This was astonishing. Delightful, yes. Charming too. But *he* was the one who'd been thinking of asking for her hand. Much as he wanted it—much as he'd decided he desperately needed it, and her, for the rest of his life—he was shocked at her asking him.

"It would be so nice if you could stay right here with us," she went on wistfully, "the way all my relatives have done."

His spirits fell. He'd misinterpreted her. Perhaps entirely?

She scowled, obviously pursuing her line of thought with displeasure, "Relatives! Sooth! In truth, was ever there such a family as ours? And all under one roof. *Ours.* True, they say they'll be on their way soon. Uncle Francis left last week and Aunt Elizabeth's making noises about returning to Sussex next week. Cousin Wilbur and his noisy brood just moved out today. The others will be back in their own homes by the new year, or so they promise. But we've still got uncles and cousins galore about the place. I only have privacy when you're here, for they're a bit wary of strangers, it seems."

Her eyes brightened. She suddenly wondered if his reticence with her was due to his worrying about her kindred! Of course. What sane man would want to align himself with a clan that stuck together like burrs?

She hurried to reassure him. "We didn't always have them with us. We're a close family, but not like this! But they all came to visit and just stayed on. At first it was amusing. After a bit, it seemed a little cramped, no matter how big the manor is. Now it's absurd. I don't think they enjoy such forced intimacy any more than I do. It must have had something to do with Father's enemy. *He* won't open his teeth on the subject. *They* say they all came for the Ball. But the truth is they came weeks before it, settled in, and haven't left."

Skye nodded. Every bedchamber in the huge house seemed occupied by some relative of hers. But they were a shy, provincial lot made uncomfortable by the gentleman from London, or else just clannish. Because they seldom did more than give him a good morning or evening before they found a reason to be away from him.

"But if you stayed here too," she went on eagerly, "how much fun it would be! And I'll wager it would be so much more comfortable than where you bide now."

"Not for me," he said, suddenly serious. "Because I think it would be torture to be so close—and yet have to remain so far—from you."

"But why . . . Oh!" she said. She blinked. And blushed, exquisitely. Then looked up at him, cocking her head to the side. " 'Tis so? But—but then, if 'tis truth . . . why don't you ever . . . well, why haven't you given me some hint, some sign?"

"I thought I had," he said, his voice grown deep.

She quickly looked away. Her heart picked up its beat, and she wished fashion still called for a lady to constantly clutch a fan. All she could do was to clench her trembling hands. Here was the thing she'd been yearning to say. The thing she'd been rehearsing with her pillow, the thing she never thought she'd dare ask, for fear of knowing the answer.

"A hint? In words, mayhap," she said, averting her eyes, "but never in deed, sir. Oh, you've pretty words a'plenty. But never an action to back them up!"

"Mirabelle!" he said, and laughed in spite of himself at her candor—and his delight. "How could I? I *am* a gentleman."

"What? I don't know how they go on in London, sirrah," she said angrily, because she was blushing so much her cheeks felt hot, "but I take leave to tell you that we don't think less of a fellow for giving a girl a sound buss now and again. Why, 'tis only tribute, everyone knows that. I don't mean I'd ever nip off to the haystacks with a lad, no, nor ever wanted to or have done. I'm no simple farm lass, or trollop neither. I'm a lady born, and know it well. But an honest buss, now and again? From a likely lad for a laughing lass? 'Tis only human nature, and so all know. And so . . . when you never so much as . . . oh!"

But then she couldn't say more, because his arms were around her and his lips were on hers. She had never tasted anything finer, and there wasn't a thing she needed to breathe except sighs of pleasure. His mouth was so warm and gentle, his body so vividly vital against hers. Her newly fashioned flimsy gown

was wonderful, she managed to think in wonder. It let
her get closer than she'd ever been to a man, and
allowed her to feel the exact shape and strength of
him against her own body. It was as thrilling as the
feel of his heart beating so quickly against her own.
She burrowed into his arms, surrendering her lips to
his, wriggling against him to discover what else he
would want of her.

He wanted everything. And she in her candid but
obviously innocent passion seemed unaware of how
close he was to taking it. So he was the one to pull
away. He touched her hair, then snatched his hand
away before it could slide down her silken cheek to
her slender neck, to the rise of those wondrous breasts
that had teased his chest. . . .

"Mirabelle," he said in a shaken voice, "I do believe
it's time to have a talk with your father."

She blinked, and licked her swollen lips. She looked
at him with stark tragedy in her luminous eyes. And
then, disbelief. "After only *one* kiss?"

His delighted laughter ended on her lips.

Skye was humming as he stepped out of the house
the next morning to get Albion from the stable. He
was so engrossed in his thoughts that it was only Albion's dancing and nickering that alerted him to a visitor
arriving. Bemused, Skye halted to watch an ornate
carriage rumble up the crooked lane and pull to a stop
in front of the house. A liveried servant, looking as
out of place as a rose in this December setting, leapt
out, lowered the steps, and the owner of the cottage
stepped out and looked around.

"Skye!" Robert called when he saw his friend. "The
Holiday's coming, but behold—your savior is already
here! Forgive the blasphemy," he chuckled, "but you

must think of me as that by now, poor fellow. Never fear! I've come to carry you away, just as I promised. Must have been counting the hours 'til I got here but it's just like you to be too stubborn to admit a mistake and write for me to come sooner, eh? Never mind. I'll pop in and have a cup of tea or something warmer—cold as the devil here, ain't it?—while you bundle up your things. Then we can get a start and be halfway to the Hall before darkness falls. Come, your exile's ended. A real Holiday awaits!"

"Robert, my friend," Skye laughed, "go in but prepare to stay the night or go on without me. Because I'm off on an important errand and can't stop to explain it right now."

"Oh no, you don't!" Robert cried. "Nothing will induce me to stay if I don't have to. Have you run mad? I offer you an instant escape and you delay it? It must be something earth-shattering. Have you got yourself involved with a debt? A duel? Or have you plain run mad? Spit out now. You owe me that at least."

"So I do," Skye sighed, sliding down from Albion's broad back. "Come in, sit by the fire, and hear my story. It's earth-shattering, all right, but not in the way you think."

Robert came into the house, and accepted the curtsies and bows from his servants absently as he shucked off his top coat and gloves and followed Skye into the parlor. He sat in awestruck silence and heard his friend out, interrupting only to thank his housekeeper when she brought him tea.

But when Skye was done, his friend sprang to his feet. "Madness!" he cried in agitation. "See what happens when I leave you in this damned place? *Eldritch?* I said. *Magical? Mystical?* I remember the words too

well, just as I remember the lure of the damned place
now. I must have been enchanted myself to have sent
you here in your state of mind. Look, my friend, you
were weary and cynical, disgusted with the war, and
the ways of city life as well. You wanted rustication?
Fine. You met a fair maiden here in the wilderness.
Natural enough that you'd be bemused. But bewitched? A few days among civilized folk will cure
this. It's like—like faery magic or somesuch, brought
on by the isolation of this devilish place. Come away,
write her letters if you must, but bide some time until
you come to your senses, man!"

"I've never been more in possession of them," Skye
said, smiling. "She's no rustic, Robert. Squire Roundeville's daughter, no less."

"Roundeville? Sounds familiar—but I don't know
the man or his family."

"Because they've been reclusive. The father had a
problem with a vengeful relative or an embittered
neighbor, I think, and kept close to home. But now
it's settled, and they're out in Society again. It's the
very manor you paused at as a boy, the one you told
me about. The one with the gate and the padlock?
You ought to have tried harder to find out what was
behind that gate. They're a delightful family. But I'm
glad you didn't stay to meet them after all. You'd
have met Mirabelle, and I doubt you'd ever have been
able to leave her, which would have complicated
things for me. Only complicated, mind. Because it's
clear she was fated for me.

"I've found my lady, Robert!" Skye said, his face
alight with animation. "She's everything I ever wanted
in a lover—a wife—mother of my children. Lovely and
clever, saucy but gentle, brash as a boy but tender as
a woman should be. Honest to a fault, with not one

sly bone in her lovely body. A sense of humor and of honor. She's scented like roses and beautiful as one too. And not a care in her head about Fashion or rank or honors. The only one who resents our meeting is Albion, since I hardly talk to him anymore. Not when I have a lady whose mind is every bit as entrancing as her face. I'm in your debt forever for sending me here."

"Thought you wanted an old-fashioned girl," Robert said, grasping at straws.

"Her manners are every bit as much that as either of my grandmamas', although she's modern in her outlook. But you know? Now I think about it, there *is* something in her that reminds me of them. Her frankness. Her absolute candor. They weren't mealymouthed and neither is she. She says what she thinks, and if she hears a warm jest, she laughs aloud—if it's a truly funny one. But she'll blush at a compliment. She's no hoyden but there aren't any missish airs about my Merrybelle! I mean to make her mine, this very day. That's where I was going. To ask her papa his permission. If I'm lucky enough to secure it, I'll ask you to pass Christmas with me. Because it will be the most joyous one yet. No—*ever*!"

"Stay *here*?" Robert said, appalled, glancing around the humble room.

"Rest easy. If I'm in luck, they'll want you as guest at the manor. If not—then my friend, I'll leave here too—though I vow my heart will always remain. Enough solemnity! I know my Mirabelle's answer. I hope I can predict her papa's."

But he couldn't. Which was why Skye was strangely ill-at-ease when he went for his interview with the squire. Robert was introduced and welcomed with pleasure because he was Skye's friend, as well as a

new link to the outside world. He stayed with Mirabelle and her mama when Skye went into Squire's
study for a private chat with him.

Skye took a glass of wine, but didn't beat about the
bush. He set down his glass and stated his case. And
waited. . . . And waited.

Squire didn't answer. He looked thoughtful. He
tapped his jaw, he glanced out the window, he stared
at the fireplace. Skye had time to review his proposal
from several angles as Squire thought about it. Every
long moment that passed seemed an hour.

"I didn't expect you to leap at my offer and fall
over me with glad cries of joy," Skye finally said in a
strangled voice, attempting a jest, "but I confess, I
thought we were friends. I don't understand your
hesitation."

"It's not you, lad," Squire said, frowning, "not
really. It's just—there's much she don't know about
your world."

"I'll teach her," Skye said.

"Oh aye, and you might find it novel. But you could
tire of it too, in time. You're used to worldly females,
foreign types and such, women who know a thing or
three. My lass is clear as running water, without an
ounce of deceit in her. Add to that the fact that I've
kept her apart from the world so long, and you might
find her innocence boring, in time, at least when
you're back among your smart London ladies."

"I came here to escape those London ladies, since
few of them were that smart, and none half so wise
as your Mirabelle."

Squire nodded, but still looked troubled.

Skye spoke in frustration. "I come from a good family, sir. I have a good income. I have good intentions.
I love her and will devote my life to making her

happy. I don't care about London fashions, I care about Mirabelle. I'll be faithful, if that's what's worrying you. It is how I was raised too. I . . ."

"It ain't so much you, lad." Squire said. He eyed Skye from under his brows. He fidgeted with his fob, and then took a deep breath. "There's things about our situation you might find . . . odd. Things that don't make sense. Things I couldn't blame you for wondering on. Not about Mirabelle, of course," he added hastily. "I mean about why we lived as we did so long. The danger's past, I promise you. But mind, I might never be able to tell you the reason I kept her close here all these years, if only because the subject still affrights her mother so. And because you might not think me wise for doing it. And because"—he hesitated—"when—if—you come to know—you mightn't believe it, neither. Well, I scarcely do. Will you be content to live with a mystery?"

"If I may live with Mirabelle, I can live with a mystery, a comedy, a tragedy, and a farce, if I must," Skye said. "Isn't that what wedlock is anyway? Or so my father told me. You'd have liked him, I think. I'd hoped to call you 'father' too. 'Squire' seems too formal, doesn't it?"

Squire finally smiled. "Clever lad. Well, then, so be it. You've my blessing, and my daughter, if she wishes it. And if you truly do."

"I wish nothing else," Skye breathed in relief as he put out his hand for Squire to shake.

"Good," Squire said with equal relief, taking his hand in a firm grip, "for wishes are treacherous things. They can be the very devil if you don't mind how they're made. Or the very making of a man, if you do."

"You've made my life for me, sir," Skye said sincerely. "I'll never give you cause to regret it."

"Humph! Well, go to it, lad, she's in the parlor, doubtless pacing a path through my finest rug. We'll talk about settlements and families and dates and such later."

But Skye met her in the great hall as she ran to him, and he lifted her up off her feet and swung her round, as all the servants cheered.

"Well, 'tis done, Mother," Squire said to his wife as they watched the happy couple embracing.

"And well done," she said, and took his arm in hers.

That night they made merry. The reclusive relatives loosened their collars and their tongues, and told gay stories at the table, becoming merrier with every toast to the couple's health.

"I only wish you had a sister," Robert told Mirabelle honestly, after he had made his seventh toast.

"I have cousins, dozens, all in better looks than me," she said mischievously, "and if you stay for Christmas, you'll meet them."

"Do stay, my lord," her mother urged him. "Christmas at the manor was always so lovely," she said wistfully. She brightened. "And will be even more so this year, of course. We'll have the Yule log. And the caroling."

"And the wassail," Squire said.

"And the mistletoe, I hope?" Skye laughed.

"Which I'll be sure to keep you away from—unless I'm the only one next to you," Mirabelle said, making a face. She turned to Robert. "And dancing, music, games, and the best puddings and minces and punch in all England and Wales! Oh do stay, it's only a few days away and will be such fun!"

"M'family expects me . . . but did you say *dozens*

of comely cousins?" Robert asked. He basked in the merriment his comment provoked.

"Dozens," Squire agreed. "Though none are as lovely as our Mirabelle—no matter what she says—many are comely enough to suit any man. And there will be friends—and well-wishers too. Yes," he said to his wife's sudden look of apprehension. "Well-wishers, my dear, from near and from far this year. For we've had our share of troubles. Our trials are ended and now only joy can ensue."

His wife glanced at the head of the table where Skye and Mirabelle sat. They were obviously deaf to the company now, and blind to everything except what they saw in each other's eyes.

"How glad I am that I found you," Skye was saying softly. "I don't know what I would have done if I had not."

"How glad I am that you did," Mirabelle sighed, "I don't know how I'd have gone on had you not. You woke me, my love, to more than the day."

Skye's gaze caressed her as he dared not in front of all the company. "You woke me to my life," he murmured.

The longing in her eyes showed him she knew. "You woke me to love."

"It's the same thing," they both said at the same time, and laughed because they had.

"Such a handsome couple," her mother sighed.

"Aye," Squire said softly, "made for each other, all right. No matter how long it took for them to find each other. Their love will answer every question, and there will be no shadows. Be of good cheer, my dear."

She blinked back happy tears and raised her glass to his.

The guests saw the toast and joined it, with quips

and congratulations anew. Their laughter rose like the
fragrant smoke from the blazing fire in the great
hearth. The piney fragrance of it melted into that of
all the other kindled hearths in the great manor, joining the scents of roast meats and pies, rising up the
many chimneys, dispersing like a cloud of warmth and
content into the frosty silent night.

The woman standing in the crooked lane in the
depths of the great forest raised her head. She sniffed
the air. And smiled. "Roast pig and goose, beef, and
venison. And Cook's pheasant pie. Ah, her steak and
kidney pudding too, gingerbreads, brandysnaps, mince,
apple and bramble pies. Lovely."

"Lovely, aye, lovely is as lovely does, though. They
didn't invite thee, lovey, did they, eh?" the old hag at
her side snickered.

"They did," the handsome woman said calmly, "for
tonight and the next day and the whole Holiday. But
I'll come on Christmas Day to see how they like my
presents. They invited you too, you know."

" 'Cause they feared not to," the crone sneered.

"No, there's no harm you can do now, and they
know it, for I've told them. Wasps have only one sting
to them. There *are* rules. So they'd nothing to fear
anymore. They invited you."

"Well, they can look for me 'til their eyes drop out,
for I ain't goin'."

"Do as you will. You always do."

"Oh, Mistress Holy and Meek. Thou doest as thou
will too," the crone said spitefully. "Thee and me,
we're peas in a pod. Only different colors. And thou
hast all the luck."

"Why do you say that?" the other asked curiously.

"Eh!" the old woman scoffed. "Just look at it. It
were clever of thee, no matter how it were done, I

grant. But it could've been ruinous too, thou knows't that right well. Think on. Had things changed too much, he'd have taken her for a loony and her family for dafties, and gone on his way with naught but a weird tale to tell of his visit to the manor. But no. Thy luck's in, as ever. It's *still* the French they're fighting! And still in Spain, no less! A hundred years only brought them from one King George to another. And both kings thinking their son George a wastrel, and rightly so, and *neither* prince caring a fig for his father or what he thinks! What are the odds on them things, I ask thee? It's thy blasted luck, as ever."

"It's only good over evil, as I've always said," the other woman said, "and so it will always be. History will bend itself to it, Nature will turn herself to it, it's what the Universe wants and will always strive to get, no matter how many years go by. Squire and his good wife share credit too, making such shrewd preparations. Gathering their loved ones together to stay the course with them, raising Mirabelle so well. Educate a child about the Past and she shall cope with the Present, and be able to face the Future. They did it well. They're worthy, and deserve their present happiness.

"You should have listened to me," the sweet-faced woman said, shaking her head. "I tried to tell you, you could have avoided all this trouble and your own frustration. But you will not change! Not your mind, nor face, speech, or attitude! You could! You didn't *have* to curse them for not inviting you. My word! With your reputation, after what you did with the princess in the castle all those years ago, what sane family would? People remember such things for generations, and they're right to. Because you tried the same thing again. Exactly the same way too, venting your spite on them even though it was only a Squire's beloved daughter this time, only a manor house, and not a kingdom. One would think you'd learn. They have. And I did too."

But the old woman wasn't listening. She was scratching her hoary head and muttering. "I had it *figgered* this time. This time, I knew thou couldst not spite nor stop me!" She counted on her gnarled fingers. "I waited 'til thou gavest thy christening present, so I could be sure there wasn't a thing thou couldst do to change mine this time. I waited 'til all the others were done giving their gifts too. I made sure of it! I even left out the spindle prick bit, for I noticed maidens don't spin so much as they used to. I made it clear, I made it easy, with no room to wriggle out. All I said was it would happen on her eighteenth birthday, will she, nil she. Eighteen years, she'd fall into a swoon, and that'd be that. *How* didst thou get 'round it this time? I must know. Thou canst tell me, for it's done, ain't it?"

"So it is," the fair woman said, "and so I shall. Remember what I said about learning from the past? You didn't. You minded all, sister . . . all but for one thing. You left in triumph, but too soon, or you would have known then. Yes, I had no Christening present left to give after I gave her the gift of Laughter, did I? But you forgot. Good will find a way. Christmas was coming, and I remembered though you forgot— if you ever did think of giving presents to gladden instead of sadden, that is. I simply gave her the best gifts for Christmas. Life. And Love. Sleep instead of Death. And love to wake her."

"Christmas gifts!" the hag raged. "It was a trick!"

"A trick? No one ever said I could only give Christening gifts, did they? And can you think of more fitting Christmas presents?"

She spoke to air. Her sister had vanished into it.

And soon, so did she.

But she was smiling. An odd smile for such a sweet-faced creature known for her good deeds. Because it looked positively wicked.

SIGNET REGENCY ROMANCE

Lord Dragoner's Wife by Lynn Kerstan

Six years ago, Delia wed Lord Dragoner, the man she'd loved from afar. But after only one night, the handsome lord mysteriously fled the country...only to return amid scandalous rumors.

Can love bloom again in the shadows of the past—and the danger of the present?

0-451-19861-1/$4.99

Double Deceit by Allison Lane

Antiquarian Alexandra Vale is more interested in artifacts than love affairs, but her diabolical father has different plans for her. Soon, Alex is caught up in a cunning deceit with a notorious rogue— but the clever twosome may learn they can't outsmart their very own hearts....

0-451-19854-9/$4.99

The Holly and the Ivy by Elisabeth Fairchild

Mary Rivers's Gran has predicted a wonderful Christmas in London. And when their usually prickly neighbor, Lord Balfour, is increasingly attentive, Gran's prediction may come true—if the merry Mary and the thorny lord can weather a scandalous misunderstanding and a chaotic Christmas Eve ball!

0-451-19841-7/$4.99

To order call: 1-800-788-6262